THE

46

WHY FRAU FROHMANN RAISED HER PRICES AND OTHER STORIES

ANTHONY TROLLOPE, the fourth of six surviving children, was born on 24 April 1815 in London. As he describes in his *Autobiography*, poverty and debt made his childhood acutely unhappy and disrupted his education: his school fees at Harrow and Winchester were frequently unpaid. His family attempted to restore their fortunes by going to America, leaving the young Anthony alone in England, but it was not until his mother, Frances, began to write that there was any improvement in the family's finances. Her success came too late for her husband, who died in exile in Belgium in 1835. Trollope was unable to afford a university education, and in 1834 he became a junior clerk in the Post Office. He achieved little until he was appointed Surveyor's Clerk in Ireland in 1841. There he worked hard, travelled widely, took up hunting and still found time for his literary career. He married Rose Heseltine, the daughter of a bank manager, in 1844; they had two sons, one of whom emigrated to Australia. Trollope frequently went abroad for the Post Office and did not settle in England again until 1859. He is still remembered as the inventor of the letter-box. In 1867 he resigned from the Post Office and became the editor of *St Paul's Magazine* for the next three years. He failed in his attempt to enter Parliament as a Liberal in 1868. Trollope took his place among London literary society and counted William Thackeray, George Eliot and G. H. Lewes among his friends. He died on 6 December 1882 as the result of a stroke.

Anthony Trollope wrote forty-seven novels and five volumes of short stories as well as travel books, biographies and collections of sketches. The Barsetshire series and the six Palliser or 'political' books were the first novel-sequences to be written in English. His works offer an unsurpassed portrait of the professional and landed classes of Victorian England. In his *Autobiography* (published posthumously in 1883) Trollope describes the self-discipline that enabled his prolific output: he would produce a given number of words per hour in the early morning, before work; he always wrote while travelling by rail or sea, and as soon as he finished one novel he began another. His efforts resulted in his becoming one of England's most successful and popular writers.

Why Frau Frohmann Raised Her Prices (1882) is the last of five volumes of Trollope's short stories to be published. They had originally appeared in the years 1877–8, printed in *Harper's Magazine* (New York) or in *Good Words* and its Christmas number, *Good Cheer*. The title story is set in the Tyrol, an area Trollope had visited with his family in 1874, while 'The Telegraph Girl' is based on his experiences when working for the Post Office.

WHY FRAU FROHMANN RAISED HER PRICES
AND OTHER STORIES

ANTHONY TROLLOPE

PENGUIN BOOKS

PENGUIN BOOKS

Published by the Penguin Group
Penguin Books Ltd, 27 Wrights Lane, London W8 5TZ, England
Penguin Books USA Inc., 375 Hudson Street, New York, New York 10014, USA
Penguin Books Australia Ltd, Ringwood, Victoria, Australia
Penguin Books Canada Ltd, 10 Alcorn Avenue, Toronto, Ontario, Canada M4V 3B2
Penguin Books (NZ) Ltd, 182–190 Wairau Road, Auckland 10, New Zealand

Penguin Books Ltd, Registered Offices: Harmondsworth, Middlesex, England

First published in one volume 1882
Published in Penguin Books 1993
1 3 5 7 9 10 8 6 4 2

Printed in England by Clays Ltd, St Ives plc

CONTENTS.

WHY FRAU FROHMANN RAISED HER PRICES.

THE LADY OF LAUNAY.

CHRISTMAS AT THOMPSON HALL.

THE TELEGRAPH GIRL.

ALICE DUGDALE.

WHY FRAU FROHMANN RAISED HER PRICES.

WHY FRAU FROHMANN RAISED HER PRICES.

CHAPTER I.

THE BRUNNENTHAL PEACOCK.

If ever there was a Tory upon earth, the Frau Frohmann was a Tory; for I hold that landed possessions, gentle blood, a gray-haired butler behind one's chair, and adherence to the Church of England, are not necessarily the distinguishing marks of Toryism. The Frau Frohmann was a woman who loved power, but who loved to use it for the benefit of those around her,—or at any rate to think that she so used it. She believed in the principles of despotism and paternal government,—but always on the understanding that she was to be the despot. In her heart of hearts she disliked education, thinking that it unfitted the minds of her humbler brethren for the duties of their lives. She hated, indeed, all changes,—changes in costume, changes in hours, changes in cookery, and changes in furniture; but of all changes she perhaps hated changes in prices the most. Gradually there had come over her a melancholy conviction that the world cannot go on altogether unaltered. There was, she felt, a fate in things,—a necessity which, in some dark way within her own mind, she connected with the fall of Adam and the general imperfection of humanity,—which demanded changes, but they were always changes for the worse; and therefore, though to those around her she was mostly silent on this matter, she was afflicted by a general idea that the world was going on towards ruin. That all things throve with herself was not sufficient for her comfort; for, being a good woman with a large heart, she was anxious for the welfare not only of herself and of her children, but for that of all who might come after her, at any rate in her own locality. Thus, when she found that there was a tendency to dine at one instead of twelve, to wear the same clothes on week days as on Sundays, to desire easy chairs, and linen that should be bleached absolutely white, thoughts as to the failing condition of the world would get the better of her and make her melancholy.

These traits are perhaps the evidences of the weakness of Toryism;—but then Frau Frohmann also had all its strength. She was thoroughly pervaded by a determination that, in as far as in her lay, all that had aught to do with herself should be "well-to-do" in the world. It was a grand ambition in her mind that every creature connected with her establishment, from the oldest and most time-honoured guest down to the last stray cat that had taken refuge under her roof, should always have enough to eat. Hunger, unsatisfied hunger, disagreeable hunger, on the part of any dependent of hers, would have been a reproach to her. Her own eating troubled her little or not at all, but the cooking of the establishment generally was a great care to her mind. In bargaining she was perhaps hard, but hard only in getting what she believed to be her own right. Aristides was not more just. Of bonds, written bonds, her neighbours knew not much; but her word for twenty miles round was as good as any bond. And though she was perhaps a little apt to domineer in her bargains,—to expect that she should fix the prices and to resent opposition,—it was only to the strong that she was tyrannical. The poor sick widow and the little orphan could generally deal with her at their own rates; on which occasions she would endeavour to hide her dealings from her own people, and would give injunctions to the favoured ones that the details of the transaction should not be made public. And then, though the Frau was, I regret to say, no better than a Papist, she was a thoroughly religious woman, believing in real truth what she professed to believe, and complying, as far as she knew how, with the ordinances of her creed.

Therefore I say that if ever there was a Tory, the Frau Frohmann was one.

And now it will be well that the reader should see the residence of the Frau, and learn something of her condition in life. In one of the districts of the Tyrol, lying some miles south of Innsbruck, between that town and Brixen, there is a valley called the Brunnenthal, a most charming spot, in which all the delights of scenery may be found without the necessity of climbing up heart-rending mountains, or sitting in oily steamboats, or paying for greedy guides, or riding upon ill-conditioned ponies. In this valley Frau Frohmann kept an hotel called the Peacock, which, however, though it was known as an inn, and was called by that name, could hardly be regarded as a house of common public entertainment. Its purpose was to afford recreation and comfort to a certain class of customers during the summer months,—persons well enough to do in the world to escape from their town work and their town residences for a short holiday, and desirous during that time of enjoying picturesque scenery, good living, moderate comfort, and some amount of society. Such institutions have now become so common that there is hardly any one who has not visited or at any rate seen such a place. They are to be found in every country in Europe, and are very common in America. Our own Scotland is full of them. But when the Peacock was first opened in Brunnenthal they were not so general.

Of the husband of the Frau there are not many records in the neighbourhood. The widow has been a widow for the last twenty years at least, and her children,—for she has a son and daughter,—have no vivid memories of their father. The house and everything in it, and the adjacent farm, and the right of cutting timber in the forests, and the neighbouring quarry, are all the undoubted property of the Frau, who has a reputation for great wealth. Though her son is perhaps nearly thirty, and is very diligent in the affairs of the establishment, he has no real authority. He is only, as it were, the out-of-doors right hand of his mother, as his sister, who is perhaps five years younger, is an in-doors right hand. But they are only hands. The brain, the intelligence, the mind, the will by which the Brunnenthal Peacock is conducted and managed, come all from the Frau Frohmann herself. To this day she can hardly endure a suggestion either from Peter her son or from her daughter Amalia, who is known among her friends as Malchen, but is called "the fraulein" by the Brunnenthal world at large. A suggestion as to the purchase of things new in their nature she will not stand at all, though she is liberal enough in maintaining the appurtenances of the house generally.

But the Peacock is more than a house. It is almost a village; and yet every shed, cottage, or barn at or near the place forms a part of the Frau's establishment. The centre or main building is a large ordinary house of three stories,—to the lower of which there is an ascent by some half-dozen stone steps,—covered with red tiles, and with gable ends crowded with innumerable windows. The ground-floor is devoted to kitchens, offices, the Frau's own uses, and the needs of the servants. On the first-story are the two living rooms of the guests, the greater and by far the more important being devoted to eating and drinking. Here, at certain hours, are collected all the forces of the establishment,—and especially at one o'clock, when, with many ringing of bells and great struggles in the culinary department, the dinner is served. For to the adoption of this hour has the Frau at last been driven by the increasing infirmities of the world around her. The scenery of the locality is lovely; the air is considered to be peculiarly health-compelling; the gossipings during the untrammelled idleness of the day are very grateful to those whose lives are generally laborious; the love-makings are frequent, and no doubt sweet; skittles and bowls and draughts and dominoes have their devotees; and the smoking of many pipes fills up the vacant hours of the men.

But, at the Brunnenthal, dinner is the great glory of the day. It would be vain for any æsthetical guest, who might conceive himself to be superior to the allurements of the table, to make little of the Frau's dinner. Such a one had better seek other quarters for his summer's holiday. At the Brunnenthal Peacock it is necessary that you should believe in the paramount importance of dinner. Not to come to it at the appointed time would create, first marvel, in the Frau's mind, then pity,—as to the state of your health,—and at last hot anger should it be found that such neglect arose from contempt. What muse will assist me to describe these dinners in a few words? They were commenced of course by soup,—real soup, not barley broth with a strong prevalence of the barley. Then would follow the boiled meats, from which the soup was supposed to have been made,—but such boiled meat, so good, that the supposition must have contained a falsehood. With this there would be always potatoes and pickled cabbages and various relishes. Then there would be two other kinds of meat, generally with accompaniment of stewed fruit; after that fish,—trout from the neighbouring stream, for the preservation of which great tanks had been made. Vegetables with unknown sauces would follow,—and then would come the roast, which consisted always of poultry, and was accompanied of course by salad. But it was after this that were made the efforts on which the Frau's fame most depended. The puddings, I think, were the subject of her greatest struggles and most complete success. Two puddings daily were, by the rules of the house, required to be eaten; not two puddings brought together so that you might choose with careless haste either one or the other; but two separate courses of puddings, with an interval between for appreciation, for thought, and for digestion. Either one or both can, no doubt, be declined. No absolute punishment,—such as notice to leave the house,—follows such abstention. But the Frau is displeased, and when dressed in her best on Sundays does not smile on those who abstain. After the puddings there is dessert, and there are little cakes to nibble if you will. They are nibbled very freely. But the heat of the battle is over with the second pudding.

They have a great fame, these banquets; so that ladies and gentlemen from Innsbruck have themselves driven out here to enjoy them. The distance each way is from two to three hours, so that a pleasant holiday is made by a visit to the Frau's establishment. There is a ramble up to the waterfall and a smoking of pipes among the rocks, and pleasant opportunities for secret whispers among young people;—but the Frau would not be well pleased if it were presumed that the great inducement for the visit were not to be found in the dinner which she provides. In this way, though the guests at the house may not exceed perhaps thirty in number, it will sometimes be the case that nearly twice as many are seated at the board. That the Frau has an eye to profit cannot be doubted. Fond of money she is certainly;—fond of prosperity generally. But, judging merely from what comes beneath his eye, the observer will be led to suppose that her sole ambition on these occasions is to see the food which she has provided devoured by her guests. A weak stomach, a halting appetite, conscientious scruples as to the over-enjoyment of victuals, restraint in reference to subsequent excesses or subsequent eatings,—all these things are a scandal to her. If you can't, or won't, or don't eat your dinner when you get it, you ought not to go to the Brunnenthal Peacock.

This banqueting-hall, or Speise-Saal, occupies a great part of the first-floor; but here also is the drawing-room, or reading-room, as it is called, having over the door "Lese-Saal" painted, so that its purpose may not be doubted. But the reading-room is not much, and the guests generally spend their time chiefly out of doors or in their bedrooms when they are not banqueting. There are two other banquets, breakfast and supper, which need not be specially described;—but of the latter it may be said that it is a curtailed dinner, having limited courses of hot meat, and only one pudding.

On this floor there is a bedroom or two, and a nest of others above; but the accommodation is chiefly afforded in other buildings, of which the one opposite is longer, though not so high, as the central house; and there is another, a little down the road, near the mill, and another as far up the stream, where the baths have been built,—an innovation to which Frau Frohmann did not lend herself without much inward suffering. And there are huge barns and many stables; for the Frau keeps a posting establishment, and a diligence passes the door three times each way in the course of the day and night, and the horses are changed at the Peacock;—or it was so, at any rate, in the days of which I am speaking, not very long ago. And there is the blacksmith's forge, and the great carpenter's shed, in which not only are the carts and carriages mended, but very much of the house furniture is made. And there is the mill, as has been said before, in which the corn is ground, and three or four cottages for married men, and a pretty little chapel, built by the Frau herself, in which mass is performed by her favourite priest once a month,—for the parish chapel is nearly three miles distant if you walk by the mountain path, but is fully five if you have yourself carried round by the coach road. It must, I think, be many years since the

Frau can have walked there, for she is a dame of portly dimensions.

Whether the buildings are in themselves picturesque I will not pretend to say. I doubt whether there has been an attempt that way in regard to any one except the chapel. But chance has so grouped them, and nature has so surrounded them, that you can hardly find anywhere a prettier spot. Behind the house, so as to leave only space for a little meadow which is always as green as irrigation can make it, a hill rises, not high enough to be called a mountain, which is pine-clad from the foot to the summit. In front and around the ground is broken, but immediately before the door there is a way up to a lateral valley, down which comes a nameless stream which, just below the house, makes its way into the Ivil, the little river which runs from the mountain to the inn, taking its course through that meadow which lies between the hill and the house. It is here, a quarter of a mile perhaps up this little stream, at a spot which is hidden by many turnings from the road, that visitors come upon the waterfall,—the waterfall which at Innsbruck is so often made to be the excuse of these outings which are in truth performed in quest of Frau Frohmann's dinners. Below the Peacock, where the mill is placed, the valley is closely confined, as the sombre pine-forests rise abruptly on each side; and here, or very little lower, is that gloomy or ghost-like pass through the rocks, which is called the Höllenthor; a name which I will not translate. But it is a narrow ravine, very dark in dark weather, and at night as black as pitch. Among the superstitious people of the valley the spot is regarded with the awe which belonged to it in past ages. To visitors of the present day it is simply picturesque and sublime. Above the house the valley spreads itself, rising, however, rapidly; and here modern engineering has carried the road in various curves and turns round knolls of hills and spurs of mountains, till the traveller as he ascends hardly knows which way he is going. From one or two points among these curves the view down upon the Peacock with its various appendages, with its dark-red roofs, and many windows glittering in the sun, is so charming, that the tourist is almost led to think that they must all have been placed as they are with a view to effect.

The Frau herself is what used to be called a personable woman. To say that she is handsome would hardly convey a proper idea. Let the reader suppose a woman of about fifty, very tall and of large dimensions. It would be unjust to call her fat, because though very large she is still symmetrical. When she is dressed in her full Tyrolese costume,—which is always the case at a certain hour on Sunday, and on other stated and by no means unfrequent days as to which I was never quite able to learn the exact rule, —when she is so dressed her arms are bare down from her shoulders, and such arms I never saw on any human being. Her back is very broad and her bust expansive. But her head stands erect upon it as the head of some old Juno, and in all her motions,—

though I doubt whether she could climb by the mountain path to her parish church,—she displays a certain stately alertness which forbids one to call her fat. Her smile,—when she really means to smile and to show thereby her good-will and to be gracious,—is as sweet as Hebe's. Then it is that you see that in her prime she must in truth have been a lovely woman. There is at these moments a kindness in her eyes and a playfulness about her mouth which is apt to make you think that you can do what you like with the Frau. Who has not at times been charmed by the frolic playfulness of the tiger? Not that Frau Frohmann has aught of the tiger in her nature but its power. But the power is all there, and not unfrequently the signs of power. If she be thwarted, contradicted, counselled by unauthorised counsellors,—above all if she be censured,—then the signs of power are shown. Then the Frau does not smile. At such times she is wont to speak her mind very plainly, and to make those who hear her understand that, within the precincts and purlieus of the Brunnenthal Peacock, she is an irresponsible despot. There have been guests there rash enough to find some trifling faults with the comforts provided for them,—whose beds perhaps have been too hard, or their towels too limited, or perhaps their hours not agreeably arranged for them. Few, however, have ever done so twice, and they who have so sinned,—and have then been told that the next diligence would take them quickly to Innsbruck if they were discontented,—have rarely stuck to their complaints and gone. The comforts of the house, and the prices charged, and the general charms of the place have generally prevailed,—so that the complainants, sometimes with spoken apologies, have in most cases sought permission to remain. In late years the Frau's certainty of victory has created a feeling that nothing is to be said against the arrangements of the Peacock. A displeased guest can exercise his displeasure best by taking himself away in silence.

The Frau of late years has had two counsellors; for though she is but ill inclined to admit advice from those who have received no authority to give it, she is not therefore so self-confident as to feel that she can live and thrive without listening to the wisdom of others. And those two counsellors may be regarded as representing—the first or elder her conscience, and the second and younger her worldly prudence. And in the matter of her conscience very much more is concerned than simple honesty. It is not against cheating or extortion that her counsellor is sharp to her; but rather in regard to those innovations which he and she think to be prejudicial to the manner and life of Brunnenthal, of Innsbruck, of the Tyrol, of the Austrian empire generally, and, indeed, of the world at large. To be as her father had been before her,—for her father, too, had kept the Peacock; to let life be cheap and simple, but yet very plentiful as it had been in his days, this was the counsel given by Father Conolin the old priest, who always spent two nights in each month at the establishment, and was not unfrequently to be seen there on other occasions. He had been opposed to many things which had been effected,—that alteration of the hour of dinner, the erection of the bathhouse, the changing of plates at each course, and especially certain notifications and advertisements by which foreigners may have been induced to come to the Brunnenthal. The kaplan, or chaplain, as he was called, was particularly averse to strangers, seeming to think that the advantages of the place should be reserved, if not altogether for the Tyrolese, at any rate for the Germans of Southern Germany, and was probably of opinion that no real good could be obtained by harbouring Lutherans. But, of late, English also had come, to whom, though he was personally very courteous, he was much averse in his heart of hearts. Such had ever been the tendency of his advice, and it had always been received with willing, nay, with loving ears. But the fate of the kaplan had been as is the fate of all such counsellors. Let the toryism of the Tory be ever so strong, it is his destiny to carry out the purposes of his opponents. So it had been, and was, with the Frau. Though she was always in spirit antagonistic to the other counsellor, it was the other counsellor who prevailed with her.

At Innsbruck for many years there had lived a lawyer; or rather a family of lawyers, men always of good repute and moderate means, named Schlessen; and in their hands had been reposed by the Frau that confidence as to business matters which almost every one in business must have in some lawyer. The first

Schlessen whom the Frau had known in her youth, and who was then a very old man, had been almost as Conservative as the priest. Then had come his son, who had been less so, but still lived and died without much either of the light of progress or contamination of revolutionary ideas from the outer world. But about three years before the date of our tale he also had passed away, and now young Fritz Schlessen sat in the chair of his forefathers. It was the opinion of Innsbruck generally that the young lawyer was certainly equal, probably superior, in attainments and intellect to any of his predecessors. He had learned his business both at Munich and Vienna, and though he was only twenty-six when he was left to manage his clients himself, most of them adhered to him. Among others so did our Frau, and this she did knowing the nature of the man and of the counsel she might expect to receive from him. For though she loved the priest, and loved her old ways, and loved to be told that she could live and thrive on the rules by which her father had lived and thriven before her,—still, there was always present to her mind the fact that she was engaged in trade, and that the first object of a tradesman must be to make money. No shoemaker can set himself to work to make shoes having as his first intention an ambition to make the feet of his customers comfortable. That may come second, and to him, as a conscientious man, may be essentially necessary. But he sets himself to work to make shoes in order that he may earn a living. That law,—almost of nature we may say,—

had become so recognised by the Frau that she felt that it must be followed, even in spite of the priest if need were, and that, in order that it might be followed, it would be well that she should listen to the advice of Herr Schlessen. She heard, therefore, all that her kaplan would say to her with gracious smiles, and something of what her lawyer would say to her, not always very graciously; but in the long-run she would take her lawyer's advice.

It will have to be told in a following chapter how it was that Fritz Schlessen had a preponderating influence in the Brunnenthal, arising from other causes than his professional soundness and general prudence. It may, however, be as well to explain here that Peter Frohmann the son sided always with the priest, and attached himself altogether to the conservative interest. But he, though he was honest, diligent, and dutiful to his mother, was lumpy, uncouth, and slow both of speech and action. He understood the cutting of timber and the making of hay,—something perhaps of the care of horses and of the nourishment of pigs; but in money matters he was not efficient. Amalia, or Malchen, the daughter, who was four or five years her brother's junior, was much brighter, and she was strong on the reforming side. British money was to her thinking as good as Austrian, or even Tyrolese. To thrive even better than her forefathers had thriven seemed to her to be desirable. She therefore, though by her brightness and feminine ways she was very dear to the priest, was generally opposed to him in the family conclaves.

It was chiefly in consequence of her persistency that the table napkins at the Peacock were now changed twice a week.

CHAPTER II.

THE BEGINNING OF TROUBLES.

Of late days, and up to the time of which we are speaking, the chief contest between the Frau, with the kaplan and Peter on one side, and Malchen with Fritz Schlessen on the other, was on that most important question whether the whole rate of charges should not be raised at the establishment. The prices had been raised, no doubt, within the last twenty years, or the Frau could not have kept her house open;—but this had been done indirectly. That the matter may not be complicated for our readers, we will assume that all charges are made at the Peacock in zwansigers and kreutzers, and that the zwansiger, containing twenty kreutzers, is worth eightpence of English money. Now it must be understood that the guests at the Peacock were entertained at the rate of six zwansigers, or four shillings, a day, and that this included everything necessary,—a bed, breakfast, dinner, a cup of coffee after dinner, supper, as much fresh milk as anybody chose to drink when the cows were milked, and the use of everything in and about the establishment. Guests who required wine or beer, of course, were charged for what they had. Those who were rich enough to be taken about in carriages paid so much per job,—each separate jaunt having been inserted in a tariff. No doubt there were other possible and probable extras; but an ordinary guest might live for his six zwansigers a day;—and the bulk of them did so live, with the addition of whatever allowance of beer each might think appropriate. From time to time a little had been added to the cost of luxuries. Wine had become dearer, and perhaps the carriages. A bath was an addition to the bill, and certain larger and more commodious rooms were supposed to be entitled to an extra zwansiger per week;—but the main charge had always remained fixed. In the time of the Frau's father guests had been entertained at, let us say, four shillings a head, and guests were so entertained now. All the world,—at any rate all the Tyrolese world south of Innsbruck,—knew that six zwansigers was the charge in the Brunnenthal. It would be like adding a new difficulty to the path of life to make a change. The Frau had always held her head high,—had never been ashamed of looking her neighbour in the face, but when she was advised to rush at once up to seven zwansigers and a half (or five shillings a day), she felt that, should she do so, she would be overwhelmed with shame. Would not her customers then have cause of complaint? Would not they have such cause that they would in truth desert her? Did she not know that Herr Weiss, the magistrate from Brixen, with his wife, and his wife's sister, and the children, who came yearly to the Peacock, could not afford to bring his family at this increased rate of expenses? And the Fraulein Tendel with her sister would never come from Innsbruck if such an announcement was made to her. It was the pride of this woman's heart to give all that was necessary for good living, to those who would come and submit themselves to her, for four shillings a day. Among the "extras" she could endure some alteration. She did not like extras, and if people would have luxuries they must be made to pay for them. But the Peacock had always been kept open for six zwansigers, and though Fritz Schlessen was very eloquent, she would not give way to him.

Fritz Schlessen simply told her that the good things which she provided for her guests cost at present more than six zwansigers, and could not therefore be sold by her at that price without a loss. She was rich, Fritz remarked, shrugging his shoulders, and having amassed property could if she pleased dispose of it gradually by entertaining her guests at a loss to herself;—only let her know what she was doing. That might be charity, might be generosity, might be friendliness; but it was not trade. Everything else in the world had become dearer, and therefore living at the Peacock should be dearer. As to the Weisses and the Tendels, no doubt they might be shocked, and perhaps hindered from coming. But their places would surely be filled by others. Was not the house always full from the 1st of June till the end of September? Were not strangers refused admittance week after week from want of accommodation? If the new prices were found to be too high for the Tyrolese and Bavarians, they would not offend the Germans from the Rhine, or the Belgians, or the English. Was it not plain to every one that people now came from greater distances than heretofore?

These were the arguments which Herr Schlessen used; and, though they were very disagreeable, they were not easily answered. The Frau repudiated altogether the idea of keeping open her house on other than true trade principles. When the young lawyer talked to her about generosity she waxed angry, and accused him of laughing at her. "Dearest Frau Frohmann," he said, "it is so necessary you should know the truth! Of course you intend to make a profit;—but if you cannot do so at your present prices, and yet will not raise them, at any rate understand what it is that you are doing." Now the last year had been a bad year, and she knew that she had not increased her store. This all took place in the month of April, when a proposition was being made as to the prices for the coming season. The lawyer had suggested that a circular should be issued, giving notice of an altered tariff.

Malchen was clearly in favour of the new idea. She could not see that the Weisses and Tendels, and other neighbours, should be entertained at a manifest loss; and, indeed, she had prepossessions in favour of foreigners, especially of the English, which, when expressed, brought down upon her head sundry hard words from her mother, who called her a "pert hussey," and implied that if Fritz Schlessen wanted to pull the house down she, Malchen, would be willing that it should be done. "Better do that, mother, than keep the roof on at a loss," said Malchen; who upon that was turned at once out of the little inner room in which the conference was being held.

Peter, who was present on the occasion, was decidedly opposed to all innovations, partly because his conservative nature so prompted him, and partly because he did not regard Herr Schlessen with a friendship so warm as that entertained by his sister. He was, perhaps, a little jealous of the lawyer. And then he had an idea that as things were prosperous to the eye, they would certainly come right at last. The fortunes of the house had been made at the rate of six zwansigers a day, and there was, he thought, no wisdom more clear than that of adhering to a line of conduct which had proved itself to be advantageous.

The kaplan was clear against any change of prices; but then he burdened his advice on the question with a suggestion which was peculiarly disagreeable to the Frau. He acknowledged the truth of much that the lawyer had said. It appeared to him that the good things provided could not in truth be sold at the terms as they were now fixed. He was quite alive to the fact that it behoved the Frau as a wise woman to make a profit. Charity is one thing, and business is another. The Frau did her charities like a Christian, generally using Father Conolin as her almoner in such matters. But, as a keeper of a house of public entertainment, it was necessary that she should live. The kaplan was as wide awake to this as was the Frau herself, or the lawyer. But he thought that the changes should not be in the direction indicated by Schlessen. The condition of the Weisses and of the Tendels should be considered. How would it be if one of the "meats" and one of the puddings were discontinued, and if the cup of coffee after dinner were made an extra? Would not that so reduce the expenditure as to leave a profit? And in that case the Weisses and the Tendels need not necessarily incur any increased charges.

When the kaplan had spoken the lawyer looked closely into the Frau's face. The proposition might no doubt for the present meet the difficulty, but he knew that it would be disagreeable. There came a cloud upon the old woman's brow, and she frowned even upon the priest.

"They'd want to be helped twice out of the one pudding, and you'd gain nothing," said Peter.

"According to that," said the lawyer, "if there were only one course the dinner would cost the same. The fewer the dishes, the less the cost, no doubt."

"I don't believe you know anything about it," said the Frau.

"Perhaps not," said the lawyer. "On those little details no doubt you are the best judge. But I think I have shown that something should be done."

"You might try the coffee, Frau Frohmann," said the priest.

"They would not take any. You'd only save the coffee," said the lawyer.

"And the sugar," said the priest.

"But then they'd never ask for brandy," suggested Peter.

The Frau on that occasion said not a word further, but after a little while got up from her chair and stood silent among them; which was known to be a sign that the conference was dismissed.

All this had taken place immediately after dinner, which at this period of the year was eaten at noon. It had simply been a family meal, at which the Frau had sat with her two children and her two friends. The kaplan on such occasions was always free. Nothing that he had in that house ever cost him a kreutzer. But the attorney paid his way like any one else. When called on for absolute work done,—not exactly for advice given in conference,—he made his charges. It might be that a time was coming in which no money would pass on either side, but that time had not arrived as yet. As soon as the Frau was left alone, she re-seated herself in her accustomed arm-chair, and set herself to work in sober and almost solemn sadness to think over it all. It was a most perplexing question. There could be no doubt that all the wealth which she at present owned had been made by a business carried on at the present prices and after the existing fashion. Why should there be any change? She was told that she must make her customers pay more because she herself was made to pay more. But why should she pay more? She could understand that in the general prosperity of the Brunnenthal those about her should have somewhat higher wages. As she had prospered, why should not they also prosper? The servants of the poor must, she thought, be poorer than the servants of the rich. But why should poultry be dearer, and meat? Some things she knew were cheaper, as tea and sugar and coffee. She had bought three horses during the winter, and they certainly had been costly. Her father had not given such prices, nor, before this, had she. But that probably had been Peter's fault, who had too rashly acceded to the demands made upon him. And now she remembered with regret that, on the 1st of January, she had acceded to a petition from the carpenter for an addition of six zwansigers to his monthly wages. He had made the request on the plea of a sixth child, adding also, that journeymen carpenters both at Brixen and at Innsbruck were getting what he asked. She had granted to the coming of the additional baby that which she would probably have denied to the other argument; but it had never occurred to her that she was really paying the additional four shillings a month because carpenters were becoming dearer throughout the world. Malchen's clothes were certainly much more costly than her own had been, when she was young; but then Malchen was a foolish girl, fond of fashion from Munich, and just at this moment was in love. It could hardly be right that those poor Tendel females, with their small and fixed means, should be made to pay more for their necessary summer excursions because Malchen would dress herself in so-called French finery, instead of adhering, as she ought, to Tyrolese customs.

The Frau on this occasion spent an hour in solitude, thinking over it all. She had dismissed the conference, but that could not be regarded as an end to the matter. Herr Schlessen had come out from Innsbruck with a written document in his pocket, which he was proposing to have printed and circulated, and which, if printed and circulated, would intimate to the world at large that the Frau Frohmann had raised her prices. Therein the new rates, seven zwansigers and a half a head, were inserted unblushingly at full length, as though such a disruption of old laws was the most natural thing in the world. There was a flippancy about it which disgusted the old woman. Malchen seemed to regard an act which would banish from the Peacock the old friends and well-known customers of the house as though it were an easy trifle; and almost desirable with that very object. The Frau's heart warmed to the well-known faces as she thought of this. Would she not have infinitely greater satisfaction in cooking good dinners for her simple Tyrolese neighbours, than for rich foreigners who, after all, were too often indifferent to what was done for them? By those Tendel ladies her puddings were recognised as real works of art. They thought of them, talked of them, ate them, and no doubt dreamed of them. And Herr Weiss—how he enjoyed her dinners, and how proud he always was as he encouraged his children around him to help themselves to every dish in succession! And the Frau

Weiss—with all her cares and her narrow means—was she to be deprived of that cheap month's holiday which was so necessary for her, in order that the Peacock and the charms of the Brunnenthal generally might be devoted to Jews from Frankfort, or rich shopkeepers from Hamburg, or, worse still, to proud and thankless Englishmen? At the end of the hour the Frau had determined that she would not raise her prices.

But yet something must be done. Had she resolved, even silently resolved, that she would carry on her business at a loss, she would have felt that she was worthy of restraint as a lunatic. To keep a house of public entertainment and to lose by it was, to her mind, a very sad idea! To work and be out of pocket by working! To her who knew little or nothing of modern speculation, such a catastrophe was most melancholy. But to work with the intention of losing could be the condition only of a lunatic. And Schlessen had made good his point as to the last season. The money spent had been absolutely more than the money received. Something must be done. And yet she would not raise her prices.

Then she considered the priest's proposition. Peter, she knew, had shown himself to be a fool. Though his feelings were good, he always was a fool. The expenses of the house no doubt might be much diminished in the manner suggested by Herr Conolin. Salt butter could be given instead of fresh at breakfast. Cheaper coffee could be procured. The courses at dinner might be reduced. The second pudding might be discontinued with economical results. But had not her success in these things been the pride of her life; and of what good would her life be to her if its pride were crushed? The Weisses no doubt would come all the same, but how would they whisper and talk of her among themselves when they found these parsimonious changes! The Tendel ladies would not complain. It was not likely that a breath of complaint would ever pass their humble lips; but she herself, she, Frau Frohmann, who was perhaps somewhat unduly proud of her character for wealth, would have to explain to them why it was that that second pudding had been abolished. She would be forced to declare that she could no longer afford to supply it, a declaration which to her would have in it something of meanness, something of degradation. No! she could not abandon the glory of her dinner. It was as though you should ask a Royal Academician to cease to exhibit his pictures, or an actor to consent to have his name withdrawn from the bills. Thus at last she came to that further resolve. The kaplan's advice must be rejected, as must that of the lawyer.

But something must be done. For a moment there came upon her a sad idea that she would leave the whole thing to others, and retire into obscurity at Schwatz, the village from whence the Frohmanns had originally come. There would be ample means for private comfort. But then who would carry on the Peacock, who would look after the farm, and the timber, and the posting, and the mill? Peter was certainly not efficient for all that. And Malchen's ambition lay elsewhere. There was, too, a cowardice in this idea of running away which was very displeasing to her.

Why need there be any raising of prices at all,—either in one direction or in the other?—Had she herself never been persuaded into paying more to others, then she would not have been driven to demand more from others. And those higher payments on her part had, she thought, not been obligatory on her. She had been soft and good-natured, and therefore it was that she was now called upon to be exorbitant. There was something abominable to her in this general greed of the world for more money. At the moment she felt almost a hatred for poor Seppel the carpenter, and regarded that new baby of his as an impertinent intrusion. She would fall back upon the old wages, the old prices for everything. There would be a difficulty with that Innsbruck butcher; but unless he would give way she would try the man at Brixen. In that matter of fowls she would not yield a kreutzer to the entreaties of her poor neighbours who brought them to her for sale.

Then she walked forth from the house to a little arbour or summer-house which was close to the chapel opposite, in which she found Schlessen smoking his pipe with a cup of coffee before him, and Malchen by his side. "I have made up my mind. Herr Schlessen," she said. It was only when she was very angry with him that she called him Herr Schlessen.

"And what shall I do?" asked the lawyer.

"Do nothing at all; but just destroy that bit of paper." So saying, the Frau walked back to the house, and Fritz Schlessen, looking round at Malchen, did destroy that bit of paper.

CHAPTER III.

THE QUESTION OF THE MITGIFT.

About two months after the events described in the last chapter, Malchen and Fritz Schlessen were sitting in the same little arbour, and he was again smoking his pipe, and again drinking his coffee. And they were again alone. When these two were seated together in the arbour, at this early period of the season, they were usually left alone, as they were known to be lovers by the guests who would then be assembled at the Peacock. When the summer had grown into autumn, and the strangers from a distance had come, and the place was crowded, then the ordinary coffee-drinkers and smokers would crowd round the arbour, regardless of the loves of Amalia and Fritz.

The whole family of the Weisses were now at the Peacock, and the two Tendel ladies and three or four others, men with their wives and daughters, from Botzen, Brunecken, and places around at no great distance. It was now the end of June; but it is not till July that the house becomes full, and it is in August that the real crowd is gathered at Frau Frohmann's board. It is then that folk from a distance cannot find beds, and the whole culinary resources of the establishment are put to their greatest stress. It was now Monday, and the lawyer had been making a holiday, having come to the Brunnenthal on the previous Saturday. On the Sunday there had been perhaps a dozen visitors from Innsbruck who had been driven out after early mass for their dinner and Sunday holiday. Everything had been done at the Peacock on the old style. There had been no diminution either in the number or in the excellence of the dishes, nor had there been any increase in the tariff. It had been the first day of the season at which there had been a full table, and the Frau had done her best. Everybody had known that the sojourners in the house were to be entertained at the old rates; but it had been hoped by the lawyer and the priest, and by Malchen,—even by Peter himself—that a zwansiger would be added to the charge for dinner demanded from the townspeople. But at the last moment word had gone forth that there should be no increase. All the morning the old lady had been very gloomy. She had heard mass in her own chapel, and had then made herself very busy in the kitchen. She had spoken no word to any one till, at the moment before dinner, she gave her instructions to Malchen, who always made out the bills, and saw that the money was duly received. There was to be no increase. Then, when the last pudding had been sent in, she went, according to her custom, to her room and decorated herself in her grand costume. When the guests had left the dining-room and were clustering about in the passages and on the seats in front of the house, waiting for their coffee, she had come forth, very fine, with her grand cap on her head, with her gold and silver ornaments, with her arms bare, and radiant with smiles. She shook Madame Weiss very graciously by the hand and stooped down and kissed the youngest child. To one fraulein after another she said a civil word. And when, as it happened, Seppel the carpenter went by, dressed in his Sunday best, with a child in each hand, she stopped him and asked kindly after the baby. She had made up her mind that, at any rate for a time, she would not submit to the humiliation of acknowledging that she was driven to the necessity of asking increased prices.

That had taken place on the Sunday, and it was on the following day that the two lovers were in the arbour together. Now it must be understood that all the world knew that these lovers were lovers, and that all the world presumed that they were to become husband and wife. There was not and never had been the least secrecy about it. Malchen was four or five and twenty, and he was perhaps thirty. They knew their own minds, and were, neither of them, likely to be persuaded by others either to marry or not to marry. The Frau had given her consent,—not with that ecstacy of joy with which sons-in-law are sometimes welcomed,—but still without reserve. The kaplan had given in his adhesion. The young lawyer was not quite the man he liked,—entertained some of the new ideas about religion, and was given to innovations; but he was respectable and well-to-do. He was a lover against whom he, as a friend of the family, could not lift up his voice. Peter did not like the man, and Peter, in his way, was fond of his sister. But he had not objected. Had he done so, it would not have mattered much. Malchen was stronger at the Brunnenthal than Peter. Thus it may be said that things generally smiled upon the lovers. But yet no one had ever heard that a day was fixed for their marriage. Madame Weiss had once asked Malchen, and Malchen had told her—not exactly to mind her own business; but that had been very nearly the meaning of what she had said.

There was, indeed, a difficulty; and this was the difficulty. The Frau had assented—in a gradual fashion, rather by not dissenting as the thing had gone on, so that it had come to be understood that the thing was to be. But she had never said a word as to the young lady's fortune—as to that "mitgift" which in such a case would certainly be necessary. Such a woman as the Frau in giving her daughter would surely have to give something with her. But the Frau was a woman who did not like parting with her money; and was such a woman that even the lawyer did not like asking the question. The fraulein had once inquired, but the mother had merely raised her eyebrows and remained silent. Then the lawyer had told the priest that in the performance of her moral duties the Frau ought to settle something in her own mind. The priest had assented, but had seemed to imply that in the performance of such a duty an old lady ought not to be hurried. A year or two, he seemed to think, would not be too much for consideration. And so the matter stood at the present moment.

Perhaps it is that the Germans are a slow people. It may be that the Tyrolese are especially so. Be that as it may, Herr Schlessen did not seem to be driven into any agony of despair by these delays. He was fondly attached to his Malchen ; but as to offering to take her without any mitgift,—quite empty-handed, just as she stood,—that was out of the question. No young man who had anything, ever among his acquaintances, did that kind of thing. Scales should be somewhat equally balanced. He had a good income, and was entitled to some substantial mitgift. He was quite ready to marry her to-morrow, if only this important question could get itself settled.

Malchen was quite as well aware as was he that her mother should be brought to do her duty in this matter; but, perhaps of the two, she was a little the more impatient. If there should at last be a slip between the cup and the lip, the effect to her would be so much more disastrous than to him! He could very easily get another wife. Young women were as plenty as blackberries. So the fraulein told herself. But she might find it difficult to suit herself, if at last this affair were to be broken off. She knew herself to be a fair, upstanding, good-looking lass, with personal attractions sufficient to make such a young man as Fritz Schlessen like her society; but she knew also that her good looks, such as they were, would not be improved by fretting. It might be possible that Fritz should change his mind some day, if he were kept waiting till he saw her becoming day by day more commonplace under his eyes. Malchen had good sense enough not to overrate her own charms, and she knew the world well enough to be aware that she would be wise to secure, if possible, a comfortable home while she was at her best. It was not that she suspected Fritz; but she did not think that she would be justified in supposing him to be more angelic than other young men simply because he was her lover. Therefore, Malchen was impatient, and for the last month or two had been making up her mind to be very "round" with her mother on the subject.

At the present moment, however, the lovers, as they were sitting in the arbour, were discussing rather the Frau's affairs in regard to the establishment than their own. Schlessen had, in truth, come to the Brunnenthal on this present occasion to see what would be done, thinking that if the thin edge of the wedge could have been got in,—if those people from the town could have been made to pay an extra zwansiger each for their Sunday dinner,—then, even yet, the old lady might be induced to raise her prices in regard to the autumn and more fashionable visitors. But she had been obstinate, and had gloried in her obstinacy, dressing herself up in her grandest ornaments and smiling her best smiles, as in triumph at her own victory.

"The fact is, you know, it won't do," said the lawyer to his love. "I don't know how I am to say any more, but anybody can see with half an eye that she will simply go on losing money year after year. It is all very fine for the Weisses and Tendels, and very fine for old Trauss,"—old Trauss was a retired linendraper from Vienna, who lived at Innsbruck, and was accustomed to eat many dinners at the Peacock; a man who could afford to pay a proper price, but who was well pleased to get a good dinner at a cheap rate,—"and very well for old Trauss," continued the lawyer, becoming more energetic as he went on, "to regale themselves at your mother's expense;—but that's what it comes to. Everybody knows that everybody has raised the price of everything. Look at the Golden Lion." The Golden Lion was the grand hotel in the town. "Do you think they haven't raised their prices during the last twenty years?"

"Why is it, Fritz?"

"Everything goes up together, of course. If you'll look into old accounts you'll see that three hundred years ago you could buy a sheep at Salzburg for two florins and a half. I saw it somewhere in a book. If a lawyer's clerk then had eighty florins a year he was well off. That would not surprise her. She can understand that there should be an enormous change in three hundred years; but she can't make out why there should be a little change in thirty years."

"But many things have got cheaper, Fritz."

"Living altogether hasn't got cheaper. Look at wages!"

"I don't know why we should pay more. Everybody says that bread is lower than it used to be."

"What sort of bread do the people eat now? Look at that man." The man was Seppel, who was dragging a cart which he had just mended out of the shed which was close by,—in which cart were seated his three eldest children, so that he might help their mother as assistant nurse even while he was at his work. "Don't you think he gets more wheaten flour into his house in a week than his grandfather did in a year? His grandfather never saw white bread."

"Why should he have it?"

"Because he likes it, and because he can get it. Do you think he'd have stayed here if his wages had not been raised?"

"I don't think Seppel ever would have moved out of the Brunnenthal, Fritz."

"Then Seppel would have been more stupid than the cow, which knows very well on which side of the field it can find the best grass. Everything gets dearer;—and if one wants to live one has to swim with the stream. You might as well try to fight with bows and arrows, or with the old-fashioned flint rifles, as to live at the same rate as your grandfather." The young lawyer, as he said this, rapped his pipe on the table to knock out the ashes, and threw himself back on his seat with a full conviction that he had spoken words of wisdom.

"What will it all come to, Fritz?" This Malchen asked with real anxiety in her voice. She was not slow to join two things together. It might well be that her mother should be induced by her pride to carry on the business for a while, so as to lose some of her money, but that she should, at last, be induced to see the error of her ways before serious damage had been done. Her financial position was too good to be brought to ruin by small losses. But during the period of her discomfiture she certainly would not be got to open her hand in that matter of the mitgift. Malchen's own little affair would never get itself settled till this other question should have arranged itself satisfactorily. There could be no mitgift from a failing business. And if the business were to continue to fail for the next year or two, where would Malchen be then? It was not, therefore, wonderful that she should be in earnest.

"Your mother is a very clever woman," said the lover.

"It seems to me that she is very foolish about this," said Malchen, whose feeling of filial reverence was not at the moment very strong.

"She is a clever woman, and has done uncommonly well in the world. The place is worth double as much as when she married your father. But it is that very success which makes her obstinate. She thinks that she can see her way. She fancies that she can compel people to work for her and deal with her at the old prices. It will take her, perhaps, a couple of years to find out that this is wrong. When she has lost three or four thousand florins she'll come round."

Fritz, as he said this, seemed to be almost contented with this view of the case,—as though it made no difference to him. But with the fraulein the matter was so essentially personal that she could not allow it to rest there. She had made up her mind to be round with her mother; but it seemed to her to be necessary, also, that something should be said to her lover. "Won't all that be very bad for you, Fritz?"

"Her business with me will go on just the same."

This was felt to be unkind and very unloverlike. But she could not afford at the present moment to quarrel with him. "I mean about our settling," she said.

"It ought not to make a difference."

"I don't know about ought;—but won't it? You don't see her as I do, but, of course, it puts her into a bad temper."

"I suppose she means to give you some fixed sum. I don't doubt but she has it all arranged in her own mind."

"Why doesn't she name it, then?"

"Ah, my dear,—mein schatz,—there is nobody who likes too well to part with his money."

"But when is there to be an end of it?"

"You should find that out. You are her child, and she has only two. That she should hang back is a matter of course. When one has the money of his own one can do anything. It is all in her own hand. See what I bear. When I tell her this or that she turns upon me as if I were nobody. Do you think I should suffer it if she were only just a client? You must persuade her, and be gentle with her; but if she would name the sum it would be a comfort, of course."

The fraulein herself did not in the least know what the sum ought to be; but she thought she did know that it was a matter which should be arranged between her lover and her parent. What she would have liked to have told him was this,—that as there were only two children, and as her mother was at any rate an honest woman, he might be sure that a proper dowry would come at last. But she was well aware that he would think that a mitgift should be a mitgift. The bride should come with it in her hand, so that she might be a comfort to her husband's household. Schlessen would not be at all willing to wait patiently for the Frau's death, or even for some final settlement of her affairs when she might make up her mind to leave the Peacock and betake herself to Schwatz. "You would not like to ask her yourself?" she said.

He was silent for a while, and then he answered her by another question. "Are you afraid of her?"

"Not afraid. But she would just tell me I was impertinent. I am not a bit afraid, but it would do no good. It would be so reasonable for you to do it."

"There is just the difference, Malchen. I am afraid of her."

"She could not bite you."

"No;—but she might say something sharp, and then I might answer her sharply. And then there might be a quarrel. If she were to tell me that she did not want to see me any more in the Brunnenthal, where should we be then? Mein schatz, if you will take my advice, you will just say a word yourself, in your softest, sweetest way." Then he got up and made his way across to the stable, where was the horse which was to take him back to Innsbruck. Malchen was not altogether well pleased with her lover, but she perceived that on the present occasion she must, perforce, follow his advice.

CHAPTER IV.

THE FRAU RETURNS TO THE SIMPLICITY OF THE OLD DAYS.

Two or three weeks went by in the Brunnenthal without any special occurrence, and Malchen had not as yet spoken to her mother about her fortune. The Frau had during this time been in more than ordinary good humour with her own household. July had opened with lovely weather, and the house had become full earlier than usual. The Frau liked to have the house full, even though there might be no profit, and therefore she was in a good humour. But she had been exceptionally busy, and was trying experiments in her housekeeping, as to which she was still in hope that they would carry her through all her difficulties. She had been both to Brixen on one side of the mountain and to Innsbruck on the other, and had changed her butcher. Her old friend Hoff, at the latter place, had altogether declined to make any reduction in his prices. Of course they had been raised within the last five or six years. Who did not know that that had been the case with butchers' meat all the world over? As it was, he charged the Frau less than he charged the people at the Golden Lion. So at least he swore; and when she told him that unless an alteration was made she must take her custom elsewhere—he bade her go elsewhere. Therefore she did make a contract with the butcher at Brixen on lower terms, and seemed to think that she had got over her difficulty. But Brixen was further than Innsbruck, and the carriage was more costly. It was whispered also about the house that the meat was not equally good. Nobody, however, had as yet dared to say a word on that subject to the Frau. And she, though in the midst of her new efforts she was good-humoured herself,—as is the case with many people while they have faith in the efforts they are making,—had become the cause of much unhappiness among others. Butter, eggs, poultry, honey, fruit, and vegetables, she was in the habit of buying from her neighbours, and had been so excellent a customer that she was as good as a market to the valley in general. There had usually been some haggling; but that, I think, by such vendors is considered a necessary and almost an agreeable part of the operation. The produce had been bought and sold, and the Frau had, upon the whole, been regarded as a kind of providence to the Brunnenthal. But now there were sad tales told at many a cottage and small farmstead around. The Frau had declared that she would give no more than three zwansigers a pair for chickens, and had insisted on having both butter and eggs at a lower price than she had paid last year. And she had succeeded, after infinite clamours. She had been their one market, their providence, and they had no other immediate customers to whom to betake themselves. The eggs and the butter, the raspberries and the currants, must be sold. She had been imperious and had succeeded, for a while. But there were deep murmurs, and already a feeling was growing up in favour of Innsbruck and a market cart. It was very dreadful. How were they to pay their taxes, how were they to pay anything, if they were to be crimped and curtailed in this way? One poor woman had already walked to Innsbruck with three dozen eggs, and had got nearly twice the money which the Frau had offered. The labour of the walk had been very hard upon her, and the economy of the proceeding generally may have been doubtful; but it had been proved that the thing could be done.

Early in July there had come a letter, addressed to Peter, from an English gentleman who, with his wife and daughter, had been at the Brunnenthal on the preceding year. Mr. Cartwright had now written to say, that the same party would be glad to come again early in August, and had asked what were the present prices. Now the very question seemed to imply a conviction on the gentleman's mind that the prices would be raised. Even Peter, when he took the letter to his mother, thought that this would be a good opportunity for taking a step in advance. These were English people, and entitled to no loving forbearance. The Cartwrights need know nothing as to the demands made on the Weisses and Tendels. Peter who had always been on his mother's side, Peter who hated changes, even he suggested that he might write back word that seven zwansigers and a half was now the tariff. "Don't you know I have settled all that?" said the old woman, turning upon him fiercely. Then he wrote to Mr. Cartwright to say that the charge would be six zwansigers a day, as heretofore. It was certainly a throwing away of money. Mr. Cartwright was a Briton, and would, therefore, almost have preferred to pay another zwansiger or two. So at least Peter thought. And he, even an Englishman, with his wife and daughter, was to be taken in and entertained at a loss! At a loss!—unless, indeed, the Frau could be successful in her new mode of keeping her house. Father Conolin in these days kept away. The complaints made by the neighbours around reached his ears,—very sad complaints,—and he hardly knew how to speak of them to the Frau. It was becoming very serious with him. He had counselled her against any rise in her own prices, but had certainly not intended that she should make others lower. That had not been his plan; and now he did not know what advice to give.

But the Frau, resolute in her attempt, and proud of her success as far as it had gone, constantly adducing the conduct of these two rival butchers as evidence of her own wisdom, kept her ground like a Trojan. All the old courses were served, and the puddings and the fruit were at first as copious as ever. If the meat was inferior in quality,—and it could not be so without her knowledge, for she had not reigned so long in the kitchen of the Peacock without having become a judge in such matters,—she was willing to pass the fault over for a time. She tried to think that there was not much difference. She almost tried to believe that second-rate meat would do as well as first-rate. There should at least be no lack of anything in the cookery. And so she toiled and struggled, and was hopeful that she might have her own way and prove to all her advisers that she knew how to manage the house better than any of them.

There was great apparent good humour. Though she had frowned upon Peter when he had shown a disposition to spoil those Egyptians the Cartwrights, she had only done so in defence of her own resolute purpose, and soon returned to her kind looks. She was, too, very civil to Malchen, omitting for the time her usual gibes and jeers as to her daughter's taste for

French finery and general rejection of Tyrolese customs. And she said nothing of the prolonged absence of her two counsellors, the priest and the lawyer. A great struggle was going on within her own bosom, as to which she in these days said not a word to anybody. One counsellor had told her to raise her prices; another had advised her to lessen the luxuries supplied. As both the one proposition and the other had gone against her spirit, she had looked about her to find some third way out of her embarrassments. She had found it, and the way was one which recommended itself to her own sense of abstract justice. The old prices should prevail in the valley everywhere. She would extort nothing from Mr. Cartwright, but then neither should her neighbours extort anything from her. Seppel's wife was ill, and she had told him that in consequence of that misfortune the increased wages should be continued for three months, but that after that she must return to the old rate. In the softness of her heart she would have preferred to say six months, but that in doing so she would have seemed to herself to have departed from the necessary rigour of her new doctrine. But when Seppel stood before her, scratching his head, a picture of wretchedness and doubt, she was not comfortable in her mind. Seppel had a dim idea of his own rights, and did not like to be told that his extra zwansigers came to him from the Frau's charity. To go away from the Brunnenthal at the end of the summer, to go away at all, would be terrible to him; but to work for less than fair wages, would that not be more terrible? Of all which the Frau, as she looked at him, understood much.

And she understood much also of the discontent and almost despair which was filling the minds of the poor women all around her. All those poor women were dear to her. It was in her nature to love those around her, and especially those who were dependent on her. She knew the story of every household,—what children each mother had reared and what she had lost, when each had been brought to affliction by a husband's illness or a son's misconduct. She had never been deaf to their troubles; and though she might have been heard in violent discussions, now with one and now with another, as to the selling value of this or that article, she had always been held by them to be a just woman and a constant friend. Now they were up in arms against her, to the extreme grief of her heart.

Nevertheless it was necessary that she should support herself by an outward appearance of tranquillity, so that the world around her might know that she was not troubled by doubts as to her own conduct. She had heard somewhere that no return can be made from evil to good courses without temporary disruptions, and that all lovers of justice are subject to unreasonable odium. Things had gone astray because there had been unintentional lapses from justice. She herself had been the delinquent when she had allowed herself to be talked into higher payments than those which had been common in the valley in her young days. She had not understood, when she made these lapses gradually, how fatal would be their result. Now she understood, and was determined to plant her foot firmly down on the old figures. All this evil had come from a departure from the old ways. There must be sorrow and trouble, and perhaps some ill blood, in this return. That going back to simplicity is always so difficult! But it should be done. So she smiled, and refused to give more than three zwansigers a pair for her chickens.

One old woman came to her with the express purpose of arguing it all out. Suse Krapp was the wife of an old woodman who lived high up above the Peacock, among the pines, in a spot which could only be reached by a long and very steep ascent, and who being old, and having a daughter and granddaughters whom she could send down with her eggs and wild fruit, did not very often make her appearance in the valley. But she had known the Frau well for many years, having been one of those to welcome her when she had arrived there as a bride, and had always been treated with exceptional courtesy. Suse Krapp was a woman who had brought up a large family, and had known troubles; but she had always been able to speak her own mind; and when she arrived at the house, empty-handed, with nothing to sell, declaring at once her purpose of remonstrating with the Frau, the Frau regarded her as a delegate from the commercial females of the valley generally; and she took the coming in good part, asking Suse into her own inner room.

After sundry inquiries on each side, respecting the children and the guests, and the state of things in the world at large, the real question was asked, "Ah, meine liebe Frau Frohmann,—my very dear Mrs. Frohmann, as one might say here,—why are you dealing with us all in the Brunnenthal after this hard fashion?"

"What do you call a hard fashion, Suse?"

"Only giving half price for everything that you buy. Why should anything be cheaper this year than it was last? Ah, alas! does not everybody know that everything is dearer?"

"Why should anything be dearer, Suse? The people who come here are not charged more than they were twenty years ago."

"Who can tell? How can an old woman say? It is all very bad. The world, I suppose, is getting worse. But it is so. Look at the taxes."

The taxes, whether imperial or municipal, was a matter on which Frau did not want to speak. She felt that they were altogether beyond her reach. No doubt there had been a very great increase in such demands during her time, and it was an increase against which nobody could make any stand at all. But, if that was all, there had been a rise in prices quite sufficient to answer that. She was willing to pay three zwansigers a pair for chickens, and yet she could remember when they were to be bought for a zwansiger each.

"Yes, taxes," she said; "they are an evil which we

must all endure. It is no good grumbling at them. But we have had the roads made for us."

This was an unfortunate admission, for it immediately gave Suse Krapp an easy way to her great argument. "Roads, yes! and they are all saying that they must make use of them to send the things into market. Josephine Bull took her eggs into the city and got two kreutzers apiece for them."

The Frau had already heard of that journey, and had also heard that poor Josephine Bull had been very much fatigued by her labours. It had afflicted her much, both that the poor woman should have been driven to such a task, and that such an innovation should have been attempted. She had never loved Innsbruck dearly, and now she was beginning to hate the place. "What good did she get by that, Suse? None, I fear. She had better have given her eggs away in the valley."

"But they will have a cart."

"Do you think a cart won't cost money? There must be somebody to drive the cart, I suppose." On this point the Frau spoke feelingly, as she was beginning to appreciate the inconvenience of sending twice a week all the way to Brixen for her meat. There was a diligence, but though the horses were kept in her own stables, she had not as yet been able to come to terms with the proprietor.

"There is all that to think of certainly," said Suse. "But——. Wouldn't you come back, meine liebe Frau, to the prices you were paying last year? Do you not know that they would sooner sell to you than to any other human being in all the world, and they must live by their little earnings?"

But the Frau could not be persuaded. Indeed had she allowed herself to be persuaded, all her purpose would have been brought to an end. Of course there must be trouble, and her refusal of such a prayer as this was a part of her trouble. She sent for a glass of kirsch-wasser to mitigate the rigour of her denial, and as Suse drank the cordial she endeavoured to explain her system. There could be no happiness, no real prosperity in the valley, till they had returned to their old ways. "It makes me unhappy," said the Frau, shaking her head, "when I see the girls making for themselves long petticoats." Suse quite agreed with the Frau as to the long petticoats; but, as she went, she declared that the butter and eggs must be taken into Innsbruck, and another allusion to the cart was the last word upon her tongue.

It was on the evening of that same day that Malchen, unaware that her mother's feelings had just then been peculiarly stirred up by an appeal from the women of the valley, came at last to the determination of asking that something might be settled as to the "mitgift." "Mother," she said, "Fritz Schlessen thinks that something should be arranged."

"Arranged as how?"

"I suppose he wants—to be married."

"If he don't, I suppose somebody else does," said the mother smiling.

"Well, mother! Of course it is not pleasant to be as we are now. You must feel that yourself. Fritz is a good young man, and there is nothing about him that I have a right to complain of. But of course, like all the rest of 'em, he expects some money when he takes a wife. Couldn't you tell him what you mean to give?"

"Not at present, Malchen."

"And why not now? It has been going on two years."

"Nina Cobard at Schwatz was ten years before her people would let it come off. Just at present I am trying a great experiment, and I can say nothing about money till the season is over." With this answer Malchen was obliged to be content, and was not slow in perceiving that it almost contained a promise that the affairs should be settled when the season was over.

CHAPTER V.

A ZWANSIGER IS A ZWANSIGER.

In the beginning of August, the Weisses and the Tendels and Herr Trauss had all left the Brunnenthal, and our friend Frau Frohmann was left with a house full of guests who were less intimately known to her, but who not the less demanded and received all her care. But, as those departed whom she had taught herself to regard as neighbours and who were therefore entitled to something warmer and more generous than mere tavern hospitality, she began to feel the hardness of her case in having to provide so sumptuously for all these strangers at a loss. There was a party of Americans in the house who had absolutely made no inquiry whatsoever as to prices till they had shown themselves at her door. Peter had been very urgent with her to mulct the Americans, who were likely, he thought, to despise the house merely because it was cheap. But she would not give way. If the American gentleman should find out the fact and turn upon her, and ask her why he was charged more than others, how would she be able to answer him? She had never yet been so placed as not to be able to answer any complaints, boldly and even indignantly. It was hard upon her; but if the prices were to be raised to any, they must be raised to all.

The whole valley now was in a hubbub. In the matter of butter there had been so great a commotion that the Frau had absolutely gone back to the making of her own, a system which had been abandoned at the Peacock a few years since, with the express object of befriending the neighbours. There had been a dairy with all its appurtenances; but it had come to pass that the women around had got cows, and that the Frau had found that without damage to herself she could buy their supplies. And in this way her own dairy had gone out of use. She had kept her cows because there had grown into use a great drinking of milk at the Peacock, and as the establishment had gradually increased, the demand for cream, custards, and such luxuries had of course increased also. Now, when, remembering this, she conceived that she had a peculiar right to receive submission as to the price of butter, and yet found more strong rebellion here than on any other point, she at once took the bull by the horns, and threw not only her energies, but herself bodily into the dairy. It was repaired and whitewashed, and scoured and supplied with all necessary furniture in so marvellously short a time, that the owners of cows around could hardly believe their ears and their eyes. Of course there was a spending of money, but there had never been any slackness as to capital at the Peacock when good results might be expected from its expenditure. So the dairy was set agoing.

But there was annoyance, even shame, and to the old woman's feeling almost disgrace, arising from this. As you cannot eat your cake and have it, so neither can you make your butter and have your cream. The supply of new milk to the milk-drinkers was at first curtailed, and then altogether stopped. The guests were not entitled to the luxury by any contract, and were simply told that as the butter was now made at home, the milk was wanted for that purpose. And then there certainly was a deterioration in the puddings. There had hitherto been a rich plenty which was now wanting. No one complained; but the Frau herself felt the falling off. The puddings now were such as might be seen at other places,—at the Golden Lion for instance. Hitherto her puddings had been unrivalled in the Tyrol.

Then there had suddenly appeared a huckster, a

pedlar, an itinerant dealer in the valley who absolutely went round to the old women's houses and bought the butter at the prices which she had refused to give. And this was a man who had been in her own employment, had been brought to the valley by herself, and had once driven her own horses! And it was reported to her that this man was simply an agent for a certain tradesman in Innsbruck. There was an ingratitude in all this which nearly broke her heart. It seemed to her that those to whom in their difficulties she had been most kind were now turning upon her in her difficulty. And she thought that there was no longer left among the people any faith, any feeling of decent economy, any principle. Disregarding right or wrong, they would all go where they could get half a zwansiger more! They knew what it was she was attempting to do; for had she not explained it all to Suse Krapp? And yet they turned against her.

The poor Frau knew nothing of that great principle of selling in the dearest market, however much the other lesson as to buying in the cheapest had been brought home to her. When a fixed price had become fixed, that, she thought, should not be altered. She was demanding no more than she had been used to demand, though to do so would have been so easy! But her neighbours, those to whom she had even been most friendly, refused to assist her in her efforts to re-establish the old and salutary simplicity. Of course when the butter was taken into Innsbruck, the chickens and the eggs went with the butter. When she learned how all this was she sent for Suse Krapp, and Suse Krapp again came down to her.

"They mean then to quarrel with me utterly?" said the Frau with her sternest frown.

"Meine liebe Frau Frohmann!" said the old woman, embracing the arm of her ancient friend.

"But they do mean it?"

"What can we do, poor wretches? We must live."

"You lived well enough before," said the Frau, raising her fist in the unpremeditated eloquence of her indignation. "Will it be better for you now to deal with strangers who will rob you at every turn? Will Karl Muntz, the blackguard that he is, advance money to any of you at your need? Well; let it be so. I too can deal with strangers. But when once I have made arrangements in the town, I will not come back to the people of the valley. If we are to be severed, we will be severed. It goes sadly against the grain with me, as I have a heart in my bosom."

"You have, you have, my dearest Frau Frohmann."

"As for the cranberries, we can do without them." Now it had been the case that Suse Krapp with her grandchildren had supplied the Peacock with wild fruits in plentiful abundance, which wild fruits, stewed as the Frau knew how to stew them, had been in great request among the guests at the Brunnenthal. Great bowls of cranberries and bilberries had always at this period of the year turned the Frau's modest suppers into luxurious banquets. But there must be an end to that now; not in any way because the price paid for the fruit was grudged, but because the quarrel, if quarrel there must be, should be internecine at all points. She had loved them all; but, if they turned against her, not the less because of her love would she punish them. Poor old Suse wiped her eyes and took her departure, without any kirsch-wasser on this occasion.

It all went on from bad to worse. Seppel the carpenter gave her notice that he would leave her service at the end of August. "Why at the end of August?" she asked, remembering that she had promised to give him the higher rate of wages up to a later date than that. Then Seppel explained, that as he must do something for himself,—that is, find another place,—the sooner he did that the better. Now Seppel the carpenter was brother to that Anton who had most wickedly undertaken the huckstering business, on the part of Karl Muntz the dealer in Innsbruck, and it turned out that Seppel was to join him. There was an ingratitude in this which almost drove the old woman frantic. If any one in the valley was more bound to her by kindly ties than another, it was Seppel, with his wife and six children. Wages! There had been no question of wages when Babette, Seppel's wife, had been ill; and Babette had always been ill. And when he had chopped his own foot with his own axe, and had gone into the hospital for six weeks, they had wanted nothing! That he should leave her for a matter of six zwansigers a month, and not only leave her, but become her active enemy, was dreadful to her. Nor was her anger at all modified when he explained it all to her. As a man, and as a carpenter who was bound to keep up his own respect among carpenters, he could not allow himself to work for less than the ordinary wages. The Frau had been very kind to him, and he and his wife and children were all grateful. But she would not therefore wish him,—this was his argument, —she would not on that account require him to work for less than his due. Seppel put his hand on his heart, and declared that his honour was concerned. As for his brother's cart and his huckstery trade and Karl Muntz, he was simply lending a hand to that till he could get a settled place as carpenter. He was doing the Frau no harm. If he did not look after the cart, somebody else would. He was very submissive and most anxious to avoid her anger; but yet would not admit that he was doing wrong. But she towered in her wrath, and would listen to no reason. It was to her all wrong. It was innovation, a spirit of change coming from the source of all evil, bringing with it unkindness, absence of charity, ingratitude! It was flat mutiny, and rebellion against their betters. For some weeks it seemed to the Frau that all the world was going to pieces.

Her position was the more painful because at the time she was without counsellors. The kaplan came indeed as usual, and was as attentive and flattering to her as of yore; but he said nothing to her about her own affairs unless he was asked; and she did not ask him, knowing that he would not give her palatable counsel. The kaplan himself was not well versed in political economy or questions of money generally; but he had a vague idea that the price of a chicken ought to be higher now than it was thirty years ago. Then why not also the price of living to the guests at the Peacock? On that matter he argued with himself that the higher prices for the chickens had prevailed for some time, and that it was at any rate impossible to go back. And perhaps the lawyer had been right in recommending the Frau to rush at once to seven zwansigers and a half. His mind was vacillating and his ideas misty; but he did agree with Suse Krapp when she declared that the poor people must live. He could not, therefore, do the Frau any good by his advice.

As for Schlessen he had not been at the Brunnenthal for a month, and had told Malchen in Innsbruck that unless he were specially wanted, he would not go to the Peacock until something had been settled as to the mitgift. "Of course she is going to lose a lot of money," said Schlessen. "Anybody can see that with half an eye. Everybody in the town is talking about it. But when I tell her so, she is only angry with me."

Malchen of course could give no advice. Every step which her mother took seemed to her to be unwise. Of course the old women would do the best they could with their eggs. The idea that any one out of gratitude should sell cheaper to a friend than to an enemy was to her monstrous. But when she found that her mother was determined to swim against the stream, to wound herself by kicking against the pricks, to set at defiance all the common laws of trade, and that in this way money was to be lost, just at that very epoch of her own life in which it was so necessary that money should be forthcoming for her own advantage,—then she became moody, unhappy, and silent. What a pity it was that all this power should be vested in her mother's hands.

As for Peter, he had been altogether converted. When he found that a cart had to be sent twice a week to Brixen, and that the very poultry which had been carried from the valley to the town had to be brought back from the town to the valley, then his spirit of conservatism deserted him. He went so far as to advise his mother to give way. "I don't see that you do any good by ruining yourself," he said.

But she turned at him very fiercely. "I suppose I may do as I like with my own," she replied.

Yes; she could do what she liked with her own. But now it was declared by all those around her, by her neighbours in the valley, and by those in Innsbruck who knew anything about her, that it was a sad thing and a bad thing that an old woman should be left with the power of ruining all those who belonged to her, and that there should be none to restrain her! And yet for the last twenty-five years previous to this it had been the general opinion in these parts that nobody had ever managed such a house as well as the Frau Frohmann. As for being ruined,—Schlessen, who was really acquainted with her affairs, knew better than that. She might lose a large sum of money, but there was no fear of ruin. Schlessen was inclined to think that all this trouble would end in the Frau retiring to Schwatz, and that the settlement of the mitgift might thus be accelerated. Perhaps he and the Frau herself were the only two persons who really knew how well she had thriven. He was not afraid, and, being naturally patient, was quite willing to let things take their course.

The worst of it to the Frau herself was that she knew so well what people were saying of her. She had enjoyed for many years all that delight which comes from success and domination. It had not been merely, nor even chiefly, the feeling that money was being made. It is not that which mainly produces the comfortable condition of mind which attends success. It is the sense of respect which it engenders. The Frau had held her head high, and felt herself inferior to none, because she had enjoyed to the full this conviction. Things had gone pleasantly with her. Nothing is so enfeebling as failure; but she, hitherto, had never failed. Now a new sensation had fallen upon her, by which at certain periods she was almost prostrated. The woman was so brave that at her worst moments she would betake herself to solitude and shed her tears where no one could see her. Then she would come out and so carry herself that none should guess how she suffered. To no ears did she utter a word of complaint, unless her indignation to Seppel, to Suse, and the others might be called complaining. She asked for no sympathy. Even to the kaplan she was silent, feeling that the kaplan, too, was against her. It was natural that he should take part with the poor. She was now, for the first time in her life, driven, alas, to feel that the poor were against her.

The house was still full, but there had of late been a great falling off in the midday visitors. It had, indeed, almost come to pass that that custom had died away. She told herself, with bitter regret, that this was the natural consequence of her deteriorated dinners. The Brixen meat was not good. Sometimes she was absolutely without poultry. And in those matters of puddings, cream, and custards, we know what a falling off there had been. I doubt, however, whether her old friends had been stopped by that cause. It may have been so with Herr Trauss, who in going to Brunnenthal, or elsewhere, cared for little else but what he might get to eat and drink. But with most of those concerned the feeling had been that things were generally going wrong in the valley, and that in existing circumstances the Peacock could not be pleasant. She at any rate felt herself to be deserted, and this feeling greatly aggravated her trouble.

"You are having beautiful weather," Mr. Cartwright said to her one day when in her full costume she came out among the coffee-drinkers in the front of the house. Mr. Cartwright spoke German, and was on friendly terms with the old lady. She was perhaps a little in awe of him as being a rich man, an Englishman, and one with a white beard and a general deportment of dignity.

"The weather is well enough, sir," she said.

"I never saw the place all round look more lovely. I was up at Sustermann's saw-mills this morning, and I and my daughter agreed that it is the most lovely spot we know."

"The saw-mill is a pretty spot, sir, no doubt."

"It seems to me that the house becomes fuller and fuller every year, Frau Frohmann."

"The house is full enough, sir; perhaps too full." Then she hesitated as though she would say something further. But the words were wanting to her in which to explain her difficulties with sufficient clearness for the foreigner, and she retreated, therefore, back into her own domains. He, of course, had heard something of the Frau's troubles, and had been willing enough to say a word to her about things in general if the occasion arose. But he had felt that the subject must be introduced by herself. She was too great a potentate to have advice thrust upon her uninvited.

A few days after this she asked Malchen whether Schlessen was ever coming out to the Brunnenthal again. This was almost tantamount to an order for his presence. "He will come directly, mother, if you want to see him," said Malchen. The Frau would do no more than grunt in answer to this. It was too much to expect that she should say positively that he must come. But Malchen understood her, and sent the necessary word to Innsbruck.

On the following day Schlessen was at the Peacock, and took a walk up to the waterfall with Malchen before he saw the Frau. "She won't ruin herself," said

Fritz. "It would take a great deal to ruin her. What she is losing in the house she is making up in the forests and in the land."

"Then it won't matter if it does go on like this?"

"It does matter because it makes her so fierce and unhappy, and because the more she is knocked about the more obstinate she will get. She has only to say the word, and all would be right to-morrow."

"What word?" asked Malchen.

"Just to acknowledge that everything has got to be twenty-five per cent. dearer than it was twenty-five years ago."

"But she does not like paying more, Fritz. That's just the thing."

"What does it matter what she pays?"

"I should think it mattered a great deal."

"Not in the least. What does matter is whether she makes a profit out of the money she spends. Florins and zwansigers are but names. What you can manage to eat, and drink, and wear, and what sort of a house you can live in, and whether you can get other people to do for you what you don't like to do yourself,—that is what you have got to look after."

"But, Fritz;—money is money."

"Just so; but it is no more than money. If she could find out suddenly that what she has been thinking was a zwansiger was in truth only half a zwansiger, then she would not mind paying two where she had hitherto paid one, and would charge two where she now charges one,—as a matter of course. That's about the truth."

"But a zwansiger is a zwansiger."

"No;—not in her sense. A zwansiger now is not much more than half what it used to be. If the change had come all at once she could have understood it better."

"But why is it changed?"

Here Schlessen scratched his head. He was not quite sure that he knew, and felt himself unable to explain clearly what he himself only conjectured dimly. "At any rate it is so. That's what she has got to be made to understand, or else she must give it up and go and live quietly in private. It'll come to that, that she won't have a servant about the place if she goes on like this. Her own grandfather and grandmother were very good sort of people, but it is useless to try and live like them. You might just as well go back further, and give up knives and forks and cups and saucers."

Such was the wisdom of Herr Schlessen; and when he had spoken it he was ready to go back from the waterfall, near which they were seated, to the house. But Malchen thought that there was another subject as to which he ought to have something to say to her. "It is all very bad for us;—isn't it, Fritz?"

"It will come right in time, my darling."

"Your darling! I don't think you care for me a bit." As she spoke she moved herself a little further away from him. "If you did, you would not take it all so easily."

"What can I do, Malchen?" She did not quite know what he could do, but she was sure that when her lover, after a month's absence, got an opportunity of sitting with her by a waterfall, he should not confine his conversation to a discussion on the value of zwansigers.

"You never seem to think about anything except money now."

"That is very unfair, Malchen. It was you asked me, and so I endeavoured to explain it."

"If you have said all that you've got to say, I suppose we may go back again."

"Of course, Malchen, I wish she'd settle what she means to do about you. We have been engaged long enough."

"Perhaps you'd like to break it off."

"You never knew me break off anything yet." That was true. She did know him to be a man of a constant, if not of an enthusiastic temperament. And now, as he helped her up from off the rock, and contrived to snatch a kiss in the process, she was restored to her good humour.

"What's the good of that?" she said, thumping him, but not with much violence. "I did speak to mother a little while ago, and asked her what she meant to do."

"Was she angry?"

"No;—not angry; but she said that everything must remain as it is till after the season. Oh, Fritz!

I hope it won't go on for another winter. I suppose she has got the money."

"Oh, yes; she has got it; but, as I've told you before, people who have got money do not like to part with it." Then they returned to the house; and Malchen, thinking of it all, felt reassured as to her lover's constancy, but was more than ever certain that, though it might be for five years, he would never marry her till the mitgift had been arranged.

Shortly afterwards he was summoned into the Frau's private room, and there had an interview with her alone. But it was very short; and, as he afterwards explained to Malchen, she gave him no opportunity of proffering any advice. She had asked him nothing about prices, and had made no allusion whatever to her troubles with her neighbours. She said not a word about the butcher, either at Innsbruck or at Brixen, although they were both at this moment very much on her mind. Nor did she tell him anything of the wickedness of Ánton, nor of the ingratitude of Seppel. She had simply wanted so many hundred florins,—for a purpose, as she said,—and had asked him how she might get them with the least inconvenience. Hitherto the money coming in, which had always gone into her own hands, had sufficed for her expenditure, unless when some new building was required. But now a considerable sum was necessary. She simply communicated her desire, and said nothing of the purpose for which it was wanted. The lawyer told her that she could have the money very easily,—at a day's notice, and without any peculiar damage to her circumstances. With that the interview was over, and Schlessen was allowed to return to his lady love, —or to the amusements of the Peacock generally.

"What did she want of you?" asked Peter.

"Only a question about business."

"I suppose it was about business. But what is she going to do?"

"You ought to know that, I should think. At any rate, she told me nothing."

"It is getting very bad here," said Peter, with a peculiarly gloomy countenance. "I don't know where we are to get anything soon. We have not milk enough, and half the time the visitors can't have eggs if they want them. And as for fowls, they have to be bought for double what we used to give. I wonder the folk here put up with it without grumbling."

"It'll come right after this season."

"Such a name as the place is getting!" said Peter. "And then I sometimes think it will drive her distracted. I told her yesterday we must buy more cows, —and, oh, she did look at me!"

CHAPTER VI.

HOFF THE BUTCHER.

THE lawyer returned to town, and on the next day the money was sent out to the Brunnenthal. Frau

Frohmann had not winced when she demanded the sum needed, nor had she shown by any contorted line in her countenance that she was suffering when she asked for it; but, in truth, the thing had not been done without great pain. Year by year she had always added something to her store, either by investing money, or by increasing her property in the valley, and it would generally be at this time of the year that some deposit was made; but now the stream, which had always run so easily and so prosperously in one direction, had begun to flow backwards. It was to her as though she were shedding her blood. But, as other heroes have shed their blood in causes that have been dear to them, so would she shed hers in this. If it were necessary that these veins of her heart should be opened, she would give them to the knife. She had scowled when Peter had told her that more cows must be bought; but before the week was over the cows were there. And she had given a large order at Innsbruck for poultry to be sent out to her, almost irrespective of price. All idea of profit was gone. It was pride now for which she was fighting. She would not give way, at any rate till the end of this season. Then—then—then! There had come upon her mind an idea that some deluge was about to flow over her; but also an idea that even among the roar of the waters she would hold her head high, and carry herself with dignity.

But there had come to her now a very trouble of troubles, a crushing blow, a misfortune which could not be got over, which could not even be endured, without the knowledge of all those around her. It was not only that she must suffer, but that her sufferings must be exposed to all the valley,—to all Innsbruck. When Schlessen was closeted with her, at that very moment, she had in her pocket a letter from that traitorous butcher at Brixen, saying that after such and such a date he could not continue to supply her with meat at the prices fixed. And this was the answer which the man had sent to a remonstrance from her as to the quality of the article! After submitting for weeks to inferior meat she had told him that there must be some improvement, and he had replied by throwing her over altogether!

What was she to do? Of all the blows which had come to her this was the worst. She must have meat. She could, when driven to it by necessity, make her own butter; but she could not kill her own beef and mutton. She could send into the town for ducks and chickens, and feel that in doing so she was carrying out her own project,—that, at any rate, she was encountering no public disgrace. But now she must own herself beaten, and must go back to Innsbruck.

And there came upon her dimly a conviction that she was bound, both by prudence and justice, to go back to her old friend Hoff. She had clearly been wrong in this matter of meat. Hoff had plainly told her that she was wrong, explaining to her that he had to give much more for his beasts and sheep than he did twenty years ago, to pay more wages to the men who killed them and cut them up, and also to make a greater profit himself, so as to satisfy the increased needs of his wife and daughters. Hoff had been outspoken, and had never wavered for a moment. But he had seemed to the Frau to be almost insolent; she would have said, too independent. When she had threatened to take away her custom he had shrugged his shoulders, and had simply remarked that he would endeavour to live without it. The words had been spoken with, perhaps, something of a jeer, and the Frau had left the shop in wrath. She had since repented herself of this, because Hoff had been an old friend, and had attended to all her wishes with friendly care. But there had been the quarrel, and her custom had been transferred to that wretch at Brixen. If it had been simply a matter of forgiving and forgetting she could have made it up with Hoff, easily enough, an hour after her anger had shown itself. But now she must own herself to have been beaten. She must confess that she had been wrong. It was in that matter of meat, from that fallacious undertaking made by the traitor at Brixen, that she, in the first instance, had been led to think that she could triumph. Had she not been convinced of the truth of her own theory by that success, she would not have been led on to quarrel with all her neighbours, and to attempt to reduce Seppel's wages. But now, when this, her great foundation, was taken away from her, she had no ground on which to stand. She had the misery of failure all around her, and, added to that, the growing feeling that, in some step of her argument, she must have been wrong. One should be very sure of all the steps before one allows oneself to be guided in important matters by one's own theories!

But after some ten days' time the supply of meat from Brixen would cease, and something therefore must be done. The Brixen traitor demanded now exactly the price which Hoff had heretofore charged. And then there was the carriage! That was not to be thought of. She would not conceal her failure from the world by submission so disgraceful as that. With the Brixen man she certainly would deal no more. She took twenty-four hours to think of it, and then she made up her mind that she would herself go into the town and acknowledge her mistake to Hoff. As to the actual difference of price, she did not now care very much about it. When a deluge is coming, one does not fret oneself as to small details of cost; but even when a deluge is coming one's heart and pride, and perhaps one's courage, may remain unchanged.

On a certain morning it was known throughout the Peacock at an early hour that the Frau was going into town that day. But breakfast was over before any one was told when and how she was to go. Such journeyings, which were not made very often, had always about them something of ceremony. On such occasions her dress would be, not magnificent as when she was arrayed for festive occasions at home, but yet very carefully arranged and equally unlike her ordinary habiliments. When she was first seen on this day,—

after her early visit to the kitchen, which was not a full-dress affair,—she was clad in what may be called the beginnings or substratum of her travelling gear. She wore a very full, rich-looking, dark-coloured merino gown, which came much lower to the ground than her usual dress, and which covered her up high round the throat. Whenever this was seen it was known as a certainty that the Frau was going to travel. Then there was the question of the carriage and the horses. It was generally Peter's duty and high privilege to drive her in to town; and as Peter seldom allowed himself a holiday, the occasion was to him always a welcome one. It was her custom to let him know what was to befall him at any rate the night before; but now not a word had been said. After breakfast, however, a message went out that the carriage and horses would be needed, and Peter prepared himself accordingly. "I don't think I need take you," said the Frau.

"Why not me? There is no one else to drive them. The men are all employed." Then she remembered that when last she had dispensed with Peter's services Anton had driven her,—that Anton who was now carrying the butter and eggs into market. She shook her head, and was silent for a while in her misery. Then she asked whether the boy, Jacob, could not take her. "He would not be safe with those horses down the mountains," said Peter. At last it was decided that Peter should go;—but she yielded unwillingly, being very anxious that no one in the valley should be informed that she was about to visit Hoff. Of course it would be known at last. Everybody about the place would learn whence the meat came. But she could not bear to think that those around her should talk of her as having been beaten in the matter.

About ten they started, and on the whole road to Innsbruck hardly a word was spoken between the mother and son. She was quite resolved that she would not tell him whither she was going, and resolved also that she would pay the visit alone. But, of course, his curiosity would be excited. If he chose to follow her about and watch her, there could be no help for that. Only he had better not speak to her on the subject, or she would pour out upon him all the vials of her wrath! In the town there was a little hostel called the Black Eagle, kept by a cousin of her late husband, which on these journeys she always frequented: there she and Peter ate their dinner. At table they sat, of course, close to each other; but still not a word was spoken as to her business. He made no inquiry, and when she rose from the table simply asked her whether there was anything for him to do. "I am going—alone—to see a friend," she said. No doubt he was curious, probably suspecting that Hoff the butcher might be the friend; but he asked no further question. She declared that she would be ready to start on the return journey at four, and then she went forth alone.

So great was her perturbation of spirit that she did not take the directest way to the butcher's house, which was not, indeed, above two hundred yards from the Black Eagle, but walked round slowly by the river, studying as she went the words with which she would announce her purpose to the man,—studying, also, by what wiles and subtlety she might get the man all to herself,—so that no other ears should hear her disgrace. When she entered the shop Hoff himself was there, conspicuous with the huge sharpening-steel which hung from his capacious girdle, as though it were the sword of his knighthood. But with him there was a crowd either of loungers or customers, in the midst of whom he stood, tall above all the others, laughing and talking. To our poor Frau it was terrible to be seen by so many eyes in that shop;—for had not her quarrel with Hoff and her dealings at Brixen been so public that all would know why she had come? "Ah, my friend, Frau Frohmann," said the butcher, coming up to her with hand extended, "this is good for sore eyes. I am delighted to see thee in the old town." This was all very well, and she gave him her hand. As long as no public reference was made to that last visit of hers, she would still hold up her head. But she said nothing. She did not know how to speak as long as all those eyes were looking at her.

The butcher understood it all, being a tender-hearted man, and intelligent also. From the first moment of her entrance he knew that there was something to be said intended only for his own ears. "Come in, come in, Frau Frohmann," he said; "we will sit down within, out of the noise of the street and the smell of the carcases." With that he led the way into an inner room, and the Frau followed him. There were congregated three or four of his children, but he sent them away, bidding them join their mother in the kitchen. "And now, my friend," he said, again taking her hand, "I am glad to see thee. Thirty years of good fellowship is not to be broken by a word." By this time the Frau was endeavouring to hide with her handkerchief the tears which were running down her face. "I was thinking I would go out to the valley one of these days, because my heart misgave me that there should be anything like a quarrel between me and thee. I should have gone, but that, day after day, there comes always something to be done. And now thou art come thyself. What, shall the price of a side of beef stand betwixt thee and me?"

Then she told her tale,—quite otherwise than as she had intended to tell it. She had meant to be dignified and very short. She had meant to confess that the Brixen arrangement had broken down, and that she would resort to the old plan and the old prices. To the saying of this she had looked forward with an agony of apprehension, fearing that the man would be unable to abstain from some killing expression of triumph,—fearing that, perhaps, he might decline her offer. For the butcher was a wealthy man, who could afford himself the luxury of nursing his enmity. But his manner with her had been so gracious that she was altogether unable to be either dignified or reticent. Before half an hour was over she had poured out to him, with many tears, all her troubles;—how she had refused to raise her rate of charges, first out of consideration for her poorer customers, and then because she did not like to demand from one class more than from another. And she explained how she had endeavoured to reduce her expenditure, and how she had failed. She told him of Seppel and Anton, of Suse Krapp and Josephine Bull,—and, above all, of that traitor at Brixen. With respect to the valley folk Hoff expressed himself with magnanimity and kindness; but in regard to the rival tradesman at Brixen his scorn was so great that he could not restrain himself from expressing wonder that a woman of such experience should have trusted to so poor a reed for support. In all other respects he heard her with excellent patience, putting in a little word here and there to encourage her, running his great steel all the while through his fingers, as he sat opposite to her on a side of the table.

"Thou must pay them for their ducks and chickens as before," he said.

"And you?"

"I will make all that straight. Do not trouble thyself about me. Thy guests at the Peacock shall once again have a joint of meat fit for the stomach of a Christian. But, my friend——!"

"My friend!" echoed the Frau, waiting to hear what further the butcher would say to her.

"Let a man who has brought up five sons and five daughters, and who has never owed a florin which he could not pay, tell thee something that shall be useful. Swim with the stream." She looked up into his face, feeling rather than understanding the truth of what he was saying. "Swim with the stream. It is the easiest and the most useful."

"You think I should raise my prices."

"Is not everybody doing so? The Tendel ladies are very good, but I cannot sell them meat at a loss. That is not selling; it is giving. Swim with the stream. When other things are dearer, let the Peacock be dearer also."

"But why are other things dearer?"

"Nay;—who shall say that? Young Schlessen is a clear-headed lad, and he was right when he told thee of the price of sheep in the old days. But why——? There I can say nothing. Nor is there reason why I should trouble my head about it. There is a man who has brought me sheep from the Achensee these thirty years,—he and his father before him. I have to pay him now,—ay, more than a third above his first prices."

"Do you give always what he asks?"

"Certainly not that, or there would be no end to his asking. But we can generally come to terms without hard words. When I pay him more for sheep, then I charge more for mutton; and if people will not pay it, then they must go without. But I do sell my meat, and I live at any rate as well now as I did when the prices were lower." Then he repeated his great advice, "Swim with the stream, my friend; swim with the stream. If you turn your head the other way, the chances are you will go backwards. At any rate you will make no progress."

Exactly at four o'clock she started on her return with her son, who, with admirable discretion, asked no question as to her employment during the day. The journey back took much longer than that coming, as the road was up hill all the way, so that she had ample time to think over the advice which had been given her as she leaned back in the carriage. She certainly was happier in her mind than she had been in the morning. She had made no step towards success in her system,—had rather been made to feel that no such step was possible. But, nevertheless, she had been comforted. The immediate trouble as to the meat had been got over without offence to her feelings. Of course she must pay the old prices,—but she had come to understand that the world around her was, in that matter, too strong for her. She knew now that she must give up the business, or else raise her own terms at the end of the season. She almost thought that she would retire to Schwatz and devote the remainder of her days to tranquillity and religion. But her immediate anxiety had reference to the next six weeks, so that when she should have gone to Schwatz it might be said of her that the house had not lost its reputation for good living up to the very last. At any rate, within a very few days, she would again have the pleasure of seeing good meat roasting in her oven.

Peter, as was his custom, had walked half the hill, and then, while the horses were slowly advancing, climbed up to his seat on the box. "Peter," she said, calling to him from the open carriage behind. Then Peter looked back. "Peter, the meat is to come from Hoff again after next Thursday."

He turned round quick on hearing the words. "That's a good thing, mother."

"It is a good thing. We were nearly poisoned by that scoundrel at Brixen."

"Hoff is a good butcher," said Peter.

"Hoff is a good man," said the Frau. Then Peter pricked up, because he knew that his mother was happy in her mind, and became eloquent about the woods, and the quarry, and the farm.

CHAPTER VII.

AND GOLD BECOMES CHEAP.

"But if there is more money, sir, that ought to make us all more comfortable." This was said by the Frau to Mr. Cartwright a few days after her return from Innsbruck, and was a reply to a statement made by him. She had listened to advice from Hoff the butcher, and now she was listening to advice from her guest. He had told her that these troubles of hers had come from the fact that gold had become more plentiful in the world than heretofore, or rather from that other fact that she had refused to accommodate herself to this increased plenty of gold. Then had come her very natural suggestion, "If there is more money that ought to make us all more comfortable."

"Not at all, Frau Frohmann."

"Well, sir!" Then she paused, not wishing to express an unrestrained praise of wealth, and so to appear too worldly-minded, but yet feeling that he certainly was wrong according to the clearly expressed opinion of the world.

"Not at all. Though you had your barn and your stores filled with gold, you could not make your guests comfortable with that. They could not eat it, nor drink it, nor sleep upon it, nor delight themselves with looking at it as we do at the waterfall, or at the mill up yonder."

"But I could buy all those things for them."

"Ah, if you could buy them! That's just the question. But if everybody had gold so common, if all the barns were tull of it, then people would not care to take it for their meat and wine."

"It never can be like that, surely."

"There is no knowing; probably not. But it is a question of degree. When you have your hay-crop here very plentiful, don't you find that hay becomes cheap?"

"That's of course."

"And gold becomes cheap. You just think it over, and you'll find how it is. When hay is plentiful, you can't get so much for a load because it becomes cheap. But you can feed more cows, and altogether you know that such plenty is a blessing. So it is with gold. When it is plentiful, you can't get so much meat for it as you used to do; but, as you can get the gold much easier, it will come to the same thing,—if you will swim with the stream, as your friend in Innsbruck counselled you."

Then the Frau again considered, and again found that she could not accept this doctrine as bearing upon her own case. "I don't think it can be like that here, sir," she said.

"Why not here as well as elsewhere?"

"Because we never see a bit of gold from one year's end to the other. Barns full of it! Why, it's so precious that you English people, and the French, and the Americans always change it for paper before you come here. If you mean that it is because bank-notes are so common——"

Then Mr. Cartwright scratched his head, feeling that there would be a difficulty in making the Frau understand the increased use of an article which, common as it had become in the great marts of the world, had not as yet made its way into her valley. "It is because bank-notes are less common." The Frau gazed at him steadfastly, trying to understand something about it. "You still use bank-notes at Innsbruck?"

"Nothing else," she said. "There is a little silver among the shops, but you never see a bit of gold."

"And at Munich?"

"At Munich they tell me the French pieces have become—well, not common, but not so very scarce."

"And at Dresden?"

"I do not know. Perhaps Dresden is the same."

"And at Paris?"

"Ah, Paris! Do they have gold there?"

"When I was young it was all silver at Paris. Gold is now as plentiful as blackberries. And at Berlin it is nearly the same. Just here in Austria, you have not quite got through your difficulties."

"I think we are doing very well in Austria;—at any rate, in the Tyrol."

"Very well, Frau Frohmann; very well indeed. Pray do not suppose that I mean anything to the contrary. But though you haven't got into the way of using gold money yourself, the world all around you has done so; and, of course, if meat is dear at Munich because gold won't buy so much there as it used to do, meat will be dearer also at Innsbruck, even though you continue to pay for it with bank-notes."

"It is dearer, sir, no doubt," said the Frau, shaking her head. She had endeavoured to contest that point gallantly, but had been beaten by the conduct of the two butchers. The higher prices of Hoff at Innsbruck had become at any rate better than the lower prices of that deceitful enemy at Brixen.

"It is dearer. For the world generally that may suffice. Your friend's doctrine is quite enough for the world at large. Swim with the stream. In buying and selling,—what we call trade,—things arrange themselves so subtly, that we are often driven to accept them without quite knowing why they are so. Then we can only swim with the stream. But, in this matter, if you want to find out the cause, if you cannot satisfy your mind without knowing why it is that you must pay more for everything, and must, therefore, charge more to other people, it is because the gold which your notes represent has become more common in the world during the last thirty years."

She did want to know. She was not satisfied to swim with the stream as Hoff had done, not caring to inquire, but simply feeling sure that as things were so, so they must be. That such changes should take place had gone much against the grain of her conservative nature. She, in her own mind, had attributed these pestilently increased expenses to elongated petticoats, French bonnets, swallow-tailed coats, and a taste for sour wine. She had imagined that Josephine Bull might have been contented with the old price for her eggs if she would also be contented with the old raiment and the old food. Grounding her resolutions on that belief, she had endeavoured not only to resist further changes, but even to go back to the good old times. But she now was quite aware that in doing so she had endeavoured to swim against the stream. Whether it ought to be so or not, she was not as yet quite sure, but she was becoming sure that such was the fact, and that the fact was too strong for her to combat.

She did not at all like swimming with the stream.

There was something conveyed by the idea which was repugnant to her sense of honour. Did it not mean that she was to increase her prices because other people increased theirs, whether it was wrong or right? She hated the doing of anything because other people did it. Was not that base propensity to imitation the cause of the long petticoats which all the girls were wearing? Was it not thus that all those vile changes were effected which she saw around her on every side? Had it not been her glory, her great resolve, to stand as fast as possible on the old ways? And now in her great attempt to do so, was she to be foiled thus easily?

It was clear to her that she must be foiled, if not in one way, then in another. She must either raise her prices, or else retire to Schwatz. She had been thoroughly beaten in her endeavour to make others carry on their trade in accordance with her theories. On every side she had been beaten. There was not a poor woman in the valley, not one of those who had wont to be so submissive and gracious to her, who had not deserted her. A proposed reduction of two kreutzers on a dozen of eggs had changed the most constant of humble friends into the bitterest foes. Seppel would have gone through fire and water for her. Anything that a man's strength or courage could do, he would have done. But a threat of going back to the old wages had conquered even Seppel's gratitude. Concurrent testimony had convinced her that she must either yield—or go. But, when she came to think of it in her solitude, she did not wish to go. Schwatz! oh yes; it would be very well to have a quiet place ready chosen for retirement when retirement should be necessary. But what did retirement mean? Would it not be to her simply a beginning of dying? A man, or a woman, should retire when no longer able to do the work of the world. But who in all the world could keep the Brunnenthal Peacock as well as she? Was she fatigued with her kitchen, or worn out with the charge of her guests, or worried inwardly by the anxieties of her position? Not in the least, not at all, but for this later misfortune which had come upon her, a misfortune which she knew how to remedy at once if only she could bring herself to apply the remedy. The kaplan had indiscreetly suggested to her that as Malchen was about to marry and be taken away into the town, it would be a good thing that Peter should take a wife, so that there might be a future mistress of the establishment in readiness. The idea caused her to arm herself instantly with renewed self-assertion. So;—they were already preparing for her departure to Schwatz! It was thus she communed with herself. They had already made up their minds that she must succumb to these difficulties and go! The idea had come simply from the kaplan without consultation with any one, but to the Frau it seemed as though the whole valley were already preparing for her departure. No, she would not go! With her strength and her energy, why should she shut herself up as ready for death? She would not go to Schwatz yet awhile.

But if not, then she must raise her prices. To waste her substance, to expend the success of her life in entertaining folk gratis who, after all, would believe that they were paying for their entertainment, would be worse even than going to Schwatz. "I have been thinking over what you were telling me," she said to Mr. Cartwright about a week after their last interview, on the day before his departure from the valley.

"I hope you do not find I was wrong, Frau Frohmann."

"As for wrong and right, that is very difficult to get at in this wicked world."

"But one can acknowledge a necessity."

"That is where it is, sir. One can see what is necessary; but if one could only see that it were right also, one would be so much more comfortable."

"There are things so hard to be seen, my friend, that let us do what we will we cannot see clearly into the middle of them. Perhaps I could have explained to you better all this about the depreciation of money, and the nominal rise in the value of everything else, if I had understood it better myself."

"I am sure you understand all about it,—which a poor woman can't ever do."

"But this at any rate ought to give you confidence, that that which you purpose to do is being done by everybody around you. You were talking to me about the Weisses. Herr Weiss, I hear, had his salary raised last spring."

"Had he?" asked the Frau with energy and a little

start. For this piece of news had not reached her before.

"Somebody was saying so the other day. No doubt it was found that he must be paid more because he had to pay more for everything he wanted. Therefore he ought to expect to have to pay you more."

This piece of information gave the Frau more comfort than anything she had yet heard. That gold should be common, what people call a drug in the market, did not come quite within the scope of her comprehension. Gold to her was gold, and a zwansiger a zwansiger. But if Herr Weiss got more for his services from the community, she ought to get more from him for her services. That did seem plain to her. But then her triumph in that direction was immediately diminished by a tender feeling as to other customers. "But what of those poor Fraulein Tendels?" she said.

"Ah, yes," said Mr. Cartwright. "There you come to fixed incomes."

"To what?"

"To people with fixed incomes. They must suffer, Frau Frohmann. There is an old saying that in making laws you cannot look after all the little things. The people who work and earn their living are the multitude, and to them these matters adjust themselves. The few who live upon what they have saved or others have saved for them must go to the wall." Neither did the Frau understand this; but she at once made up her mind that, however necessary it might be to raise her prices against the Weisses and the rest of the world, she would never raise them against those two poor desolate frauleins.

So Herr Weiss had had his salary raised, and had said nothing to her about it, no doubt prudently wishing to conceal the matter! He had said nothing to her about it, although he had talked to her about her own affairs, and had applauded her courage and her old conservatism in that she would not demand that extra zwansiger and a half! This hardened her heart so much that she felt she would have a pleasure in sending a circular to him as to the new tariff. He might come or let it alone, as he pleased,—certainly he ought to have told her that his own salary had been increased!

But there was more to do than sending out the new circular to her customers. How was she to send a circular round the valley to the old women and the others concerned? How was she to make Seppel, and Anton, and Josephine Bull understand that they should be forgiven, and have their old prices and their increased wages if they would come back to their allegiance, and never say a word again as to the sad affairs of the past summer? This circular must be of a nature very different from that which would serve for her customers. Thinking over it, she came to the opinion that Suse Krapp would be the best circular. A day or two after the Cartwrights were gone, she sent for Suse.

Suse was by no means a bad diplomate. When gaining her point she had no desire to triumph outwardly. When feeling herself a conqueror, she was quite ready to flatter the conquered one. She had never been more gracious, more submissive, or more ready to declare that in all matters the Frau's will was the law of the valley than now, when she was given to understand that everything should be bought on the same terms as heretofore, that the dairy should be discontinued during the next season, and that the wild fruits of the woods and mountains should be made welcome at the Peacock as had heretofore always been the case.

"To-morrow will be the happiest day that ever was in the valley," said Suse in her enthusiasm. "And as for Seppel, he was telling me only yesterday that he would never be a happy man again till he could find himself once more at work in the old shed behind the chapel."

Then Suse was told that Seppel might come as soon as he pleased.

"He'll be there the morning after next if I'm a living woman," continued Suse energetically; and then she said another word, "Oh, meine liebe Frau Frohmann, it broke my heart when they told me you were going away."

"Going away!" said the Frau, as though she had been stung. "Who said that I was going away?"

"I did hear it."

"Psha! it was that stupid priest." She had never before been heard to say a word against the kaplan; but now she could hardly restrain herself. "Why should I go away?"

"No, indeed!"

"I am not thinking of going away. It would be a bad thing if I were to be driven out of my house by a little trouble as to the price of eggs and butter! No, Suse Krapp, I am not going away."

"It will be the best word we have all of us heard this many a day, Frau Frohmann. When it came to that, we were all as though we would have broken our hearts." Then she was sent away upon her mission, not, upon this occasion, without a full glass of kirsch-wasser.

On the very day following Seppel was back. There was nothing said between him and his mistress, but he waited about the front of the house till he had an opportunity of putting his hand up to his cap and smiling at her as she stood upon the doorstep. And then, before the week was over, all the old women and all the young girls were crowding round the place with little presents which, on this their first return to their allegiance, they brought to the Frau as peace-offerings.

The season was nearly over when she signified to Malchen her desire that Fritz Schlessen should come out to the valley. This she did with much good humour, explaining frankly that Fritz would have to prepare the new circulars, and that she must discuss with him the nature of the altered propositions which were to be made to the public. Fritz of course came, and was closeted with her for a full hour, during which he absolutely prepared the document for the Innsbruck printer. It was a simple announcement that for the future the charge made at the Brunnenthal Peacock would be seven and a half zwansigers per head per day. It then went on to declare that, as heretofore, the Frau Frohmann would endeavour to give satisfaction to all those who would do her the honour of visiting her establishment. And instructions were given to Schlessen as to sending the circulars out to the public. "But whatever you do," said the Frau, "don't send one to those Tendel ladies."

And something else was settled at this conference. As soon as it was over Fritz Schlessen was encountered by Malchen, who on such occasions would never be far away. Though the spot on which they met was one which might not have been altogether secure from intrusive eyes, he took her fondly by the waist and whispered a word in her ear.

"And will that do?" asked Malchen anxiously; to which question his reply was made by a kiss. In that whisper he had conveyed to her the amount now fixed for the mitgift.

CHAPTER VIII.

IT DOESN'T MAKE ANY DIFFERENCE TO ANY OF THEM.

AND so Frau Frohmann had raised her prices, and had acknowledged herself to all the world to have been beaten in her enterprise. There are, however, certain misfortunes which are infinitely worse in their anticipation than in their reality; and this, which had been looked forward to as a terrible humiliation, was soon found to be one of them. No note of triumph was sounded; none at least reached her ear. Indeed, it so fell out that those with whom she had quarrelled for awhile seemed now to be more friendly with her than ever. Between her and Hoff things were so sweet that no mention was ever made of money. The meat was sent and the bills were paid with a reticence which almost implied that it was not trade, but an amiable giving and taking of the good things of the world. There had never been a word of explanation with Seppel; but he was late and early about the carts and the furniture, and innumerable little acts of kindnesses made their way up to the mother and her many children. Suse and Josephine had never been so brisk, and the eggs had never been so fresh or the vegetables so good. Except from the working of her own mind, she received no wounds.

But the real commencement of the matter did not take place till the following summer,—the commencement as regarded the public. The circulars were sent out, but to such letters no answers are returned; and up to the following June the Frau was ignorant what effect the charge would have upon the coming of her customers. There were times at which she thought that her house would be left desolate, that the extra charge would turn away from her the hearts of her visitors, and that in this way she would be compelled to retire to Schwatz.

"Suppose they don't come at all," she said to Peter one day.

"That would be very bad," said Peter, who also had his fears in the same direction.

"Fritz Schlessen thinks it won't make any difference," said the Frau.

"A zwansiger and a half a day does make a difference to most men," replied Peter uncomfortably.

This was uncomfortable; but when Schlessen came out he raised her spirits.

"Perhaps old Weiss won't come," he said, "but then there will be plenty in his place. There are houses like the Peacock all over the country now, in the Engadine, and the Bregenz, and the Salzkammergut; and it seems to me the more they charge the fuller they are."

"But they are for the grand folk."

"For anybody that chooses. It has come to that, that the more money people are charged the better they like it. Money has become so plentiful with the rich, that they don't know what to do with it."

This was a repetition of Mr. Cartwright's barn full of gold. There was something in the assertion that money could be plentiful, in the idea that gold could be a drug, which savoured to her of innovation, and was therefore unpleasant. She still felt that the old times were good, and that no other times could be so good as the old times. But if the people would come and fill her house, and pay her the zwansiger and a half extra without grumbling, there would be some consolation in it.

Early in June Malchen made a call at the house of the Frauleins Tendel. Malchen at this time was known to all Innsbruck as the handsome Frau Schlessen who had been brought home in the winter to her husband's house with so very comfortable a mitgift in her hand. That was now quite an old story, and there were people in the town who said that the young wife already knew quite as much about her husband's business as she had ever done about her mother's. But at this moment she was obeying one of her mother's commands.

"Mother hopes you are both coming out to the Brunnenthal this year," said Malchen. The elder fraulein shook her head sadly. "Because——" Then Malchen paused, and the younger of the two ladies shook her head. "Because you always have been there."

"Yes, we have."

"Mother means this. The change in the price won't have anything to do with you if you will come."

"We couldn't think of that, Malchen."

"Then mother will be very unhappy;—that's all. The new circular was not sent to you."

"Of course we heard of it."

"If you don't come mother will take it very bad." Then of course the ladies said they would come, and so that little difficulty was overcome.

This took place in June. But at that time the young wife was staying out in the valley with her mother, and had only gone into Innsbruck on a visit. She was with her mother preparing for the guests; but perhaps, as the Frau too often thought, preparing for guests who would never arrive. From day to day, however, there came letters bespeaking rooms as usual, and when the 21st of June came there was Herr Weiss with all his family.

She had taught herself to regard the coming of the Weisses as a kind of touchstone by which she might judge of the success of what she had done. If he remained away it would be because, in spite of the increase in his salary, he could not encounter the higher cost of this recreation for his wife and family. He was himself too fond of the good living of the Peacock not to come if he could afford it. But if he could not pay so much, then neither could others in his rank of life; and it would be sad indeed to the Frau if her house were to be closed to her neighbour Germans, even though she might succeed in filling it with foreigners from a distance. But now the Weisses had come, not having given their usual notice, but having sent a message for rooms only two days before their arrival. And at once there was a little sparring match between Herr Weiss and the Frau.

"I didn't suppose that there would be much trouble as to finding rooms," said Herr Weiss.

"Why shouldn't there be as much trouble as usual?" asked the Frau in return. She had felt that there was some slight in this arrival of the whole family without the usual preliminary inquiries,—as though there would never again be competition for rooms at the Peacock.

"Well, my friend, I suppose that that little letter which was sent about the country will make a difference."

"That's as people like to take it. It hasn't made any difference with you, it seems."

"I had to think a good deal about it, Frau Frohmann; and I suppose we shall have to make our stay shorter. I own I am a little surprised to see the Tendel women here. A zwansiger and a half a day comes to a deal of money at the end of a month, when there are two or three."

"I am happy to think it won't hurt you, Herr Weiss, as you have had your salary raised."

"That is neither here nor there, Frau Frohmann," said the magistrate, almost with a touch of anger. All the world knew, or ought to know, how very insufficient was his stipend when compared with the invaluable public services which he rendered. Such at least was the light in which he looked at the question.

"At any rate," said the Frau as he stalked away, "the house is like to be as full as ever."

"I am glad to hear it. I am glad to hear it." These were his last words on the occasion. But before the day was over he told his wife that he thought the place was not as comfortable as usual, and that the Frau with her high prices was more upsetting than ever.

His wife, who took delight in being called Madame Weiss at Brixen, and who considered herself to be in some degree a lady of fashion, had nevertheless been very much disturbed in her mind by the increased prices, and had suggested that the place should be abandoned. A raising of prices was in her eyes extortion;—though a small raising of salary was simply justice, and, as she thought, inadequate justice. But the living at the Peacock was good. Nobody could deny that. And when a middle-aged man is taken away from the comforts of his home, how is he to console himself in the midst of his idleness unless he has a good dinner? Herr Weiss had therefore determined to endure the injury, and as usual to pass his holiday in the Brunnenthal. But when Madame Weiss saw those two frauleins from Innsbruck in the house, whose means she knew down to the last kreutzer, and who certainly could not afford the increased demand, she thought that there must be something not apparent to view. Could it be possible that the Frau should be so unjust, so dishonest, so extortious as to have different prices for different neighbours! That an Englishman, or even a German from Berlin, should be charged something extra, might not perhaps be unjust or extortious. But among friends of the same district, to put a zwansiger and a half on to one and not to another seemed to Madame Weiss to be a sin for which there should be no pardon. "I am so glad to see you here," she said to the younger fraulein.

"That is so kind of you. But we always are here, you know."

"Yes;—yes. But I feared that perhaps—— I know that with us we had to think more than once about it before we could make up our minds to pay the increased charges. The 'Magistrat' felt a little hurt about it." To this the fraulein at first answered nothing, thinking that perhaps she ought not to make public the special benevolence shown by the Frau to herself and her sister. "A zwansiger and a half each is a great deal of money to add on," said Madame Weiss.

"It is, indeed."

"We might have got it cheaper elsewhere. And then I thought that perhaps you might have done so too."

"She has made no increase to us," said the poor lady, who at last was forced to tell the truth, as by not doing so she would have been guilty of a direct falsehood in allowing it to be supposed that she and her sister paid the increased price.

"Soh—oh—oh!" exclaimed Madame Weiss, clasping her hands together and bobbing her head up and down. "Soh—oh—oh!" She had found it all out.

Then, shortly after that,—the next day,—there was an uncomfortable perturbation of affairs at the Peacock, which was not indeed known to all the guests, but which to those who heard it, or heard of it, seemed for the time to be very terrible. Madame Weiss and the Frau had,—what is commonly called,—a few words together.

"Frau Frohmann," said Madame Weiss, "I was quite astonished to hear from Agatha Tendel that you were only charging them the old prices."

"Why shouldn't I charge them just what I please,—or nothing at all, if I pleased?" asked the Frau sharply.

"Of course you can. But I do think, among neighbours, there shouldn't be one price to one and one to another."

"Would it do you any good, Frau Weiss, if I were to charge those ladies more than they can pay? Does it do you any harm if they live here at a cheap rate?"

"Surely there should be one price—among neighbours!"

"Herr Weiss got my circular, no doubt. He knew. I don't suppose he wants to live here at a rate less than it costs me to keep him. You and he can do what you like about coming. And you and he can do what you like about staying away. You knew my prices. I have not made any secret about the change. But as for interference between me and my other customers, it is what I won't put up with. So now you know all about it."

By the end of her speech the Frau had worked herself up into a grand passion, and spoke aloud, so that all near her heard her. Then there was a great commotion in the Peacock, and it was thought that the Weisses would go away. But they remained for their allotted time.

This was the only disturbance which took place, and it passed off altogether to the credit of the Frau. Something in a vague way came to be understood about fixed incomes;—so that Peter and Malchen, with the kaplan, even down to Seppel and Suse Krapp, were aware that the two frauleins ought not to be made to pay as much as the prosperous magistrate who had had his salary raised. And then it was quite understood that the difference made in favour of those two poor ladies was a kindness shown to them, and could not therefore be an injury to any one else.

Later in the year, when the establishment was full and everything was going on briskly, when the two puddings were at the very height of their glory, and the wild fruits were brought up on the supper-table in huge bowls, when the Brunnenthal was at its loveliest, and the Frau was appearing on holidays in her gayest costume, the Cartwrights returned to the valley. Of course they had ordered their rooms much beforehand; and the Frau, trusting altogether to the wisdom of those counsels which she did not even yet quite understand, had kept her very best apartments for them. The greeting between them was most friendly,—the Frau condescending to put on something of her holiday costume to add honour to their arrival;—a thing which she had never been known to do before on behalf of any guests. Of course there was not then time for conversation; but a day or two had not passed before she made known to Mr. Cartwright her later experience. "The people have come, sir, just the same," she said.

"So I perceive."

"It don't seem to make any difference to any of them."

"I didn't think it would. And I don't suppose anybody has complained."

"Well;—there was a little said by one lady, Mr. Cartwright. But that was not because I charged her more, but because another old friend was allowed to pay less."

"She didn't do you any harm, I dare say."

"Harm;—oh dear no! She couldn't do me any harm if she tried. But I thought I'd tell you, sir, because you said it would be so. The people don't seem to think any more of seven zwansigers and a half than they do of six! It's very odd,—very odd, indeed. I suppose it's all right, sir?" This she asked, still thinking that there must be something wrong in the world when so monstrous a condition of things seemed to prevail.

"They'd think a great deal of it if you charged them more than they believed sufficient to give you a fair profit for your outlay and trouble."

"How can they know anything about it, Mr. Cartwright?"

"Ah,—indeed. How do they? But they do. You and I, Frau Frohmann, must study these matters very closely before we can find out how they adjust themselves. But we may be sure of this, that the world will never complain of fair prices, will never long endure unfair prices, and will give no thanks at all to those who sell their goods at a loss."

The Frau curtseyed and retired,—quite satisfied that she had done the right thing in raising her prices; but still feeling that she had many a struggle to make before she could understand the matter.

THE LADY OF LAUNAY.

THE LADY OF LAUNAY.

CHAPTER I.

HOW BESSY PRYOR BECAME A YOUNG LADY OF IMPORTANCE.

HOW great is the difference between doing our duty and desiring to do it; between doing our duty and a conscientious struggle to do it; between duty really done and that satisfactory state of mind which comes from a conviction that it has been performed. Mrs. Miles was a lady who through her whole life had thought of little else than duty. Though she was possessed of wealth and social position, though she had been a beautiful woman, though all phases of self-indulgent life had been open to her, she had always adhered to her own idea of duty. Many delights had tempted her. She would fain have travelled, so as to see the loveliness of the world; but she had always remained at home. She could have enjoyed the society of intelligent sojourners in capitals; but she had confined herself to that of her country neighbours. In early youth she had felt herself to be influenced by a taste for dress; she had consequently compelled herself to use raiment of extreme simplicity. She would buy no pictures, no gems, no china, because when young she found that she liked such things too well. She would not leave the parish church to hear a good sermon elsewhere, because even a sermon might be a snare. In the early days of her widowed life it became, she thought, her duty to adopt one of two little motherless, fatherless girls, who had been left altogether unprovided for in the world; and having the choice between the two, she took the plain one, who had weak eyes and a downcast, unhappy look, because it was her duty to deny herself. It was not her fault that the child, who was so unattractive at six, had become beautiful at sixteen, with sweet soft eyes, still downcast occasionally, as though ashamed of their own loveliness; nor was it her fault that Bessy Pryor had so ministered to her in her advancing years as almost to force upon her the delights of self-indulgence. Mrs. Miles had struggled manfully against these wiles, and, in the performance of her duty, had fought with them, even to an attempt to make herself generally disagreeable to the young child. The child, however, had conquered, having wound herself into the old woman's heart of hearts. When Bessy at fifteen was like to die, Mrs. Miles for awhile broke down altogether. She lingered by the bedside, caressed the thin hands, stroked the soft locks, and prayed to the Lord to stay his hand, and to alter his purpose. But when Bessy was strong again she strove to return to her wonted duties. But

Bessy, through it all, was quite aware that she was loved.

Looking back at her own past life, and looking also at her days as they were passing, Mrs. Miles thought that she did her duty as well as it is given to frail man or frail woman to perform it. There had been lapses, but still she was conscious of great strength. She did believe of herself that should a great temptation come in her way she would stand strong against it. A great temptation did come in her way, and it is the purport of this little story to tell how far she stood and how far she fell.

Something must be communicated to the reader of her condition in life, and of Bessy's; something, but not much. Mrs. Miles had been a Miss Launay, and, by the death of four brothers almost in their infancy, had become heiress to a large property in Somersetshire. At twenty-five she was married to Mr. Miles, who had a property of his own in the next county, and who at the time of their marriage represented that county in Parliament. When she had been married a dozen years she was left a widow, with two sons, the younger of whom was then about three years old. Her own property, which was much the larger of the two, was absolutely her own; but was intended for Philip, who was her younger boy. Frank Miles, who was eight years older, inherited the other. Circumstances took him much away from his mother's wings. There were troubles among trustees and executors; and the father's heir, after he came of age, saw but little of his mother.

She did her duty, but what she suffered in doing it may be imagined.

Philip was brought up by his mother, who, perhaps, had some consolation in remembering that the younger boy, who was always good to her, would become a man of higher standing in the world than his brother. He was called Philip Launay, the family name having passed on through the mother to the intended heir of the Launay property. He was thirteen when Bessy Pryor was brought home to Launay Park, and, as a schoolboy, had been good to the poor little creature, who for the first year or two had hardly dared to think her life her own amidst the strange huge spaces of the great house. He had despised her, of course; but had not been boyishly cruel to her, and had given her his old playthings. Everybody at Launay had at first despised Bessy Pryor; though the mistress of the house had been thoroughly good to her. There was no real link between her and Launay. Mrs. Pryor had, as a humble friend, been under great obligations to Mrs. Launay, and these obligations, as is their wont, had produced deep love in the heart of the person conferring them. Then both Mr. and Mrs. Pryor had died, and Mrs. Miles had declared that she would take one of the children. She fully intended to bring the girl up sternly and well, with hard belongings, such as might suit her condition. But there had been lapses, occasioned by those unfortunate female prettinesses, and by that equally unfortunate sickness. Bessy never rebelled, and gave, therefore, no scope to an exhibition of extreme duty; and she had a way of kissing her adopted mamma which Mrs. Miles knew to be dangerous. She struggled not to be kissed, but ineffectually. She preached to herself, in the solitude of her own room, sharp sermons against the sweet softness of the girl's caresses; but she could not put a stop to them. "Yes; I will," the girl would say, so softly, but so persistently! Then there would be a great embrace, which Mrs. Miles felt to be as dangerous as a diamond, as bad as a box at the opera.

Bessy had been despised at first all around Launay. Unattractive children are despised, especially when, as in this case, they are nobodies. Bessy Pryor was quite nobody. And certainly there had never been a child more powerless to assert herself. She was for a year or two inferior to the parson's children, and was not thought much of by the farmers' wives. The servants called her Miss Bessy, of course; but it was not till after that illness that there existed among them any of that reverence which is generally felt in the servants' hall for the young ladies of the house. It was then, too, that the parson's daughters found that Bessy was nice to walk with, and that the tenants began to make much of her when she called. The old lady's secret manifestations in the sick bedroom had, perhaps, been seen. The respect paid to Mrs. Miles in that and the next parish was of the most reverential kind. Had she chosen that a dog sbould be treated as one of the Launays, the dog would have received all the family honours. It must be acknowledged of her that in the performance of her duty she had become a rural tyrant. She gave away many petticoats; but they all had to be stitched according to her idea of stitching a petticoat. She administered physic gratis to the entire estate; but the estate had to take the doses as she chose to have them mixed. It was because she had fallen something short of her acknowledged duty in regard to Bessy Pryor that the parson's daughters were soon even proud of an intimacy with the girl, and that the old butler, when she once went away for a week in the winter, was so careful to wrap her feet up warm in the carriage.

In this way, during the two years subsequent to Bessy's illness, there had gradually come up an altered condition of life at Launay. It could not have been said before that Bessy, though she had been Miss Bessy, was as a daughter in the house. But now a daughter's privileges were accorded to her. When the old squiress was driven out about the county, Bessy was expected, but was asked rather than ordered to accompany her. She always went; but went because she decided on going, not because she was told. And she had a horse to ride; and she was allowed to arrange flowers for the drawing-room; and the gardener did what she told him. What daughter could have more extensive privileges? But poor Mrs. Miles had her misgivings, often asking herself what would come of it all.

When Bessy had been recovering from her illness, Philip, who was seven years her senior, was making a grand tour about the world. He had determined to see, not Paris, Vienna, and Rome, which used to make a grand tour, but Japan, Patagonia, and the South Sea Islands. He had gone in such a way as to ensure the consent of his mother. Two other well-minded young men of fortune had accompanied him, and they had been intent on botany, the social condition of natives, and the progress of the world generally. There had been no harum-scarum rushing about without an object. Philip had been away for more than two years, and had seen all there was to be seen in Japan, Patagonia, and the South Sea Islands. Between them, the young men had written a book, and the critics had been unanimous in observing how improved in those days were the aspirations of young men. On his return he came to Launay for a week or two, and then went up to London. When, after four months, he returned to his mother's house, he was twenty-seven years of age; and Bessy was just twenty. Mrs. Miles knew that there was cause for fear; but she had already taken steps to prevent the danger which she had foreseen.

CHAPTER II.

HOW BESSY PRYOR WOULDN'T MARRY THE PARSON.

Of course there would be danger. Mrs. Miles had been aware of that from the commencement of things. There had been to her a sort of pleasure in feeling that she had undertaken a duty which might possibly lead to circumstances which would be altogether heart-breaking. The duty of mothering Bessy was so much more a duty because, even when the little girl was blear-eyed and thin, there was present to her mind all the horror of a love affair between her son and the little girl. The Mileses had always been much, and the Launays very much in the west of England. Bessy had not a single belonging that was anything. Then she had become beautiful and attractive, and worse than that, so much of a person about the house that Philip himself might be tempted to think that she was fit to be his wife!

Among the duties prescribed to herself by Mrs. Miles was none stronger than that of maintaining the family position of the Launays. She was one of those who not only think that blue blood should remain blue, but that blood not blue should be allowed no azure mixture. The proper severance of classes was a religion to her. Bessy was a gentlewoman, so much had been admitted, and therefore she had been brought into the drawing-room instead of being relegated among the servants, and had thus grown up to be, oh, so dangerous! She was a gentlewoman, and fit to be a gentleman's wife, but not fit to be the wife of the heir of the Launays. The reader will understand, perhaps, that I, the writer of this little history, think her to have been fit to become the wife of any man who might have been happy enough to win her young heart, however blue his blood. But Mrs. Miles had felt that precautions and remedies and arrangements were necessary.

Mrs. Miles had altogether approved of the journey to Japan. That had been a preventive, and might probably afford time for an arrangement. She had even used her influence to prolong the travelling till the arrangements should be complete; but in this she had failed. She had written to her son, saying that, as his sojourn in strange lands would so certainly tend to the amelioration of the human races generally—for she had heard of the philanthropic inquiries, of the book, and the botany—she would by no means press upon him her own natural longings. If another year was required, the necessary remittances should be made with a liberal hand. But Philip, who had chosen to go because he liked it, came back when he liked it, and there he was at Launay before a certain portion of the arrangements had been completed, as to which Mrs. Miles had been urgent during the last six months of his absence.

A good-looking young clergyman in the neighbourhood, with a living of £400 a year, and a fortune of £6,000 of his own, had during the time been proposed to Bessy by Mrs. Miles. Mr. Morrison, the Rev. Alexander Morrison, was an excellent young man; but it may be doubted whether the patronage by which he was put into the living of Budcombe at an early age, over the head of many senior curates, had been exercised with sound clerical motives. Mrs. Miles was herself the patroness, and, having for the last six years felt the necessity of providing a husband for Bessy, had looked about for a young man who should have good gifts and might probably make her happy. A couple of thousand pounds added had at first suggested itself to Mrs. Miles. Then love had ensnared her, and Bessy had become dear to every one, and money was plenty. The thing should be made so beautiful to all concerned that there should be no doubt of its acceptance. The young parson didn't doubt. Why should he? The living had been a wonderful stroke of luck for him! The portion proposed would put him at once among the easy-living gentlemen of the county; and then the girl herself! Bessy had loomed upon him as feminine perfection from the first moment he had seen her. It was to him as though the heavens were raining their choicest blessings on his head.

Nor had Mrs. Miles any reason to find fault with Bessy. Had Bessy jumped into the man's arms directly he had been offered to her as a lover, Mrs. Miles would herself have been shocked. She knew enough of Bessy to be sure that there would be no such jumping. Bessy had at first been startled, and, throwing herself into her old friend's arms, had pleaded her youth. Mrs. Miles had accepted the embrace, had acknowledged the plea, and had expressed herself quite satisfied, simply saying that Mr. Morrison would be allowed to come about the house, and use his own efforts to make himself agreeable. The young parson had come about the house, and had shown himself to be good-humoured and pleasant. Bessy never said a word against him;

did in truth try to persuade herself that it would be nice to have him as a lover; but she failed. "I think he is very good," she said one day, when she was pressed by Mrs. Miles.

"And he is a gentleman."

"Oh, yes," said Bessy.

"And good-looking."

"I don't know that that matters."

"No, my dear, no; only he is handsome. And then he is very fond of you." But Bessy would not commit herself, and certainly had never given any encouragement to the gentleman himself.

This had taken place just before Philip's return. At that time his stay at Launay was to be short; and during his sojourn his hands were to be very full. There would not be much danger during that fortnight, as Bessy was not prone to put herself forward in any man's way. She met him as his little pet of former days, and treated him quite as though he were a superior being. She ran about for him as he arranged his botanical treasures, and took in all that he said about the races. Mrs. Miles, as she watched them, still trusted that there might be no danger. But she went on with her safeguards. "I hope you like Mr. Morrison," she said to her son.

"Very much indeed, mother; but why do you ask?"

"It is a secret; but I'll tell you. I think he will become the husband of our dear Bessy."

"Marry Bessy!"

"Why not?" Then there was a pause. "You

know how dearly I love Bessy. I hope you will not think me wrong when I tell you that I propose to give what will be for her a large fortune, considering all things."

"You should treat her just as though she were a daughter and a sister," said Philip.

"Not quite that! But you will not begrudge her six thousand pounds?"

"It is not half enough."

"Well, well. Six thousand pounds is a large sum of money to give away. However, I am sure we shall not differ about Bessy. Don't you think Mr. Morrison would make her a good husband?" Philip looked very serious, knitted his brows, and left the room, saying that he would think about it.

To make him think that the marriage was all but arranged would be a great protection. There was a protection to his mother also in hearing him speak of Bessy as being almost a sister. But there was still a further protection. Down away in Cornwall there was another Launay heiress coming up, some third or fourth cousin, and it had long since been settled among certain elders that the Launay properties should be combined. To this Philip had given no absolute assent; had even run away to Japan just when it had been intended that he should go to Cornwall. The Launay heiress had then only been seventeen, and it had been felt to be almost as well that there should be delay, so that the time was not passed by the young man in dangerous neighbourhoods. The South Sea Islands and Patagonia had been safe. And now when the idea of combining the properties was again mooted, he at first said nothing against it. Surely such precautions as these would suffice, especially as Bessy's retiring nature would not allow her to fall in love with any man within the short compass of a fortnight.

Not a word more was said between Mrs. Miles and her son as to the prospects of Mr. Morrison; not a word more then. She was intelligent enough to perceive that the match was not agreeable to him; but she attributed this feeling on his part to an idea that Bessy ought to be treated in all respects as though she were a daughter of the house of Launay. The idea was absurd, but safe. The match, if it could be managed, would of course go on, but should not be mentioned to him again till it could be named as a thing absolutely arranged. But there was no present danger. Mrs. Miles felt sure that there was no present danger. Mrs. Miles had seen Bessy grow out of meagre thinness and early want of ruddy health, into gradual proportions of perfect feminine loveliness; but, having seen the gradual growth, she did not know how lovely the girl was. A woman hardly ever does know how omnipotent may be the attraction which some feminine natures, and some feminine forms, diffuse unconsciously on the young men around them.

But Philip knew, or rather felt. As he walked about the park he declared to himself that Alexander Morrison was an insufferably impudent clerical prig; for which assertion there was, in truth, no ground whatsoever. Then he accused his mother of a sordid love of money and property, and swore to himself that he would never stir a step towards Cornwall. If they chose to have that red-haired Launay girl up from the far west, he would go away to London, or perhaps back to Japan. But what shocked him most was that such a girl as Bessy, a girl whom he treated always just like his own sister, should give herself to such a man as that young parson at the very first asking! He struck the trees among which he was walking with his stick as he thought of the meanness of feminine nature. And then such a greasy, ugly brute! But Mr. Morrison was not at all greasy, and would have been acknowledged by the world at large to be much better looking than Philip Launay.

Then came the day of his departure. He was going up to London in March to see his book through the press, make himself intimate at his club, and introduce himself generally to the ways of that life which was to be his hereafter. It had been understood that he was to pass the season in London, and that then the combined-property question should come on in earnest. Such was his mother's understanding; but by this time, by the day of his departure, he was quite determined that the combined-property question should never receive any consideration at his hands.

Early on that day he met Bessy somewhere about the house. She was very sweet to him on this occasion, partly because she loved him dearly,—as her adopted brother; partly because he was going; partly because it was her nature to be sweet! "There is one question I want to ask you," he said suddenly, turning round upon her with a frown. He had not meant to frown, but it was his nature to do so when his heart frowned within him.

"What is it, Philip?" She turned pale as she spoke, but looked him full in the face.

"Are you engaged to that parson?" She went on looking at him, but did not answer a word. "Are you going to marry him? I have a right to ask." Then she shook her head. "You certainly are not?" Now as he spoke his voice was changed, and the frown had vanished. Again she shook her head. Then he got hold of her hand, and she left her hand with him, not thinking of him as other than a brother. "I am so glad. I detest that man."

"Oh, Philip; he is very good!"

"I do not care two-pence for his goodness. You are quite sure?" Now she nodded her head. "It would have been most awful, and would have made me miserable; miserable. Of course, my mother is the best woman in the world; but why can't she let people alone to find husbands and wives for themselves?" There was a slight frown, and then with a visible effort he completed his speech. "Bessy, you have grown to be the loveliest woman that ever I looked upon."

She withdrew her hand very suddenly. "Philip, you should not say such a thing as that."

"Why not, if I think it?"

"People should never say anything to anybody about themselves."

"Shouldn't they?"

"You know what I mean. It is not nice. It's the sort of stuff which people who ain't ladies and gentlemen put into books."

"I should have thought I might say anything."

"So you may; and of course you are different. But there are things that are so disagreeable!"

"And I am one of them?"

"No, Philip, you are the truest and best of brothers."

"At any rate you won't——" Then he paused.

"No, I won't."

"That's a promise to your best and dearest brother?" She nodded her head again, and he was satisfied.

He went away, and when he returned to Launay at the end of four months he found that things were not going on pleasantly at the Park. Mr. Morrison had been refused, with a positive assurance from the young lady that she would never change her mind, and Mrs. Miles had become more stern than ever in the performance of her duty to her family.

CHAPTER III.

HOW BESSY PRYOR CAME TO LOVE THE HEIR OF LAUNAY.

MATTERS became very unpleasant at the Park soon after Philip went away. There had been something in his manner as he left, and a silence in regard to him on Bessy's part, which created, not at first surprise, but uneasiness in the mind of Mrs. Miles. Bessy hardly mentioned his name, and Mrs. Miles knew enough of the world to feel that such restraint must have a cause. It would have been natural for a girl so circumstanced to have been full of Philip and his botany. Feeling this she instigated the parson to renewed attempts; but the parson had to tell her that there was no chance for him. "What has she said?" asked Mrs. Miles.

"That it can never be."

"But it shall be," said Mrs. Miles, stirred on this occasion to an assertion of the obstinacy which was in her nature. Then there was a most unpleasant scene between the old lady and her dependent. "What is it that you expect?" she asked.

"Expect, aunt!" Bessy had been instructed to call Mrs. Miles her aunt.

"What do you think is to be done for you?"

"Done for me! You have done everything. May I not stay with you?" Then Mrs. Miles gave utterance to a very long lecture, in which many things were explained to Bessy. Bessy's position was said to be one very peculiar in its nature. Were Mrs. Miles to die there would be no home for her. She could not hope to find a home in Philip's house as a real sister might have done. Everybody loved her because she had been good and gracious, but it was her duty to marry—especially her duty—so that there might be no future difficulty. Mr. Morrison was exactly the man that such a girl as Bessy ought to want as a husband. Bessy through her tears declared that she didn't want any husband, and that she certainly did not want Mr. Morrison.

"Has Philip said anything?" asked the imprudent old woman. Then Bessy was silent. "What has Philip said to you?"

"I told him, when he asked, that I should never marry Mr. Morrison." Then it was—in that very moment—that Mrs. Miles in truth suspected the blow that was to fall upon her; and in that same moment she resolved that, let the pain be what it might to any or all of them, she would do her duty by her family.

"Yes," she said to herself, as she sat alone in the unadorned, unattractive sanctity of her own bedroom, "I will do my duty at any rate now." With deep remorse she acknowledged to herself that she had been remiss. For a moment her anger was very bitter. She had warmed a reptile in her bosom. The very words came to her thoughts, though they were not pronounced. But the words were at once rejected. The girl had been no reptile. The girl had been true. The girl had been as sweet a girl as had ever brightened the hearth of an old woman. She acknowledged so much to herself even in this moment of her agony. But not the less would she do her duty by the family of the Launays. Let the girl do what she might, she must be sent away—got rid of—sacrificed in any way rather than that Philip should be allowed to make himself a fool.

When for a couple of days she had turned it all in

her mind she did not believe that there was as yet any understanding between the girl and Philip. But still she was sure that the danger existed. Not only had the girl refused her destined husband—just such a man as such a girl as Bessy ought to have loved—but she had communicated her purpose in that respect to Philip. There had been more of confidence between them than between her and the girl. How could they two have talked on such a subject unless there had been between them something of stricter, closer friendship even than that of brother and sister? There had been something of a conspiracy between them against her—her who at Launay was held to be omnipotent, against her who had in her hands all the income, all the power, all the ownership—the mother of one of them, and the protectress and only friend of the other! She would do her duty, let Bessy be ever so sweet. The girl must be made to marry Mr. Morrison—or must be made to go.

But whither should she go, and if that "whither" should be found, how should Philip be prevented from following her? Mrs. Miles, in her agony, conceived an idea that it would be easier to deal with the girl herself than with Philip. A woman, if she thinks it to be a duty, will more readily sacrifice herself in the performance of it than will a man. So at least thought Mrs. Miles, judging from her own feelings; and Bessy was very good, very affectionate, very grateful, had always been obedient. If possible she should be driven into the arms of Mr. Morrison. Should she stand firm against such efforts as could be made in that direction, then an appeal should be made to herself. After all that had been done for her, would she ruin the family of the Launays for the mere whim of her own heart?

During the process of driving her into Mr. Morrison's arms—a process which from first to last was altogether hopeless—not a word had been said about Philip. But Bessy understood the reticence. She had been asked as to her promise to Philip, and never forgot that she had been asked. Nor did she ever forget those words which at the moment so displeased her—"You have grown to be the loveliest woman that I have ever looked upon." She remembered now that he had held her hand tightly while he had spoken them, and that an effort had been necessary as she withdrew it. She had been perfectly serious in decrying the personal compliment; but still, still, there had been a flavour of love in the words which now remained among her heartstrings. Of course he was not her brother—not even her cousin. There was not a touch of blood between them to warrant such a compliment as a joke. He, as a young man, had told her that he thought her, as a young woman, to be lovely above all others. She was quite sure of this—that no possible amount of driving should drive her into the arms of Mr. Morrison.

The old woman became more and more stern. "Dear aunt," Bessy said to her one day, with an air of firmness which had evidently been assumed purposely for the occasion, "indeed, indeed, I cannot love

Mr. Morrison." Then Mrs. Miles had resolved that she must resort to the other alternative. Bessy must go. She did believe that when everything should be explained Bessy herself would raise no difficulty as to her own going. Bessy had no more right to live at Launay than had any other fatherless, motherless, penniless living creature. But how to explain it? What reason should be given? And whither should the girl be sent?

Then there came delay, caused by another great trouble. On a sudden Mrs. Miles was very ill. This began about the end of May, when Philip was still up in London inhaling the incense which came up from the success of his book. At first she was very eager that her son should not be recalled to Launay. "Why should a young man be brought into the house with a sick old woman? Of course she was eager. What evils might not happen if they two were brought together during her illness? At the end of three weeks, however, she was worse—so much worse that the people around her were afraid; and it became manifest to all of them that the truth must be told to Philip in spite of her injunctions. Bessy's position became one of great difficulty, because words fell from Mrs. Miles which explained to her almost with accuracy the condition of her aunt's mind. "You should not be here," she said over and over again. Now, it had been the case, as a matter of course, that Bessy, during the old lady's illness, had never left her bedside day or night. Of course she had been the nurse, of course she had tended the invalid in everything. It had been so much a matter of course that the poor lady had been impotent to prevent it, in her ineffectual efforts to put an end to Bessy's influence. The servants, even the doctors, obeyed Bessy in regard to the household matters. Mrs. Miles found herself quite unable to repel Bessy from her bedside. And then, with her mind always intent on the necessity of keeping the young people apart, and when it was all but settled that Philip should be summoned, she said again and again, "You should not be here, Bessy. You must not be here, Bessy."

But whither should she go? No place was even suggested to her. And were she herself to consult some other friend as to a place—the clergyman of their own parish for instance, who out of that house was her most intimate friend—she would have to tell the whole story, a story which could not be told by her lips. Philip had never said a word to her, except that one word: "You have grown to be the loveliest woman that ever I looked upon." The word was very frequent in her thoughts, but she could tell no one of that!

If he did think her lovely, if he did love her, why should not things run smoothly? She had found it to be quite out of the question that she should be driven into the arms of Mr. Morrison, but she soon came to own to herself that she might easily be enticed into those other arms. But then perhaps he had meant nothing—so probably had meant nothing! But if not, why should she be driven away from Launay? As her aunt became worse and worse, and when Philip came down from London, and with Philip a London physician, nothing was settled about poor Bessy, and nothing was done. When Philip and Bessy stood together at the sick woman's bedside she was nearly insensible, wandering in her mind, but still with that care heavy at her heart. "No, Philip; no, no, no," she said. "What is it, mother?" asked Philip. Then Bessy escaped from the room and resolved that she would always be absent when Philip was by his mother's bedside.

There was a week in which the case was almost hopeless; and then a week during which the mistress of Launay crept slowly back to life. It could not but be that they two should see much of each other during such weeks. At every meal they sat together. Bessy was still constant at the bedside of her aunt, but now and again she was alone with Philip. At first she struggled to avoid him, but she struggled altogether in vain. He would not be avoided. And then of course he spoke. "Bessy, I am sure you know that I love you."

"I am sure I hope you do," she replied, purposely misinterpreting him.

Then he frowned at her. "I am sure, Bessy, you are above all subterfuges."

"What subterfuges? Why do you say that?"

"You are no sister of mine; no cousin even. You know what I mean when I say that I love you. Will you be my wife?"

Oh! if she might only have knelt at his feet and hidden her face among her hands, and have gladly answered him with a little "Yes," extracted from amidst her happy blushes! But, in every way, there was no time for such joys. "Philip, think how ill your mother is," she said.

"That cannot change it. I have to ask you whether you can love me. I am bound to ask you whether you will love me." She would not answer him then; but during that second week in which Mrs. Miles was creeping back to life she swore that she did love him, and would love him, and would be true to him for ever and ever.

CHAPTER IV.

HOW BESSY PRYOR OWNED THAT SHE WAS ENGAGED.

When these pretty oaths had been sworn, and while Mrs. Miles was too ill to keep her eyes upon them or to separate them, of course the two lovers were much together. For whispering words of love, for swearing oaths, for sweet kisses and looking into each other's eyes, a few minutes now and again will give ample opportunities. The long hours of the day and night were passed by Bessy with her aunt; but there were short moments, heavenly moments, which sufficed to lift her off the earth into an Elysium of joy. His love for her was so perfect, so assured! "In a matter such as this," he said in his fondly serious air, "my mother can have no right to interfere with me."

"But with me she may," said Bessy, foreseeing in the midst of her Paradise the storm which would surely come.

"Why should she wish to do so? Why should she not allow me to make myself happy in the only way in which it is possible?" There was such an ecstacy of bliss coming from such words as these, such a perfection of the feeling of mutual love, that she could not but be exalted to the heavens, although she knew that the storm would surely come. If her love would make him happy, then, then, surely he should be happy. "Of course she has given up her idea about that parson," he said.

"I fear she has not, Philip."

"It seems to me too monstrous that any human being should go to work and settle whom two other human beings are to marry."

"There was never a possibility of that."

"She told me it was to be so."

"It never could have been," said Bessy with great emphasis. "Not even for her, much as I love her—not even for her to whom I owe everything—could I consent to marry a man I did not love. But——"

"But what?"

"I do not know how I shall answer her when she bids me give you up. Oh, my love, how shall I answer her?"

Then he told her at considerable length what was

the answer which he thought should in such circumstances be made to his mother. Bessy was to declare that nothing could alter her intentions, that her own happiness and that of her lover depended on her firmness, and that they two did, in fact, intend to have their own way in this matter sooner or later. Bessy, as she heard the lesson, made no direct reply, but she knew too well that it could be of no service to her. All that it would be possible for her to say, when the resolute old woman should declare her purpose, would be that come what might she must always love Philip Launay; that she never, never, never could become the wife of any other man. So much she thought she would say. But as to asserting her right to her lover, that she was sure would be beyond her.

Everyone in the house except Mrs. Miles was aware that Philip and Bessy were lovers, and from the dependents of the house the tidings spread through the parish. There had been no special secrecy. A lover does not usually pronounce his vows in public. Little half-lighted corners and twilight hours are chosen, or banks beneath the trees supposed to be safe from vulgar eyes, or lonely wanderings. Philip had followed the usual way of the world in his love-making, but had sought his secret moments with no special secrecy. Before the servants he would whisper to Bessy with that look of thorough confidence in his eyes which servants completely understand; and thus while the poor old woman was still in her bed, while she was unaware both of the danger and of her own immediate impotence, the secret—as far as it was a secret—became known to all Launay. Mr. Morrison heard it over at Budcombe, and, with his heart down in his boots, told himself that now certainly there could be no chance for him. At Launay Mr. Gregory was the rector, and it was with his daughters that Bessy had become intimate. Knowing much of the mind of the first lady of the parish, he took upon himself to say a word or two to Philip. "I am so glad to hear that your mother is much better this morning."

"Very much better."

"It has been a most serious illness."

"Terribly serious, Mr. Gregory."

Then there was a pause, and sundry other faltering allusions were made to the condition of things up at the house, from which Philip was aware that words of counsel or perhaps reproach were coming. "I hope you will excuse me, Philip, if I tell you something."

"I think I shall excuse anything from you."

"People are saying about the place that during your mother's illness you have engaged yourself to Bessy Pryor."

"That's very odd," said Philip.

"Odd!" repeated the parson.

"Very odd indeed, because what the people about the place say is always supposed to be untrue. But this report is true."

"It is true?"

"Quite true, and I am proud to be in a position to

assure you that I have been accepted. I am really sorry for Mr. Morrison, you know."

"But what will your mother say?"

"I do not think that she or anyone can say that Bessy is not fit to be the wife of the finest gentleman in the land." This he said with an air of pride which showed plainly enough that he did not intend to be talked out of his purpose.

"I should not have spoken, but that your dear mother is so ill," rejoined the parson.

"I understand that. I must fight my own battle and Bessy's as best I may. But you may be quite sure, Mr. Gregory, that I mean to fight it."

Nor did Bessy deny the fact when her friend Mary Gregory interrogated her. The question of Bessy's marriage with Mr. Morrison had, somewhat cruelly in regard to her and more cruelly still in regard to the gentleman, become public property in the neighbourhood. Everybody had known that Mrs. Miles intended to marry Bessy to the parson of Budcombe, and everybody had thought that Bessy would, as a matter of course, accept her destiny. Everybody now knew that Bessy had rebelled; and, as Mrs. Miles's autocratic disposition was well understood, everybody was waiting to see what would come of it. The neighbourhood generally thought that Bessy was unreasonable and ungrateful. Mr. Morrison was a very nice man, and nothing could have been more appropriate. Now, when the truth came out, everybody was very much interested indeed. That Mrs. Miles should assent to a marriage between the heir and Bessy Pryor was quite out of the question. She was too well known to leave a doubt on the mind of anyone either in Launay or Budcombe on that matter. Men and women drew their breath and looked at each other. It was just when the parishes thought that she was going to die that the parishioners first heard that Bessy would not marry Mr. Morrison because of the young squire. And now, when it was known that Mrs. Miles was not going to die, it was known that the young squire was absolutely engaged to Bessy Pryor. "There'll be a deal o' vat in the voir," said the old head ploughman of Launay, talking over the matter with the wife of Mr. Gregory's gardener. There was going to be "a deal of fat in the fire."

Mrs. Miles was not like other mothers. Everything in respect to present income was in her hands. And Bessy was not like other girls. She had absolutely no "locus standi" in the world, except what came to her from the bounty of the old lady. By favour of the Lady of Launay she held her head among the girls of that part of the country as high as any girl there. She was only Bessy Pryor; but, from love and kindness, she was the recognised daughter of the house of Launay. Everybody knew it all. Everybody was aware that she had done much towards reaching her present position by her own special sweetness. But should Mrs. Miles once frown, Bessy would be nobody. "Oh, Bessy, how is this all to be?" asked Mary Gregory.

"As God pleases," said Bessy, very solemnly.

"What does Mrs. Miles say?"

"I don't want anybody to ask me about it," said Bessy. "Of course I love him. What is the good of denying it? But I cannot talk about it." Then Mary Gregory looked as though some terrible secret had been revealed to her—some secret of which the burden might probably be too much for her to bear.

The first storm arose from an interview which took place between the mother and son as soon as the mother found herself able to speak on a subject which was near her heart. She sent for him and once again besought him to take steps towards that combining of the properties which was so essential to the Launay interests generally. Then he declared his purpose very plainly. He did not intend to combine the properties. He did not care for the red-haired Launay cousin. It was his intention to marry—Bessy Pryor; yes—he had proposed to her and she had accepted him. The poor sick mother was at first almost overwhelmed with despair. "What can I do but tell you the truth when you ask me?" he said.

"Do!" she screamed. "What could you do? You could have remembered your honour! You could have remembered your blood! You could have remembered your duty!" Then she bade him leave her, and after an hour passed in thought she sent for Bessy. "I have had my son with me," she said, sitting bolt upright in her bed, looking awful in her wanness, speaking with low, studied, harsh voice, with her two hands before her on the counterpane. "I have had my son with me and he has told me." Bessy felt that she was trembling. She was hardly able to support herself. She had not a word to say. The sick old woman was terrible in her severity. "Is it true?"

"Yes, it is true," whispered Bessy.

"And this is to be my return?"

"Oh, my dearest, my darling, oh, my aunt, dear, dearest, dearest aunt! Do not speak like that! Do not look at me like that! You know I love you. Don't you know I love you?" Then Bessy prostrated herself on the bed, and getting hold of the old woman's hand covered it with kisses. Yes, her aunt did know that the girl loved her, and she knew that she loved the girl perhaps better than any other human being in the world. The eldest son had become estranged from her. Even Philip had not been half so much to her as this girl. Bessy had wound herself round her very heartstrings. It made her happy even to sit and look at Bessy. She had denied herself all pretty things; but this prettiest of all things had grown up beneath her eyes. She did not draw away her hand; but, while her hand was being kissed, she made up her mind that she would do her duty.

"Of what service will be your love," she said, "if this is to be my return?" Bessy could only lie and sob and hide her face. "Say that you will give it up." Not to say that, not to give him up, was the only resolution at which Bessy had arrived. "If you will not say so, you must leave me, and I shall send you word what you are to do. If you are my enemy you shall not remain here."

"Pray—pray do not call me an enemy."

"You had better go." The woman's voice as she said this was dreadful in its harshness. Then Bessy, slowly creeping down from the bed, slowly slunk out of the room.

CHAPTER V.

HOW BESSY PRYOR CEASED TO BE A YOUNG LADY OF IMPORTANCE.

WHEN the old woman was alone she at once went to work in her own mind resolving what should be her course of proceeding. To yield in the matter, and to confirm the happiness of the young people, never occurred to her. Again and again she repeated to herself that she would do her duty; and again and again she repeated to herself that in allowing Philip and Bessy to come together she had neglected her duty. That her duty required her to separate them, in spite of their love, in spite of their engagement, though all the happiness of their lives might depend upon it, she did not in the least doubt. Duty is duty. And it was her duty to aggrandise the house of Launay, so that the old autocracy of the land might, so far as in her lay, be preserved. That it would be a good and pious thing to do,—to keep them apart, to force Philip to marry the girl in Cornwall, to drive Bessy into Mr. Morrison's arms, was to her so certain that it required no further thought. She had never indulged herself. Her life had been so led as to maintain the power of her own order, and relieve the wants of those below her. She had done nothing for her own pleasure. How should it occur to her that it would be well for her to change the whole course of her life in order that she might administer to the joys of a young man and a young woman?

It did not occur to her to do so. Lying thus all alone, white, sick, and feeble, but very strong of heart, she made her resolutions. As Bessy could not well be sent out of the house till a home should be provided for her elsewhere, Philip should be made to go. As that was to be the first step, she again sent for Philip that day. "No, mother; not while you are so ill." This he said in answer to her first command that he should leave Launay at once. It had not occurred to him that the house in which he had been born and bred, the house of his ancestors, the house which he had always supposed was at some future day to be his own, was not free to him. But, feeble as she was, she soon made him understand her purpose. He must go,—because she ordered him, because the house was hers and not his, because he was no longer welcome there as a guest unless he would promise to abandon Bessy. "This is tyranny, mother," he said.

"I do not mean to argue the question," said Mrs. Miles, leaning back among the pillows, gaunt, with hollow cheeks, yellow with her long sickness, seeming to be all eyes as she looked at him. "I tell you that you must go."

"Mother!"

Then, at considerable length, she explained her intended arrangements. He must go, and live upon the very modest income which she proposed. At any rate he must go, and go at once. The house was hers, and she would not have him there. She would have no one in the house who disputed her will. She had been an over-indulgent mother to him, and this had been the return made to her! She had condescended to explain to him her intention in regard to Bessy, and he had immediately resolved to thwart her. When she was dead and gone it might perhaps be in his power to ruin the family if he chose. As to that she would take further thought. But she, as long as she lived, would do her duty. "I suppose I may understand," she said, "that you will leave Launay early after breakfast to-morrow."

"Do you mean to turn me out of the house?"

"I do," she said, looking full at him, all eyes, with her grey hair coming dishevelled from under the large frill of her nightcap, with cheeks gaunt and yellow. Her extended hands were very thin. She had been very near death, and seemed, as he gazed at her, to be very near it now. If he went it might be her fate never to see him again.

"I cannot leave you like this," he said.

"Then obey me."

"Why should we not be married, mother?"

"I will not argue. You know as well as I do. Will you obey me?"

"Not in this, mother. I could not do so without perjuring myself."

"Then go you out of this house at once." She was sitting now bolt upright on her bed, supporting herself on her hands behind her. The whole thing was so dreadful that he could not endure to prolong the interview, and he left the room.

Then there came a message from the old housekeeper to Bessy, forbidding her to leave her own room. It was thus that Bessy first understood that her great sin was to be made public to all the household. Mrs. Knowl, who was the head of the domestics, had been told, and now felt that a sort of authority over Bessy had been confided to her. "No, Miss Bessy; you are not to go into her room at all. She says that she will not see you till you promise to be said by her."

"But why, Mrs. Knowl?"

"Well, miss; I suppose it's along of Mr. Philip. But you know that better than me. Mr. Philip is to go to-morrow morning and never come back any more."

"Never come back to Launay?"

"Not while things is as they is, miss. But you are to stay here and not go out at all. That's what Madam says." The servants about the place all called Mrs. Miles Madam.

There was a potency about Mrs. Miles which enabled her to have her will carried out, although she was lying ill in bed,—to have her will carried out as far as the immediate severance of the lovers was concerned. When the command had been brought by the mouth of a servant, Bessy determined that she would not see Philip again before he went. She understood that she was bound by her position, bound by gratitude, bound by a sense of propriety, to so much obedience as that. No earthly authority could be sufficient to make her abandon her troth. In that she could not allow even her aunt to sway her,—her aunt though she were sick and suffering, even though she were dying! Both her love and her vow were sacred to her. But obedience at the moment she did owe, and she kept her room. Philip came to the door, but she sat mute and would not speak to him. Mrs. Knowl, when she brought her some food, asked her whether she intended to obey the order. "Your aunt wants a promise from you, Miss Bessy?"

"I am sure my aunt knows that I shall obey her," said Bessy.

On the following morning Philip left the house. He sent a message to his mother, asking whether she would see him; but she refused. "I think you had better not disturb her, Mr. Philip," said Mrs. Knowl. Then he went, and as the waggonette took him away from the door, Bessy sat and listened to the sound of the wheels on the gravel.

All that day and all the next passed on and she was not allowed to see her aunt. Mrs. Knowl repeated that she could not take upon herself to say that Madam was better. No doubt the worry of the last day or two had been a great trouble to her. Mrs. Knowl grew much in self-importance at the time, and felt that she was overtopping Miss Bessy in the affairs of Launay.

It was no less true than singular that all the sympathies of the place should be on the side of the old woman. Her illness probably had something to do with it. And then she had been so autocratic, all Launay and Budcombe had been so accustomed to bow down to her, that rebellion on the part of anyone seemed to be shocking. And who was Bessy Pryor that she should dare to think of marrying the heir? Who, even, was the supposed heir that he should dare to think of marrying anyone in opposition to the actual owner of the acres? Heir though he was called, he was not necessarily the heir. She might do as she pleased with all Launay and all Budcombe, and there were those who thought that if Philip was still obstinate she would leave everything to her elder son. She did not love her elder son. In these days she never saw him. He was a gay man of the world, who had never been dutiful to her. But he might take the name of Launay, and the family would be perpetuated as well that way as the other. Philip was very foolish. And as for Bessy; Bessy was worse than foolish. That was the verdict of the place generally.

I think Launay liked it. The troubles of our neighbours are generally endurable, and any subject for conversation is a blessing. Launay liked the excitement; but, nevertheless, felt itself to be compressed into whispers and a solemn demeanour. The Gregory girls were solemn, conscious of the iniquity of their friend, and deeply sensitive of the danger to which poor Philip was exposed. When a rumour came to the vicarage that a fly had been up at the great house, it was immediately conceived that Mr. Jones, the lawyer from Taunton, had been sent for, with a view to an alteration of the will. This suddenness, this anger, this disruption of all things was dreadful! But when it was discovered that the fly contained no one but the doctor there was disappointment.

On the third day there came a message from Mrs. Miles to the rector. Would Mr. Gregory step up and see Mrs. Miles? Then it was thought at the rectory that the dear old lady was again worse, and that she had sent for her clergyman that she might receive the last comforts of religion. But this again was wrong. "Mr. Gregory," she said very suddenly, "I want to consult you as to a future home for Bessy Pryor."

"Must she go from this?"

"Yes; she must go from this. You have heard, perhaps, about her and my son." Mr. Gregory acknowledged that he had heard. "Of course she must go. I cannot have Philip banished from the house which is to be his own. In this matter he probably has been the most to blame."

"They have both, perhaps, been foolish."

"It is wickedness rather than folly. But he has been the wickeder. It should have been a duty to him, a great duty, and he should have been the stronger. But he is my son, and I cannot banish him."

"Oh, no!"

"But they must not be brought together. I love Bessy Pryor dearly, Mr. Gregory; oh, so dearly! Since she came to me, now so many years ago, she has been like a gleam of sunlight in the house. She has always been gentle with me. The very touch of her hand is sweet to me. But I must not on that account sacrifice the honour of the family. I have a duty to do; and I must do it, though I tear my heart in pieces. Where can I send her?"

"Permanently?"

"Well, yes; permanently. If Philip were married, of course she might come back. But I will still trust that she herself may be married first. I do not mean to cast her off;—only she must go. Anything that may be wanting in money shall be paid for her. She shall be provided for comfortably. You know what I had hoped about Mr. Morrison. Perhaps he may even yet be able to persuade her; but it must be away from here. Where can I send her?"

This was a question not very easy to answer, and Mr. Gregory said that he must take time to think of it. Mrs. Miles, when she asked the question, was aware that Mr. Gregory had a maiden sister, living at Avranches in Normandy, who was not in opulent circumstances.

CHAPTER VI.

HOW BESSY PRYOR WAS TO BE BANISHED.

When a man is asked by his friend if he knows of a horse to be sold he does not like immediately to suggest a transfer of the animal which he has in his own stable, though he may at the moment be in want of money and anxious to sell his steed. So it was with Mr. Gregory. His sister would be delighted to take as a boarder a young lady for whom liberal payment would be made; but at the first moment he had hesitated to make an offer by which his own sister would be benefited. On the next morning, however, he wrote as follows:—

"Dear Mrs. Miles,—My sister Amelia is living at Avranches, where she has a pleasant little house on the outskirts of the town, with a garden. An old friend was living with her, but she died last year, and my sister is now alone. If you think that Bessy would like to sojourn for awhile in Normandy, I will write to Amelia and make the proposition. Bessy will find my sister good-tempered and kind-hearted.—Faithfully yours, Joshua Gregory."

Mrs. Miles did not care much for the good temper and the kind heart. Had she asked herself whether she wished Bessy to be happy she would no doubt have answered herself in the affirmative. She would probably have done so in regard to any human being or animal in the world. Of course, she wanted them all to be happy. But happiness was to her thinking of much less importance than duty; and at the present moment her duty and Bessy's duty and Philip's duty were so momentous that no idea of happiness ought to be considered in the matter at all. Had Mr. Gregory written to say that his sister was a woman of severe morals, of stern aspect, prone to repress all youthful ebullitions, and supposed to be disagreeable because of her temper, all that would have been no obstacle. In the present condition of things suffering would be better than happiness; more in accord with the feelings and position of the person concerned. It was quite intelligible to Mrs. Miles that Bessy should really love Philip almost to the breaking of her heart, quite intelligible that Philip should have set his mind upon the untoward marriage with all the obstinacy of a proud man. When young men and young women neglect their duty, hearts have to be broken. But it is not a soft and silken operation, which can be made pleasant by good temper and social kindness. It was necessary, for certain quite adequate reasons, that Bessy should be put on the wheel, and be racked and tormented. To talk to her of the good temper of the old woman who would have to turn the wheel would be to lie to her. Mrs. Miles did not want her to think that things could be made pleasant for her.

Soon after the receipt of Mr. Gregory's letter she

sent for Bessy, who was then brought into the room under the guard, as it were, of Mrs. Knowl. Mrs. Knowl accompanied her along the corridor, which was surely unnecessary, as Bessy's door had not been locked upon her. Her imprisonment had only come from obedience. But Mrs. Knowl felt that a great trust had been confided to her, and was anxious to omit none of her duties. She opened the door so that the invalid on the bed could see that this duty had been done, and then Bessy crept into the room. She crept in, but very quickly, and in a moment had her arms round the old woman's back and her lips pressed to the old woman's forehead. "Why may not I come and be with you?" she said.

"Because you are disobedient."

"No, no; I do all that you tell me. I have not stirred from my room, though it was hard to think you were ill so near me, and that I could do nothing. I did not try to say a word to him, or even to look at him; and now that he has gone, why should I not be with you?"

"It cannot be."

"But why not, aunt? Even though you would not speak to me I could be with you. Who is there to read to you?"

"There is no one. Of course it is dreary. But there are worse things than dreariness."

"Why should not I come back, now that he has gone?" She still had her arm round the old woman's back, and had now succeeded in dragging herself on to the bed and in crouching down by her aunt's side. It was her perseverance in this fashion that had so often forced Mrs. Miles out of her own ordained method of life, and compelled her to leave for a moment the strictness which was congenial to her. It was this that had made her declare to Mr. Gregory, in the midst of her severity, that Bessy had been like a gleam of sunshine in the house. Even now she knew not how to escape from the softness of an embrace which was in truth so grateful to her. It was a consciousness of this,—of the potency of Bessy's charm even over herself,—which had made her hasten to send her away from her. Bessy would read to her all the day, would hold her hand when she was half dozing, would assist in every movement with all the patience and much more than the tenderness of a waiting-maid. There was no voice so sweet, no hand so cool, no memory so mindful, no step so soft as Bessy's. And now Bessy was there, lying on her bed, caressing her, more closely bound to her than had ever been any other being in the world, and yet Bessy was an enemy from whom it was imperatively necessary that she should be divided.

"Get down, Bessy," she said; "go off from me."

"No, no, no," said Bessy, still clinging to her and kissing her.

"I have that to say to you which must be said calmly."

"I am calm,—quite calm. I will do whatever you tell me; only pray, pray, do not send me away from you."

"You say that you will obey me."

"I will; I have. I always have obeyed you."

"Will you give up your love for Philip?"

"Could I give up my love for you, if anybody told me? How can I do it? Love comes of itself. I did not try to love him. Oh, if you could know how I tried not to love him! If somebody came and said I was not to love you, would it be possible?"

"I am speaking of another love."

"Yes; I know. One is a kind of love that is always welcome. The other comes first as a shock, and one struggles to avoid it. But when it has come, how can it be helped? I do love him, better than all the world." As she said this she raised herself upon the bed, so as to look round upon her aunt's face; but still she kept her arm upon the old woman's shoulder. "Is it not natural? How could I have helped it?"

"You must have known that it was wrong."

"No!"

"You did not know that it would displease me?"

"I knew that it was unfortunate,—not wrong. What did I do that was wrong? When he asked me, could I tell him anything but the truth?"

"You should have told him nothing." At this reply Bessy shook her head. "It cannot be that you should think that in such a matter there should be no restraint. Did you expect that I should give my consent to such a marriage? I want to hear from yourself what you thought of my feelings."

"I knew you would be angry."

"Well?"

"I knew you must think me unfit to be Philip's wife."

"Well?"

"I knew that you wanted something else for him, and something else also for me."

"And did such knowledge go for nothing?"

"It made me feel that my love was unfortunate,—but not that it was wrong. I could not help it. He had come to me, and I loved him. The other man came, and I could not love him. Why should I be shut up for this in my own room? Why should I be sent away from you, to be miserable because I know that you want things done? He is not here. If he were here and you bade me not to go near him, I would not go. Though he were in the next room I would not see him. I would obey you altogether, but I must love him. And as I love him I cannot love another. You would not wish me to marry a man when my heart has been given to another."

The old woman had not at all intended that there should be such arguments as these. It had been her purpose simply to communicate her plan, to tell Bessy that she would have to live probably for a few years at Avranches, and then to send her back to her prison. But Bessy had again got the best of her, and then had come caressing, talking, and excuses. Bessy had been nearly an hour in her room before Mrs. Miles had disclosed her purpose, and had hovered round her aunt, doing as had been her wont when she was recognised as having all the powers of head nurse in her hands.

Then at last, in a manner very different from that which had been planned, Mrs. Miles proposed the Normandy scheme. She had been, involuntarily, so much softened that she condescended even to repeat what Mr. Gregory had said as to the good temper and general kindness of his maiden sister. "But why should I go?" asked Bessy, almost sobbing.

"I wonder that you should ask."

"He is not here."

"But he may come."

"If he came ever so I would not see him if you bade me not. I think you hardly understand me, aunt. I will obey you in everything. I am sure you will not now ask me to marry Mr. Morrison."

She could not say that Philip would be more likely to become amenable and marry the Cornish heiress if Bessy were away at Avranches than if she still remained shut up at Launay. But that was her feeling. Philip, she knew, would be less obedient than Bessy. But then, too, Philip might be less obstinate of purpose. "You cannot live here, Bessy, unless you will say that you will never become the wife of my son."

"Never?"

"Never!"

"I cannot say that." There was a long pause before she found the courage to pronounce these words, but she did pronounce them at last.

"Then you must go."

"I may stay and nurse you till you are well. Let me do that. I will go whenever you may bid me."

"No. There shall be no terms between us. We must be friends, Bessy, or we must be enemies. We cannot be friends as long as you hold yourself to be engaged to Philip Launay. While that is so I will not take a cup of water from your hands. No, no," for the girl was again trying to embrace her. "I will not have your love, nor shall you have mine."

"My heart would break were I to say it."

"Then let it break! Is my heart not broken? What is it though our hearts do break,—what is it though we die,—if we do our duty? You owe this for what I have done for you."

"I owe you everything."

"Then say that you will give him up."

"I owe you everything, except this. I will not speak to him, I will not write to him, I will not even look at him, but I will not give him up. When one loves, one cannot give it up." Then she was ordered to go back to her room, and back to her room she went.

CHAPTER VII.

HOW BESSY PRYOR WAS BANISHED TO NORMANDY.

THERE was nothing for it but to go, after the interview described in the last chapter. Mrs. Miles sent a message to the obstinate girl, informing her that she need not any longer consider herself as a prisoner, but that she had better prepare her clothes so as to be ready to start within a week. The necessary correspondence had taken place between Launay and Avranches, and within ten days from the time at which Mr. Gregory had made the proposition,—in less than a fortnight from the departure of her lover,—Bessy came down from her room all equipped, and took her place in the same waggonette which so short a time before had taken her lover away from her. During the week she had had liberty to go where she pleased, except into her aunt's room. But she had, in truth, been almost as much a prisoner as before. She did for a few minutes each day go out into the garden, but she would not go beyond the garden into the park, nor did she accept an invitation from the Gregory girls to spend an evening at the rectory. It would be so necessary, one of them wrote, that everything should be told to her as to the disposition and ways of life of Aunt Amelia! But Bessy would not see the Gregory girls. She was being sent away from home because of the wickedness of her love, and all Launay knew it. In such a condition of things she could not go out to eat sally-lunn and pound-cake, and to be told of the delights of a small Norman town. She would not even see the Gregory girls when they came up to the house, but wrote an affectionate note to the elder of them explaining that her misery was too great to allow her to see any friend.

She was in truth very miserable. It was not only because of her love, from which she had from the first been aware that misery must come,—undoubted misery, if not misery that would last through her whole life. But now there was added to this the sorrow of absolute banishment from her aunt. Mrs. Miles would not see her again before she started. Bessy was well aware of all that she owed to the mistress of Launay; and, being intelligent in the reading of character, was aware also that through many years she had succeeded in obtaining from the old woman more than the intended performance of an undertaken duty. She had forced the old woman to love her, and was aware that by means of that love the old woman's life had been brightened. She had not only received, but had conferred kindness, —and it is by conferring kindness that love is created. It was an agony to her that she should be compelled to leave this dearest friend, who was still sick and infirm, without seeing her. But Mrs. Miles was inexorable. These four words written on a scrap of paper were brought to her on that morning:—"Pray, pray, see me!" She was still inexorable. There had been long pencil-written notes between them on the previous day. If Bessy would pledge herself to give up her lover all might yet be changed. The old woman at Avranches should be compensated for her disappointment. Bessy should be restored to all her privileges at Launay. "You shall be my own, own child," said Mrs. Miles. She condescended even to promise that not a word more should be said about Mr. Morrison. But Bessy also could be inexorable. "I cannot say that I will give him up," she wrote. Thus it came to pass that she had to get into the waggonette without seeing her old friend. Mrs. Knowl went with her, having received instructions to wait upon Miss Bessy all the way to Avranches. Mrs. Knowl felt that she was sent as a guard against the lover. Mrs. Miles had known Bessy too well to have fear of that kind, and had sent Mrs. Knowl as general guardian against the wild beasts which are supposed to be roaming about the world in quest of unprotected young females.

In the distribution of her anger Mrs. Miles had for the moment been very severe towards Philip as to pecuniary matters. He had chosen to be rebellious, and therefore he was not only turned out of the house, but told that he must live on an uncomfortably small income. But to Bessy Mrs. Miles was liberal. She had astounded Miss Gregory by the nobility of the terms she had proposed, and on the evening before the journey had sent ten five-pound notes in a blank envelope to Bessy. Then in a subsequent note she had said that a similar sum would be paid to her every half-year. In none of these notes was there any expression of endearment. To none of them was there even a signature. But they all conveyed evidence of the amount of thought which Mrs. Miles was giving to Bessy and her affairs.

Bessy's journey was very comfortless. She had learned to hate Mrs. Knowl, who assumed all the airs of a duenna. She would not leave Bessy out of sight for a moment, as though Philip might have been hidden behind every curtain or under every table. Once or twice the duenna made a little attempt at persuasion herself: "It ain't no good, miss, and it had better be give up." Then Bessy looked at her, and desired that she might be left alone. This had been at the hotel at Dover. Then again Mrs. Knowl spoke as the carriage was approaching Avranches: "If you wish to come back, Miss Bessy, the way is open." "Never mind my wishes, Mrs. Knowl," said Bessy. When, on her return to Launay, Mrs. Knowl once attempted to intimate to her mistress that Miss Bessy was very obstinate, she was silenced so sternly, so shortly, that the housekeeper began to doubt whether she might not have made a mistake and whether Bessy would not at last prevail. It was evident that Mrs. Miles would not hear a word against Bessy.

On her arrival at Avranches Miss Gregory was very kind to her. She found that she was received not at all as a naughty girl who had been sent away from home in order that she might be subjected to severe treatment. Miss Gregory fulfilled all the promises which her brother had made on her behalf, and was thoroughly kind and good-tempered. For nearly a month not a word was said about Philip or the love affairs. It seemed to be understood that Bessy had come to Avranches quite at her own desire. She was introduced to the genteel society with which that place abounds, and was conscious that a much freer life was vouchsafed to her than she had ever known before. At Launay she had of course been subject to Mrs. Miles. Now she was subject to no one. Miss Gregory exercised no authority over her,—was indeed rather subject to Bessy, as being recipient of the money paid for Bessy's board and lodging.

But by the end of the month there had grown up so much of friendship between the elder and the younger lady, that something came to be said about Philip. It was impossible that Bessy should be silent as to her past life. By degrees she told all that Mrs. Miles had done for her; how she herself had been a penniless orphan; how Mrs. Miles had taken her in from simple charity; how love had grown up between them two,—the warmest, truest love; and then how that other love had grown! The telling of secrets begets the telling of secrets. Miss Gregory, though she was now old, with the marks of little feeble crow's-feet round her gentle eyes, though she wore a false front and was much withered, had also had her love affair. She took delight in pouring forth her little tale; how she had loved an officer and had been beloved; how there had been no money; how the officer's parents had besought her to set the officer free, so that he might marry money; how she had set the officer free, and how, in consequence, the officer had married money and was now a major-general, with a large family, a comfortable house, and the gout. "And I have always thought it was right," said the excellent spinster. "What could I have done for him?"

"It couldn't be right if he loved you best," said Bessy.

"Why not, my dear? He has made an excellent

husband. Perhaps he didn't love me best when he stood at the altar."

"I think love should be more holy."

"Mine has been very holy,—to me, myself. For a time I wept; but now I think I am happier than if I had never seen him. It adds something to one's life to have been loved once."

Bessy, who was of a stronger temperament, told herself that happiness such as that would not suffice for her. She wanted not only to be happy herself, but also to make him so. In the simplicity of her heart she wondered whether Philip would be different from that easy-changing major-general; but in the strength of her heart she was sure he would be very different. She would certainly not release him at the request of any parent;—but he should be free as air at the slightest hint of a request from himself. She did not believe for a moment that such a request would come; but, if it did,—if it did,—then there should be no difficulty. Then would she submit to banishment,—at Avranches or elsewhere as it might be decided for her,—till it might please the Lord to release her from her troubles.

At the end of six weeks Miss Gregory knew the whole secret of Philip and Bessy's love, and knew also that Bessy was quite resolved to persevere. There were many discussions about love, in which Bessy always clung to the opinion that when it was once offered and taken, given and received, it ought to be held as more sacred than any other bond. She owed much to Mrs. Miles;—she acknowledged that;—but she thought that she owed more to Philip. Miss Gregory would never quite agree with her;—was strong in her own opinion that women are born to yield and suffer and live mutilated lives, like herself; but not the less did they become fast friends. At the end of six weeks it was determined between them that Bessy should write to Mrs. Miles. Mrs. Miles had signified her wish not to be written to, and had not herself written. Messages as to the improving state of her health had come from the Gregory girls, but no letter had as yet passed. Then Bessy wrote as follows, in direct disobedience to her aunt's orders:

"Dearest Aunt,—I cannot help writing a line because I am so anxious about you. Mary Gregory says you have been up and out on the lawn in the sunshine, but it would make me so happy if I could see the words in your own dear handwriting. Do send me one little word. And though I know what you told me, still I think you will be glad to hear that your poor affectionate loving Bessy is well. I will not say that I am quite happy. I cannot be quite happy away from Launay and you. But Miss Gregory has been very, very kind to me, and there are nice people here. We live almost as quietly as at Launay, but sometimes we see the people. I am reading German and making lace, and I try not to be idle.

"Good-bye, dear, dearest aunt. Try to think kindly of me. I pray for you every morning and night. If you will send me a little note from yourself it will fill me with joy."—Your most affectionate and devoted niece, BESSY PRYOR."

This was brought up to Mrs. Miles when she was still in bed, for as yet she had not returned to the early hours of her healthy life. When she had read it she at first held it apart from her. Then she put it close to her bosom, and wept bitterly as she thought how void of sunshine the house had been since that gleam had been turned away from it.

CHAPTER VIII.

HOW BESSY PRYOR RECEIVED TWO LETTERS FROM LAUNAY.

THE same post brought Bessy two letters from England about the middle of August, both of which the reader shall see;—but first shall be given that which Bessy read the last. It was from Mrs. Miles, and had been sent when she was beginning to think that her aunt was still resolved not to write to her. The letter was as follows, and was written on square paper, which in these days is only used even by the old-fashioned when the letter to be sent is supposed to be one of great importance.

"My dear Bessy,—Though I had told you not to write to me, still I am glad to hear that you are well, and that your new home has been made as comfortable for you as circumstances will permit. Launay has not been comfortable since you went. I miss you very much. You have become so dear to me that my life is sad without you. My days have never been bright, but now they are less so than ever. I should scruple to admit so much as this to you, were it not that I intend it as a prelude to that which will follow.

"We have been sent into this world, my child, that we may do our duties, independent of that fleeting feeling which we call happiness. In the smaller affairs of life I am sure you would never seek a pleasure at the cost of your conscience. If not in the smaller things, then certainly should you not do so in the greater. To deny yourself, to remember the welfare of others, when temptation is urging you to do wrong, then do that which you know to be right,—that is your duty as a Christian, and especially your duty as a woman. To sacrifice herself is the special heroism which a woman can achieve. Men who are called upon to work may gratify their passions and still be heroes. A woman can soar only by suffering.

"You will understand why I tell you this. I and my son have been born into a special degree of life which I think it to be my duty and his to maintain. It is not that I or that he may enjoy any special delights that I hold fast to this opinion, but that I may do my part towards maintaining that order of things which has made my country more blessed than others. It would take me long to explain all this, but I know you will believe me when I say that an imperative sense of duty is my guide. You have not been born into that degree. That this does not affect my own personal feeling to you, you must know. You have had many signs how dear you are to me. At this moment my days are heavy to bear because I have not my Bessy with me,—my Bessy who has been so good to me, so loving, such an infinite blessing that to see the hem of her garments, to hear the sound of her foot, has made things bright around me. Now, there is nothing to see, nothing to hear, that is not unsightly and harsh of sound. Oh, Bessy, if you could come back to me!

"But I have to do that duty of which I have spoken, and I shall do it. Though I were never to see you again I shall do it. I am used to suffering, and sometimes think it wrong even to wish that you were back with me. But I write to you thus that you may understand everything. If you will say that you will give him up, you shall return to me and be my own, own beloved child. I tell you that you are not of the same degree. I am bound to tell you so. But you shall be so near my heart that nothing shall separate us.

"You two cannot marry while I am living. I do not think it possible that you should be longing to be made happy by my death. And you should remember that he cannot be the first to break away from this foolish engagement without dishonour. As he is the wealthy one, and the higher born, and as he is the man, he ought not to be the first to say the word.

You may say it without falsehood and without disgrace. You may say it, and all the world will know that you have been actuated only by a sense of duty. It will be acknowledged that you have sacrificed yourself,—as it becomes a woman to do.

"One word from you will be enough to assure me. Since you came to me you have never been false. One word, and you shall come back to me and to Launay, my friend and my treasure! If it be that there must be suffering, we will suffer together. If tears are necessary there shall be joint tears. Though I am old still I can understand. I will acknowledge the sacrifice. But, Bessy, my Bessy, dearest Bessy, the sacrifice must be made.

"Of course he must live away from Launay for awhile. The fault will have been his, and what of inconvenience there may be he must undergo. He shall not come here till you yourself shall say that you can bear his presence without an added sorrow.

"I know you will not let this letter be in vain. I know you will think it over deeply, and that you will not keep me too long waiting for an answer. I need hardly tell you that I am

"Your most loving friend,

"M. MILES."

When Bessy was reading this, when the strong words with which her aunt had pleaded her cause were harrowing her heart, she had clasped in her hand this other letter from her lover. This too was written from Launay.

"My own dearest Bessy,—It is absolutely only now that I have found out where you are, and have done so simply because the people at the rectory could not keep the secret. Can anything be more absurd than supposing that my mother can have her way by whisking you away, and shutting you up in Normandy? It is too foolish! She has sent for me, and I have come like a dutiful son. I have, indeed, been rejoiced to see her looking again so much like herself. But I have not extended my duty to obeying her in a matter in which my own future happiness is altogether bound up; and in which, perhaps, the happiness of another person may be slightly concerned. I have told her that I would venture to say nothing of the happiness of the other person. The other person might be indifferent, though I did not believe it was so; but I was quite sure of my own. I have assured her that I know what I want myself, and that I do not mean to abandon my hope of achieving it. I know that she is writing to you. She can of course say what she pleases.

"The idea of separating two people who are as old as you and I, and who completely know our own minds,—you see that I do not really doubt as to yours,—is about as foolish as anything well can be. It is as though we were going back half a dozen centuries into the tyrannies of the middle ages. My object shall be to induce her to let you come home and be married properly from Launay. If she will not consent by the end of this month I shall go over to you, and we must contrive to be married at Avranches. When the thing has been once done all this rubbish will be swept away. I do not believe for a moment that my mother will punish us by any injustice as to money.

"Write and tell me that you agree with me, and be sure that I shall remain, as I am, always altogether your own,

"Truly and affectionately,

"PHILIP MILES."

When Bessy Pryor began to consider these two letters together, she felt that the task was almost too much for her. Her lover's letter had been the first read. She had known his handwriting, and of course had read his the first. And as she had read it everything seemed to be of rose colour. Of course she had been filled with joy. Something had been done by the warnings of Miss Gregory, something, but not much, to weaken her strong faith in her lover. The major-general had been worldly and untrue, and it had been possible that her Philip should be as had been the major-general. There had been moments of doubt in which her heart had fainted a little; but as she read her lover's words she acknowledged to herself how wrong she had been to faint at all. He declared it to be "a matter in which his own future happiness was altogether bound up." And then there had been his playful allusion to her happiness, which was not the less pleasant to her because he had pretended to think that the "other person might be indifferent." She pouted her lips at him, as though he were present while she was reading, with a joyous affectation of disdain. No, no; she could not consent to an immediate marriage at Avranches. There must be some delay. But she would write to him and explain all that. Then she read her aunt's letter.

It moved her very much. She had read it all twice before there came upon her a feeling of doubt, an acknowledgment to herself that she must reconsider the matter. But even when she was only reading it, before she had begun to consider, her former joy was repressed and almost quenched. So much of it was too true, terribly true. Of course her duty should be paramount. If she could persuade herself that duty required her to abandon Philip, she must abandon him, let the suffering to herself or to others be what it might. But then, what was it that duty required of her? "To sacrifice herself is the special heroism which a woman can achieve." Yes, she believed that. But then, how about sacrificing Philip, who, no doubt, was telling the truth when he said that his own happiness was altogether bound up in his love?

She was moved too by all that which Mrs. Miles said as to the grandeur of the Launay family. She had learned enough of the manners of Launay to be quite alive to the aristocratic idiosyncrasies of the old woman, She, Bessy Pryor, was nobody. It would have been well that Philip Launay should have founded his happiness on some girl of higher birth. But he had not done so. King Cophetua's marriage had been recognised by the world at large. Philip was no more than King Cophetua, nor was she less than the beggar-girl. Like to like in marriages was no doubt expedient,—but not indispensable. And though she was not Philip's equal, yet she was a lady. She would not disgrace him at his table, or among his friends. She was sure that she could be a comfort to him in his work.

But the parts of the old woman's letter which moved her most were those in which she gave full play to her own heart, and spoke, without reserve, of her own love for her dearest Bessy. "My days are heavy to bear because I have not my Bessy with me." It was impossible to read this and not to have some desire to yield. How good this lady had been to her! Was it not through her that she had known Philip? But for Mrs. Miles, what would her own life have been? She thought that had she been sure of Philip's happiness, could she have satisfied herself that he would bear the blow, she would have done as she was asked. She would have achieved her heroism, and shown the strength of her gratitude, and would have taken her delight in administering to the comforts of her old friend,—only that Philip had her promise. All that she could possibly owe to all the world beside must be less, so infinitely less, than what she owed to him.

She would have consulted Miss Gregory, but she knew so well what Miss Gregory would have advised. Miss Gregory would only have mentioned the major-general and her own experiences. Bessy determined, therefore, to lie awake and think of it, and to take no other counsellor beyond her own heart.

CHAPTER IX.

HOW BESSY PRYOR ANSWERED THE TWO LETTERS, AND WHAT CAME OF IT.

THE letters were read very often, and that from Mrs. Miles I think the oftener. Philip's love was plainly expressed, and what more is expected from a lover's letter than a strong, manly expression of love? It was quite satisfactory, declaring the one important fact that his happiness was bound up in hers. But Mrs. Miles' was the stronger letter, and by far the more suggestive. She had so mingled hardness and softness, had enveloped her stern lesson of feminine duty in so sweet a frame of personal love, that it was hardly possible that such a girl as Bessy Pryor should not be shaken by her arguments. There were moments during the night in which she had almost resolved to yield. "A woman can soar only by suffering." She was not sure that she wanted to soar, but she certainly did want to do her duty, even though suffering should come of it. But there was one word in her aunt's letter which militated against the writer's purpose rather than assisted it. "Since you first came to me, you have never been false." False! no; she hoped she had not been false. Whatever might be the duty of a man or a woman, that duty should be founded on truth. Was it not her special duty at this moment to be true to Philip? I do not know that she was altogether logical. I do not know but that in so supporting herself in her love there may have been a bias of personal inclination. Bessy perhaps was a little prone to think that her delight and her duty went together. But that flattering assurance, that she had never yet been false, strengthened her resolution to be true, now, to Philip.

She took the whole of the next day to think, abstaining during the whole day from a word of confidential conversation with Miss Gregory. Then on the following morning she wrote her letters. That to Philip would be easily written. Words come readily when one has to give a hearty assent to an eager and welcome proposition. But to deny, to make denial to one loved and respected, to make denial of that which the loved one has a right to ask, must be difficult. Bessy, like a brave girl, went to the hard task first, and she rushed instantly at her subject, as a brave horseman rides at his fence without craning.

"Dearest Aunt,—I cannot do as you bid me. My word to him is so sacred to me that I do not dare to break it. I cannot say that I won't be his when I feel that I have already given myself to him.

"Dear, dearest aunt, my heart is very sad as I write

this, because I feel that I am separating myself from you almost for ever. You know that I love you. You know that I am miserable because you have banished me from your side. All the sweet kind words of your love to me are like daggers to me, because I cannot show my gratitude by doing as you would have me. It seems so hard! I know it is probable that I may never see him again, and yet I am to be separated from you, and you will be my enemy. In all the world there are but two that I really love. Though I cannot and will not give him up, I desire to be back at Launay now only that I might be with you. My love for him would be contented with a simple permission that it should exist. My love for you cannot be satisfied unless I am allowed to be close to you once again. You say that a woman's duty consists in suffering. I am striving to do my duty, but I know how great is my suffering in doing it. However angry you may be with your Bessy, you will not think that she can appear even to be ungrateful without a pang.

"Though I will not give him up, you need not fear that I shall do anything. Should he come here I could not, I suppose, avoid seeing him, but I should ask him to go at once; and I should beg Miss Gregory to tell him that she could not make him welcome to her house. In all things I will do as though I were your daughter—though I know so well how far I am from any right to make use of so dear a name!

"But dear, dear aunt, no daughter could love you better, nor strive more faithfully to be obedient.

"I shall always be, even when you are most angry with me, your own, poor, loving, most affectionate

"BESSY."

The other letter need perhaps be not given in its entirety. Even in such a chronicle as this there seems to be something of treachery, something of a want of that forbearance to which young ladies are entitled, in making public the words of love which such a one may write to her lover. Bessy's letter was no doubt full of love, but it was full of prudence also. She begged him not to come to Avranches. As to such a marriage as that of which he had spoken, it was, she assured him, quite impossible. She would never give him up, and so she had told Mrs. Miles. In that respect her duty to him was above her duty to her aunt. But she was so subject to her aunt that she would not in any other matter disobey her. For his sake—for Philip's sake—only for Philip's sake, she grieved that there should be more delay. Of course she was aware that it might possibly be a trouble in life too many for him to bear. In that case he might make himself free from it without a word of reproach from her. Of that he alone must be the judge. But, for the present, she could be no partner to any plans for the future. Her aunt had desired her to stay at Avranches, and at Avranches she must remain. There were words of love, no doubt; but the letter, taken altogether, was much sterner and less demonstrative of affection than that written to her aunt.

There very soon came a rejoinder from Mrs. Miles, but it was so curt and harsh as almost to crush Bessy by its laconic severity. "You are separated from me, and I am your enemy." That was all. Beneath that one line the old woman had signed her name, M. Miles, in large, plain angry letters. Bessy, who knew every turn of the woman's mind, understood exactly how it had been with her when she wrote those few words, and when, with care, she had traced that indignant signature. "Then everything shall be broken, and though there was but one gleam of sunshine left to me, that gleam shall be extinguished. No one shall say that I, as Lady of Launay, did not do my duty." It was thus the Lady of Launay had communed with herself when she penned that dreadful line. Bessy understood it all, and could almost see the woman as she wrote it.

Then in her desolation she told everything to Miss Gregory—showed the two former letters, showed that dreadful denunciation of lasting wrath, and described exactly what had been her own letter, both to Mrs. Miles and to her lover. Miss Gregory had but one recipe to offer in such a malady; that, namely, which she had taken herself in a somewhat similar sickness. The gentleman should be allowed to go forth into the world and seek a fitter wife, whereas Bessy should content herself, for the remainder of her life, with the pleasures of memory. Miss Gregory thought that it was much even to have been once loved by the major-general. When Bessy almost angrily declared that this would not be enough for her, Miss Gregory very meekly suggested that possibly affection might change in the lapse of years, and that some other suitor —perhaps Mr. Morrison—might in course of time suffice. But at the idea Bessy became indignant, and Miss Gregory was glad to confine herself to the remedy pure and simple which she acknowledged to have been good for herself.

Then there passed a month—a month without a line from Launay or from Philip. That Mrs. Miles should not write again was to be expected. She had declared her enmity, and there was an end of everything. During the month there had come a cheque to Miss Gregory from some man of business, and with the cheque there had been no intimation that the present arrangement was to be brought to a close. It appeared therefore that Mrs. Miles, in spite of her enmity, intended to provide for the mutinous girl a continuation of the comforts which she now enjoyed. Certainly nothing more than this could have been expected from her. But, in regard to Philip, though Bessy had assured herself, and had assured Miss Gregory also, that she did not at all desire a correspondence in the present condition of affairs, still she felt so total a cessation of all tidings to be hard to bear. Mary Gregory, when writing to her aunt, said nothing of Philip—merely remarked that Bessy Pryor would be glad to know that her aunt had nearly recovered her health, and was again able to go out among the poor. Then Bessy began to think—not that Philip was like the major-general, for to that idea she would not give way at all—but that higher and nobler motives had induced him to yield to his mother. If so she would never reproach him. If so she would forgive him in her heart of hearts. If so she would accept her destiny and entreat her old friend to allow her to return once more to Launay, and thenceforth to endure the evil thing which fate would have done to her in patient submission. If once the word should have come to her from Philip, then would she freely declare that everything should be over, then and for always, between her and her lover. After such suffering as that, while she was undergoing agony so severe, surely her friend would forgive her. That terrible word, "I am your enemy," would surely then be withdrawn.

But if it were to be so, if this was to be the end of her love, Philip, at least, would write. He would not leave her in doubt, after such a decision on his own part. That thought ought to have sustained her; but it was explained to her by Miss Gregory that the major-general had taken three months before he had been inspirited to send the fatal letter, and to declare his purpose of marrying money. There could be but little doubt, according to Miss Gregory, that Philip was undergoing the same process. It was, she thought, the natural end to such an affair. This was the kind of thing which young ladies without dowry, but with hearts to love, are doomed to suffer. There could be no doubt that Miss Gregory regarded the termination of the affair with a certain amount of sympathetic satisfaction. Could she have given Bessy all Launay, and her lover, she would have done so. But sadness and disappointment were congenial to her, and a heart broken, but still constant, was, to her thinking, a pretty feminine acquisition. She was to herself the heroine of her own romance, and she thought it good to be a heroine. But Bessy was indignant; not that Philip should be false, but that he should not dare to write and say so. "I think he ought to write," was on her lips, when the door was opened, and, lo, all of a sudden, Philip Miles was in the room.

CHAPTER X.

HOW BESSY PRYOR'S LOVER ARGUED HIS CASE.

We must now go back to Launay. It will be remembered that Bessy received both her letters on the same day—those namely from Mrs. Miles and from Philip—and that they both came from Launay. Philip had been sent away from the place when the fact of his declared love was first made known to the old lady, as though into a banishment which was to be perpetual till he should have repented of his sin. Such certainly had been his mother's intention. He was to be sent one way, and the girl another, and everyone concerned was to be made to feel the terrible weight of her displeasure, till repentance and retractation should come.

He was to be starved into obedience by a minimised allowance, and she by the weariness of her life at Avranches. But the person most grievously punished by these arrangements was herself. She had declared to herself that she would endure anything, everything, in the performance of her duty. But the desolation of her life was so extreme that it was very hard to bear. She did not shrink and tell herself that it was unendurable, but after awhile she persuaded herself that now that Bessy was gone there could be no reason why Philip also should be exiled. Would not her influence be more potent over Philip if he were at Launay? She therefore sent for him, and he came. Thus it was that the two letters were written from the same house.

Philip obeyed his mother's behest in coming as he had obeyed it in going; but he did not hesitate to show her that he felt himself to be aggrieved. Launay of course belonged to her. She could leave it and all the property to some hospital if she chose. He was well aware of that. But he had been brought up as the heir, and he could not believe that there should come such a ruin of heaven and earth as would be produced by any change in his mother's intentions as to the Launay property. Touching his marriage, he felt that he had a right to marry whom he pleased, as long as she was a lady, and that any dictation from his mother in such a matter was a tyranny not to be endured. He had talked it all over with the rector before he went. Of course it was possible that his mother should commit such an injustice as that at which the rector hinted. "There are," said Philip, "no bounds to possibilities." It was, however, he thought, all but impossible; and whether probable or improbable, no fear of such tyranny should drive him from his purpose. He was a little magniloquent, perhaps, in what he said, but he was very resolved.

It was, therefore, with some feeling of an injury inflicted upon him that he first greeted his mother on his return to the house. For a day or two not a word passed about Bessy. "Of course, I am delighted to be with you, and glad enough to have the shooting," he said, in answer to some word of hers. "I shouldn't have gone, as you know, unless you had driven me away." This was hard on the old woman; but she bore it, and, for some days, was simply affectionate and gentle to her son—more gentle than was her wont. Then she wrote to Bessy, and told her son that she was writing. "It is so impossible," she said, "that I cannot conceive that Bessy should not obey me when she comes to regard it at a distance."

"I see no impossibility; but Bessy can, of course, do as she pleases," replied Philip, almost jauntily. Then he determined that he also would write.

There were no further disputes on the matter till Bessy's answer came, and then Mrs. Miles was very angry indeed. She had done her best so to write her letter that Bessy should be conquered both by the weight of her arguments and by the warmth of her love. If reason would not prevail, surely gratitude would compel her to do as she was bidden. But the very first words of Bessy's letter contained a flat refusal. "I cannot do as you bid me." Who was this girl, that had been picked out of a gutter, that she should persist in the right of becoming the mistress of Launay? In a moment the old woman's love was turned into a feeling of condemnation, nearly akin to hatred. Then she sent off her short rejoinder, declaring herself to be Bessy's enemy.

On the following morning regret had come, and perhaps remorse. She was a woman of strong passion, subject to impulses which were, at the time, uncontrollable; but she was one who was always compelled by her conscience to quick repentance, and sometimes to an agonising feelirg of wrong done by herself. To declare that Bessy was her enemy—Bessy, who for so many years had prevented all her wishes, who had never been weary of well-doing to her, who had been patient in all things, who had been her gleam of sunshine, of whom she had sometimes said to herself in her closet that the child was certainly nearer to perfection than any other human being that she had known! True, it was not fit that the girl should become mistress of Launay! A misfortune had happened which must be cured—if even by the severance of persons so dear to each other as she and her Bessy. But she knew that she had sinned in declaring one so good, and one so dear, to be her enemy.

But what should she do next? Days went on and she did nothing. She simply suffered. There was no pretext on which she could frame an affectionate letter to her child. She could not write and ask to be forgiven for the harshness of her letter. She could not simply revoke the sentence she had pronounced without any reference to Philip and his love. In great misery, with a strong feeling of self-degradation because she had allowed herself to be violent in her wrath, she went on, repentant but still obstinate, till Philip himself forced the subject upon her.

"Mother," he said one day, "is it not time that things should be settled?"

"What things, Philip?"

"You know my intention."

"What intention?"

"As to making Bessy my wife."

"That can never be."

"But it will be. It has to be. If as regards my own feelings I could bring myself to yield to you, how could I do so with honour in regard to her? But, for myself, nothing on earth would induce me to change my mind. It is a matter on which a man has to judge for himself, and I have not heard a word from you or from anyone to make me think that I have judged wrongly."

"Do birth and rank go for nothing?"

He paused a moment, and then he answered her very seriously, standing up and looking down upon her as he did so. "For very much—with me. I do not think that I could have brought myself to choose a wife, whatever might have been a woman's charms, except among ladies. I found this one to be the chosen companion and dearest friend of the finest lady I know." At this the old woman, old as she was, first blushed, and then, finding herself to be sobbing, turned her face away from him. "I came across a girl of whose antecedents I could be quite sure, of whose bringing up I knew all the particulars, as to whom I could be certain that every hour of her life had been passed among the best possible associations. I heard testimony as to her worth and her temper which I could not but believe. As to her outward belongings, I had eyes of my own to judge. Could I be wrong in asking such a one to be my wife? Can I be regarded as unhappy in having succeeded with her? Could I be acquitted of dishonour if I were to desert her? Shall I be held to be contemptible if I am true to her?"

At every word he spoke he grew in her esteem. At this present crisis of her life she did not wish to think specially well of him, though he was her son, but she could not help herself. He became bigger before her than he had ever been before, and more of a man. It was, she felt, almost vain for a woman to lay her commands, either this way or that, upon a man who could speak to her as Philip had spoken.

But not the less was the power in her hands. She could bid him go and marry—and be a beggar. She could tell him that all Launay should go to his brother, and she could instantly make a will to that effect. So strong was the desire for masterdom upon her that she longed to do it. In the very teeth of her honest wish to do what was right, there was another wish—a longing to do what she knew to be wrong. There was a struggle within, during which she strove to strengthen herself for evil. But it was vain. She knew of herself that were she to swear to-day to him that he was disinherited, were she to make a will before nightfall carrying out her threat, the pangs of conscience would be so heavy during the night that she would certainly change it all on the next morning. Of what use is a sword in your hand if you have not the heart to use it? Why seek to be turbulent with a pistol if your bosom be of such a nature that your finger cannot be forced to pull the trigger? Power was in her possession—but she could not use it. The power rather was in her hands. She could not punish her boy, even though he had deserved it. She had punished her girl, and from that moment she had been crushed by torments, because of the thing that she had done. Others besides Mrs. Miles have felt, with something of regret, that they have lacked the hardness necessary for cruelty and the courage necessary for its doing.

"How shall it be, mother?" asked Philip. As she knew not what to answer she rose slowly from her chair, and leaving the room went to the seclusion of her own chamber.

Days again passed before Philip renewed his question, and repeated it in the same words: "How shall it be, mother?" Wistfully she looked up at him, as though even yet something might be accorded by him to pity; as though the son might even yet be induced to accede to his mother's prayers. It was not that she thought so. No. She had thought much, and was aware that it could not be so. But as a dog will ask with its eyes when it knows that asking is in vain, so did she ask. "One word from you, mother, will make us all happy."

"No; not all of us."

"Will not my happiness make you happy?" Then he stooped over her and kissed her forehead. "Could you be happy if you knew that I were wretched?"

"I do not want to be happy. It should be enough that one does one's duty."

"And what is my duty? Can it be my duty to betray the girl I love in order that I may increase an estate which is already large enough?"

"It is for the family."

"What is a family but you, or I, or whoever for the moment may be its representative? Say that it shall be as I would have it, and then I will go to her and let her know that she may come back to your arms."

Not then, or on the next day, or on the next, did she yield; though she knew well during all these hours that it was her fate to yield. She had indeed yielded. She had confessed to herself that it must be so, and as she did so she felt once more the soft pressure of Bessy's arms as they would cling round her neck, and she could see once more the brightness of Bessy's eyes as the girl would hang over her bed early in the morning. "I do not want to be happy," she had said; but she did want, sorely want, to see her girl. "You may go and tell her," she said one night as she was preparing to go to her chamber. Then she turned quickly away, and was out of the room before he could answer her with a word.

CHAPTER XI.

HOW BESSY PRYOR RECEIVED HER LOVER.

MISS GREGORY was certainly surprised when, on the entrance of the young man, Bessy jumped from her chair and rushed into his arms. She knew that Bessy had no brother, and her instinct rather than her experience told her that the greeting which she saw was more than fraternal,—more than cousinly. She did not doubt but that the young man was Philip Launay, and knowing what she knew she was not disposed to make spoken complaints. But when Bessy lifted her face to be kissed, Miss Gregory became red and very uneasy. It is probable that she herself had never progressed as far as this with the young man who afterwards became the major-general.

Bessy herself, had a minute been allowed to her for reflection, would have been less affectionate. She knew nothing of tho cause which had brought Philip to Avranches. She only knew that her dear friend at Launay had declared her to be an enemy, and that she had determined that she could not, for years, become the wife of Philip Launay, without the consent of her who had used that cruel word. And at the moment of Philip's entering the room her heart had been sore with reproaches against him. "He ought at any rate to write." The words had been on her lips as the door had been opened, and the words had been spoken in the soreness of heart coming from a fear that she was to be abandoned.

Then he was there. In the moment that sufficed for the glance of his eye to meet hers she knew that she was not abandoned. With whatever tidings he had come that was not to be the burden of his news. No man desirous of being released from his vows ever looked like that. So up she jumped and flew to him, not quite knowing what she intended, but filled with delight when she found herself pressed to his bosom. Then she had to remember herself, and to escape from his arms. "Philip," she said, "this is Miss Gregory. Miss Gregory, I do not think you ever met Mr. Launay."

Then Miss Gregory had to endeavour to look as though nothing particular had taken place,—which was a trial. But Bessy bore her part, if not without a struggle, at least without showing it. "And now, Philip," she said, "how is my aunt?"

"A great deal stronger than when you left her."

"Quite well?"

"Yes; for her, I think I may say quite well."

"She goes out every day?"

"Every day,—after the old plan. The carriage

toddles round to the door at three, and then toddles about the parish at the rate of four miles an hour, and toddles home exactly at five. The people at Launay, Miss Gregory, don't want clocks to tell them the hour in the afternoon."

"I do love punctuality," said Miss Gregory.

"I wish I were with her," said Bessy.

"I have come to take you," said Philip.

"Have you?" Then Bessy blushed,—for the first time. She blushed as a hundred various thoughts rushed across her mind. If he had been sent to take her back, sent by her aunt, instead of Mrs. Knowl, what a revulsion of circumstances must there not have been at Launay! How could it all have come to pass? Even to have been sent for at all, to be allowed to go back even in disgrace, would have been an inexpressible joy. Had Knowl come for her, with a grim look and an assurance that she was to be brought back because a prison at Launay was thought to be more secure than a prison at Avranches, the prospect of a return would have been hailed with joy. But now,—to be taken back by Philip to Launay! There was a whole heaven of delight in the thought of the very journey.

Miss Gregory endeavoured to look pleased, but in truth the prospect to her was not so pleasant as to Bessy. She was to be left alone again. She was to lose her pensioner. After so short a fruition of the double bliss of society and pay, she was to be deserted without a thought. But to be deserted without many thoughts had been her lot in life, and now she bore her misfortune like a heroine. "You will be glad to go back to your aunt, Bessy ; will you not?"

"Glad!" The ecstacy was almost unkind, but poor Miss Gregory bore it, and maintained that pretty smile of gratified serenity as though everything were well with all of them.

But Bessy felt that she had as yet heard nothing of the real news, and that the real news could not be told in the presence of Miss Gregory. It had not even yet occurred to her that Mrs. Miles had actually given her sanction to the marriage. "This is a very pretty place," said Philip.

"What, Avranches?" said Miss Gregory, mindful of future possible pensioners. "Oh, delightful. It is the prettiest place in Normandy, and I think the most healthy town in all France."

"It seemed nice as I came up from the hotel. Suppose we go out for a walk, Bessy. We have to start back to-morrow."

"To-morrow!" ejaculated Bessy. She would have been ready to go in half an hour had he demanded it.

"If you can manage it. I promised my mother to be as quick as I could; and, when I arranged to come, I had ever so many engagements."

"If she must go to-morrow, she won't have much time for walking," said Miss Gregory, with almost a touch of anger in her voice. But Bessy was determined to have her walk. All her fate in life was to be disclosed to her within the next few minutes. She was already exultant, but she was beginning to think that there was a heaven, indeed, opening for her. So she ran away for her hat and gloves, leaving her lover and Miss Gregory together.

"It is very sudden," said the poor old lady with a gasp.

"My mother felt that, and bade me tell you that, of course, the full twelvemonth——"

"I was not thinking about that," said Miss Gregory. "I did not mean to allude to such a thing. Mrs. Miles has always been so kind to my brother, and anything I could have done I should have been so happy, without thinking of money. But——" Philip sat with the air of an attentive listener, so that Miss Gregory could get no answer to her question without absolutely asking it. "But there seems to be a change."

"Yes, there is a change, Miss Gregory."

"We were afraid that Mrs. Miles had been offended."

"It is the old story, Miss Gregory. Young people and old people very often will not think alike: but it is the young people who generally have their way."

She had not had her way. She remembered that at the moment. But then, perhaps, the major-general had had his. When a period of life has come too late for success, when all has been failure, the expanding triumphs of the glorious young, grate upon the feelings even of those who are generous and self-denying. Miss Gregory was generous by nature and self-denying by practice, but Philip's pæan and Bessy's wondrous prosperity were for a moment a little hard upon her.

There had been a comfort to her in the conviction that Philip was no better than the major-general. "I suppose it is so," she said. "That is, if one of them has means."

"Exactly."

"But if they are both poor, I don't see how their being young can enable them to live upon nothing." She intended to imply that Philip probably would have been another major-general, but that he was heir to Launay.

Philip, who had never heard of the major-general, was a little puzzled; nevertheless, he acceded to the proposition, not caring, however, to say anything as to his own circumstances on so very short an acquaintance.

Then Bessy came down with her hat, and they started for their walk. "Now tell me all about it," she said, in a fever of expectation, as soon as the front door was closed behind them.

"There is nothing more to tell," said he.

"Nothing more?"

"Unless you want me to say that I love you."

"Of course I do."

"Well, then,—I love you. There!"

"Philip, you are not half nice to me."

"Not after coming all the way from Launay to say that?"

"There must be so much to tell me? Why has my aunt sent for me?"

"Because she wants you."

"And why has she sent you?"

"Because I want you too."

"But does she want me?"

"Certainly she does."

"For you?" If he could say this, then everything would have been said. If he could say this truly, then everything would have been done necessary for the perfection of her happiness. "Oh, Philip, do tell me. It is so strange that she should send for me! Do you know what she said to me in her last letter? It was not a letter. It was only a word. She said that I was her enemy."

"All that is changed."

"She will be glad to have me again?"

"Very glad. I fancy that she has been miserable without you."

"I shall be as glad to be with her again, Philip. You do not know how I love her. Think of all she has done for me!"

"She has done something now that I hope will beat everything else."

"What has she done?"

"She has consented that you and I shall be man and wife. Isn't that more than all the rest?"

"But has she? Oh, Philip, has she really done that?"

Then at last he told his whole story. Yes; his mother had yielded. From the moment in which she had walked out of the room, having said that he might "go and tell her," she had never endeavoured to renew the fight. When he had spoken to her, endeavouring to draw from her some warmth of assent, she had generally been very silent. She had never brought herself absolutely to wish him joy. She had not as yet so crucified her own spirit in the matter as to be able to tell him that he had chosen his wife well; but she had shown him in a hundred ways that her anger was at an end, and that if any feeling was left opposed to his own happiness, it was simply one of sorrow. And there were signs which made him think that even that was not deep-seated. She would pat him, stroking his hair, and leaning on his shoulder, administering to his comforts with a nervous accuracy as to little things which was peculiar to her. And then she gave him an infinity of directions as to the way in which it would be proper that Bessy should travel, being anxious at first to send over a maid for her behoof,—not Mrs. Knowl, but a younger woman, who would have been at Bessy's command. Philip, however, objected to the maid. And when Mrs. Miles remarked that if it was Bessy's fate to become mistress of Launay, Bessy ought to have a maid to attend her, Philip said that that would be very well a month or two hence, when Bessy would have become,—not mistress of Launay, which was a place which he trusted might not be vacant for many a long day,—but first lieutenant to the mistress, by right of marriage. He refused altogether to take the maid with him, as he explained to Bessy with much laughter. And so they came to understand each other thoroughly, and Bessy knew that the great trouble of her life, which had been as a mountain in her way, had disappeared suddenly, as might some visionary mountain. And then, when they thoroughly understood each other, they started back to England and to Launay together.

CHAPTER XII.

HOW BESSY PRYOR WAS BROUGHT BACK, AND WHAT THEN BECAME OF HER.

Bessy understood the condition of the old woman much better than did her son. "I am sad a little," she said, on her way home, "because of her disappointment."

"Sad, because she is to have you,—you yourself,—for her daughter-in-law?"

"Yes, indeed, Philip; because I know that she has not wanted me. She will be kind because I shall belong to you, and perhaps partly because she loves me; but she will always regret that that young lady down in Cornwall has not been allowed to add to the honour and greatness of the family. The Launays are everything to her, and what can I do for the Launays?" Of course he said many pretty things to her in answer to this, but he could not eradicate from her mind the feeling that, in regard to the old friend who had been so kind to her, she was returning evil for good.

But even Bessy did not quite understand the old woman. When she found that she had yielded, there was disappointment in the old woman's heart. Who can have indulged in a certain longing for a lifetime, in a special ambition, and seen that ambition and that longing crushed and trampled on, without such a feeling? And she had brought this failure on herself,—by her own weakness, as she told herself. Why had she given way to Bessy and to Bessy's blandishments? It was because she had not been strong to do her duty that this ruin had fallen upon her hopes. The power in her own hands had been sufficient. But for her Philip need never have seen Bessy Pryor. Might not Bessy Pryor have been sent somewhere out of the way when it became evident that she had charms of her own with which to be dangerous? And even after the first evil had been done her power had been sufficient. She need not have sent for Philip back. She need have written no letter to Bessy. She might have been calm and steady in her purpose, so that there should have been no violent ebullition of anger,—so violent as to induce repentance, and with repentance renewed softness and all the pangs of renewed repentance.

When Philip had left her on his mission to Normandy her heart was heavy with regret, and heavy also with anger. But it was with herself that she was angry. She had known her duty and she had not done it. She had known her duty, and had neglected it,—because Bessy had been soft to her, and dear, and pleasant. It was here that Bessy did not quite understand her friend. Bessy reproached herself because she had made to her friend a bad return to all the kindness she had received. The old woman would not allow herself to entertain any such a thought. Once she had spoken to herself of having warmed a serpent in her bosom; but instantly, with infinite self-scorn, she had declared to herself that Bessy was no serpent. For all that she had done for Bessy, Bessy had made ample return, the only possible return that could be full enough. Bessy had loved her. She too had loved Bessy, but that should have had no weight. Though they two had been linked together by their very heart-strings, it had been her duty to make a severance because their joint affection had been dangerous. She had allowed her own heart to over-ride her own sense of duty, and therefore she was angry,—not with Bessy, but with herself.

But the thing was done. To quarrel with Philip had been impossible to her. One feeling coming upon another, her own repentance, her own weakness, her acknowledgment of a certain man's strength on the part of her son, had brought her to such a condition that she had yielded. Then it was natural that she should endeavour to make the best of it. But even the doing of that was a trial to her. When she told herself that as far as the woman went, the mere woman, Philip could not have found a better wife had he searched the world all round, she found that she was being tempted from her proper path even in that. What right could she have to look for consolation there? For other reasons, which she still felt to be adequate, she had resolved that something else should be done. That something else had not been done, because she had failed in her duty. And now she was trying to salve the sore by the very poison which had created the wound. Bessy's sweet temper, and Bessy's soft voice, and Bessy's bright eye, and Bessy's devotion to the delight of others, were all so many temptations. Grovelling as she was in sackcloth and ashes because she had yielded to them, how could she console herself by a prospect of these future enjoyments either for herself or her son?

But there were various duties to which she could attend, grievously afflicted as she was by her want of attention to that great duty. As Fate had determined that Bessy Pryor was to become mistress of Launay, it was proper that all Launay should know and recognise its future mistress. Bessy certainly should not be punished by any want of earnestness in this respect. No one should be punished but herself. The new mistress should be made as welcome as though she had been the red-haired girl from Cornwall. Knowl was a good deal put about because Mrs. Miles, remembering a few hard words which Knowl had allowed herself to use in the days of the imprisonment, became very stern. "It is settled that Miss Pryor is to become Mrs. Philip Launay, and you will obey her just as myself." Mrs. Knowl, who had saved a little money, began to consider whether it would not be as well to retire into private life.

When the day came on which the two travellers were to reach Launay Mrs. Miles was very much disturbed in her mind. In what way should she receive the girl? In her last communication,—her very last,—she had called Bessy her enemy; and now Bessy was being brought home to be made her daughter-in-law under her own roof. How sweet it would be to stand at the door and welcome her in the hall, among all the smiling servants, to make a tender fuss and hovering over her, as would be so natural with a mother-in-law who loved an adopted daughter as tenderly as Mrs. Miles loved Bessy! How pleasant to take her by the hand and lead her away into some inner sanctum where warm kisses as between mother and child would be given and taken; to hear her praises of Philip, and then to answer again with other praises; to tell her with words half serious and half drollery that she must now buckle on her armour and do her work, and take upon herself the task of managing the household! There was quite enough of softness in the old woman to make all this delightful. Her imagination revelled in thinking of it even at the moment in which she was telling herself that it was impossible. But it was impossible. Were she to force such a change upon herself Bessy would not believe in the sincerity of the change. She had told Bessy that she was her enemy!

At last the carriage which had gone to the station was here; not the waggonette on this occasion, but the real carriage itself, the carriage which was wont to toddle four miles an hour about the parish. "This is an honour meant for the prodigal daughter," said

Philip, as he took his seat. "If you had never been naughty, we should only have had the waggonette, and we then should have been there in half the time." Mrs. Miles, when she heard the wheels on the gravel, was even yet uncertain where she would place herself. She was fluttered, moving about from the room into the hall and back, when the old butler spoke a careful word: "Go into the library, madam, and Mr. Philip will bring her to you there." Then she obeyed the butler,—as she had probably never done in her life before.

Bessy, as soon as her step was off the carriage, ran very quickly into the house. "Where is my aunt?" she said. The butler was there showing the way, and in a moment she had thrown her arms round the old woman. Bessy had a way of making her kisses obligatory, from which Mrs. Miles had never been able to escape. Then, when the old woman was seated, Bessy was at once upon her knees before her. "Say that you love me, aunt. Say that at once! Say that first of all!"

"You know I love you."

"I know I love you. Oh, I am so glad to have you again. It was so hard not to be with you when I thought that you were ill. I did not know how sick it would make me to be away from you." Neither then nor at any time afterwards was there a word spoken on the one side or the other as to that declaration of enmity.

There was nothing then said in way of explanation.

There was nothing perhaps necessary. It was clear to Bessy that she was received at Launay as Philip's future wife,—not only by Mrs. Miles herself, but by the whole household,—and that all the honours of the place were to be awarded to her without stint. For herself that would have sufficed. To her any explanation of the circumstances which had led to a change so violent was quite unnecessary. But it was not so with Mrs. Miles herself. She could not but say some word in justification of herself,—in excuse rather than justification. She had Bessy into her bedroom that night, and said the word, holding between her two thin hands the hand of the girl she addressed. "You have known, Bessy, that I did not wish this." Bessy muttered that she did know it. "And I think you knew why."

"How could I help it, aunt?"

Upon this the old woman patted the hand. "I suppose he could not help it. And, if I had been a young man, I could not have helped it. I could not help it as I was, though I am an old woman. I think I am as foolish as he is."

"Perhaps he is foolish, but you are not."

"Well; I do not know. I have my misgivings about that, my dear. I had objects which I thought were sacred and holy, to which I had been wedded through many years. They have had to be thrust aside."

"Then you will hate me!"

"No, my child; I will love you with all my heart. You will be my son's wife now, and, as such, you will be dear to me, almost as he is dear. And you will still be my own Bessy, my gleam of sunlight, without whom the house is so gloomy that it is like a prison to me. For myself, do you think I could want any other young woman about the house than my own dear Bessy;—that any other wife for Philip could come as near my heart as you do?"

"But if I have stood in the way?"

"We will not think of it any more. You, at any rate, need not think of it," added the old woman, as she remembered all the circumstances. "You shall be made welcome with all the honours and all the privileges due to Philip's wife; and if there be a regret, it shall never trouble your path. It may be a comfort to you to hear me say that you, at least, in all things have done your duty." Then, at last, there were more tears, more embracings, and, before either of them went to their rest, a perfect ecstacy of love.

Little or nothing more is necessary for the telling of the story of the Lady of Launay. Before the autumn had quite gone, and the last tint had left the trees, Bessy Pryor became Bessy Launay, under the hand of Mr. Gregory, in the Launay parish church. Everyone in the neighbourhood around was there, except Mr. Morrison, who had taken this opportunity of having a holiday and visiting Switzerland. But even he, when he returned, soon became reconciled to the arrangement, and again became a guest in the dining-room of the mansion. I hope I shall have no reader who will not think that Philip Launay did well in not following the example of the major-general.

CHRISTMAS AT THOMPSON HALL.

CHRISTMAS AT THOMPSON HALL.

CHAPTER I.

MRS. BROWN'S SUCCESS.

EVERYONE remembers the severity of the Christmas of 187—. I will not designate the year more closely, lest I should enable those who are too curious to investigate the circumstances of this story, and inquire into details which I do not intend to make known. That winter, however, was especially severe, and the cold of the last ten days of December was more felt, I think, in Paris than in any part of England. It may, indeed, be doubted whether there is any town in any country in which thoroughly bad weather is more afflicting than in the French capital. Snow and hail seem to be colder there, and fires certainly are less warm, than in London. And then there is a feeling among visitors to Paris that Paris ought to be gay; that gaiety, prettiness, and liveliness are its aims, as money, commerce, and general business are the aims of London,—which with its outside sombre darkness does often seem to want an excuse for its ugliness. But on this occasion, at this Christmas of 187—, Paris was neither gay nor pretty nor lively. You could not walk the streets without being ankle deep, not in snow, but in snow that had just become slush; and there was falling throughout the day and night of the 23rd of December a succession of damp half-frozen abominations from the sky which made it almost impossible for men and women to go about their business.

It was at ten o'clock on that evening that an English lady and gentleman arrived at the Grand Hotel on the Boulevard des Italiens. As I have reasons for concealing the names of this married couple I will call them Mr. and Mrs. Brown. Now I wish it to be understood that in all the general affairs of life this gentleman and this lady lived happily together, with all the amenities which should bind a husband and a wife. Mrs. Brown was one of a wealthy family, and Mr. Brown, when he married her, had been relieved from the necessity of earning his bread. Nevertheless she had at once yielded to him when he expressed a desire to spend the winters of their life in the south of France; and he, though he was by disposition somewhat idle, and but little prone to the energetic occupations of life, would generally allow himself, at other periods of the year, to be carried hither and thither by her, whose more robust nature delighted in the excitement of travelling. But on this occasion there had been a little difference between them.

Early in December an intimation had reached Mrs. Brown at Pau that on the coming Christmas there was to be a great gathering of all the Thompsons in the Thompson family hall at Stratford-le-Bow, and that she who had been a Thompson was desired to join the party with her husband. On this occasion her only sister was desirous of introducing to the family generally a most excellent young man to whom she had recently become engaged. The Thompsons,—the real name, however, is in fact concealed,—were a numerous and a thriving people. There were uncles and cousins and brothers who had all done well in the world, and who were all likely to do better still. One had lately been returned to Parliament for the Essex Flats, and was at the time of which I am writing a conspicuous member of the gallant Conservative majority. It was partly in triumph at this success that the great Christmas gathering of the Thompsons was to be held, and an opinion had been expressed by the legislator himself that should Mrs. Brown, with her husband, fail to join the family on this happy occasion she and he would be regarded as being but *fainéant* Thompsons.

Since her marriage, which was an affair now nearly eight years old, Mrs. Brown had never passed a Christmas in England. The desirability of doing so had often been mooted by her. Her very soul craved the festivities of holly and mince-pies. There had ever been meetings of the Thompsons at Thompson Hall, though meetings not so significant, not so important to the family, as this one which was now to be collected. More than once had she expressed a wish to see old Christmas again in the old house among the old faces. But her husband had always pleaded a certain weakness about his throat and chest as a reason for remaining among the delights of Pau. Year after year she had yielded, and now this loud summons had come.

It was not without considerable trouble that she had induced Mr. Brown to come as far as Paris. Most unwillingly had he left Pau; and then, twice on his journey,—both at Bordeaux and Tours,—he had made an attempt to return. From the first moment he had pleaded his throat, and when at last he had consented to make the journey he had stipulated for sleeping at those two towns and at Paris. Mrs. Brown, who, without the slightest feeling of fatigue, could have made the journey from Pau to Stratford without stopping, had assented to everything,—so that they might be at Thompson Hall on Christmas Eve. When Mr. Brown uttered his unavailing complaints at the two first towns at which they stayed, she did not perhaps quite believe all that he said of his own condition. We know how prone the strong are to suspect the weakness of the weak,—as the weak are to be disgusted by the strength of the strong. There were perhaps a few words between them on the journey, but the result had hitherto been in favour of the lady. She had succeeded in bringing Mr. Brown as far as Paris.

Had the occasion been less important, no doubt she would have yielded. The weather had been bad even when they left Pau, but as they had made their way northwards it had become worse and still worse. As they left Tours Mr. Brown, in a hoarse whisper, had declared his conviction that the journey would kill him. Mrs. Brown, however, had unfortunately noticed half an hour before that he had scolded the waiter on the score of an overcharged franc or two with a loud and clear voice. Had she really believed that there was danger, or even suffering, she would have yielded; —but no woman is satisfied in such a matter to be taken in by false pretences. She observed that he ate a good dinner on his way to Paris, and that he took a small glass of cognac with complete relish,—which a man really suffering from bronchitis surely would not do. So she persevered, and brought him into Paris, late in the evening, in the midst of all that slush and snow. Then, as they sat down to supper, she thought that he did speak hoarsely, and her loving feminine heart began to misgive her.

But this now was at any rate clear to her,—that he could not be worse off by going on to London than he would be should he remain in Paris. If a man is to be ill he had better be ill in the bosom of his family than at an hotel. What comfort could he have, what relief, in that huge barrack? As for the cruelty of the weather, London could not be worse than Paris, and then she thought she had heard that sea air is good for a sore throat. In that bedroom which had been allotted to them au quatrième, they could not even get a decent fire. It would in every way be wrong now to forego the great Christmas gathering when nothing could be gained by staying in Paris.

She had perceived that as her husband became really ill he became also more tractable and less disputatious. Immediately after that little glass of cognac he had declared that he would be —— if he would go beyond Paris, and she began to fear that, after all, everything would have been done in vain. But as they went down to supper between ten and eleven he was more subdued, and merely remarked that this journey would, he was sure, be the death of him. It was half-past eleven when they got back to their bedroom, and then he seemed to speak with good sense,—and also with much real apprehension. "If I can't get something to relieve me I know I shall never make my way on," he said. It was intended that they should leave the hotel at half-past five the next morning, so as to arrive at Stratford, travelling by the tidal train, at half-past seven on Christmas Eve. The early hour, the long journey, the infamous weather, the prospect of that horrid gulf between Boulogne and Folkestone, would have been as nothing to Mrs. Brown, had it not been for that settled look of anguish which had now pervaded her husband's face. "If you don't find something to relieve me I shall never live through it," he said again, sinking back into the questionable comfort of a Parisian hotel arm-chair.

"But, my dear, what can I do?" she asked, almost

in tears, standing over him and caressing him. He was a thin, genteel-looking man, with a fine long, soft brown beard, a little bald at the top of the head, but certainly a genteel-looking man. She loved him dearly, and in her softer moods was apt to spoil him with her caresses. "What can I do, my dearie? You know I would do anything if I could. Get into bed, my pet, and be warm, and then to-morrow morning you will be all right." At this moment he was preparing himself for his bed, and she was assisting him. Then she tied a piece of flannel round his throat, and kissed him, and put him in beneath the bed-clothes.

"I'll tell you what you can do," he said very hoarsely. His voice was so bad now that she could hardly hear him. So she crept close to him, and bent over him. She would do anything if he would only say what. Then he told her what was his plan. Down in the salon he had seen a large jar of mustard standing on a sideboard. As he left the room he had observed that this had not been withdrawn with the other appurtenances of the meal. If she could manage to find her way down there, taking with her a handkerchief folded for the purpose, and if she could then appropriate a part of the contents of that jar, and, returning with her prize, apply it to his throat, he thought that he could get some relief, so that he might be able to leave his bed the next morning at five. "But I am afraid it will be very disagreeable for you to go down all alone at this time of night," he croaked out in a piteous whisper.

"Of course I'll go," said she. "I don't mind going in the least. Nobody will bite me," and she at once began to fold a clean handkerchief. "I won't be two minutes, my darling, and if there is a grain of mustard in the house I'll have it on your chest immediately." She was a woman not easily cowed, and the journey down into the salon was nothing to her. Before she went she tucked the clothes carefully up to his ears, and then she started.

To run along the first corridor till she came to a flight of stairs was easy enough, and easy enough to descend them. Then there was another corridor, and another flight, and a third corridor, and a third flight, and she began to think that she was wrong. She found herself in a part of the hotel which she had not hitherto visited, and soon discovered by looking through an open door or two that she had found her way among a set of private sitting-rooms which she had not seen before. Then she tried to make her way back, up the same stairs and through the same passages, so that she might start again. She was beginning to think that she had lost herself altogether, and that she would be able to find neither the salon nor her bedroom, when she happily met the night-porter. She was dressed in a loose white dressing-gown, with a white net over her loose hair, and with white worsted slippers. I ought perhaps to have described her personal appearance sooner. She was a large woman, with a commanding bust, thought by some to be handsome, after the manner of Juno. But with strangers there was a certain severity of manner about her,—a fortification, as it were, of her virtue against all possible attacks,—a declared determination to maintain, at all points, the beautiful character of a British matron, which, much as it had been appreciated at Thompson Hall, had met with some ill-natured criticism among French men and women. At Pau she had been called La Fière Anglaise. The name had reached her own ears and those of her husband. He had been much annoyed, but she had taken it in good part,—had, indeed, been somewhat proud of the title,—and had endeavoured to live up to it. With her husband she could, on occasion, be soft, but she was of opinion that with other men a British matron should be stern. She was now greatly in want of assistance; but, nevertheless, when she met the porter she remembered her character. "I have lost my way wandering through these horrid passages," she said, in her severest tone. This was in answer to some question from him,—some question to which her reply was given very slowly. Then when he asked where Madame wished to go, she paused, again thinking what destination she would announce. No doubt the man could take her back to her bedroom, but if so, the mustard must be renounced, and with the mustard, as she now feared, all hope of reaching Thompson Hall on Christmas Eve. But she, though she was in many respects a brave woman, did not dare to tell the man that she was prowling about the hotel in order that she might make a midnight raid upon the mustard pot. She paused, therefore, for a moment, that she might collect her thoughts, erecting her head as she did so in her best Juno fashion, till the porter was lost in admiration. Thus she gained time to fabricate a tale. She had, she said, dropped her handkerchief under the supper-table; would he show her the way to the salon, in order that she might pick it up? But the porter did more than that, and accompanied her to the room in which she had supped.

Here, of course, there was a prolonged, and, it need hardly be said, a vain search. The good-natured man insisted on emptying an enormous receptacle of soiled table-napkins, and on turning them over one by one, in order that the lady's property might be found. The lady stood by unhappy, but still patient, and, as the man was stooping to his work, her eye was on the mustard pot. There it was, capable of containing enough to blister the throats of a score of sufferers. She edged off a little towards it while the man was busy, trying to persuade herself that he would surely forgive her if she took the mustard, and told him her whole story. But the descent from her Juno bearing would have been so great! She must have owned, not only to the quest for mustard, but also to a fib,—and she could not do it. The porter was at last of opinion that Madame must have made a mistake, and Madame acknowledged that she was afraid it was so.

With a longing, lingering eye, with an eye turned back, oh! so sadly, to the great jar, she left the room, the porter leading the way. She assured him that she could find it by herself, but he would not leave her till he had put her on to the proper passage. The journey seemed to be longer now even than before, but as she ascended the many stairs she swore to herself that she would not even yet be baulked of her object. Should her husband want comfort for his poor throat, and the comfort be there within her reach, and he not have it? She counted every stair as she went up, and marked every turn well. She was sure now that she would know the way, and that she could return to the room without fault. She would go back to the salon. Even though the man should encounter her again, she would go boldly forward and seize the remedy which her poor husband so grievously required.

"Ah, yes," she said, when the porter told her that her room, No. 333, was in the corridor which they had then reached, "I know it all now. I am so much obliged. Do not come a step further." He was anxious to accompany her up to the very door, but she stood in the passage and prevailed. He lingered awhile —naturally. Unluckily she had brought no money with her, and could not give him the two-franc piece which he had earned. Nor could she fetch it from her room, feeling that were she to return to her husband without the mustard no second attempt would be possible. The disappointed man turned on his heel at last, and made his way down the stairs and along the passage. It seemed to her to be almost an eternity while she listened to his still audible footsteps. She had gone on, creeping noiselessly up to the very door of her room, and there she stood, shading the candle in her hand, till she thought that the man must have wandered away into some furthest corner of that endless building. Then she turned once more and retraced her steps.

There was no difficulty now as to the way. She knew it, every stair. At the head of each flight she stood and listened, but not a sound was to be heard, and then she went on again. Her heart beat high with anxious desire to achieve her object, and at the same time with fear. What might have been explained so easily at first would now be as difficult of explanation. At last she was in the great public vestibule, which she was now visiting for the third time, and of which, at her last visit, she had taken the bearings accurately. The door was there—closed, indeed, but it opened easily to the hand. In the hall, and on the stairs, and along the passages, there had been gas, but here there was no light beyond that given by the little taper which she carried. When accompanied by the porter she had not feared the darkness, but now there was something in the obscurity which made her dread to walk the length of the room up to the mustard jar. She paused, and listened, and trembled. Then she thought of the glories of Thompson Hall, of the genial warmth of a British Christmas, of that proud legislator who was her first cousin, and with a rush she made good the distance, and laid her hand upon the copious delf. She looked round, but there was no one there; no sound was heard; not the distant creak of a shoe, not a rattle from one of those thousand doors. As she paused with her fair hand upon the top of the jar, while the other held the white cloth on which the medicinal compound was to be placed, she looked like Lady Macbeth as she listened at Duncan's chamber door.

There was no doubt as to the sufficiency of the contents. The jar was full nearly up to the lips. The mixture was, no doubt, very different from that good wholesome English mustard which your cook makes fresh for you, with a little water, in two minutes. It was impregnated with a sour odour, and was, to English eyes, unwholesome of colour. But still it was mustard. She seized the horn spoon, and without further delay spread an ample sufficiency on the folded square of the handkerchief. Then she commenced to hurry her return.

But still there was a difficulty, no thought of which had occurred to her before. The candle occupied one hand, so that she had but the other for the sustenance of her treasure. Had she brought a plate or saucer from the salon, it would have been all well. As it was she was obliged to keep her eye intent on her right hand, and to proceed very slowly on her return journey. She was surprised to find what an aptitude the thing had to slip from her grasp. But still she progressed slowly, and was careful not to miss a turning. At last she was safe at her chamber door. There it was, No. 333.

CHAPTER II.

MRS. BROWN'S FAILURE.

WITH her eye still fixed upon her burden, she glanced up at the number of the door—333. She had been determined all through not to forget that. Then she turned the latch and crept in. The chamber also was dark after the gaslight on the stairs, but that was so much the better. She herself had put out the two candles on the dressing-table before she had left her husband. As she was closing the door behind her she paused, and could hear that he was sleeping. She was well aware that she had been long absent,—quite long enough for a man to fall into slumber who was given that way. She must have been gone, she thought, fully an hour. There had been no end to that turning over of napkins which she had so well known to be altogether vain. She paused at the centre table of the room, still looking at the mustard, which she now delicately dried from off her hand. She had had no idea that it would have been so difficult to carry so light and so small an affair. But there it was, and nothing had been lost. She took some small instrument from the washing-stand, and with the handle collected the flowing fragments into the centre. Then the question occurred to her whether, as her husband was sleeping so sweetly, it would be well to disturb him. She listened again, and felt that the slight murmur of a snore with which her ears were regaled was altogether free from any real malady in the throat. Then it occurred to her, that after all, fatigue perhaps had only made him cross. She bethought herself how, during the whole journey, she had failed to believe in his illness. What meals he had eaten! How thoroughly he had been able to enjoy his full complement of cigars! And then that glass of brandy, against which she had raised her voice slightly in feminine opposition. And now he was sleeping there like an infant, with full, round, perfected, almost sonorous workings of the throat. Who does not know that sound, almost of two rusty bits of iron scratching against each other, which comes from a suffering windpipe? There was no semblance of that here. Why disturb him when he was so thoroughly enjoying that rest which, more certainly than anything else, would fit him for the fatigue of the morrow's journey?

I think that, after all her labour, she would have left the pungent cataplasm on the table, and have crept gently into bed beside him, had not a thought suddenly struck her of the great injury he had been doing her if he were not really ill. To send her down there, in a strange hotel, wandering among the passages, in the middle of the night, subject to the contumely of anyone who might meet her, on a commission which, if it were not sanctified by absolute necessity, would be so thoroughly objectionable! At this moment she hardly did believe that he had ever really been ill. Let him have the cataplasm; if not as a remedy, then as a punishment. It could, at any rate, do him no harm. It was with an idea of avenging rather than of justifying the past labours of the night that she proceeded at once to quick action.

Leaving the candle on the table so that she might steady her right hand with the left, she hurried stealthily to the bedside. Even though he was behaving badly to her, she would not cause him discomfort by waking him roughly. She would do a wife's duty to him as a British matron should. She would not only put the warm mixture on his neck, but would sit carefully by him for twenty minutes, so that she might relieve him from it when the proper period should have come for removing the counter irritation from his throat. There would doubtless be some little difficulty in this,—in collecting the mustard after it had served her purpose. Had she been at home, surrounded by her own comforts, the application would have been made with some delicate linen bag, through which the pungency of the spice would have penetrated with strength sufficient for the purpose. But the circumstance of the occasion had not admitted this. She had, she felt, done wonders in achieving so much success as this which she had obtained. If there should be anything disagreeable in the operation he must submit to it. He had asked for mustard for his throat, and mustard he should have.

As these thoughts passed quickly through her mind, leaning over him in the dark, with her eye fixed on the mixture lest it should slip, she gently raised his flowing beard with her left hand, and with her other inverted rapidly, steadily but very softly fixed the handkerchief on his throat. From the bottom of his chin to the spot at which the collar bones meeting together form the orifice of the chest it covered the whole noble expanse. There was barely time for a glance, but never had she been more conscious of the grand proportions of that manly throat. A sweet feeling of pity came upon her, causing her to determine to relieve his sufferings in the shorter space of fifteen minutes. He had been lying on his back, with his lips apart, and, as she held back his beard, that and her hand nearly covered the features of his face. But he made no violent effort to free himself from the encounter. He did not even move an arm or a leg. He simply emitted a snore louder than any that had come before. She was aware that it was not his wont to be so loud—that there was generally something more delicate and perhaps more querulous in his nocturnal voice, but then the present circumstances were exceptional. She dropped the beard very softly—and there on the pillow before her lay the face of a stranger. She had put the mustard plaster on the wrong man.

Not Priam wakened in the dead of night, not Dido when first she learned that Æneas had fled, not Othello when he learned that Desdemona had been chaste, not Medea when she became conscious of her slaughtered children, could have been more struck with horror than was this British matron as she stood for a moment gazing with awe on that stranger's bed. One vain, half-completed, snatching grasp she made at the handkerchief, and then drew back her hand. If she were to touch him would he not wake at once, and find her standing there in his bedroom? And then how could she explain it? By what words could she so quickly make him know the circumstances of that strange occurrence that he should accept it all before he had said a word that might offend her? For a moment she stood all but paralyzed after that faint ineffectual movement of her arm. Then he stirred his head uneasily on the pillow, opened wider his lips, and twice in rapid succession snored louder than before. She started back a couple of paces, and with her body placed between him and the candle, with her face averted, but with her hand still resting on the foot of the bed, she endeavoured to think what duty required of her.

She had injured the man. Though she had done it most unwittingly, there could be no doubt but that she had injured him. If for a moment she could be brave, the injury might in truth be little; but how disastrous might be the consequences if she were now in her cowardice to leave him, who could tell? Applied for fifteen to twenty minutes a mustard plaster may be the salvation of a throat ill at ease, but if left there throughout the night upon the neck of a strong man, ailing nothing, only too prone in his strength to slumber soundly, how sad, how painful, for aught she knew how dangerous might be the effects! And surely it was an error which any man with a heart in his bosom would pardon! Judging from what little she had seen of him she thought that he must have a heart in his bosom. Was it not her duty to wake him, and then quietly to extricate him from the embarrassment which she had brought upon him?

But in doing this what words should she use? How should she wake him? How should she make him understand her goodness, her beneficence, her sense of duty, before he should have jumped from the bed and rushed to the bell, and have summoned all above and all below to the rescue? "Sir, sir, do not move, do not stir, do not scream. I have put a mustard plaster on your throat, thinking that you were my husband. As yet no harm has been done. Let me take it off, and then hold your peace for ever." Where is the man of such native constancy and grace of spirit that, at the first moment of waking with a shock, he could hear these words from the mouth of an unknown woman by his bedside, and at once obey them to the letter? Would he not surely jump from his bed, with that horrid compound falling about him,—from which there could be no complete relief unless he would keep his present attitude without a motion? The picture which presented itself to her mind as to his probable conduct was so terrible that she found herself unable to incur the risk.

Then an idea presented itself to her mind. We all know how in a moment quick thoughts will course through the subtle brain. She would find that porter and send him to explain it all. There should be no concealment now. She would tell the story and would bid him to find the necessary aid. Alas! as she told herself that she would do so, she knew well that she was only running from the danger which it was her duty to encounter. Once again she put out her hand as though to return along the bed. Then thrice he snorted louder than before, and moved up his knee uneasily beneath the clothes as though the sharpness of the mustard were already working upon his skin. She watched him for a moment longer, and then, with the candle in her hand, she fled.

Poor human nature! Had he been an old man, even a middle-aged man, she would not have left him to his unmerited sufferings. As it was, though she completely recognised her duty, and knew what justice and goodness demanded of her, she could not do it. But there was still left to her that plan of sending the night-porter to him. It was not till she was out of the room and had gently closed the door behind her, that she began to bethink herself how she had made the mistake. With a glance of her eye she looked up, and then saw the number on the door: 353. Remarking to herself, with a Briton's natural criticism on things French, that those horrid foreigners do not know how to make their figures, she scudded rather than ran along the corridor, and then down some stairs and along another passage,—so that she might not be found in the neighbourhood should the poor man in his agony rush rapidly from his bed.

In the confusion of her first escape she hardly ventured to look for her own passage,—nor did she in the least know how she had lost her way when she came upstairs with the mustard in her hand. But at the present moment her chief object was the night-porter. She went on descending till she came again to that vestibule, and looking up at the clock saw that it was now past one. It was not yet midnight when she left her husband, but she was not at all astonished at the lapse of time. It seemed to her as though she had passed a night among these miseries. And, oh, what a night! But there was yet much to be done. She must find that porter, and then return to her own suffering husband. Ah,—what now should she say to him? If he should really be ill, how should she assuage him? And yet how more than ever necessary was it that they should leave that hotel early in the morning,—that they should leave Paris by the very earliest and quickest train that would take them as fugitives from their present dangers! The door of the salon was open, but she had no courage to go in search of a second supply. She would have lacked strength to carry it up the stairs. Where now, oh, where, was that man? From the vestibule she made her way into the hall, but everything seemed to be deserted. Through the glass she could see a light in the court beyond, but she could not bring herself to endeavour even to open the hall doors.

And now she was very cold,—chilled to her very bones. All this had been done at Christmas, and during such severity of weather as had never before been experienced by living Parisians. A feeling of great pity for herself gradually came upon her. What wrong had she done that she should be so grievously punished? Why should she be driven to wander about in this way till her limbs were failing her? And then, so absolutely important as it was that her strength should support her in the morning! The man would not die even though he were left there without aid, to rid himself of the cataplasm as best he might. Was it absolutely necessary that she should disgrace herself?

But she could not even procure the means of disgracing herself, if that telling her story to the night-porter would have been a disgrace. She did not find him, and at last resolved to make her way back to her own room without further quest. She began to think that she had done all that she could do. No man was ever killed by a mustard plaster on his throat. His discomfort at the worst would not be worse than hers had been—or too probably than that of her poor husband. So she went back up the stairs and along the passages, and made her way on this occasion to the door of her room without any difficulty. The way was so well known to her that she could not but wonder that she had failed before. But now her hands had been empty, and her eyes had been at her full command. She looked up, and there was the number, very manifest on this occasion,—333. She opened the door most gently, thinking that her husband might be sleeping as soundly as that other man had slept, and she crept into the room.

CHAPTER III.

MRS. BROWN ATTEMPTS TO ESCAPE.

But her husband was not sleeping. He was not even in bed, as she had left him. She found him sitting there before the fire-place, on which one half-burned log still retained a spark of what had once pretended to be a fire. Nothing more wretched than his appearance could be imagined. There was a single lighted candle on the table, on which he was leaning with his two elbows, while his head rested between his hands. He had on a dressing-gown over his night-shirt, but otherwise was not clothed. He shivered audibly, or rather shook himself with the cold, and made the table to chatter as she entered the room. Then he groaned, and let his head fall from his hands on to the table. It occurred to her at the moment as she recognised the tone of his querulous voice, and as she saw the form of his neck, that she must have been deaf and blind when she had mistaken that stalwart stranger for her husband. "Oh, my dear," she said, "why are you not in bed?" He answered nothing in words, but only groaned again. "Why did you get up? I left you warm and comfortable"

"Where have you been all night?" he half whispered, half croaked, with an agonising effort.

"I have been looking for the mustard."

"Have been looking all night and haven't found it? Where have you been?"

She refused to speak a word to him till she had got him into bed, and then she told her story! But, alas, that which she told was not the true story! As she was persuading him to go back to his rest, and while she arranged the clothes again around him, she with difficulty made up her mind as to what she would do and what she would say. Living or dying he must be made to start for Thompson Hall at half-past five on the next morning. It was no longer a question of the amenities of Christmas, no longer a mere desire to satisfy the family ambition of her own people, no longer an anxiety to see her new brother-in-law. She was conscious that there was in that house one whom she had deeply injured, and from whose vengeance, even from whose aspect, she must fly. How could she endure to see that face which she was so well sure that she would recognise, or to hear the slightest sound of that voice which would be quite familiar to her ears, though it had never spoken a word in her hearing? She must certainly fly on the wings of the earliest train which would carry her towards the old house; but in order that she might do so she must propitiate her husband.

So she told her story. She had gone forth, as he had bade her, in search of the mustard, and then had suddenly lost her way. Up and down the house she had wandered, perhaps nearly a dozen times. "Had she met no one?" he asked in that raspy, husky whisper. "Surely there must have been some one about the hotel! Nor was it possible that she could have been roaming about all those hours." "Only one hour, my dear," she said. Then there was a question about the duration of time, in which both of them waxed angry, and as she became angry her husband waxed stronger, and as he became violent beneath the clothes the comfortable idea returned to her that he was not perhaps so ill as he would seem to be. She found herself driven to tell him something about the porter, having to account for that lapse of time by explaining how she had driven the poor man to search for the handkerchief which she had never lost.

"Why did you not tell him you wanted the mustard?"

"My dear!"

"Why not? There is nothing to be ashamed of in wanting mustard."

"At one o'clock in the morning! I couldn't do it. To tell you the truth, he wasn't very civil, and I thought that he was,—perhaps a little tipsy. Now, my dear, do go to sleep."

"Why didn't you get the mustard?"

"There was none there,—nowhere at all about the room. I went down again and searched everywhere. That's what took me so long. They always lock up those kind of things at these French hotels. They are too close-fisted to leave anything out. When you first spoke of it I knew that it would be gone when I got there. Now, my dear, do go to sleep, because we positively must start in the morning."

"That is impossible," said he, jumping up in bed.

"We must go, my dear. I say that we must go.

After all that has passed I wouldn't not be with Uncle John and my cousin Robert to-morrow evening for more,—more,—more than I would venture to say."

"Bother!" he exclaimed.

"It's all very well for you to say that, Charles, but you don't know. I say that we must go to-morrow, and we will."

"I do believe you want to kill me, Mary."

"That is very cruel, Charles, and most false, and most unjust. As for making you ill, nothing could be so bad for you as this wretched place, where nobody can get warm either day or night. If anything will cure your throat for you at once it will be the sea air. And only think how much more comfortable they can make you at Thompson Hall than anywhere in this country. I have so set my heart upon it, Charles, that I will do it. If we are not there to-morrow night Uncle John won't consider us as belonging to the family."

"I don't believe a word of it."

"Jane told me so in her letter. I wouldn't let you know before because I thought it so unjust. But that has been the reason why I've been so earnest about it all through."

It was a thousand pities that so good a woman should have been driven by the sad stress of circumstances to tell so many fibs. One after another she was compelled to invent them, that there might be a way open to her of escaping the horrors of a prolonged sojourn in that hotel. At length, after much grumbling, he became silent, and she trusted that he was sleeping. He had not as yet said that he would start at the required hour in the morning, but she was perfectly determined in her own mind that he should be made to do so. As he lay there motionless, and as she wandered about the room pretending to pack her things, she more than once almost resolved that she would tell him everything. Surely then he would be ready to make any effort. But there came upon her an idea that he might perhaps fail to see all the circumstances, and that, so failing, he would insist on remaining that he might tender some apology to the injured gentleman. An apology might have been very well had she not left him there in his misery—but what apology would be possible now? She would have to see him and speak to him, and everyone in the hotel would know every detail of the story. Everyone in France would know that it was she who had gone to the strange man's bedside, and put the mustard plaster on the strange man's throat in the dead of night! She could not tell the story even to her husband, lest even her husband should betray her.

Her own sufferings at the present moment were not light. In her perturbation of mind she had foolishly resolved that she would not herself go to bed. The tragedy of the night had seemed to her too deep for personal comfort. And then how would it be were she to sleep, and have no one to call her? It was imperative that she should have all her powers ready for thoroughly arousing him. It occurred to her that the servant of the hotel would certainly run her too short of time. She had to work for herself and for him too, and therefore she would not sleep. But she was very cold, and she put on first a shawl over her dressing-gown and then a cloak. She could not consume all the remaining hours of the night in packing one bag and one portmanteau, so that at last she sat down on the narrow red cotton velvet sofa, and, looking at her watch, perceived that as yet it was not much past two o'clock. How was she to get through those other three long, tedious, chilly hours?

Then there came a voice from the bed—"Ain't you coming?"

"I hoped you were asleep, my dear."

"I haven't been asleep at all. You'd better come, if you don't mean to make yourself as ill as I am."

"You are not so very bad, are you, darling?"

"I don't know what you call bad. I never felt my throat so choked in my life before!" Still as she listened she thought that she remembered his throat to have been more choked. If the husband of her bosom could play with her feelings and deceive her on such an occasion as this,—then, then,—then she thought that she would rather not have any husband of her bosom at all. But she did creep into bed, and lay down beside him without saying another word.

Of course she slept, but her sleep was not the sleep of the blest. At every striking of the clock in the quadrangle she would start up in alarm, fearing that she had let the time go by. Though the night was so short it was very long to her. But he slept like an infant. She could hear from his breathing that he was not quite so well as she could wish him to be, but still he was resting in beautiful tranquillity. Not once did he move when she started up, as she did so frequently. Orders had been given and repeated over and over again that they should be called at five. The man in the office had almost been angry as he assured Mrs. Brown for the fourth time that Monsieur and Madame would most assuredly be wakened at the appointed time. But still she would trust to no one, and was up and about the room before the clock had struck half-past four.

In her heart of hearts she was very tender towards her husband. Now, in order that he might feel a gleam of warmth while he was dressing himself, she collected together the fragments of half-burned wood, and endeavoured to make a little fire. Then she took out from her bag a small pot, and a patent lamp, and some chocolate, and prepared for him a warm drink, so that he might have it instantly as he was awakened. She would do anything for him in the way of ministering to his comfort,—only he must go! Yes, he certainly must go!

And then she wondered how that strange man was bearing himself at the present moment. She would fain have ministered to him too had it been possible; but ah!—it was so impossible! Probably before this he would have been aroused from his troubled slumbers. But then—how aroused? At what time in the night would the burning heat upon his chest have awakened him to a sense of torture which must have been so altogether incomprehensible to him? Her strong imagination showed to her a clear picture of the scene, —clear, though it must have been done in the dark. How he must have tossed and hurled himself under the clothes; how those strong knees must have worked themselves up and down before the potent god of sleep would allow him to return to perfect consciousness; how his fingers, restrained by no reason, would have trampled over his feverish throat, scattering everywhere that unhappy poultice! Then when he should have sat up wide awake, but still in the dark—with her mind's eye she saw it all—feeling that some fire as from the infernal regions had fallen upon him, but whence he would know not, how fiercely wild would be the working of his spirit! Ah, now she knew, now she felt, now she acknowledged how bound she had been to awaken him at the moment, whatever might have been the personal inconvenience to herself! In such a position what would he do—or rather what had he done? She could follow much of it in her own thoughts;—how he would scramble madly from his bed, and, with one hand still on his throat, would snatch hurriedly at the matches with the other. How the light would come, and how then he would rush to the mirror. Ah, what a sight he would behold! She could see it all to the last widespread daub.

But she could not see, she could not tell herself, what in such a position a man would do;—at any rate, not what that man would do. Her husband, she thought, would tell his wife, and then the two of them, between them, would—put up with it. There are misfortunes which, if they be published, are simply aggravated by ridicule. But she remembered the features of the stranger as she had seen them at that instant in which she had dropped his beard, and she thought that there was a ferocity in them, a certain tenacity of self-importance, which would not permit their owner to endure such treatment in silence. Would he not storm and rage, and ring the bell, and call all Paris to witness his revenge?

But the storming and the raging had not reached her yet, and now it wanted but a quarter to five. In three-quarters of an hour they would be in that demi-omnibus which they had ordered for themselves, and in half an hour after that they would be flying towards Thompson Hall. Then she allowed herself to think of the coming comforts,—of those comforts so sweet, if only they would come! That very day now present to her was the 24th December, and on that very evening she would be sitting in Christmas joy among all her uncles and cousins, holding her new brother-in-law affectionately by the hand. Oh, what a change from Pandemonium to Paradise;—from that wretched room, from that miserable house in which there was such ample cause for fear, to all the domestic Christmas bliss of the home of the Thompsons! She resolved that she would not, at any rate, be deterred by any light opposition on the part of her husband. "It wants just a quarter to five," she said, putting her hand steadily upon his shoulder, "and I'll get a cup of chocolate for you, so that you may get up comfortably."

"I've been thinking about it," he said, rubbing his eyes with the back of his hands. "It will be so much better to go over by the mail train to-night. We should be in time for Christmas just the same."

"That will not do at all," she answered, energetically. "Come, Charles, after all the trouble do not disappoint me."

"It is such a horrid grind."

"Think what I have gone through,—what I have done for you! In twelve hours we shall be there, among them all. You won't be so little like a man as not to go on now." He threw himself back upon the bed, and tried to readjust the clothes round his neck. "No, Charles, no," she continued; "not if I know it. Take your chocolate and get up. There is not a moment to be lost." With that she laid her hand upon his shoulder, and made him clearly understand that he would not be allowed to take further rest in that bed.

Grumbling, sulky, coughing continually, and declaring that life under such circumstances was not worth having, he did at last get up and dress himself. When once she knew that he was obeying her she became again tender to him, and certainly took much more than her own share of the trouble of the proceedings. Long before the time was up she was ready, and the porter had been summoned to take the luggage downstairs. When the man came she was rejoiced to see that it was not he whom she had met among the passages during her nocturnal rambles. He shouldered the box, and told them that they would find coffee and bread and butter in the small salle-à-manger below.

"I told you that it would be so, when you would boil that stuff," said the ungrateful man, who had nevertheless swallowed the hot chocolate when it was given to him.

They followed their luggage down into the hall; but as she went, at every step, the lady looked around her. She dreaded the sight of that porter of the night; she feared lest some potential authority of the hotel should come to her and ask her some horrid question; but of all her fears her greatest fear was that there should arise before her an apparition of that face which she had seen recumbent on its pillow.

As they passed the door of the great salon, Mr. Brown looked in. "Why, there it is still!" said he.

"What?" said she, trembling in every limb.

"The mustard-pot!"

"They have put it in there since," she exclaimed energetically, in her despair. "But never mind. The omnibus is here. Come away." And she absolutely took him by the arm.

But at that moment a door behind them opened, and Mrs. Brown heard herself called by her name. And there was the night-porter,—with a handkerchief in his hand. But the further doings of that morning must be told in a further chapter.

CHAPTER IV.

MRS. BROWN DOES ESCAPE.

IT had been visible to Mrs. Brown from the first moment of her arrival on the ground floor that "something was the matter," if we may be allowed to use such a phrase; and she felt all but convinced that this something had reference to her. She fancied that the people of the hotel were looking at her as she swallowed, or tried to swallow, her coffee. When her husband was paying the bill there was something disagreeable in the eye of the man who was taking the money. Her sufferings were very great, and no one sympathised with her. Her husband was quite at his ease, except that he was complaining of the cold. When she was anxious to get him out into the carriage, he still stood there leisurely, arranging shawl after shawl around his throat. "You can do that quite as well in an omnibus," she had just said to him very crossly, when there appeared upon the scene through a side door that very night-porter whom she dreaded, with a soiled pocket-handkerchief in his hand.

Even before the sound of her own name met her ears Mrs. Brown knew it all. She understood the full horror of her position from that man's hostile face, and from the little article which he held in his hand. If during the watches of the night she had had money in her pocket, if she had made a friend of this greedy fellow by well-timed liberality, all might have been so different! But she reflected that she had allowed him to go unfee'd after all his trouble, and she knew that he was her enemy. It was the handkerchief that she feared. She thought that she might have brazened out anything but that. No one had seen her enter or leave that strange man's room. No one had seen her dip her hands in that jar. She had, no doubt, been found wandering about the house while the slumberer had been made to suffer so strangely, and there might have been suspicion, and perhaps accusation. But she would have been ready with frequent protestations to deny all charges made against her, and, though no one might have believed her, no one could have convicted her. Here, however, was evidence against which she would be unable to stand for a moment. At the first glance she acknowledged the potency of that damning morsel of linen.

During all the horrors of the night she had never given a thought to the handkerchief, and yet she ought to have known that the evidence it would bring against her was palpable and certain. Her name, "M. Brown," was plainly written on the corner. What a fool she had been not to have thought of this! Had she but remembered the plain marking which she, as a careful, well-conducted British matron, had put upon all her clothes, she would at any hazard have recovered the article. Oh that she had waked the man, or bribed the porter, or even told her husband! But now she was, as it were, friendless, without support, without a word that she could say in her own defence, convicted of having committed this assault upon a strange man in his own bedroom, and then of having left him! The thing must be explained by the truth; but how to explain such truth, how to tell such story in a way to satisfy injured folk, and she with only barely time sufficient to catch the train! Then it occurred to her that they could have no legal right to stop her because the pocket-handkerchief had been found in a strange gentleman's bedroom. "Yes, it is mine," she said, turning to her husband, as the porter, with a loud voice, asked if she were not Madame Brown. "Take it, Charles, and come on." Mr. Brown naturally stood still in astonishment. He did put out his hand, but the porter would not allow the evidence to pass so readily out of his custody.

"What does it all mean?" asked Mr. Brown.

"A gentleman has been—eh—eh—. Something has been done to a gentleman in his bedroom," said the clerk.

"Something done to a gentleman!" repeated Mr. Brown.

"Something very bad indeed," said the porter. "Look here," and he showed the condition of the handkerchief.

"Charles, we shall lose the train," said the affrighted wife.

"What the mischief does it all mean?" demanded the husband.

"Did Madame go into the gentleman's room?" asked

the clerk. Then there was an awful silence, and all eyes were fixed upon the lady.

"What does it all mean?" demanded the husband. "Did you go into anybody's room?"

"I did," said Mrs. Brown with much dignity, looking round upon her enemies as a stag at bay will look upon the hounds which are attacking him. "Give me the handkerchief." But the night-porter quickly put it behind his back. "Charles, we cannot allow ourselves to be delayed. You shall write a letter to the keeper of the hotel, explaining it all." Then she essayed to swim out, through the front door, into the courtyard in which the vehicle was waiting for them. But three or four men and women interposed themselves, and even her husband did not seem quite ready to continue his journey. "To-night is Christmas Eve," said Mrs. Brown, "and we shall not be at Thompson Hall! Think of my sister!"

"Why did you go into the man's bedroom, my dear?" whispered Mr. Brown in English.

But the porter heard the whisper, and understood the language;—the porter who had not been "tipped." "Ye'es;—vy?" asked the porter.

"It was a mistake, Charles; there is not a moment to lose. I can explain it all to you in the carriage." Then the clerk suggested that Madame had better postpone her journey a little. The gentleman upstairs had certainly been very badly treated, and had demanded to know why so great an outrage had been perpetrated. The clerk said that he did not wish to send for the police—here Mrs. Brown gasped terribly and threw herself on her husband's shoulder,—but he did not think he could allow the party to go till the gentleman upstairs had received some satisfaction. It had now become clearly impossible that the journey could be made by the early train. Even Mrs. Brown gave it up herself, and demanded of her husband that she should be taken back to her own bedroom.

"But what is to be said to the gentleman?" asked the porter.

Of course it was impossible that Mrs. Brown should be made to tell her story there in the presence of them all. The clerk, when he found he had succeeded in preventing her from leaving the house, was satisfied with a promise from Mr. Brown that he would inquire from his wife what were these mysterious circumstances, and would then come down to the office and give some explanation. If it were necessary, he would see the strange gentleman,—whom he now ascertained to be a certain Mr. Jones returning from the east of Europe. He learned also that this Mr. Jones had been most anxious to travel by that very morning train which he and his wife had intended to use,—that Mr. Jones had been most particular in giving his orders accordingly, but that at the last moment he had declared himself to be unable even to dress himself, because of the injury which had been done him during the night. When Mr. Brown heard this from the clerk just before he was allowed to take his wife upstairs, while she was sitting on a sofa in a corner with her face hidden, a look of awful gloom came over his own countenance. What could it be that his wife had done to the man of so terrible a nature? "You had better come up with me," he said to her with marital severity, and the poor cowed woman went with him tamely as might have done some patient Grizel. Not a word was spoken till they were in the room and the door was locked. "Now," said he, "what does it all mean?"

It was not till nearly two hours had passed that Mr. Brown came down the stairs very slowly,—turning it all over in his mind. He had now gradually heard the absolute and exact truth, and had very gradually learned to believe it. It was first necessary that he should understand that his wife had told him many fibs during the night; but as she constantly alleged to him when he complained of her conduct in this respect, they had all been told on his behalf. Had she not struggled to get the mustard for his comfort, and when she had secured the prize had she not hurried to put it on,—as she had fondly thought,—his throat? And though she had fibbed to him afterwards, had she not done so in order that he might not be troubled? "You are not angry with me because I was in that man's room?" she asked, looking full into his eyes, but not quite without a sob. He paused a moment and then declared, with something of a true husband's confidence in his tone, that he was not in the least angry with her on that account. Then she kissed him, and bade him remember that after all no one could really injure them. "What harm has been done, Charles? The gentleman won't die because he has had a mustard plaster on his throat. The worst is about Uncle John and dear Jane. They do think so much of Christmas Eve at Thompson Hall!"

Mr. Brown, when he again found himself in the clerk's office, requested that his card might be taken up to Mr. Jones. Mr. Jones had sent down his own card, which was handed to Mr. Brown: "Mr. Barnaby Jones." "And how was it all, sir?" asked the clerk, in a whisper—a whisper which had at the same time something of authoritative demand and something also of submissive respect. The clerk of course was anxious to know the mystery. It is hardly too much to say that everyone in that vast hotel was by this time anxious to have the mystery unravelled. But Mr. Brown would tell nothing to anyone. "It is merely a matter to be explained between me and Mr. Jones," he said. The card was taken upstairs, and after awhile he was ushered into Mr. Jones' room. It was, of course, that very 353 with which the reader is already acquainted. There was a fire burning, and the remains of Mr. Jones' breakfast were on the table. He was sitting in his dressing-gown and slippers, with his shirt open in the front, and a silk handkerchief very loosely covering his throat. Mr. Brown, as he entered the room, of course looked with considerable anxiety at the gentleman of whose condition he had heard so sad an account; but he could only observe some considerable stiffness of movement and demeanour as Mr. Jones turned his head round to greet him.

"This has been a very disagreeable accident, Mr. Jones," said the husband of the lady.

"Accident! I don't know how it could have been an accident. It has been a most—most—most—a most monstrous,—er,—er,—I must say, interference with a gentleman's privacy, and personal comfort."

"Quite so, Mr. Jones, but,—on the part of the lady, who is my wife—"

"So I understand. I myself am about to become a married man, and I can understand what your feelings must be. I wish to say as little as possible to harrow them." Here Mr. Brown bowed. "But,—there's the fact. She did do it."

"She thought it was—me!"

"What!"

"I give you my word as a gentleman, Mr. Jones. When she was putting that mess upon you she thought it was me! She did, indeed."

Mr. Jones looked at his new acquaintance and shook his head. He did not think it possible that any woman would make such a mistake as that.

"I had a very bad sore throat," continued Mr. Brown, "and indeed you may perceive it still,"—in saying this, he perhaps aggravated a little the sign of his distemper, "and I asked Mrs. Brown to go down and get one,—just what she put on you."

"I wish you'd had it," said Mr. Jones, putting his hand up to his neck.

"I wish I had,—for your sake as well as mine,—

and for hers, poor woman. I don't know when she will get over the shock."

"I don't know when I shall. And it has stopped me on my journey. I was to have been to-night, this very night, this Christmas Eve, with the young lady I am engaged to marry. Of course I couldn't travel. The extent of the injury done nobody can imagine at present."

"It has been just as bad to me, sir. We were to have been with our family this Christmas Eve. There were particular reasons,—most particular. We were only hindered from going by hearing of your condition."

"Why did she come into my room at all? I can't understand that. A lady always knows her own room at an hotel."

"353—that's yours; 333—that's ours. Don't you see how easy it was? She had lost her way, and she was a little afraid lest the thing should fall down."

"I wish it had, with all my heart."

"That's how it was. Now I'm sure, Mr. Jones, you'll take a lady's apology. It was a most unfortunate mistake,—most unfortunate; but what more can be said?"

Mr. Jones gave himself up to reflection for a few moments before he replied to this. He supposed that he was bound to believe the story as far as it went. At any rate, he did not know how he could say that he did not believe it. It seemed to him to be almost incredible,—especially incredible in regard to that personal mistake, for, except that they both had long beards and brown beards, Mr. Jones thought that there was no point of resemblance between himself and Mr. Brown. But still, even that, he felt, must be accepted. But then why had he been left, deserted, to undergo all those torments? "She found out her mistake at last, I suppose?"

"Oh, yes."

"Why didn't she wake a fellow and take it off again?"

"Ah!"

"She can't have cared very much for a man's comfort when she went away and left him like that."

"Ah! there was the difficulty, Mr. Jones."

"Difficulty! Who was it that had done it? To come to me, in my bedroom, in the middle of the night, and put that thing on me, and then leave it there and say nothing about it! It seems to me deuced like a practical joke."

"No, Mr. Jones!"

"That's the way I look at it," said Mr. Jones, plucking up his courage.

"There isn't a woman in all England, or in all France, less likely to do such a thing than my wife. She's as steady as a rock, Mr. Jones, and would no more go into another gentleman's bedroom in joke than—— Oh dear no! You're going to be a married man yourself."

"Unless all this makes a difference," said Mr. Jones, almost in tears. "I had sworn that I would be with her this Christmas Eve."

"Oh, Mr. Jones, I cannot believe that will interfere

with your happiness. How could you think that your wife, as is to be, would do such a thing as that in joke?"

"She wouldn't do it at all;—joke or anyway."

"How can you tell what accident might happen to anyone?"

"She'd have wakened the man then afterwards. I'm sure she would. She would never have left him to suffer in that way. Her heart is too soft. Why didn't she send you to wake me, and explain it all? That's what my Jane would have done; and I should have gone and wakened him. But the whole thing is impossible," he said, shaking his head as he remembered that he and his Jane were not in a condition as yet to undergo any such mutual trouble. At last Mr. Jones was brought to acknowledge that nothing more could be done. The lady had sent her apology, and told her story, and he must bear the trouble and inconvenience to which she had subjected him. He still, however, had his own opinion about her conduct generally, and could not be brought to give any sign of amity. He simply bowed when Mr. Brown was hoping to induce him to shake hands, and sent no word of pardon to the great offender.

The matter, however, was so far concluded that there was no further question of police interference, nor any doubt but that the lady with her husband was to be allowed to leave Paris by the night train. The nature of the accident probably became known to all. Mr. Brown was interrogated by many, and though he professed to declare that he would answer no question, nevertheless he found it better to tell the clerk something of the truth than to allow the matter to be shrouded in mystery. It is to be feared that Mr. Jones, who did not once show himself through the day, but who employed the hours in endeavouring to assuage the injury done him, still lived in the conviction that the lady had played a practical joke on him. But the subject of such a joke never talks about it, and Mr. Jones could not be induced to speak even by the friendly adherence of the night-porter.

Mrs. Brown also clung to the seclusion of her own bedroom, never once stirring from it till the time came in which she was to be taken down to the omnibus. Upstairs she ate her meals, and upstairs she passed her time in packing and unpacking, and in requesting that telegrams might be sent repeatedly to Thompson Hall. In the course of the day two such telegrams were sent, in the latter of which the Thompson family were assured that the Browns would arrive, probably in time for breakfast on Christmas Day, certainly in time for church. She asked more than once tenderly after Mr. Jones' welfare, but could obtain no information. "He was very cross, and that's all I know about it," said Mr. Brown. Then she made a remark as to the gentleman's Christian name, which appeared on the card as "Barnaby." "My sister's husband's name will be Burnaby," she said. "And this man's Christian name is Barnaby; that's all the difference," said her husband, with ill-timed jocularity.

We all know how people under a cloud are apt to

fail in asserting their personal dignity. On the former day a separate vehicle had been ordered by Mr. Brown to take himself and his wife to the station, but now, after his misfortunes, he contented himself with such provision as the people at the hotel might make for him. At the appointed hour he brought his wife down, thickly veiled. There were many strangers as she passed through the hall, ready to look at the lady who had done that wonderful thing in the dead of night, but none could see a feature of her face as she stepped across the hall, and was hurried into the omnibus. And there were many eyes also on Mr. Jones, who followed very quickly, for he also, in spite of his sufferings, was leaving Paris on the evening in order that he might be with his English friends on Christmas Day. He, as he went through the crowd, assumed an air of great dignity, to which, perhaps, something was added by his endeavours, as he walked, to save his poor throat from irritation. He, too, got into the same omnibus, stumbling over the feet of his enemy in the dark. At the station they got their tickets, one close after the other, and then were brought into each other's presence in the waiting-room. I think it must be acknowledged that here Mr. Jones was conscious, not only of her presence, but of her consciousness of his presence, and that he assumed an attitude, as though he should have said, "Now do you think it possible for me to believe that you mistook me for your husband?" She was perfectly quiet, but sat through that quarter of an hour with her face continually veiled. Mr.

Brown made some little overture of conversation to Mr. Jones, but Mr. Jones, though he did mutter some reply, showed plainly enough that he had no desire for further intercourse. Then came the accustomed stampede, the awful rush, the internecine struggle in which seats had to be found. Seats, I fancy, are regularly found, even by the most tardy, but it always appears that every British father and every British husband is actuated at these stormy moments by a conviction that unless he proves himself a very Hercules he and his daughters and his wife will be left desolate in Paris. Mr. Brown was quite Herculean, carrying two bags and a hat-box in his own hands, besides the cloaks, the coats, the rugs, the sticks, and the umbrellas. But when he had got himself and his wife well seated, with their faces to the engine, with a corner seat for her,—there was Mr. Jones immediately opposite to her. Mr. Jones, as soon as he perceived the inconvenience of his position, made a scramble for another place, but he was too late. In that contiguity the journey as far as Calais had to be made. She, poor woman, never once took up her veil. There he sat, without closing an eye, stiff as a ramrod, sometimes showing by little uneasy gestures that the trouble at his neck was still there, but never speaking a word, and hardly moving a limb.

Crossing from Calais to Dover the lady was, of course, separated from her victim. The passage was very bad, and she more than once reminded her husband how well it would have been with them now had they pursued their journey as she had intended,—as though they had been detained in Paris by his fault! Mr. Jones, as he laid himself down on his back, gave himself up to wondering whether any man before him had ever been made subject to such absolute injustice. Now and again he put his hand up to his own beard, and began to doubt whether it could have been moved, as it must have been moved, without waking him. What if chloroform had been used? Many such suspicions crossed his mind during the misery of that passage.

They were again together in the same railway carriage from Dover to London. They had now got used to the close neighbourhood, and knew how to endure each the presence of the other. But as yet Mr. Jones had never seen the lady's face. He longed to know what were the features of the woman who had been so blind —if indeed that story were true. Or if it were not true, of what like was the woman who would dare in the middle of the night to play such a trick as that? But still she kept her veil close over her face.

From Cannon Street the Browns took their departure in a cab for the Liverpool Street Station, whence they would be conveyed by the Eastern Counties Railway to Stratford. Now at any rate their troubles were over. They would be in ample time, not only for Christmas Day church, but for Christmas Day breakfast. "It will be just the same as getting in there last night," said Mr. Brown, as he walked across the platform to place his wife in the carriage for Stratford. She entered it the first, and as she did so there she saw Mr. Jones seated in the corner! Hitherto she had borne his presence well, but now she could not restrain herself from a little start and a little scream. He bowed his head very slightly, as though acknowledging the compliment, and then down she dropped her veil. When they arrived at Stratford, the journey being over in a quarter of an hour, Jones was out of the carriage even before the Browns.

"There is Uncle John's carriage," said Mrs. Brown, thinking that now, at any rate, she would be able to free herself from the presence of this terrible stranger. No doubt he was a handsome man to look at, but on no face so sternly hostile had she ever before fixed her eyes. She did not, perhaps, reflect that the owner of no other face had ever been so deeply injured by herself.

CHAPTER V.

MRS. BROWN AT THOMPSON HALL.

"PLEASE, sir, we were to ask for Mr. Jones," said the servant, putting his head into the carriage after both Mr. and Mrs. Brown had seated themselves.

"Mr. Jones!" exclaimed the husband.

"Why ask for Mr. Jones?" demanded the wife. The servant was about to tender some explanation when Mr. Jones stepped up and said that he was Mr. Jones. "We are going to Thompson Hall," said the lady with great vigour.

"So am I," said Mr. Jones, with much dignity. It was, however, arranged that he should sit with the coachman, as there was a rumble behind for the other servant. The luggage was put into a cart, and away all went for Thompson Hall.

"What do you think about it, Mary?" whispered Mr. Brown, after a pause. He was evidently awe-struck by the horror of the occasion.

"I cannot make it out at all. What do you think?"

"I don't know what to think. Jones going to Thompson Hall?"

"He's a very good-looking young man," said Mrs. Brown.

"Well;—that's as people think. A stiff, stuck-up fellow, I should say. Up to this moment he has never forgiven you for what you did to him."

"Would you have forgiven his wife, Charles, if she'd done it to you?"

"He hasn't got a wife,—yet."

"How do you know?"

"He is coming home now to be married," said Mr. Brown. "He expects to meet the young lady this very Christmas Day. He told me so. That was one of the reasons why he was so angry at being stopped by what you did last night."

"I suppose he knows Uncle John, or he wouldn't be going to the Hall," said Mrs. Brown.

"I can't make it out," said Mr. Brown, shaking his head.

"He looks quite like a gentleman," said Mrs. Brown,

"though he has been so stiff. Jones! Barnaby Jones! You're sure it was Barnaby?"

"That was the name on the card."

"Not Burnaby?" asked Mrs. Brown.

"It was Barnaby Jones on the card,—just the same as 'Barnaby Rudge,' and as for looking like a gentleman, I'm by no means quite so sure. A gentleman takes an apology when it's offered."

"Perhaps, my dear, that depends on the condition of his throat. If you had had a mustard plaster on all night, you might not have liked it. But here we are at Thompson Hall at last."

Thompson Hall was an old brick mansion, standing within a huge iron gate, with a gravel sweep before it. It had stood there before Stratford was a town, or even a suburb, and had then been known by the name of Bow Place. But it had been in the hands of the present family for the last thirty years, and was now known far and wide as Thompson Hall,—a comfortable, roomy, old-fashioned place, perhaps a little dark and dull to look at, but much more substantially built than most of our modern villas. Mrs. Brown jumped with alacrity from the carriage, and with a quick step entered the home of her forefathers. Her husband followed her more leisurely, but he, too, felt that he was at home at Thompson Hall. Then Mr. Jones walked in also; —but he looked as though he were not at all at home. It was still very early, and no one of the family was as yet down. In these circumstances it was almost necessary that something should be said to Mr. Jones.

"Do you know Mr. Thompson?" asked Mr. Brown.

"I never had the pleasure of seeing him,—as yet," answered Mr. Jones, very stiffly.

"Oh,—I didn't know;—because you said you were coming here."

"And I have come here. Are you friends of Mr. Thompson?"

"Oh, dear, yes," said Mrs. Brown. "I was a Thompson myself before I married."

"Oh,—indeed!" said Mr. Jones. "How very odd,—very odd, indeed."

During this time the luggage was being brought into the house, and two old family servants were offering them assistance. Would the new comers like to go up to their bedrooms? Then the housekeeper, Mrs. Green, intimated with a wink that Miss Jane would, she was sure, be down quite immediately. The present moment, however, was still very unpleasant. The lady probably had made her guess as to the mystery; but the two gentlemen were still altogether in the dark. Mrs. Brown had no doubt declared her parentage, but Mr. Jones, with such a multitude of strange facts crowding on his mind, had been slow to understand her. Being somewhat suspicious by nature, he was beginning to think whether possibly the mustard had been put by this lady on his throat with some reference to his connexion with Thompson Hall. Could it be that she, for some reason of her own, had wished to prevent his coming, and had contrived this untoward stratagem out of her brain? or had she wished to make him ridiculous to the Thompson family,—to whom, as a family, he was at present unknown? It was becoming more and more improbable to him that the whole thing should have been an accident. When, after the first horrid torments of that morning in which he had in his agony invoked the assistance of the night-porter, he had begun to reflect on his situation, he had determined that it would be better that nothing further should be said about it. What would life be worth to him if he were to be known wherever he went as the man who had been mustard-plastered in the middle of the night by a strange lady? The worst of a practical joke is that the remembrance of the absurd condition sticks so long to the sufferer! At the hotel that night-porter, who had possessed himself of the handkerchief and had read the name, and had connected that name with the occupant of 333 whom he had found wandering about the house with some strange purpose, had not permitted the thing to sleep. The porter had pressed the matter home against the Browns, and had produced the interview which has been recorded. But during the whole of that day Mr. Jones had been resolving that he would never again either think of the Browns or speak of them. A great injury had been done to him,—a most outrageous injustice;—but it was a thing which had to be endured. A horrid woman had come across him like a nightmare. All he could do was to endeavour to forget the terrible visitation. Such had been his resolve,—in making which he had passed that long day in Paris. And now the Browns had stuck to him from the moment of his leaving his room! he had been forced to travel with them, but had travelled with them as a stranger. He had tried to comfort himself with the reflection that at every fresh stage he would shake them off. In one railway after another the vicinity had been bad,—but still they were strangers. Now he found himself in the same house with them,—where of course the story would be told. Had not the thing been done on purpose that the story might be told there at Thompson Hall?

Mrs. Brown had acceded to the proposition of the housekeeper, and was about to be taken to her room when there was heard a sound of footsteps along the passage above and on the stairs, and a young lady came bounding on to the scene. "You have all of you come a quarter of an hour earlier than we thought possible," said the young lady. "I did so mean to be up to receive you!" With that she passed her sister on the stairs,—for the young lady was Miss Jane Thompson, sister to our Mrs. Brown,—and hurried down into the hall. Here Mr. Brown, who had ever been on affectionate terms with his sister-in-law, put himself forward to receive her embraces; but she, apparently not noticing him in her ardour, rushed on and threw herself on to the breast of the other gentleman. "This is my Charles," she said. "Oh, Charles, I thought you never would be here."

Mr. Charles Burnaby Jones, for such was his name since he had inherited the Jones property in Pembrokeshire, received into his arms the ardent girl of his heart with all that love and devotion to which she was entitled, but could not do so without some external shrinking from her embrace. "Oh, Charles, what is it?" she said.

"Nothing, dearest—only—only—." Then he looked piteously up into Mrs. Brown's face, as though imploring her not to tell the story.

"Perhaps, Jane, you had better introduce us," said Mrs. Brown.

"Introduce you! I thought you had been travelling together, and staying at the same hotel—and all that."

"So we have; but people may be in the same hotel without knowing each other. And we have travelled all the way home with Mr. Jones without in the least knowing who he was."

"How very odd! Do you mean you have never spoken?"

"Not a word," said Mrs. Brown.

"I do so hope you'll love each other," said Jane.

"It shan't be my fault if we don't," said Mrs. Brown.

"I'm sure it shan't be mine," said Mr. Brown, tendering his hand to the other gentleman. The various feelings of the moment were too much for Mr. Jones, and he could not respond quite as he should have done. But as he was taken upstairs to his room he determined that he would make the best of it.

The owner of the house was old Uncle John. He was a bachelor, and with him lived various members of the family. There was the great Thompson of them all,

Cousin Robert, who was now member of Parliament for the Essex Flats, and young John, as a certain enterprising Thompson of the age of forty was usually called, and then there was old Aunt Bess, and among other young branches there was Miss Jane Thompson, who was now engaged to marry Mr. Charles Burnaby Jones. As it happened, no other member of the family had as yet seen Mr. Burnaby Jones, and he, being by nature of a retiring disposition, felt himself to be ill at ease when he came into the breakfast parlour among all the Thompsons. He was known to be a gentleman of good family and ample means, and all the Thompsons had approved of the match, but during the first Christmas breakfast he did not seem to accept his condition jovially. His own Jane sat beside him, but then on the other side sat Mrs. Brown. She assumed an immediate intimacy,—as women know how to do on such occasions,—being determined from the very first to regard her sister's husband as a brother; but he still feared her. She was still to him the woman who had come to him in the dead of night with that horrid mixture,—and had then left him.

"It was so odd that both of you should have been detained on the very same day," said Jane.

"Yes, it was odd," said Mrs. Brown, with a smile looking round upon her neighbour.

"It was abominably bad weather you know," said Brown.

"But you were both so determined to come," said the old gentleman. "When we got the two telegrams at the same moment, we were sure that there had been some agreement between you."

"Not exactly an agreement," said Mrs. Brown; whereupon Mr. Jones looked as grim as death.

"I'm sure there is something more than we understand yet," said the Member of Parliament.

Then they all went to church, as a united family ought to do on Christmas Day, and came home to a fine old English early dinner at three o'clock,—a sirloin of beef a foot-and-a-half broad, a turkey as big as an ostrich, a plum-pudding bigger than the turkey, and two or three dozen mince-pies. "That's a very large bit of beef," said Mr. Jones, who had not lived much in England latterly. "It won't look so large," said the old gentleman, "when all our friends downstairs have had their say to it." "A plum-pudding on Christmas Day can't be too big," he said again, "if the cook will but take time enough over it. I never knew a bit go to waste yet."

By this time there had been some explanation as to past events between the two sisters. Mrs. Brown had indeed told Jane all about it, how ill her husband had been, how she had been forced to go down and look for the mustard, and then what she had done with the mustard. "I don't think they are a bit alike you know, Mary, if you mean that," said Jane.

"Well, no; perhaps not quite alike. I only saw his beard, you know. No doubt it was stupid, but I did it."

"Why didn't you take it off again?" asked the sister.

"Oh, Jane, if you'd only think of it! Could you?"

Then of course all that occurred was explained, how they had been stopped on their journey, how Brown had made the best apology in his power, and how Jones had travelled with them and had never spoken a word. The gentleman had only taken his new name a week since, but of course had had his new card printed immediately. "I'm sure I should have thought of it if they hadn't made a mistake with the first name. Charles said it was like Barnaby Rudge."

"Not at all like Barnaby Rudge," said Jane; "Charles Burnaby Jones is a very good name."

"Very good indeed, — and I'm sure that after a little bit he won't be at all the worse for the accident."

Before dinner the secret had been told no further, but still there had crept about among the Thompsons, and, indeed, downstairs also, among the retainers, a feeling that there was a secret. The old housekeeper was sure that Miss Mary, as she still called Mrs. Brown, had something to tell if she could only be induced to tell it, and that this something had reference to Mr. Jones' personal comfort. The head of the family, who was a sharp old gentleman, felt this also, and the member of Parliament, who had an idea that he specially should never be kept in the dark, was almost angry. Mr. Jones, suffering from some kindred feeling throughout the dinner, remained silent and unhappy. When two or three toasts had been drunk, — the Queen's health, the old gentleman's health, the young couple's health, Brown's health, and the general health of all the Thompsons, then tongues were loosened and a question was asked, "I know that there has been something doing in Paris between these young people that we haven't heard as yet," said the uncle. Then Mrs. Brown laughed, and Jane, laughing too, gave Mr. Jones to understand that she at any rate knew all about it.

"If there is a mystery I hope it will be told at once," said the member of Parliament, angrily.

"Come, Brown, what is it?" asked another male cousin.

"Well, there was an accident. I'd rather Jones should tell," said he.

Jones' brow became blacker than thunder, but he did not say a word. "You mustn't be angry with Mary," Jane whispered into her lover's ear.

"Come, Mary, you never were slow at talking," said the uncle.

"I do hate this kind of thing," said the member of Parliament.

"I will tell it all," said Mrs. Brown, very nearly in tears, or else pretending to be very nearly in tears. "I know I was very wrong, and I do beg his pardon, and if he won't say that he forgives me I never shall be happy again." Then she clasped her hands, and turning round, looked him piteously in the face.

"Oh yes; I do forgive you," said Mr. Jones.

"My brother," said she, throwing her arms round him and kissing him. He recoiled from the embrace, but I think that he attempted to return the kiss. "And now I will tell the whole story," said Mrs. Brown. And she told it, acknowledging her fault with true contrition, and swearing that she would atone for it by life-long sisterly devotion.

"And you mustard-plastered the wrong man!" said the old gentleman, almost rolling off his chair with delight.

"I did," said Mrs. Brown, sobbing, "and I think that no woman ever suffered as I suffered."

"And Jones wouldn't let you leave the hotel?"

"It was the handkerchief stopped us," said Brown.

"If it had turned out to be anybody else," said the member of Parliament, "the results might have been most serious,—not to say discreditable."

"That's nonsense, Robert," said Mrs. Brown, who was disposed to resent the use of so severe a word, even from the legislator cousin.

"In a strange gentleman's bedroom!" he continued. "It only shows that what I have always said is quite true. You should never go to bed in a strange house without locking your door."

Nevertheless it was a very jovial meeting, and before the evening was over Mr. Jones was happy, and had been brought to acknowledge that the mustard-plaster would probably not do him any permanent injury.

THE TELEGRAPH GIRL.

THE TELEGRAPH GIRL.

CHAPTER I.

LUCY GRAHAM AND SOPHY WILSON.

THREE shillings a day to cover all expenses of life, food, raiment, shelter, a room in which to eat and sleep, and fire and light,—and recreation if recreation there might be,—is not much; but when Lucy Graham, the heroine of this tale, found herself alone in the world, she was glad to think that she was able to earn so much by her work, and that thus she possessed the means of independence if she chose to be independent. Her story up to the date with which we are dealing shall be very shortly told. She had lived for many years with a married brother, who was a bookseller in Holborn,—in a small way of business, and burdened with a large family, but still living in decent comfort. In order, however, that she might earn her own bread she had gone into the service of the Crown as a "Telegraph Girl" in the Telegraph Office.* And

* I presume my readers to be generally aware that the headquarters of the National Telegraph Department are held at the top of one of the great buildings belonging to the General Post Office, in St. Martin's-le-Grand.

there she had remained till the present time, and there she was earning eighteen shillings a week by eight hours' continual work daily. Her life had been full of occupation, as in her spare hours she had been her brother's assistant in his shop, and had made herself familiar with the details of his trade. But the brother had suddenly died, and it had been quickly decided that the widow and the children should take themselves off to some provincial refuge.

Then it was that Lucy Graham had to think of her independence and her eighteen shillings a week on the one side, and of her desolation and feminine necessities on the other. To run backwards and forwards from High Holborn to St. Martin's-le-Grand had been very well as long as she could comfort herself with the companionship of her sister-in-law and defend herself with her brother's arm;—but how would it be with her if she were called upon to live all alone in London? She was driven to consider what else she could do to earn her bread. She might become a nursemaid, or perhaps a nursery governess. Though she had been well and in some respects carefully educated, she knew that she could not soar above that. Of music she did not know a note. She could draw a little and understood enough French,—not to read it, but to teach herself to read it. With English literature she was better acquainted than is usual with young women of her age and class; and, as her only personal treasures, she had managed to save a few books which had become hers through her brother's kindness. To be a servant was distasteful to her, not through any idea that service was disreputable, but from a dislike to be subject at all hours to the will of others. To work and work hard she was quite willing, so that there might be some hours of her life in which she might not be called upon to obey.

When, therefore, it was suggested to her that she had better abandon the Telegraph Office and seek the security of some household, her spirit rebelled against the counsel. Why should she not be independent, and respectable, and safe? But then the solitude! Solitude would certainly be hard, but absolute solitude might not perhaps be necessary. She was fond too of the idea of being a government servant, with a sure and fixed salary,—bound of course to her work at certain hours, but so bound only for certain hours. During a third of the day she was, as she proudly told herself, a servant of the Crown. During the other two-thirds she was lord,—or lady,—of herself.

But there was a quaintness, a mystery, even an awe, about her independence which almost terrified her. During her labours she had eight hundred female companions, all congregated together in one vast room, but as soon as she left the Post Office she was to be all alone! For a few months after her brother's death she continued to live with her sister-in-law, during which time this great question was being discussed. But then the sister-in-law and the children disappeared, and it was incumbent on Lucy to fix herself somewhere. She must begin life after what seemed to her to be a most unfeminine fashion,—"just as though she were a young man,"—for it was thus that she described to herself her own position over and over again.

At this time Lucy Graham was twenty-six years old. She had hitherto regarded herself as being stronger and more steadfast than are women generally of that age. She had taught herself to despise feminine weaknesses, and had learned to be almost her brother's equal in managing the affairs of his shop in his absence. She had declared to herself, looking forward then to some future necessity which had become present to her with terrible quickness, that she would not be feckless, helpless, and insufficient for herself as are so many females. She had girded herself up for a work-a-day life,—looking forward to a time when she might leave the telegraphs and become a partner with her brother. A sudden disruption had broken up all that.

She was twenty-six, well made, cheery, healthy, and to some eyes singularly good-looking, though no one probably would have called her either pretty or handsome. In the first place her complexion was—brown. It was impossible to deny that her whole face was brown, as also was her hair, and generally her dress. There was a pervading brownness about her which left upon those who met her a lasting connection between Lucy Graham and that serviceable, long-enduring colour. But there was nobody so convinced that she was brown from head to foot as was she herself. A good lasting colour she would call it,—one that did not require to be washed every half-hour in order that it might be decent, but could bear real washing when it was wanted; for it was a point of her inner creed, of her very faith of faith, that she was not to depend upon feminine good looks, or any of the adventitious charms of dress for her advance in the world. "A good strong binding," she would say of certain dark-visaged books, "that will stand the gas, and not look disfigured even though a blot of ink should come in its way." And so it was that she regarded her own personal binding.

But for all that she was to some observers very attractive. There was not a mean feature in her face. Her forehead was spacious and well formed. Her eyes, which were brown also, were very bright, and could sparkle with anger or solicitude, or perhaps with love. Her nose was well formed, and delicately shaped enough. Her mouth was large, but full of expression, and seemed to declare without speech that she could be eloquent. The form of her face was oval, and complete, not as though it had been moulded by an inartistic thumb, a bit added on here and a bit there. She was somewhat above the average height of women, and stood upon her legs,—or walked upon them,—as though she understood that they had been given to her for real use.

Two years before her brother's death there had been a suitor for her hand,—as to whose suit she had in truth doubted much. He also had been a bookseller, a man in a larger way of business than her brother, some fifteen years older than herself,—a widower, with a family. She knew him to be a good man, with a comfortable house, an adequate income, and a kind heart. Had she gone to him she would not have been required then to live among the bookshelves or the telegraphs. She had doubted much whether she would not go to him. She knew she could love the children. She thought that she could buckle herself to that new work with a will. But she feared,—she feared that she could not love him.

Perhaps there had come across her heart some idea of what might be the joy of real, downright, hearty love. If so it was only an idea. No personage had come across her path thus to disturb her. But the idea, or the fear, had been so strong with her that she had never been able to induce herself to become the wife of this man; and when he had come to her after her brother's death, in her worst desolation,—when the prospect of service in some other nursery had been strongest before her eyes,—she had still refused him. Perhaps there had been a pride in this,—a feeling that as she had rejected him in her comparative prosperity, she should not take him now when the renewal of his offer might probably be the effect of generosity. But she did refuse him; and the widowed bookseller had to look elsewhere for a second mother for his children.

Then there arose the question, how and where she should live? When it came to the point of settling herself, that idea of starting in life like a young man became very awful indeed. How was she to do it? Would any respectable keeper of lodgings take her in upon that principle? And if so, in what way should she plan out her life? Sixteen hours a day were to be her own. What should she do with them? Was she or was she not to contemplate the enjoyment of any social pleasures; and if so, how were they to be found of such a nature as not to be discreditable? On rare occasions she had gone to the play with her brother, and had then enjoyed the treat thoroughly. Whether it had been *Hamlet* at the Lyceum, or *Lord Dundreary* at the Haymarket, she had found herself equally able to be happy. But there could not be for her now even such rare occasions as these. She thought that she knew that a young woman all alone could not go to the theatre with propriety, let her be ever so brave. And then those three shillings a day, though sufficient for life, would hardly be more than sufficient.

But how should she begin? At last chance assisted her. Another girl, also employed in the Telegraph Office, with whom there had been some family acquaintance over and beyond that formed in the office, happened at this time to be thrown upon the world in some such fashion as herself, and the two agreed to join their forces.

She was one Sophy Wilson by name,—and it was agreed between them that they should club their means together and hire a room for their joint use. Here would be a companionship,—and possibly, after awhile, sweet friendship. Sophy was younger than herself, and might probably need, perhaps be willing to accept, assistance. To be able to do something that should be of use to somebody would, she felt, go far towards giving her life that interest which it would otherwise lack.

When Lucy examined her friend, thinking of the closeness of their future connection, she was startled by the girl's prettiness and youth, and thorough unlikeness to herself. Sophy had long, black, glossy curls, large eyes, a pink complexion, and was very short. She seemed to have no inclination for that strong, serviceable brown binding which was so valuable in Lucy's eyes; but rather to be wedded to bright colours and soft materials. And it soon became evident to the elder young woman that the younger looked upon her employment simply as a stepping-stone to a husband. To get herself married as soon as possible was unblushingly declared by Sophy Wilson to be the one object of her ambition,—and as she supposed that of every other girl in the telegraph department. But she seemed to be friendly and at first docile, to have been brought up with aptitudes for decent life, and to be imbued with the necessity of not spending more than her three shillings a day. And she was quick enough at her work in the office,—quicker even than Lucy herself,—which was taken by Lucy as evidence that her new friend was clever, and would therefore probably be an agreeable companion.

They took together a bedroom in a very quiet street in Clerkenwell,—a street which might be described as genteel because it contained no shops; and here they began to keep house, as they called it. Now the nature of their work was such that they were not called upon to be in their office till noon, but that then they were required to remain there till eight in the evening. At two a short space was allowed them for dinner, which was furnished to them at a cheap rate in a room adjacent to that in which they worked. Here for eightpence each they could get a good meal, or if they preferred it they could bring their food with them, and even have it cooked upon the premises. In the evening tea and bread and butter were provided for them by the officials; and then at eight or a few minutes after they left the building and walked home. The keeping of house was restricted in fact to providing tea and bread and butter for the morning meal, and perhaps when they could afford it for the repetition of such comfort later in the evening. There was the Sunday to be considered,—as to which day they made a contract with the keeper of the lodging-house to sit at her table and partake of her dishes. And so they were established.

From the first Lucy Graham made up her mind that it was her duty to be a very friend of friends to this new companion. It was as though she had consented to marry that widowed bookseller. She would then have considered herself bound to devote herself to his welfare. It was not that she could as yet say that she loved Sophy Wilson. Love with her could not be so immediate as that. But the nature of the bond between them was such, that each might possibly do so much either for the happiness, or the unhappiness of the other!

And then, though Sophy was clever,—for as to this Lucy did not doubt,—still she was too evidently in many things inferior to herself, and much in want of such assistance as a stronger nature could give her. Lucy in acknowledging this put down her own greater strength to the score of her years and the nature of the life which she had been called upon to lead. She had early in her days been required to help herself, to hold her own, and to be as it were a woman of business. But the weakness of the other was very apparent to her. That doctrine as to the necessity of a husband, which had been very soon declared, had,—well,—almost disgusted Lucy. And then she found cause to lament the peculiar arrangement which the requirements of the office had made as to their hours. At first it had seemed to her to be very pleasant that they should have their morning hours for needlework, and perhaps for a little reading; but when she found that Sophy would lie in bed till ten because early rising was not obligatory, then she wished that they had been classed among those whose presence was demanded at eight.

After awhile, there was a little difference between them as to what might or what might not be done with propriety after their office hours were over. It must be explained that in that huge room in which eight hundred girls were at work together, there was also a sprinkling of boys and young men. As no girls were employed there after eight there would always be on duty in the afternoon an increasing number of the other sex, some of whom remained there till late at night,—some indeed all night. Now, whether by chance,—or as Lucy feared by management,—Sophy Wilson had her usual seat next to a young lad with whom she soon contracted a certain amount of intimacy. And from this intimacy arose a proposition that they two should go with Mr. Murray,—he was at first called Mister, but the formal appellation soon degenerated into a familiar Alec,—to a Music Hall! Lucy Graham at once set her face against the Music Hall.

"But why?" asked the other girl. "You don't mean to say that decent people don't go to Music Halls?"

"I don't mean to say anything of the kind, but then they go decently attended."

"How decently? We should be decent."

"With their brothers," said Lucy;—"or something of that kind."

"Brothers!" ejaculated the other girl with a tone of thorough contempt. A visit to a Music Hall with her brother was not at all the sort of pleasure to which Sophy was looking forward. She did her best to get over objections which to her seemed to be fastidious and absurd, observing, "that if people were to feel like that there would be no coming together of people at all." But when she found that Lucy could not be instigated to go to the Music Hall, and that the idea of Alec Murray and herself going to such a place unattended by others was regarded as a proposition too monstrous to be discussed, Sophy for awhile gave way.

But she returned again and again to the subject, thinking to prevail by asserting that Alec had a friend, a most excellent young man, who would go with them,—and bring his sister. Alec was almost sure that the sister would come. Lucy, however, would have nothing to do with it. Lucy thought that there should be very great intimacy indeed before anything of that kind should be permitted.

And so there was something of a quarrel. Sophy declared that such a life as theirs was too hard for her, and that some kind of amusement was necessary. Unless she were allowed some delight she must go mad, she must die, she must throw herself off Waterloo Bridge. Lucy, remembering her duty, remembering how imperative it was that she should endeavour to do good to the one human being with whom she was closely concerned, forgave her, and tried to comfort her;—forgave her even though at last she refused to be guided by her monitress. For Sophy did go to the Music Hall with Alec Murray,—reporting, but reporting falsely, that they were accompanied by the friend and the friend's sister. Lucy, poor Lucy, was constrained by certain circumstances to disbelieve this false assertion. She feared that Sophy had gone with Alec alone,—as was the fact. But yet she forgave her friend. How are we to live together at all if we cannot forgive each other's offences?

CHAPTER II.

ABRAHAM HALL.

As there was no immediate repetition of the offence the forgiveness soon became complete, and Lucy found the interest of her life in her endeavours to be good to this weak child whom chance had thrown in her way. For Sophy Wilson was but a weak child. She was full of Alec Murray for awhile, and induced Lucy to make the young man's acquaintance. The lad was earning twelve shillings a week, and if these two poor young creatures chose to love each other and get themselves married, it would be respectable, though it might be unfortunate. It would at any rate be the way of the world, and was a natural combination with which she would have no right to interfere. But she found that Alec was a mere boy, and with no idea beyond the enjoyment of a bright scarf and a penny cigar, with a girl by his side at a Music Hall. "I don't think it can be worth your while to go much out of your way for his sake," said Lucy.

"Who is going out of her way? Not I. He's as good as anybody else, I suppose. And one must have somebody to talk to sometimes." These last words she uttered so plaintively, showing so plainly that she was unable to endure the simple unchanging dulness of a life of labour, that Lucy's heart was thoroughly softened towards her. She had the great gift of being not the less able to sympathize with the weakness of the weak because of her own abnormal strength. And so it came to pass that she worked for her friend,—stitching and mending when the girl ought to have stitched and mended for herself,—reading to her, even though but little of what was read might be understood,—yielding to her and assisting her in all things, till at last it came to pass that in truth she loved her. And such love and care were much wanted, for the elder girl soon found that the younger was weak in health as well as weak in spirit. There were days on which she could not,—or at any rate did not go to her office. When six months had passed by Lucy had not once been absent since she had begun her new life.

"Have you seen that man who has come to look at our house?" asked Sophy one day as they were walking down to the office. Lucy had seen a strange man, having met him on the stairs. "Isn't he a fine fellow?"

"For anything that I know. Let us hope that he is very fine," said Lucy laughing.

"He's about as handsome a chap as I think I ever saw."

"As for being a chap the man I saw must be near forty."

"He is a little old I should say, but not near that. I don't think he can have a wife or he wouldn't come here. He's an engineer, and he has the care of a steam-engine in the City Road,—that great printing place. His name is Abraham Hall, and he's earning three or four pounds a week. A man like that ought to have a wife."

"How did you learn all about him?"

"It's all true. Sally heard it from Mrs. Green." Mrs. Green was the keeper of the lodging-house and Sally was the maid. "I couldn't help speaking to him yesterday because we were both at the door together. He talked just like a gentleman although he was all smutty and greasy."

"I am glad he talked like a gentleman."

"I told him we lodged here and that we were telegraph girls, and that we never got home till half-past eight. He would be just the beau for you because he is such a big steady-looking fellow."

"I don't want a beau," said Lucy angrily.

"Then I shall take him myself," said Sophy as she entered the office.

Soon after that it came to pass that there did arise a slight acquaintance between both the girls and Abraham Hall, partly from the fact of their near neighbourhood, partly perhaps from some little tricks on Sophy's part. But the man seemed to be so steady, so solid, so little given to lightnesses of flirtation or to dangerous delights, that Lucy was inclined to welcome the accident. When she saw him on a Sunday morning free from the soil of his work, she could perceive that he was still a young man, probably not much over thirty;—but there was a look about him as though he were well inured to the cares of the world, such as is often produced by the possession of a wife and family, —not a look of depression by any means, but seeming to betoken an appreciation of the seriousness of life.

From all this Lucy unconsciously accepted an idea of security in the man, feeling that it might be pleasant to have some strong one near her, from whom in case of need assistance might be asked without fear. For this man was tall and broad and powerful, and seemed to Lucy's eyes to be a very pillar of strength when he would stand still for a moment to greet her in the streets.

But poor Sophy, who had so graciously offered the man to her friend at the beginning of their intercourse, seemed soon to change her mind and to desire his attention for herself. He was certainly much more worthy than Alec Murray. But to Lucy, to whom it was a rule of life as strong as any in the commandments that a girl should not throw herself at a man, but should be sought by him, it was a painful thing to see how many of poor Sophy's much-needed sixpences were now spent in little articles of finery by which it was hoped that Mr. Hall's eyes might be gratified, and how those glossy ringlets were brushed and made to shine with pomatum, and how the little collars were washed and re-washed and starched and re-starched, in order that she might be smart for him. Lucy, who was always neat, endeavoured to become browner and browner. This she did by way of reproach and condemnation, not at all surmising that Mr. Hall might possibly prefer a good solid wearing colour to glittering blue and pink gewgaws.

At this time Sophy was always full of what Mr. Hall had last said to her; and after awhile broached an idea that he was some gentleman in disguise. "Why in disguise? Why not a gentleman not in disguise?" asked Lucy, who had her own ideas, perhaps a little exaggerated, as to Nature's gentlemen. Then Sophy explained herself. A gentleman, a real gentleman, in disguise would be very interesting;—one who had quarrelled with his father, perhaps, because he would not endure paternal tyranny, and had then determined to earn his own bread till he might happily come into the family honours and property in a year or two. Perhaps instead of being Abraham Hall he was in reality the Right Honourable Russell Howard Cavendish; and if, during his temporary abeyance, he should prove his thorough emancipation from the thraldom of his aristocracy by falling in love with a telegraph girl, how fine it would be! When Lucy expressed an opinion that Mr. Hall might be a very fine fellow though he were fulfilling no more than the normal condition of his life at the present moment, Sophy would not be contented, declaring that her friend, with all her reading, knew nothing of poetry. In this way they talked very frequently about Abraham Hall, till Lucy would often feel that such talking was indecorous. Then she would be silent for awhile herself, and rebuke the other girl for her constant mention of the man's name. Then again she would be brought back to the subject;—for in all the little intercourse which took place between them and the man, his conduct was so simple and yet so civil, that she could not really feel him to be unworthy of a place in her thoughts. But Sophy soon declared frankly to her friend that she was absolutely in love with the man. "You wouldn't have him, you know," she said when Lucy scolded her for the avowal.

"Have him! How can you bring yourself to talk in such a way about a man? What does he want of either of us?"

"Men do marry you know,—sometimes," said Lucy; "and I don't know how a young man is to get a wife unless some girl will show that she is fond of him."

"He should show first that he is fond of her."

"That's all very well for talkee-talkee," said Sophy; "but it doesn't do for practice. Men are awfully shy. And then though they do marry sometimes, they don't want to get married particularly,—not as we do. It comes like an accident. But how is a man to fall into a pit if there's no pit open?"

In answer to this Lucy used many arguments and much scolding. But to very little effect. That the other girl should have thought so much about it and be so ready with her arguments was horrid to her. "A pit open!" ejaculated Lucy; "I would rather never speak to a man again than regard myself in such a light." Sophy said that all that might be very well, but declared that it "would not wash."

The elder girl was so much shocked by all this that there came upon her gradually a feeling of doubt whether their joint life could be continued. Sophy declared her purpose openly of entrapping Abraham

Hall into a marriage, and had absolutely induced him to take her to the theatre. He had asked Lucy to join them; but she had sternly refused, basing her refusal on her inability to bear the expense. When he offered to give her the treat, she told him with simple gravity that nothing would induce her to accept such a favour from any man who was not either a very old friend or a near relation. When she said this he so looked at her that she was sure that he approved of her resolve. He did not say a word to press her;—but he took Sophy Wilson, and, as Lucy knew, paid for Sophy's ticket.

All this displeased Lucy so much that she began to think whether there must not be a separation. She could not continue to live on terms of affectionate friendship with a girl whose conduct she so strongly disapproved. But then again, though she could not restrain the poor light thing altogether, she did restrain her in some degree. She was doing some good by her companionship. And then, if it really was in the man's mind to marry the girl, that certainly would be a good thing,—for the girl. With such a husband she would be steady enough. She was quite sure that the idea of preparing a pit for such a one as Abraham Hall must be absurd. But Sophy was pretty and clever, and if married would at any rate love her husband. Lucy thought she had heard that steady, severe, thoughtful men were apt to attach themselves to women of the butterfly order. She did not like the way in which Sophy was doing this; but then, who was she that she should be a judge? If Abraham Hall liked it, would not that be much more to the purpose? Therefore she resolved that there should be no separation at present;—and, if possible, no quarrelling.

But soon it came to pass that there was another very solid reason against separation. Sophy, who was often unwell, and would sometimes stay away from the office for a day or two on the score of ill-health, though by doing so she lost one of her three shillings on each such day, gradually became worse. The superintendent at her department had declared that in case of further absence a medical certificate must be sent, and the doctor attached to the office had called upon her. He had looked grave, had declared that she wanted considerable care, had then gone so far as to recommend rest,—which meant absence from work,—for at least a fortnight, and ordered her medicine. This of course meant the loss of a third of her wages. In such circumstances and at such a time it was not likely that Lucy should think of separation.

While Sophy was ill Abraham Hall often came to the door to inquire after her health;—so often that Lucy almost thought that her friend had succeeded. The man seemed to be sympathetic and anxious, and would hardly have inquired with so much solicitude had he not really been anxious as to poor Sophy's health. Then, when Sophy was better, he would come in to see her, and the girl would deck herself out with some little ribbon and would have her collar always starched and ironed, ready for his reception. It certainly did seem to Lucy that the man was becoming fond of her foolish little friend.

During this period Lucy of course had to go to the office alone, leaving Sophy to the care of the lodging-house keeper. And, in her solitude, troubles were heavy on her. In the first place Sophy's illness had created certain necessarily increased expenses; and at the same time their joint incomes had been diminished by one shilling a week out of six. Lucy was in general matters allowed to be the dispenser of the money; but on occasions the other girl would assert her rights,—which always meant her right to some indulgence out of their joint incomes which would be an indulgence to her and her alone. Even those bright ribbons could not be had for nothing. Lucy wanted no bright ribbons. When they were fairly prosperous she had not grudged some little expenditure in this direction. She had told herself that young girls like to be bright in the eyes of men, and that she had no right even to endeavour to make her friend look at all these things with her eyes. She even confessed to herself some deficiency on her own part, some want of womanliness in that she did not aspire to be attractive,—still owning to herself, vehemently declaring to herself, that to be attractive in the eyes of a man whom she could love would of all delights be the most delightful. Thinking of all this she had endeavoured not to be angry with poor Sophy; but when she became pinched for shillings and sixpences and to feel doubtful whether at the end of each fortnight there would be money to pay Mrs. Green for lodgings and coal, then her heart became sad within her, and she told herself that Sophy, though she was ill, ought to be more careful.

And there was another trouble which for awhile was very grievous. Telegraphy is an art not yet perfected among us and is still subject to many changes. Now it was the case at this time that the pundits of the office were in favour of a system of communicating messages by ear instead of by eye. The little dots and pricks which even in Lucy's time had been changed more than once, had quickly become familiar to her. No one could read and use her telegraphic literature more rapidly or correctly than Lucy Graham. But now that this system of little tinkling sounds was coming up,—a system which seemed to be very pleasant to those females who were gifted with musical aptitudes,—she found herself to be less quick, less expert, less useful than her neighbours. This was very sad, for she had always been buoyed up by an unconscious conviction of her own superior intelligence. And then, though there had been neither promises nor threats, she had become aware,—at any rate had thought that she was aware,—that those girls who could catch and use the tinkling sounds would rise more quickly to higher pay than the less gifted ones. She had struggled therefore to overcome the difficulty. She had endeavoured to force her ears to do that which her ears were not capable of accomplishing. She had failed, and to-day had owned to herself that she must fail. But Sophy had been one of the first to catch the tinkling sounds. Lucy came back to her room sad and down at heart and full of troubles. She had a long task of needlework before her, which had been put by for awhile through causes consequent on Sophy's illness. "Now she is better perhaps he will marry her and take her away, and I shall be alone again," she said to herself, as though declaring that such a state of things would be a relief to her, and almost a happiness.

"He has just been here," said Sophy to her as soon as she entered the room. Sophy was painfully, cruelly smart, clean and starched, and shining about her locks,—so prepared that, as Lucy thought, she must have evidently expected him.

"Well;—and what did he say?"

"He has not said much yet, but it was very good of him to come and see me,—and he was looking so handsome. He is going out somewhere this evening to some political meeting with two or three other men, and he was got up quite like a gentleman. I do like to see him look like that."

"I always think a working man looks best in his working clothes," said Lucy. "There's some truth about him then. When he gets into a black coat he is pretending to be something else, but everybody can see the difference."

There was a severity, almost a savageness in this, which surprised Sophy so much that at first she hardly knew how to answer it. "He is going to speak at the meeting," she said after a pause. "And of course he had to make himself tidy. He told me all that he is going to say. Should you not like to hear him speak?"

"No," said Lucy very sharply, setting to work instantly upon her labours, not giving herself a moment for preparation or a moment for rest. Why should she like to hear a man speak who could condescend to love so empty and so vain a thing as that? Then she became gradually ashamed of her own feelings. "Yes," she said; "I think I should like to hear him speak;—only if I were not quite so tired. Mr. Hall is a man of good sense, and well educated, and I think I should like to hear him speak."

"I should like to hear him say one thing I know," said Sophy. Then Lucy in her rage tore asunder some fragment of a garment on which she was working.

CHAPTER III.

SOPHY WILSON GOES TO HASTINGS.

Sophy went back to her work, and in a very few days was permanently moved from the seat which she had hitherto occupied next to Alec Murray and near to Lucy, to a distant part of the chamber in which the tinkling instruments were used. And as a part of the arrangement consequent on this she was called on to attend from ten till six instead of from noon till eight.

And her hour for dining was changed also. In this way a great separation between the girls was made, for neither could they walk to the office together, nor walk from it. To Lucy, though she was sometimes inclined to be angry with her friend, this was very painful. But Sophy triumphed in it greatly. "I think we are to have a step up to 21*s.* in the musical box," she said laughing. For it was so that she called the part of the room in which the little bells were always ringing. "Won't it be nice to have 3*s.* 6*d.* instead of 3*s.*?" Lucy said solemnly that any increase of income was always nice, and that when such income was earned by superiority of acquirement it was a matter of just pride. This she enunciated with something of a dogmatic air; having schooled herself to give all due praise to Sophy, although it had to be given at the expense of her own feelings. But when Sophy said in reply that that was just what she had been thinking herself, and that as she could do her work by ear she was of course worth more than those who could not, then the other could only with difficulty repress the soreness of her heart.

But to Sophy I think the new arrangements were most pleasant because it enabled her to reach the street in which she lived just when Abraham Hall was accustomed to return from his work. He would generally come home,—to clean himself as she called it,—and would then again go out for his employment or amusement for the evening; and now, by a proper system of lying in wait, by creeping slow or walking quick, and by watching well, she was generally able to have a word or two with him. But he was so very bashful! He would always call her Miss Wilson; and she of course was obliged to call him Mr. Hall. "How is Miss Graham?" he asked one evening.

"She is very well. I think Lucy is always well. I never knew anybody so strong as she is."

"It is a great blessing. And how are you yourself?"

"I do get so tired at that nasty office. Though of course I like what I am doing now better than the other. It was that rolling up the bands that used to kill me. But I don't think I shall ever really be strong till I get away from the telegraphs. I suppose you have no young ladies where you are?"

"There are I believe a lot of them in the building, stitching bindings; but I never see them."

"I don't think you care much for young ladies, Mr. Hall."

"Not much—now."

"Why not now? What does that mean?"

"I dare say I never told you or Miss Graham before. But I had a wife of my own for a time."

"A wife! You!"

"Yes indeed. But she did not stay with me long. She left me before we had been a year married."

"Left you!"

"She died," he said, correcting very quickly the false impression which his words had been calculated to make.

"Dear me! Died before a year was out. How sad!"

"It was very sad."

"And you had no,—no,—no baby, Mr. Hall?"

"I wish she had had none, because then she would have been still living. Yes, I have a boy. Poor little mortal! It is two years old I think to-day."

"I should so like to see him. A little boy! Do bring him some day, Mr. Hall." Then the father explained that the child was in the country, down in Hertfordshire; but nevertheless he promised that he would some day bring him up to town and show him to his new friends.

Surely having once been married and having a child he must want another wife! And yet how little apt he was to say or do any of those things by saying and doing which men are supposed to express their desire in that direction! He was very slow at making love;—so slow that Sophy hardly found herself able to make use of her own little experiences with him. Alec Murray, who, however, in the way of a husband was not worth thinking of, had a great deal more to say for himself. She could put on her ribbons for Mr. Hall, and wait for him in the street, and look up into his face, and call him Mr. Hall;—but she could not tell him how dearly she would love that little boy and what an excellent mother she would be to him, unless he gave her some encouragement.

When Lucy heard that he had been a married man and that he had a child she was gratified, though she knew not why. "Yes, I should like to see him of course," she said, speaking of the boy. "A child, if you have not the responsibility of taking care of it, is always nice."

"I should so like to take care of it."

"I should not like to ask him to bring the boy up out of the country." She paused a moment, and then added, "He is just the man whom I should have thought would have married, and just the man to be made very serious by the grief of such a loss. I am coming to think it does a person good to have to bear troubles."

"You would not say that if you always felt as sick as I do after your day's work."

About a week after that Sophy was so weak in the middle of the day that she was obliged to leave the office and go home. "I know it will kill me," she said that evening, "if I go on with it. The place is so stuffy and nasty, and then those terrible stairs. If I could get out of it and settle down, then I should be quite well. I am not made for that kind of work;—not like you are."

"I think I was made for it certainly."

"It is such a blessing to be strong," said poor Sophy.

"Yes; it is a blessing. And I do bless God that he has made me so. It is the one good thing that has been given to me, and it is better, I think, than all the others." As she said this she looked at Sophy and thought that she was very pretty; but she thought also that prettiness had its dangers and its temptations; and that good strong serviceable health might perhaps be better for one who had to earn her bread.

But through all these thoughts there was a great struggle going on within her. To be able to earn one's bread without personal suffering is very good. To be tempted by prettiness to ribbons, pomatum, and vanities which one cannot afford is very bad. To do as Sophy was doing in regard to this young man, setting her cap at him and resolving to make prey of him as a fowler does of a bird, was, to her way of thinking, most unseemly. But to be loved by such a man as Abraham Hall, to be chosen by him as his companion, to be removed from the hard, outside, unwomanly work of the world to the indoor occupations which a husband would require from her; how much better a life according to her real tastes would that be, than anything which she now saw before her! It was all very well to be brown and strong while the exigencies of her position were those which now surrounded her; but she could not keep herself from dreaming of something which would have been much better than that.

A month or two passed away during which the child had on one occasion been brought up to town on a Saturday evening, and had been petted and washed and fed and generally cared for by the two girls during the Sunday,—all which greatly increased their intimacy with the father. And now, as Lucy quickly observed, Abraham Hall called Sophy by her christian name. When the word was first pronounced in Lucy's presence Sophy blushed and looked round at her friend. But she never said that the change had been made at her own request. "I do so hate to be called Miss Wilson," she had said. "It seems among friends as though I were a hundred years old." Then he had called her Sophy. But she did not dare,—not as yet,—to call him Abraham. All which the other girl watched very closely, saying nothing.

But during these two months Sophy had been away from her office more than half the time. Then the doctor said she had better leave town for awhile. It was September, and it was desired that she should pass that month at Hastings. Now it should be explained that in such emergencies as this the department has provided a most kindly aid for young women. Some five or six at a time are sent out for a month to Hastings or to Brighton, and are employed in the telegraph offices in those towns. Their railway fares are paid for them, and a small extra allowance is made to them to enable them to live away from their homes. The privilege is too generally sought to be always at the command of her who wants it; nor is it accorded except on the doctor's certificate. But in the September Sophy Wilson was sent down to Hastings.

In spite, however, of the official benevolence which greatly lightened the special burden which illness must always bring on those who have to earn their bread, and which in Sophy Wilson's case had done so much for her, nevertheless the weight of the misfortune fell heavily on poor Lucy. Some little struggle had to be made as to clothes before the girl could be sent away from her home; and, though the sick one was enabled to support herself at Hastings, the cost of the London lodgings which should have been divided fell entirely upon Lucy. Then at the end of the month there came worse tidings. The doctor at Hastings declared that the girl was unfit to go back to her work,—was, indeed, altogether unfit for such effort as eight hours' continued attendance required from her. She wanted at any rate some period of perfect rest, and therefore she remained down at the seaside without the extra allowance which was so much needed for her maintenance.

Then the struggle became very severe with Lucy,—so severe that she began to doubt whether she could long endure it. Sophy had her two shillings a day, the two-thirds of her wages, but she could not subsist on that. Something had to be sent to her in addition, and this something could only come from Lucy's wages. So at least it was at first. In order to avoid debt she gave up her more comfortable room and went upstairs into a little garret. And she denied herself her accustomed dinner at the office, contenting herself with bread and cheese,—or often simply with bread,—which she could take in her pocket. And she washed her own clothes and mended even her own boots, so that still she might send a part of her earnings to the sick one.

"Is she better?" Abraham asked her one day.

"It is hard to know, Mr. Hall. She writes just as

she feels at the moment. I am afraid she fears to return to the office."

"Perhaps it does not suit her."

"I suppose not. She thinks some other kind of life would be better for her. I dare say it would."

"Could I do anything?" asked the man very slowly.

Could he do anything? well; yes. Lucy at least thought that he could do a great deal. There was one thing which, if he would do it, would make Sophy at any rate believe herself to be well. And this sickness was not organic,—was not, as it appeared, due to any cause which could be specified. It had not as yet been called by any name,—such as consumption. General debility had been spoken of both by the office doctor and by him at Hastings. Now Lucy certainly thought that a few words from Mr. Hall would do more than all the doctors in the way of effecting a cure. Sophy hated the telegraph office, and she lacked the strength of mind necessary for doing that which was distasteful to her. And that idea of a husband had taken such hold of her, that nothing else seemed to her to give a prospect of contentment. "Why don't you go down and see her, Mr. Hall?" she said.

Then he was silent for awhile before he answered,—silent and very thoughtful. And Lucy as the sound of her own words rested on her ears felt she had done wrong in asking such a question. Why should he go down, unless indeed he were in love with the girl and prepared to ask her to be his wife? If he were to go down expressly to visit her at Hastings unless he were so prepared, what false hopes he would raise; what damage he would do instead of good! How indeed could he possibly go down on such a mission without declaring to all the world that he intended to make the girl his wife? But it was necessary that the question should be answered. "I could do no good by that," he said.

"No; perhaps not. Only I thought——"

"What did you think?" Now he asked a question and showed plainly by his manner that he expected an answer.

"I don't know," said Lucy blushing. "I suppose I ought not to have thought anything. But you seemed to be so fond of her."

"Fond of her! Well; one does get fond of kind neighbours. I suppose you would think me impertinent, Miss Lucy,"—he had never made even this approach to familiarity before,—"if I were to say that I am fond of both of you."

"No indeed," she replied, thinking that as a fondness declared by a young man for two girls at one and the same moment could not be interesting, so neither could it be impertinent.

"I don't think I should do any good by going down. All that kind of thing costs so much money."

"Of course it does, and I was very wrong."

"But I should like to do something, Miss Lucy." And then he put his hand into his trousers pocket, and Lucy knew that he was going to bring forth money.

She was very poor; but the idea of taking money from him was shocking to her. According to her theory of life, even though Sophy had been engaged to the man as his promised wife, she should not consent to accept maintenance from him or pecuniary aid till she had been made, in very truth, flesh of his flesh, and bone of his bone. Presents an engaged girl might take of course, but hardly even presents of simple utility. A shawl might be given, so that it was a pretty thing and not a shawl merely for warmth. An engaged girl should rather live on bread and water up to her marriage, than take the means of living from the man she loved, till she could take it by right of having become his wife. Such were her feelings, and now she knew that this man was about to offer her money. "We shall do very well," she said, "Sophy and I together."

"You are very hard pinched," he replied. "You have given up your room."

"Yes, I have done that. When I was alone I did not want so big a place."

"I suppose I understand all about it," he said somewhat roughly, or, perhaps, gruffly would be the better word. "I think there is one thing poor people ought never to do. They ought never to be ashamed of being poor among themselves."

Then she looked up into his face, and as she did so a tear formed itself in each of her eyes. "Am I ashamed of anything before you?" she asked.

"You are afraid of telling the truth lest I should

offer to help you. I know you don't have your dinner regular as you used."

"Who has dared to tell you that, Mr. Hall? What is my dinner to anybody?"

"Well. It is something to me. If we are to be friends of course I don't like seeing you go without your meals. You'll be ill next yourself."

"I am very strong."

"It isn't the way to keep so, to work without the victuals you're used to." He was talking to her now in such a tone as to make her almost feel that he was scolding her. "No good can come of that. You are sending your money down to Hastings to her."

"Of course we share everything."

"You wouldn't take anything from me for yourself I dare say. Anybody can see how proud you are. But if I leave it for her I don't think you have a right to refuse it. Of course she wants it if you don't." With that he brought out a sovereign and put it down on the table.

"Indeed I couldn't, Mr. Hall," she said.

"I may give it to her if I please."

"You can send it her yourself," said Lucy, not knowing how else to answer him.

"No, I couldn't. I don't know her address." Then without waiting for another word he walked out of the room, leaving the sovereign on the table. This occurred in a small back parlour on the ground floor, which was in the occupation of the landlady, but was used sometimes by the lodgers for such occasional meetings.

What was she to do with the sovereign? She would be very angry if any man were to send her a sovereign; but it was not right that she should measure Sophy's feelings by her own. And then it might still be that the man was sending the present to the girl whom he intended to make his wife. But why—why—why, had he asked about her dinner? What were her affairs to him? Would she not have gone without her dinner for ever rather than have taken it at his hands? And yet, who was there in all the world of whom she thought so well as of him? And so she took the sovereign upstairs with her into her garret.

CHAPTER IV.

MR. BROWN THE HAIRDRESSER.

LUCY, when she got up to her own little room with the sovereign, sat for awhile on the bed, crying. But she could not in the least explain to herself why it was that she was shedding tears at this moment. It was not because Sophy was ill, though that was cause to her of great grief; nor because she herself was so hard put to it for money to meet her wants. It may be doubted whether grief or pain ever does of itself produce tears, which are rather the outcome of some emotional feeling. She was not thinking much of Sophy as she cried, nor certainly were her own wants present to her mind. The sovereign was between her fingers, but she did not at first even turn her mind to that, or consider what had best be done with it. But what right had he to make inquiry as to her poverty? It was that, she told herself, which now provoked her to anger so that she wept from sheer vexation. Why should he have searched into her wants and spoken to her of her need of victuals? What had there been between them to justify him in tearing away that veil of custom which is always supposed to hide our private necessities from our acquaintances till we ourselves feel called upon to declare them? He had talked to her about her meals. He ought to know that she would starve rather than accept one from him. Yes;—she was very angry with him, and would henceforth keep herself aloof from him.

But still, as she sat, there were present to her eyes and ears the form and words of an heroic man. He had seemed to scold her; but there are female hearts which can be better reached and more surely touched by the truth of anger than by the patent falseness of flattery. Had he paid her compliments she would not now have been crying, nor would she have complained to herself of his usage; but she certainly would not have sat thinking of him, wondering what sort of woman had been that young wife to whom he had first given himself, wondering whether it was possible that Sophy should be good enough for him.

Then she got up, and looking down upon her own hand gazed at the sovereign till she had made up her mind what she would do with it. She at once sat down and wrote to Sophy. She had made up her mind. There should be no diminution in the contribution made from her own wages. In no way should any portion of that sovereign administer to her own comfort. Though she might want her accustomed victuals ever so badly, they should not come to her from his earnings. So she told Sophy in the letter that Mr. Hall had expressed great anxiety for her welfare, and had begged that she would accept a present from him. She was to get anything with the sovereign that might best tend to her happiness. But the shilling a day which Lucy contributed out of her own wages was sent with the sovereign.

For an entire month she did not see Abraham Hall again so as to do more than just speak to him on the stairs. She was almost inclined to think that he was cold and unkind in not seeking her;—and yet she wilfully kept out of his way. On each Sunday it would at any rate have been easy for her to meet him; but with a stubborn purpose which she did not herself understand she kept herself apart, and when she met him on the stairs, which she would do occasionally when she returned from her work, she would hardly stand till she had answered his inquiries after Sophy. But at the end of the month one evening he came up and knocked at her door. "I am sorry to intrude, Miss Lucy."

"It is no intrusion, Mr. Hall. I wish I had a place to ask you to sit down in."

"I have come to bring another trifle for Miss Sophy."

"Pray do not do it. I cannot send it her. She ought not to take it. I am sure you know that she ought not to take it."

"I know nothing of the kind. If I know anything, it is that the strong should help the weak, and the healthy the sick. Why should she not take it from me as well as from you?"

It was necessary that Lucy should think a little before she could answer this;—but, when she had thought, her answer was ready. "We are both girls."

"Is there anything which ought to confine kindness to this or the other sex? If you were knocked down in the street would you let no one but a woman pick you up?"

"It is not the same. I know you understand it, Mr. Hall. I am sure you do."

Then he also paused to think what he would say, for he was conscious that he did "understand it." For a young woman to accept money from a man seemed to imply that some return of favours would be due. But,—he said to himself,—that feeling came from what was dirty and not from what was noble in the world. "You ought to lift yourself above all that," he said at last. "Yes; you ought. You are very good, but you would be better if you would do so. You say that I understand, and I think that you, too, understand."

This again was said in that voice which seemed to scold, and again her eyes became full of tears. Then he was softer on a sudden. "Good night, Miss Lucy. You will shake hands with me;—will you not?" She put her hand in his, being perfectly conscious at the moment that it was the first time that she had ever done so. What a mighty hand it seemed to be as it held hers for a moment! "I will put the sovereign on the table," he said, again leaving the room and giving her no option as to its acceptance.

But she made up her mind at once that she would not be the means of sending his money to Sophy Wilson. She was sure that she would take nothing from him for her own relief, and therefore sure that neither ought Sophy to do so,—at any rate unless there had been more between them than either of them had told to her. But Sophy must judge for herself. She sent, therefore, the sovereign back to Hall with a little note as follows:—

"DEAR MR. HALL,—Sophy's address is at
"Mrs. Pike's,
"19, Paradise Row,
"Fairlight, near Hastings.

"You can do as you like as to writing to her. I am obliged to send back the money which you have so *very generously* left for her, because I do not think she ought to accept it. If she were quite in want it might be different, but we have still five shillings a day between us. If a young woman were starving perhaps it ought to be the same as though she were being run over in the street, but it is not like that. In my next letter I shall tell Sophy all about it.

"Yours truly,

"LUCY GRAHAM."

The following evening, when she came home, he was standing at the house door evidently waiting for her. She had never seen him loitering in that way before, and she was sure that he was there in order that he might speak to her.

"I thought I would let you know that I got the sovereign safely," he said. "I am so sorry that you should have returned it."

"I am sure that I was right, Mr. Hall."

"There are cases in which it is very hard to say what is right and what is wrong. Some things seem right because people have been wrong so long. To give and take among friends ought to be right."

"We can only do what we think right," she said, as she passed in through the passage upstairs.

She felt sure from what had passed that he had not sent the money to Sophy. But why not? Sophy had said that he was bashful. Was he so far bashful that he did not dare himself to send the money to the girl he loved, though he had no scruple as to giving it to her through another person? And, as for bashfulness, it seemed to her that the man spoke out his mind clearly enough. He could scold her, she thought, without any difficulty, for it still seemed that his voice and manner were rough to her. He was never rough to Sophy; but then she had heard so often that love will alter a man amazingly!

Then she wrote her letter to Sophy, and explained as well as she could the whole affair. She was quite sure that Sophy would regret the loss of the money. Sophy, she knew, would have accepted it without scruple. People, she said to herself, will be different. But she endeavoured to make her friend understand that she, with her feelings, could not be the medium of sending on presents of which she disapproved. "I have given him your address," she said, "and he can suit himself as to writing to you." In this letter she enclosed a money order for the contribution made to Sophy's comfort out of her own wages.

Sophy's answer, which came in a day or two, surprised her very much. "As to Mr. Hall's money," she began, "as things stand at present perhaps it is as well that you didn't take it." As Lucy had expected that grievous fault would be found with her, this was comfortable. But it was after that, that the real news came. Sophy was a great deal better; that was also good tidings;—but she did not want to leave Hastings just at present. Indeed she thought that she did not want to leave it at all. A very gentlemanlike young man, who was just going to be taken into partnership in a hairdressing establishment, had proposed to her;—and she had accepted him. Then there were two wishes expressed;—the first was that Lucy would go on a little longer with her kind generosity, and the second,—that Mr. Hall would not feel it very much.

As regarded the first wish, Lucy resolved that she would go on at least for the present. Sophy was still on sick leave from the office, and, even though she might be engaged to a hairdresser, was still to be regarded as an invalid. But as to Mr. Hall, she thought that she could do nothing. She could not even tell him,—at any rate till that marriage at Hastings was quite a settled thing. But she thought that Mr. Hall's future happiness would not be lessened by the event. Though she had taught herself to love Sophy, she had been unable not to think that her friend was not a fitting wife for such a man. But in telling herself that he would have an escape, she put it to herself as though the fault lay chiefly in him. "He is so stern and so hard that he would have crushed her, and she never would have understood his justness and honesty." In her letter of congratulation, which was very kind, she said not a word of Abraham Hall, but she promised to go on with her own contribution till things were a little more settled.

In the meantime she was very poor. Even brown dresses won't wear for ever, let them be ever so brown, and in the first flurry of sending Sophy off to Hastings,—with that decent apparel which had perhaps been the means of winning the hairdresser's heart,—she had got somewhat into debt with her landlady. This she was gradually paying off, even on her reduced wages, but the effort pinched her closely. Day by day, in spite of all her efforts with her needle, she became sensible of a deterioration in her outward appearance which was painful to her at the office, and which made her most careful to avoid any meeting with Abraham Hall. Her boots were very bad, and she had now for some time given up even the pretence of gloves as she went backwards and forwards to the office. But perhaps it was her hat that was most vexatious. The brown straw hat which had lasted her all the summer and autumn could hardly be induced to keep its shape now when November was come.

One day, about three o'clock in the afternoon, Abraham Hall went to the Post Office, and, having inquired among the messengers, made his way up to the telegraph department at the top of the building. There he asked for Miss Graham, and was told by the doorkeeper that the young ladies were not allowed to receive visitors during office hours. He persisted, however, explaining that he had no wish to go into the room, but that it was a matter of importance, and that he was very anxious that Miss Graham should be asked to come out to him. Now it is a rule that the staff of the department who are engaged in sending and receiving messages, the privacy of which may be of vital importance, should be kept during the hours of work as free as possible from communication with the public. It is not that either the girls or the young men would be prone to tell the words which they had been the means of passing on to their destination, but that it might be worth the while of some sinner to offer great temptation, and that the power of offering it should be lessened as much as possible. Therefore, when Abraham Hall pressed his request the door-keeper told him that it was quite impossible.

"Do you mean to say that if it were an affair of life and death she could not be called out?" Abraham asked in that voice which had sometimes seemed to Lucy to be so impressive. "She is not a prisoner!"

"I don't know as to that," replied the man; "you would have to see the superintendent, I suppose."

"Then let me see the superintendent." And at last he did succeed in seeing some one whom he so convinced of the importance of his message as to bring Lucy to the door.

"Miss Graham," he said, when they were at the top of the stairs, and so far alone that no one else could hear him, "I want you to come out with me for half an hour."

"I don't think I can. They won't let me."

"Yes they will. I have to say something which I must say now."

"Will not the evening do, Mr. Hall?"

"No; I must go out of town by the mail train from Paddington, and it will be too late. Get your hat and come with me for half an hour."

Then she remembered her hat, and she snatched a glance at her poor stained dress, and she looked up at him. He was not dressed in his working clothes, and his face and hands were clean, and altogether there was a look about him of well-to-do manly tidiness which added to her feeling of shame.

"If you will go on to the house I will follow you," she said.

"Are you ashamed to walk with me?"

"I am, because——"

He had not understood her at first, but now he understood it all. "Get your hat," he said, "and come with a friend who is really a friend. You must come; you must, indeed." Then she felt herself compelled to obey, and went back and got her old hat and followed him down the stairs into the street. "And so Miss Wilson is going to be married," were the first words he said in the street.

"Has she written to you?"

"Yes; she has told me all about it. I am so glad that she should be settled to her liking, out of town. She says that she is nearly well now. I hope that Mr. Brown is a good sort of man, and that he will be kind to her."

It could hardly be possible, Lucy thought, that he should have taken her away from the office merely to talk to her of Sophy's prospects. It was evident that he was strong enough to conceal any chagrin which might have been caused by Sophy's apostacy. Could it, however, be the case that he was going to leave London because his feelings had been too much disturbed to allow of his remaining quiet? "And so you are going away? Is it for long?" "Well, yes; I suppose it is for always." Then there came upon her a sense of increased desolation. Was he not her only friend? And then, though she had refused all pecuniary assistance, there had been present to her a feeling that there was near to her a strong human being whom she could trust, and who in any last extremity could be kind to her.

"For always! And you go to-night!" Then she thought that he had been right to insist on seeing her. It would certainly have been a great blow to her if he had gone without a word of farewell.

"There is a man wanted immediately to look after the engines at a great establishment on the Wye, in the Forest of Dean. They have offered me four pounds a week."

"Four pounds a week!"

"But I must go at once. It has been talked about for some time, and now it has come all in a clap. I have to be off without a day's notice, almost before I know where I am. As for leaving London, it is just what I like. I love the country."

"Oh, yes," said Lucy, "that will be nice;—and about your little boy?" Could it be that she was to be asked to do something for the child?

They were now at the door of their house.

"Here we are," he said, "and perhaps I can say better inside what I have got to say." Then she followed him into the back sitting-room on the ground floor.

CHAPTER V.

ABRAHAM HALL MARRIED.

"YES;" he said;—"about my little boy. I could not say what I had to say in the street, though I had thought to do so." Then he paused, and she sat herself down, feeling, she did not know why, as though she would lack strength to hear him if she stood. It was then the case that some particular service was to be demanded from her,—something that would show his confidence in her. The very idea of this seemed at once to add a grace to her life. She would have the child to love. There would be something for her to do. And there must be letters between her and him. It would certainly add a grace to her life. But how odd that he should not take his child with him! He had paused a moment while she thought of all this, and she was aware that he was looking at her. But she did not dare to return his gaze, or even to glance up at his face. And then gradually she felt that she was shivering and trembling. What was it that ailed her,—just now when it would be so necessary that she should speak out with some strength? She had eaten nothing since her breakfast when he had come to her, and she was afraid that she would show herself to be weak. "Will you be his mother?" he said.

What did it mean? How was she to answer him? She knew that his eyes were on her, but hers were more than ever firmly fixed upon the floor. And she was aware that she ought briskly to have acceded to his request,—so as to have shown by her ready alacrity that she had attributed no other meaning to the words than they had been intended to convey,—that she had not for a moment been guilty of rash folly. But though it was so imperative upon her to say a word, yet she could not speak. Everything was swimming round her. She was not even sure that she could sit upon her chair. "Lucy," he said;—then she thought she would have fallen;—"Lucy, will you be my wife?"

There was no doubt about the word. Her sense of hearing was at any rate not deficient. And there came upon her at once a thorough conviction that all her troubles had been changed for ever and a day into joys and blessings. The word had been spoken from which he certainly would never go back, and which of course,—of course,—must be a commandment to her. But yet there was an unfitness about it which disturbed her, and she was still powerless to speak. The remembrance of the meanness of her clothes and poorness of her position came upon her,—so that it would be her duty to tell him that she was not fit for him; and yet she could not speak.

"If you will say that you want time to think about it, I shall be contented," he said. But she did not want a moment to think about it. She could not have confessed to herself that she had learned to love him, —oh, so much too dearly,—if it were not for this most unexpected, most unthought of, almost impossible revelation. But she did not want a moment to make herself sure that she did love him. Yet she could not speak. "Will you say that you will think of it for a month?"

Then there came upon her an idea that he was not asking this because he loved her, but in order that he might have a mother whom he could trust for his child. Even that would have been flattering, but that would not have sufficed. Then when she told herself what she was, or rather what she thought herself to be, she felt sure that he could not really love her. Why should such a man as he love such a woman? Then her mouth was opened. "You cannot want me for myself," she said.

"Not for yourself! Then why? I am not the man to seek any girl for her fortune, and you have none." Then again she was dumfounded. She could not explain what she meant. She could not say,—because I am brown, and because I am plain, and because I have become thin and worn from want, and because my clothes are old and shabby. "I ask you," he said, "because with all my heart I love you."

It was as though the heavens had been opened to her. That he should speak a word that was not true was to her impossible. And, as it was so, she would not coy her love to him for a moment. If only she could have found words with which to speak to him! She could not even look up at him, but she put out her hand so as to touch him. "Lucy," he said, "stand up and come to me." Then she stood up and with one little step crept close to his side. "Lucy, can you love me?" And as he asked the question his arm was pressed round her waist, and as she put up her hand to welcome rather than to restrain his embrace, she again felt the strength, the support, and the warmth of his grasp. "Will you not say that you love me?"

"I am such a poor thing," she replied.

"A poor thing, are you? Well, yes; there are different ways of being poor. I have been poor enough in my time, but I never thought myself a poor thing And you must not say it ever of yourself again."

"No?"

"My girl must not think herself a poor thing. May I not say, my girl?" Then there was just a little murmur, a sound which would have been "yes" but for the inability of her lips to open themselves. "And if my girl, then my wife. And shall my wife be called a poor thing? No, Lucy. I have seen it all. I don't think I like poor things;—but I like you."

"Do you?"

"I do. And now I must go back to the City Road and give up charge and take my money. And I must leave this at seven—after a cup of tea. Shall I see you again?"

"See me again! Oh, to-day, you mean. Indeed you shall. Not see you off? My own, own, own man?"

"What will they say at the office?"

"I don't care what they say. Let them say what they like. I have never been absent a day yet without leave. What time shall I be here?" Then he named an hour. "Of course I will have your last words. Perhaps you will tell me something that I must do."

"I must leave some money with you."

"No; no; no; not yet. That shall come after." This she said smiling up at him, with a sparkle of a tear in each eye, but with such a smile! Then he caught her in his arms and kissed her. "That may come at present at any rate," he said. To this, though it was repeated once and again, there was no opposition. Then in his own masterful manner he put on his hat and stalked out of the room without any more words.

She must return to the office that afternoon, of course, if only for the sake of explaining her wish to absent herself the rest of the day. But she could not go forth into the streets just yet. Though she had been able to smile at him and to return his caress, and for a moment so to stand by him that she might have something of the delight of his love, still she was too much flurried, too weak from the excitement of the last half-hour, to walk back to the Post Office without allowing herself some minutes to recruit her strength and collect her thoughts. She went at once up to her own room and cut for herself a bit of bread which she began to eat,—just as one would trim one's lamp carefully for some night work, even though oppressed by heaviest sorrow, or put fuel on the fire that would be needed. Then having fed herself, she leaned back in her chair, throwing her handkerchief over her face, in order that she might think of it.

Oh,—how much there was to fill her mind with many thoughts! Looking back to what she had been even an hour ago, and then assuring herself with infinite delight of the certain happiness of her present position, she told herself that all the world had been altered to her within that short space. As for loving him;—there was no doubt about that! Now she could own to herself that she had long since loved him, even when she thought that he might probably take that other girl as his wife. That she should love him, —was it not a matter of course, he being what he was? But that he should love her,—that, that was the marvel! But he did. She need not doubt that. She could remember distinctly each word of assurance that he had spoken to her. "I ask you, because with all my heart I love you." "May I not say my girl;—and, if my girl, then my wife?" "I do not think that I like poor things; but I like you." No. If she were regarded by him as good enough to be his wife then she would certainly never call herself a poor thing again.

In her troubles and her poverty,—especially in her solitude, she had often thought of that other older man who had wanted to make her his wife,—sometimes almost with regret. There would have been duties for her and a home, and a mode of life more fitting to her feminine nature than this solitary tedious existence. And there would have been something for her to love, some human being on whom to spend her human solicitude and sympathies. She had leagued herself with Sophy Wilson, and she had been true to the bond; but it had had in it but little satisfaction. The other life, she had sometimes thought, would have been better. But she had never loved the man, and could not have loved him as a husband should, she thought, be loved by his wife. She had done what was right in refusing the good things which he had offered her,—and now she was rewarded! Now had come to her the bliss of which she had dreamed, that of belonging to a man to whom she felt that she was bound by all the chords of her heart. Then she repeated his name to herself,—Abraham Hall, and tried in a lowest whisper the sound of that other name, —Lucy Hall. And she opened her arms wide as she sat upon the chair as though in that way she could take his child to her bosom.

She had been sitting so nearly an hour when she started up suddenly and again put on her old hat and hurried off towards her office. She felt now that as regarded her clothes she did not care about herself. There was a paradise prepared for her so dear and so near that the present was made quite bright by merely being the short path to such a future. But for his sake she cared. As belonging to him she would fain, had it been possible, not have shown herself in a garb unfitting for his wife. Everything about him had always been decent, fitting, and serviceable! Well! It was his own doing. He had chosen her as she was.

She would not run in debt to make herself fit for his notice, because such debts would have been debts to be paid by him. But if she could squeeze from her food what should supply her with garments fit at any rate to stand with him at the altar it should be done.

Then, as she hurried on to the office, she remembered what he had said about money. No! She would not have his money till it was hers of right. Then with what perfect satisfaction would she take from him whatever he pleased to give her, and how hard would she work for him in order that he might never feel that he had given her his good things for nothing!

It was five o'clock before she was at the office, and she had promised to be back in the lodgings at six, to get for him his tea. It was quite out of the question that she should work to-day. "The truth is, ma'am," she said to the female superintendent, "I have received and accepted an offer of marriage this afternoon. He is going out of town to-night, and I want to be with him before he goes." This is a plea against which official rigour cannot prevail. I remember once when a young man applied to a saturnine pundit who ruled matters in a certain office for leave of absence for a month to get married. "To get married!" said the saturnine pundit. "Poor fellow! But you must have the leave." The lady at the telegraph office was no doubt less caustic, and dismissed our Lucy for the day with congratulations rather than pity.

She was back at the lodging before her lover, and had borrowed the little back parlour from Mrs. Green, and had spread the tea-things, and herself made the toast in the kitchen before he came. "There's something I suppose more nor friendship betwixt you and Mr. Hall, and better," said the landlady smiling. "A great deal better, Mrs. Green," Lucy had replied, with her face intent upon the toast. "I thought it never could have been that other young lady," said Mrs. Green.

"And now, my dear, about money," said Abraham as he rose to prepare himself for the journey. Many things had been settled over that meal,—how he was to get a house ready, and was then to say when she should come to him, and how she should bring the boy with her, and how he would have the banns called in the church, and how they would be married as soon as possible after her arrival in the new country. "And now, my dear, about money?"

She had to take it at last. "Yes," she said, "it is right that I should have things fit to come to you in. It is right that you shouldn't be disgraced."

"I'd marry you in a sack from the poor-house, if it were necessary," he said with vehemence.

"As it is not necessary, it shall not be so. I will get things;—but they shall belong to you always; and I will not wear them till the day that I also shall belong to you."

She went with him that night to the station, and kissed him openly as she parted from him on the platform. There was nothing in her love now of which she was ashamed. How, after some necessary interval, she followed him down into Gloucestershire, and how she became his wife standing opposite to him in the bright raiment which his liberality had supplied, and how she became as good a wife as ever blessed a man's household, need hardly here be told.

That Miss Wilson recovered her health and married the hairdresser may be accepted by all anxious readers as an undoubted fact.

ALICE DUGDALE.

ALICE DUGDALE.

CHAPTER I.

THE DOCTOR'S FAMILY.

IT used to be said in the village of Beetham that nothing ever went wrong with Alice Dugdale,—the meaning of which, perhaps, lay in the fact that she was determined that things should be made to go right. Things as they came were received by her with a gracious welcome, and "things," whatever they were, seemed to be so well pleased with the treatment afforded to them, that they too for most part made themselves gracious in return.

Nevertheless she had had sorrows, as who has not? But she had kept her tears for herself, and had shown her smiles for the comfort, of those around her. In this little story it shall be told how in a certain period of her life she had suffered much;—how she still smiled, and how at last she got the better of her sorrow.

Her father was the country doctor in the populous and straggling parish of Beetham. Beetham is one of those places so often found in the south of England, half village, half town, for the existence of which there seems to be no special reason. It had no mayor, no municipality, no market, no pavements, and no gas. It was therefore no more than a village;—but it had a doctor, and Alice's father, Dr. Dugdale, was the man. He had been established at Beetham for more than thirty years, and knew every pulse and every tongue for ten miles round. I do not know that he was very great as a doctor;—but he was a kind-hearted, liberal man, and he enjoyed the confidence of the Beethamites, which is everything. For thirty years he had worked hard and had brought up a large family without want. He was still working hard, though turned sixty, at the time of which we are speaking. He had even in his old age many children dependent on him, and though he had fairly prospered, he had not become a rich man.

He had been married twice, and Alice was the only child left at home by his first wife. Two elder sisters were married, and an elder brother was away in the world. Alice had been much younger than they, and had been the only child living with him when he had brought to his house a second mother for her. She was then fifteen. Eight or nine years had since gone, and almost every year had brought an increase to the doctor's family. There were now seven little Dugdales in and about the nursery; and what the seven would do when Alice should go away the folk of Beetham always declared that they were quite at a loss even to guess. For Mrs. Dugdale was one of those women who succumb to difficulties,—who seem originally to have been made of soft material and to have become warped, out of joint, tattered, and almost useless under the wear of the world. But Alice had been constructed of thoroughly seasoned timber, so that, let her be knocked about as she might, she was never out of repair. Now the doctor, excellent as he was at doctoring, was not very good at household matters,—so that the folk at Beetham had reason to be at a loss when they bethought themselves as to what would happen when Alice should "go away."

Of course there is always that prospect of a girl's "going away." Girls not unfrequently intend to go away. Sometimes they "go away" very suddenly, without any previous intention. At any rate such a girl as Alice cannot be regarded as a fixture in a house. Binding as may be her duties at home, it is quite understood that should any adequate provocation to "go away" be brought within her reach, she will go, let the duties be what they may. Alice was a thoroughly good girl,—good to her father, good to her little brothers and sisters, unutterably good to that poor foolish stepmother;—but, no doubt she would "go away" if duly asked.

When that vista of future discomfort in the doctor's house first made itself clearly apparent to the Beethamites, an idea that Alice might perhaps go very soon had begun to prevail in the village. The eldest son of the vicar, Parson Rossiter, had come back from India as Major Rossiter, with an appointment, as some said, of £2,000 a year;—let us put it down as £1,500; —and had renewed his acquaintance with his old playfellow. Others, more than one or two, had endeavoured before this to entice Alice to "go away," but it was said that the dark-visaged warrior, with his swarthy face and black beard, and bright eyes,—probably, too, something in him nobler than those outward bearings,—had whispered words which had prevailed. It was supposed that Alice now had a fitting lover, and that therefore she would "go away."

There was no doubt in the mind of any single inhabitant of Beetham as to the quality of the lover. It was considered on all sides that he was fitting,—so fitting that Alice would of course go when asked. John Rossiter was such a man that every Beethamite looked upon him as a hero,—so that Beetham was proud to have produced him. In small communities a man will come up now and then as to whom it is surmised that any young lady would of course accept him. This man, who was now about ten years older than Alice, had everything to recommend him. He was made up of all good gifts of beauty, conduct, dignity, good heart,—and fifteen hundred a year at the very least. His official duties required him to live in London, from which Beetham was seventy miles distant; but those duties allowed him ample time for visiting the parsonage. So very fitting he was to take any girl away upon whom he might fix an eye of approbation, that there were others, higher than Alice in the world's standing, who were said to grudge the young lady of the village so great a prize. For Alice Dugdale was a young lady of the village and no more; whereas there were county families around, with daughters, among whom the Rossiters had been in the habit of mixing. Now that such a Rossiter had come to the fore, the parsonage family was held to be almost equal to county people.

To whatever extent Alice's love affairs had gone, she herself had been very silent about them; nor had her lover as yet taken the final step of being closeted for ten minutes with her father. Nevertheless everybody had been convinced in Beetham that it would be so,—unless it might be Mrs. Rossiter. Mrs. Rossiter was ambitious for her son, and in this matter sympathised with the county people. The county people certainly were of opinion that John Rossiter might do better, and did not altogether see what there was in Alice Dugdale to make such a fuss about. Of course she had a sweet countenance, rather brown, with good eyes. She had not, they said, another feature in her face which could be called handsome. Her nose was broad. Her mouth was large. They did not like that perpetual dimpling of the cheek which, if natural, looked as if it were practised. She was stout, almost stumpy, they thought. No doubt she danced well, having a good ear and being active and healthy; but with such a waist no girl could really be graceful. They acknowledged her to be the best nursemaid that ever a mother had in her family; but they thought it a pity that she should be taken away from duties for which her presence was so much desired, at any rate by such a one as John Rossiter. I, who knew Beetham well, and who though turned the hill of middle life had still an eye for female charms, used to declare to myself that Alice, though she was decidedly village and not county, was far, far away the prettiest girl in that part of the world.

The old parson loved her, and so did Miss Rossiter,—Miss Janet Rossiter,—who was four or five years older than her brother, and therefore quite an old maid. But John was so great a man that neither of them dared to say much to encourage him,—as neither did Mrs. Rossiter to use her eloquence on the other side. It was felt by all of them that any persuasion might have on John anything but the intended effect. When a man at the age of thirty-three is Deputy Assistant Inspector General of Cavalry, it is not easy to talk him this way or that in a matter of love. And John Rossiter, though the best fellow in the world, was apt to be taciturn on such a subject. Men frequently marry almost without thinking about it at all. "Well; perhaps I might as well. At any rate I cannot very well help it." That too often is the frame of mind. Rossiter's discussion to himself was of a higher nature than that, but perhaps not quite what it should have been. "This is a thing of such moment that it requires to be pondered again and again. A man has to think of himself, and of her, and of the children which have to come after him;—of the total good or total bad which may come of such a decision." As in the one manner there is too much of negligence, so in the other there may be too much of care. The "perhaps I might as wells,"—so good is Providence,—are sometimes more successful than those careful, long-pondering heroes. The old parson was very sweet to Alice, believing that she would be his daughter-in-law, and so was Miss Rossiter, thoroughly approving of such a sister. But Mrs. Rossiter was a little cold;—all of which Alice could read plainly and digest, without saying a word. If it was to be, she would welcome her happy lot with heartfelt acknowledgment of the happiness provided for her; but if it was not to be, no human being should know that she had sorrowed. There should be nothing lack-a-daisical in her life or conduct. She had her work to do, and she knew that as long as she did that, grief would not overpower her.

In her own house it was taken for granted that she was to "go," in a manner that distressed her. "You'll never be here to lengthen 'em," said her stepmother to her, almost whining, when there was a question as to flounces in certain juvenile petticoats which might require to be longer than they were first made before they should be finally abandoned.

"That I certainly shall if Tiny grows as she does now."

"I suppose he'll pop regularly when he next comes down," said Mrs. Dugdale.

There was ever so much in this which annoyed Alice. In the first place, the word "pop" was to her abominable. Then she was almost called upon to deny that he would "pop," when in her heart she thought it very probable that he might. And the word, she knew, had become intelligible to the eldest of her little sister's who was present. Moreover, she was most unwilling to discuss the subject at all, and could hardly leave it undiscussed when such direct questions were asked. "Mamma," she said, "don't let us think about anything of the kind." This did not at all satisfy herself. She ought to have repudiated the lover altogether; and yet she could not bring herself to tell the necessary lie.

"I suppose he will come—some day," said Minnie, the child old enough to understand the meaning of such coming.

"For men may come and men may go,
But I go on for ever,—for ever,"

said or sang Alice, with a pretence of drollery, as she turned herself to her little sister. But even in her little song there was a purpose. Let any man come or let any man go, she would go on, at any rate apparently untroubled, in her walk of life.

"Of course he'll take you away, and then what am I to do?" said Mrs. Dugdale moaning. It is sad enough for a girl thus to have her lover thrown in her face when she is by no means sure of her lover.

A day or two afterwards another word, much more painful, was said to her up at the parsonage. Into the parsonage she went frequently to show that there was nothing in her heart to prevent her visiting her old friends as had been her wont.

"John will be down here next week," said the parson, whom she met on the gravel drive just at the hall door.

"How often he comes! What do they do at the Horse Guards, or wherever it is that he goes to?"

"He'll be more steady when he has taken a wife," said the old man.

"In the meantime what becomes of the cavalry?"

"I dare say you'll know all about that before long," said the parson laughing.

"Now, my dear, how can you be so foolish as to fill the girl's head with nonsense of that kind?" said Mrs. Rossiter, who at that moment came out from the front door. "And you're doing John an injustice. You are making people believe that he has said that which he has not said."

Alice at the moment was very angry,—as angry as she well could be. It was certain that Mrs. Rossiter did not know what 'her son had said or had not said. But it was cruel that she who had put forward no claim, who had never been forward in seeking her lover, should be thus almost publicly rebuked. Quiet as she wished to be, it was necessary that she should say one word in her own defence. "I don't think Mr. Rossiter's little joke will do John any injustice or me any harm," she said. "But, as it may be taken seriously, I hope he will not repeat it."

"He could not do better for himself. That's my opinion," said the old man, turning back into the house. There had been words before on the subject between him and his wife, and he was not well pleased with her at this moment.

"My dear Alice, I am sure you know that I mean everything the best for you," said Mrs. Rossiter.

"If nobody would mean anything, but just let me alone, that would be best. And as for nonsense, Mrs. Rossiter, don't you know of me that I'm not likely to be carried away by foolish ideas of that kind?"

"I do know that you are very good."

"Then why should you talk at me as though I were very bad?" Mrs. Rossiter felt that she had been reprimanded, and was less inclined than ever to accept Alice as a daughter-in-law.

Alice, as she walked home, was low in spirits, and angry with herself because it was so. People would be fools. Of course that was to be expected. She had known all along that Mrs. Rossiter wanted a grander wife for her son, whereas the parson was anxious to have her for his daughter-in-law. Of course she loved the parson better than his wife. But why was it that she felt at this moment that Mrs. Rossiter would prevail?

"Of course it will be so," she said to herself. "I see it now. And I suppose he is right. But then certainly he ought not to have come here. But perhaps he comes because he wishes to—see Miss Wanless." She went a little out of her road home, not only to dry a tear, but to rid herself of the effect of it, and then spent the remainder of the afternoon swinging her brothers and sisters in the garden.

CHAPTER II.

MAJOR ROSSITER.

"PERHAPS he is coming here to see Miss Wanless," Alice had said to herself. And in the course of that week she found that her surmise was correct. John Rossiter stayed only one night at the parsonage, and then went over to Brook Park where lived Sir Walter Wanless and all the Wanlesses. The parson had not so declared when he told Alice that his son was coming, but John himself said on his arrival that this was a special visit made to Brook Park, and not to Beetham. It had been promised for the last three months, though only fixed lately. He took the trouble to come across to the doctor's house with the express purpose of explaining the fact. "I suppose you have always been intimate with them," said Mrs. Dugdale, who was sitting with Alice and a little crowd of the children round them. There was a tone of sarcasm in the words not at all hidden. "We all know that you are a great deal finer than we mere village folk. We don't know the Wanlesses, but of course you do. You'll find yourself much more at home at Brook Park than you can in such a place as this." All that, though not spoken, was contained in the tone of the lady's speech.

"We have always been neighbours," said John Rossiter.

"Neighbours ten miles off!" said Mrs Dugdale.

"I dare say the Good Samaritan lived thirty miles off," said Alice.

"I don't think distance has much to do with it," said the Major.

"I like my neighbours to be neighbourly. I like Beetham neighbours," said Mrs. Dugdale. There was a reproach in every word of it. Mrs. Dugdale had heard of Miss Georgiana Wanless, and Major Rossiter knew that she had done so. After her fashion the lady was accusing him for deserting Alice.

Alice understood it also, and yet it behoved her to hold herself well up and be cheerful. "I like Beetham people best myself," she said, "but then it is because I don't know any other. I remember going to Brook Park once, when there was a party of children, a hundred years ago, and I thought it quite a paradise. There was a profusion of strawberries by which my imagination has been troubled ever since. You'll just be in time for the strawberries, Major Rossiter." He had always been John till quite lately,—John with the memories of childhood; but now he had become Major Rossiter.

She went out into the garden with him for a moment as he took his leave,—not quite alone, as a little boy of two years old was clinging to her hand. "If I had my way," she said, "I'd have my neighbours everywhere,—at any distance. I envy a man chiefly for that."

"Those one loves best should be very near, I think."

"Those one loves best of all? Oh yes, so that one may do something. It wouldn't do not to have you every day, would it, Bobby?" Then she allowed the willing little urchin to struggle up into her arms and to kiss her, all smeared as was his face with bread-and-butter.

"Your mother meant to say that I was running away from my old friends."

"Of course she did. You see, you loom so very large to us here. You are—such a swell, as Dick says, that we are a little sore when you pass us by. Everybody likes to be bowed to by royalty. Don't you know that? Brook Park is, of course, the proper place for you; but you don't expect but what we are going to express our little disgusts and little prides when we find ourselves left behind!" No words could have less declared her own feelings on the matter than those she was uttering; but she found herself compelled to laugh at him, lest, in the other direction, something of tenderness might escape her, whereby he might be injured worse than by her raillery. In nothing that she might say could there be less of real reproach to him than in this.

"I hate that word 'swell,'" he said.

"So do I."

"Then why do you use it?"

"To show you how much better Brook Park is than Beetham. I am sure they don't talk about swells at Brook Park."

"Why do you throw Brook Park in my teeth?"

"I feel an inclination to make myself disagreeable to-day. Are you never like that?"

"I hope not."

"And then I am bound to follow up what poor dear mamma began. But I won't throw Brook Park in your teeth. The ladies I know are very nice. Sir Walter Wanless is a little grand;—isn't he?"

"You know," said he, "that I should be much happier here than there."

"Because Sir Walter is so grand?"

"Because my friends here are dearer friends. But still it is right that I should go. One cannot always be where one would be happiest."

"I am happiest with Bobby," said she; "and I can always have Bobby." Then she gave him her hand at the gate, and he went down to the parsonage.

That night Mrs. Rossiter was closeted for awhile with her son before they both went to bed. She was supposed, in Beetham, to be of a higher order of intellect,—of a higher stamp generally,—than her husband or daughter, and to be in that respect nearly on a par with her son. She had not travelled as he had done, but she was of an ambitious mind and had thoughts beyond Beetham. The poor dear parson cared for little outside the bounds of his parish. "I am so glad you are going to stay for awhile over at Brook Park," she said.

"Only for three days."

"In the intimacy of a house three days is a lifetime. Of course I do not like to interfere." When this was said the Major frowned, knowing well that his mother was going to interfere. "But I cannot help thinking how much a connection with the Wanlesses would do for you."

"I don't want anything from any connection."

"That is all very well, John, for a man to say; but in truth we all depend on connections one with another. You are beginning the world."

"I don't know about that, mother."

"To my eyes you are. Of course, you look upwards."

"I take all that as it comes."

"No doubt; but still you must have it in your mind to rise. A man is assisted very much by the kind of wife he marries. Much would be done for a son-in-law of Sir Walter Wanless."

"Nothing, I hope, ever for me on that score. To succeed by favour is odious."

"But even to rise by merit, so much outside assistance is often necessary! Though you will assuredly deserve all that you will ever get, yet you may be more likely to get it as a son-in-law to Sir Walter Wanless than if you were married to some obscure girl. Men who make the most of themselves in the world do think of these things. I am the last woman in the world to recommend my boy to look after money in marriage."

"The Miss Wanlesses will have none."

"And therefore I can speak the more freely. They will have very little,—as coming from such a family. But he has great influence. He has contested the county five times. And then—where is there a handsomer girl than Georgiana Wanless?" The Major thought that he knew one, but did not answer the question. "And she is all that such a girl ought to be. Her manners are perfect,—and her conduct. A constant performance of domestic duties is of course admirable. If it comes to one to have to wash linen, she who washes her linen well is a good woman. But among mean things high spirits are not to be found."

"I am not so sure of that."

"It must be so. How can the employment of every hour in the day on menial work leave time for the mind to fill itself? Making children's frocks may be a duty, but it must also be an impediment."

"You are speaking of Alice."

"Of course I am speaking of Alice."

"I would wager my head that she has read twice more in the last two years than Georgiana Wanless. But, mother, I am not disposed to discuss either the one young lady or the other. I am not going to Brook Park to look for a wife; and if ever I take one, it will be simply because I like her best, and not because I wish to use her as a rung of a ladder by which to climb upwards into the world." That all this and just this would be said to her Mrs. Rossiter had been aware; but still she had thought that a word in season might have its effect.

And it did have its effect. John Rossiter, as he was driven over to Brook Park on the following morning, was unconsciously mindful of that allusion to the washerwoman. He had seen that Alice's cheek had been smirched by the greasy crumbs from her little brother's mouth, he had seen that the tips of her fingers showed the mark of the needle; he had seen fragments of thread about her dress, and the mud even from the children's boots on her skirts. He had seen this, and had been aware that Georgiana Wanless was free from all such soil on her outward raiment. He liked the perfect grace of unspotted feminine apparel, and he had, too, thought of the hours in which Alice might probably be employed amidst the multifarious needs of a nursery, and had argued to himself much as his mother had argued. It was good and homely,—worthy of a thousand praises; but was it exactly that which he wanted in a wife? He had repudiated with scorn his mother's cold, worldly doctrine; but yet he had felt that it would be a pleasant thing to have it known in London that his wife was the daughter of Sir Walter Wanless. It was true that she was wonderfully handsome,—a complexion perfectly clear, a nose cut as out of marble, a mouth delicate as of a goddess, with a waist quite to match it. Her shoulders were white as alabaster. Her dress was at all times perfect. Her fingers were without mark or stain. There might perhaps be a want of expression; but faces so symmetrical are seldom expressive. And then, to crown all this, he was justified in believing that she was attached to himself. Almost as much had been said to him by Lady Wanless herself,—a word which would amount to as much, coupled as it was with an immediate invitation to Brook

Park. Of this he had given no hint to any human being; but he had been at Brook Park once before, and some rumour of something between him and Miss Georgiana Wanless had reached the people at Beetham, —had reached, as we have seen, not only Mrs. Rossiter, but also Alice Dugdale.

There had been moments up in London when his mind had veered round towards Miss Wanless. But there was one little trifle which opposed the action of his mind, and that was his heart. He had begun to think that it might be his duty to marry Georgiana; —but the more he thought so the more clearly would the figure of Alice stand before him, so that no veil could be thrown over it. When he tried to summon to his imagination the statuesque beauty of the one girl, the bright eyes of the other would look at him, and the words from her speaking mouth would be in his ears. He had once kissed Alice, immediately on his return, in the presence of her father, and the memory of the halcyon moment was always present to him. When he thought most of Miss Wanless he did not think much of her kisses. How grand she would be at his dining-table, how glorious in his drawing-room! But with Alice how sweet would it be to sit by some brook side and listen to the waters!

And now since he had been at Beetham, from the nature of things which sometimes make events to come from exactly contrary causes, a new charm had been added to Alice, simply by the little effort she had made to annoy him. She had talked to him of "swells," and had pretended to be jealous of the Wanlesses, just because she had known that he would hate to hear such a word from her lips, and that he would be vexed by exhibition of such a feeling on her part! He was quite sure that she had not committed these sins because they belonged to her as a matter of course. Nothing could be more simple than her natural language or her natural feelings. But she had chosen to show him that she was ready to run into little faults which might offend him. The reverse of her ideas came upon him. She had said, as it were,—"See how little anxious I must be to dress myself in your mirror when I put myself in the same category with my poor stepmother." Then he said to himself that he could see her as he was fain to see her, in her own mirror, and he loved her the better because she had dared to run the risk of offending him.

As he was driven up to the house at Brook Park he knew that it was his destiny to marry either the one girl or the other; and he was afraid of himself,—that before he left the house he might be engaged to the one he did not love. There was a moment in which he thought he would turn round and go back. "Major Rossiter," Lady Wanless had said, "you know how glad we are to see you here. There is no young man of the day of whom Sir Walter thinks so much." Then he had thanked her. "But—may I say a word in warning?"

"Certainly."

"And I may trust to your honour?"

"I think so, Lady Wanless."

"Do not be much with that sweet darling of mine, —unless indeed—" And then she had stopped. Major Rossiter, though he was a major and had served some years in India, blushed up to his eyebrows and was unable to answer a word. But he knew that Georgiana Wanless had been offered to him, and was entitled to believe that the young lady was prone to fall in love with him. Lady Wanless, had she been asked for an excuse for such conduct, would have said that the young men of the present day were slow in managing their own affairs, unless a little help were given to them.

When the Major was almost immediately invited to return to Brook Park, he could not but feel that, if he were so to make his choice, he would be received there as a son-in-law. It may be that unless he intended so to be received, he should not have gone. This he felt as he was driven across the park, and was almost minded to return to Beetham.

CHAPTER III.

LADY WANLESS.

Sir Walter Wanless was one of those great men who never do anything great, but achieve their greatness partly by their tailors, partly by a breadth of eyebrow and carriage of the body,—what we may call deportment,—and partly by the outside gifts of fortune. Taking his career altogether we must say that he had been unfortunate. He was a baronet with a fine house and park,—and with an income hardly sufficient for the place. He had contested the county four times on old Whig principles, and had once been in Parliament for two years. There he had never opened his mouth; but in his struggle to get there had greatly embarrassed his finances. His tailor had been well chosen, and had always turned him out as the best dressed old baronet in England. His eyebrow was all his own, and certainly commanded respect from those with whom eyebrows are efficacious. He never read; he eschewed farming, by which he had lost money in early life; and had, so to say, no visible occupation at all. But he was Sir Walter Wanless, and what with his tailor and what with his eyebrow he did command a great deal of respect in the country round Beetham. He had, too, certain good gifts for which people were thankful as coming from so great a man. He paid his bills, he went to church, he was well behaved, and still maintained certain old-fashioned family charities, though money was not plentiful with him.

He had two sons and five daughters. The sons were in the army, and were beyond his control. The daughters were all at home, and were altogether under the control of their mother. Indeed everything at Brook Park was under the control of Lady Wanless,—though no man alive gave himself airs more autocratic than Sir Walter. It was on her shoulders that fell the burden of the five daughters, and of maintaining with straitened means the hospitality of Brook Park on their behoof. A hard-worked woman was Lady Wanless, in doing her duty,—with imperfect lights no doubt, but to the best of her abilities with such lights as she possessed. She was somewhat fine in her dress, not for any comfort that might accrue to herself, but from a feeling that an alliance with the Wanlesses would not be valued by the proper sort of young men unless she were grand herself. The girls were beautifully dressed; but oh, with such care and economy and daily labour among them, herself, and the two lady's-maids upstairs! The father, what with his election and his farming, and a period of costly living early in his life, had not done well for the family. That she knew, and never rebuked him. But it was for her to set matters right, which she could only do by getting husbands for the daughters. That this might be achieved the Wanless prestige must be maintained; and with crippled means it is so hard to maintain a family prestige! A poor duke may do it, or perhaps an earl; but a baronet is not high enough to give bad wines to his guests without serious detriment to his unmarried daughters.

A beginning to what might be hoped to be a long line of successes had already been made. The eldest girl, Sophia, was engaged. Lady Wanless did not look very high, knowing that failure in such operations will bring with it such unutterable misfortune. Sophia was engaged to the eldest son of a neighbouring Squire,—whose property indeed was not large, nor was the squire likely to die very soon; but there were the means of present living and a future rental of £4,000 a year. Young Mr. Cobble was now staying at the house, and had been duly accepted by Sir Walter himself. The youngest girl, who was only nineteen, had fallen in love with a young clergyman in the neighbourhood. That would not do at all, and the young clergyman was not allowed within the Park. Georgiana was the beauty; and for her, if for any, some great destiny might have been hoped. But it was her turn, a matter of which Lady Wanless thought a great deal, and the Major was too good to be allowed to escape. Georgiana, in her cold, impassive way, seemed to like the Major, and therefore Lady Wanless paired them off instantly with that decision which was necessary amidst the labours of her life. She had no scruples in what she did, feeling sure that her daughters would make honest, good wives, and that the blood of the Wanlesses was a dowry in itself.

The Major had been told to come early, because a party was made to visit certain ruins about eight miles off,—Castle Owless, as it was called,—to which Lady Wanless was accustomed to take her guests, because the family history declared that the Wanlesses had lived there at some very remote period. It still belonged to Sir Walter, though unfortunately the intervening lands had for the most part fallen into other hands. Owless and Wanless were supposed to be the same, and thus there was room for a good deal of family tattle.

"I am delighted to see you at Brook Park," said Sir

Walter as they met at the luncheon table. "When I was at Christchurch your father was at Wadham, and I remember him well." Exactly the same words had been spoken when the Major, on a former occasion, had been made welcome at the house, and clearly implied a feeling that Christchurch, though much superior, may condescend to know Wadham—under certain circumstances. Of the Baronet nothing further was heard or seen till dinner.

Lady Wanless went in the open carriage with three daughters, Sophie being one of them. As her affair was settled it was not necessary that one of the two side-saddles should be allotted to her use. Young Cobble, who had been asked to send two horses over from Cobble Hall so that Rossiter might ride one, felt this very hard. But there was no appeal from Lady Wanless. "You'll have plenty enough of her all the evening." said the mother, patting him affectionately, "and it is so necessary just at present that Georgiana and Edith should have horse exercise." In this way it was arranged that Georgiana should ride with the Major, and Edith, the third daughter, with young Burmeston, the son of Cox and Burmeston, brewers at the neighbouring town of Slowbridge. A country brewer is not quite what Lady Wanless would have liked; but with difficulties such as hers a rich young brewer might be worth having. All this was hard upon Mr. Cobble, who would not have sent his horses over had he known it.

Our Major saw at a glance that Georgiana rode well.

He liked ladies to ride, and doubted whether Alice had ever been on horseback in her life. After all, how many advantages does a girl lose by having to pass her days in a nursery! For a moment some such idea crossed his mind. Then he asked Georgiana some question as to the scenery through which they were passing. "Very fine, indeed," said Georgiana. She looked square before her, and sat with her back square to the horse's tail. There was no hanging in the saddle, no shifting about in uneasiness. She could rise and fall easily, even gracefully, when the horse trotted. "You are fond of riding I can see," said the Major. "I do like riding," answered Georgiana. The tone in which she spoke of her present occupation was much more lively than that in which she had expressed her approbation of scenery.

At the ruin they all got down, and Lady Wanless told them the entire story of the Owlesses and the Wanlesses, and filled the brewer's mind with wonder as to the antiquity and dignity of the family. But the Major was the fish just at this moment in hand. "The Rossiters are very old, too," she said smiling; "but perhaps that is a kind of thing you don't care for."

"Very much indeed," said he. Which was true,—for he was proud of knowing that he had come from the Rossiters who had been over four hundred years in Herefordshire. "A remembrance of old merit will always be an incitement to new."

"It is just that, Major Rossiter. It is strange how very nearly in the same words Georgiana said the same thing to me yesterday." Georgiana happened to overhear this, but did not contradict her mother, though she made a grimace to her sister which was seen by no one else. Then Lady Wanless slipped aside to assist the brewer and Edith, leaving the Major and her second daughter together. The two younger girls, of whom the youngest was the wicked one with the penchant for the curate, were wandering among the ruins by themselves.

"I wonder whether there ever were any people called Owless," said Rossiter, not quite knowing what subject of conversation to choose.

"Of course there were. Mamma always says so."

"That settles the question;—does it not?"

"I don't see why there shouldn't be Owlesses. No; I won't sit on the wall, thank you, because I should stain my habit."

"But you'll be tired."

"Not particularly tired. It is not so very far. I'd go back in the carriage, only of course we can't because of the habits. Oh, yes; I'm very fond of dancing,—very fond indeed. We always have two balls every year at Slowbridge. And there are some others about the county. I don't think you ever have balls at Beetham."

"There is no one to give them."

"Does Miss Dugdale ever dance?"

The Major had to think for a moment before he could answer the question. Why should Miss Wanless ask as to Alice's dancing? "I am sure she does. Now

I think of it I have heard her talk of dancing. You don't know Alice Dugdale?" Miss Wanless shook her head. "She is worth knowing."

"I am quite sure she is. I have always heard that you thought so. She is very good to all those children; isn't she?"

"Very good indeed."

"She would be almost pretty if she wasn't so,—so, so dumpy I should say." Then they got on their horses again and rode back to Brook Park. Let Georgiana be ever so tired she did not show it, but rode in under the portico with perfect equestrian grace.

"I'm afraid you took too much out of her," said Lady Wanless to the Major that evening. Georgiana had gone to bed a little earlier than the others.

This was in some degree hard upon him, as he had not proposed the ride,—and he excused himself. "It was you arranged it all, Lady Wanless."

"Yes indeed," said she, smiling. "I did arrange the little excursion, but it was not I who kept her talking the whole day." Now this again was felt to be unfair, as nearly every word of conversation between the young people has been given in this little chronicle.

On the following day the young people were again thrust together, and before they parted for the night another little word was spoken by Lady Wanless which indicated very clearly that there was some special bond of friendship between the Major and her second daughter. "You are quite right," she had said in answer to some extracted compliment; "she does ride very well. When I was up in town in May I thought I saw no one with such a seat in the row. Miss Green, who taught the Duchess of Ditchwater's daughters, declared that she knew nothing like it."

On the third morning he returned to Beetham early, as he intended to go up to town the same afternoon. Then there was prepared for him a little valedictory opportunity in which he could not but press the young lady's fingers for a moment. As he did so no one was looking at him, but then he knew that it was so much the more dangerous because no one was looking. Nothing could be more knowing than the conduct of the young lady, who was not in any way too forward. If she admitted that slight pressure, it was done with a retiring rather than obtrusive favour. It was not by her own doing that she was alone with him for a moment. There was no casting down or casting up of her eyes. And yet it seemed to him as he left her and went out into the hall that there had been so much between them that he was almost bound to propose to her. In the hall there was the Baronet to bid him farewell,—an honour which he did to his guests only when he was minded to treat them with great distinction. "Lady Wanless and I are delighted to have had you here," he said. "Remember me to your father, and tell him that I remember him very well when I was at Christchurch and he was at Wadham." It was something to have had one's hand taken in so paternal a manner by a baronet with such an eyebrow, and such a coat.

And yet when he returned to Beetham he was not in a good-humour with himself. It seemed to him that he had been almost absorbed among the Wanlesses without any action or will of his own. He tried to comfort himself by declaring that Georgiana was, without doubt, a remarkably handsome young woman, and that she was a perfect horsewoman,—as though all that were a matter to him of any moment! Then he went across to the doctor's house to say a word of farewell to Alice.

"Have you had a pleasant visit?" she asked.

"Oh, yes; all very well."

"That second Miss Wanless is quite beautiful; is she not?"

"She is handsome certainly."

"I call her lovely," said Alice. "You rode with her the other day over to that old castle."

Who could have told this of him already? "Yes; there was a party of us went over."

"When are you going there again?" Now something had been said of a further visit, and Rossiter had almost promised that he would return. It is impossible not to promise when undefined invitations are given. A man cannot declare that he is engaged for ever and ever. But how was it that Alice knew all that had been said and done? "I cannot say that I have fixed any exact day," he replied almost angrily.

"I've heard all about you, you know. That young Mr. Burmeston was at Mrs. Tweed's and told them what a favourite you are. If it be true I will congratulate you, because I do really think that the young lady is the most beautiful that I ever saw in my life." This she said with a smile and a good-humoured little shake of the head. If it was to be that her heart must be broken he at least should not know it. And she still hoped, she still thought, that by being very constant at her work she might get over it.

CHAPTER IV.

THE BEETHAMITES.

It was told all through Beetham before a week was over that Major Rossiter was to marry the second Miss Wanless, and Beetham liked the news. Beetham was proud that one of her sons should be introduced into the great neighbouring family, and especially that he should be honoured by the hand of the acknowledged beauty. Beetham, a month ago, had declared that Alice Dugdale, a Beethamite herself from her babyhood,—who had been born and bred at Beetham and had ever lived there,—was to be honoured by the hand of the young hero. But it may be doubted whether Beetham had been altogether satisfied with the arrangement. We are apt to envy the good luck of those who have always been familiar with us. Why should it have been Alice Dugdale any more than one of the Tweed girls, or Miss Simkins, the daughter of the attorney, who would certainly have a snug little fortune of her own,—which unfortunately would not be the case with Alice Dugdale? It had been felt that Alice was hardly good enough for their hero,—Alice who had been seen about with all the Dugdale children, pushing them in perambulators almost every day since the eldest was born! We prefer the authority of a stranger to that of one chosen from among ourselves. As the two Miss Tweeds, and Miss Simkins, with Alice and three or four others, could not divide the hero among them, it was better then that the hero should go from among them, and choose a fitting mate in a higher realm. They all felt the greatness of the Wanlesses, and argued with Mrs. Rossiter that the rising star of the village should obtain such assistance in rising as would come to him from an almost noble marriage.

There had been certainly a decided opinion that Alice was to be the happy woman. Mrs. Dugdale, the stepmother, had boasted of the promotion; and old Mr. Rossiter had whispered his secret conviction into the ear of every favoured parishioner. The doctor himself had allowed his patients to ask questions about it. This had become so common that Alice herself had been inwardly indignant,—would have been outwardly indignant but that she could not allow herself to discuss the matter. That having been so, Beetham ought to have been scandalised by the fickleness of her hero. Beetham ought to have felt that her hero was most unheroic. But, at any rate among the ladies, there was no shadow of such a feeling. Of course such a man as the Major was bound to do the best for himself. The giving away of his hand in marriage was a very serious thing, and was not to be obligatory on a young hero because he had been carried away by the fervour of old friendship to kiss a young lady immediately on his return home. The history of the kiss was known all over Beetham, and was declared by competent authorities to have amounted to nothing. It was a last lingering touch of childhood's happy embracings, and if Alice was such a fool as to take it for more, she must pay the penalty of her folly. "It was in her father's presence," said Mrs. Rossiter, defending her son to Mrs. Tweed, and Mrs. Tweed had expressed her opinion that the kiss ought to go for nothing. The Major was to be acquitted,—and the fact of the acquittal made its way even to the doctor's nursery; so that Alice knew that the man might marry that girl at Brook Park with clean hands. That, as she declared to herself, did not increase her sorrow. If the man were minded to marry the girl he was welcome for her. And she apologised for him to her own heart. What a man generally wants, she said, is a beautiful wife; and of the beauty of Miss Georgiana Wanless there could be no doubt. Only,—only—only, there had been a dozen words which he should have left unspoken!

That which riveted the news on the minds of the Beethamites was the stopping of the Brook Park carriage at the door of the parsonage one day about a week after the Major's visit. It was not altogether an unprecedented occurrence. Had there been no precedent it could hardly have been justified on the present occasion. Perhaps once in two years Lady Wanless would call at the parsonage, and then there would be a return visit during which a reference would always be made to Wadham and Christchurch. The visit was now out of its order, only nine months having elapsed,—of which irregularity Beetham took due notice. On this occasion Miss Wanless and the third young lady accompanied their mother, leaving Georgiana at home. What was whispered between the two old ladies Beetham did not quite know,—but made its surmises. It was in this wise. "We were so glad to have the Major over with us," said her ladyship.

"It was so good of you," said Mrs. Rossiter.

"He is a great favourite with Sir Walter."

"That is so good of Sir Walter."

"And we are quite pleased to have him among our young people." That was all, but it was quite sufficient to tell Mrs. Rossiter that John might have Georgiana Wanless for the asking, and that Lady Wanless expected him to ask. Then the parting was much more affectionate than it had ever been before, and there was a squeezing of the hand and a nodding of the head which meant a great deal.

Alice held her tongue, and did her work and attempted to be cheery through it all. Again and again she asked herself,—what did it matter? Even though she were unhappy, even though she felt a keen, palpable, perpetual aching at her heart, what would it matter so long as she could go about and do her business? Some people in this world had to be unhappy;—perhaps most people. And this was a sorrow which, though it might not wear off, would by wearing become dull enough to be bearable. She distressed herself in that there was any sorrow. Providence had given to her a certain condition of life to which many charms were attached. She thoroughly loved the people about her,—her father, her little brothers and sisters, even her overworn and somewhat idle stepmother. She was a queen in the house, a queen among her busy toils; and she liked being a queen, and liked being busy. No one ever scolded her or crossed her or contradicted her. She had the essential satisfaction of the consciousness of usefulness. Why should not that suffice to her? She despised herself because there was a hole in her heart,—because she felt herself to shrink all over when the name of Georgiana Wanless was mentioned in her hearing. Yet she would mention the name herself, and speak with something akin to admiration of the Wanless family. And she would say how well it was that men should strive to rise in the world, and how that the world progressed through such individual efforts. But she would not mention the name of John Rossiter, nor would she endure that it should be mentioned in her hearing with any special reference to herself.

Mrs. Dugdale, though she was overworn and idle,—a warped and almost useless piece of furniture, made, as was said before, of bad timber,—yet saw more of this than anyone else, and was indignant. To lose Alice, to have no one to let down those tucks and take up those stitches, would be to her the loss of all her comforts. But, though she was feckless, she was true-hearted, and she knew that Alice was being wronged. It was Alice that had a right to the hero, and not that stuck-up young woman at Brook Park. It was thus she spoke of the affair to the doctor, and after awhile found herself unable to be silent on the subject to Alice herself. "If what they say does take place I shall think worse of John Rossiter than I ever did of any man I ever knew." This she said in the presence both of her husband and her step-daughter.

"John Rossiter will not be very much the worse for that," said Alice without relaxing a moment from her work. There was a sound of drolling in her voice, as though she were quizzing her stepmother for her folly.

"It seems to me that men may do anything now," continued Mrs. Dugdale.

"I suppose they are the same now as they always were," said the doctor. "If a man chose to be false he could always be false."

"I call it unmanly," said Mrs. Dugdale. "If I were a man I would beat him."

"What would you beat him for?" said Alice, getting up, and as she did so throwing down on the table before her the little frock she was making. "If you had the power of beating him, why would you beat him?"

"Because he is ill-using you."

"How do you know that? Did I ever tell you so?

Have you ever heard a word that he has said to me, either direct from himself, or second-hand, that justifies you in saying that he has ill-used me? You ill-use me when you speak like that."

"Alice, do not be so violent," said the doctor.

"Father, I will speak of this once, and once for all;—and then pray, pray, let there be no further mention of it. I have no right to complain of anything in Major Rossiter. He has done me no wrong. Those who love me should not mention his name in reference to me."

"He is a villain," said Mrs. Dugdale.

"He is no villain. He is a gentleman, as far as I know, from the crown of his head to the sole of his foot. Does it ever occur to you how little you make of me when you talk of him in this way? Dismiss it all from your mind, father, and let things be as they were. Do you think that I am pining for any man's love? I say that Major Rossiter is a true man and a gentleman;—but I would not give my Bobby's little finger for all his whole body." Then there was silence, and afterwards the doctor told his wife that the Major's name had better not be mentioned again among them. Alice on this occasion was, or appeared to be, very angry with Mrs. Dugdale; but on that evening and the next morning there was an accession of tenderness in her usually sweet manner to her stepmother. The expression of her mother's anger against the Major had been wrong;—but the feeling of anger was not the less endearing.

Some time after that, one evening, the parson came

upon Alice as she was picking flowers in one of the Beetham lanes. She had all the children with her, and was filling Minnie's apron with roses from the hedge. Old Mr. Rossiter stopped and talked to them, and after awhile succeeded in getting Alice to walk on with him. "You haven't heard from John?" he said.

"Oh, no," replied Alice, almost with a start. And then she added quickly, "There is no one at our house likely to hear from him. He does not write to any-one there."

"I did not know whether any message might have reached you."

"I think not."

"He is to be here again before long," said the parson.

"Oh, indeed." She had but a moment to think of it all; but, after thinking, she continued, "I suppose he will be going over to Brook Park."

"I fear he will."

"Fear;—why should you fear, Mr. Rossiter? If that is true, it is the place where he ought to be."

"But I doubt its truth, my dear."

"Ah! I know nothing about that. If so he had better stay up in London, I suppose."

"I don't think John can care much for Miss Wanless."

"Why not? She is the most thoroughly beautiful young woman I ever saw."

"I don't think he does, because I believe his heart is elsewhere. Alice, you have his heart."

"No."

"I think so, Alice."

"No, Mr. Rossiter. I have not. It is not so. I know nothing of Miss Wanless, but I can speak of myself."

"It seems to me that you are speaking of him now."

"Then why does he go there?"

"That is just what I cannot answer. Why does he go there? Why do we do the worst thing so often, when we see the better?"

"But we don't leave undone the thing which we wish to do, Mr. Rossiter."

"That is just what we do do,—under constraint. Alice, I hope, I hope that you may become his wife." She endeavoured to deny that it could ever be so;—she strove to declare that she herself was much too heart-free for that; but the words would not come to her lips, and she could only sob while she struggled to retain her tears. "If he does come to you give him a chance again, even though he may have been untrue to you for a moment."

Then she was left alone among the children. She could dry her tears and suppress her sobs, because Minnie was old enough to know the meaning of them if she saw them; but she could not for awhile go back into the house. She left them in the passage and then went out again, and walked up and down a little pathway that ran through the shrubs at the bottom of the garden. "I believe his heart is elsewhere." Could it be that it was so? And if so, of what nature can be a man's love, if when it be given in one direction, he can go in another with his hand? She could understand that there had not been much heart in it;—that he, being a man and not a woman, could have made this turning point of his life an affair of calculation, and had taken himself here or there without much love at all; that as he would seek a commodious house, so would he also a convenient wife. Resting on that suggestion to herself, she had dared to declare to her father and mother that Major Rossiter was, not a villain, but a perfect gentleman. But all that was not compatible with his father's story. "Alice, you have his heart," the old man had said. How had it come to pass that the old man had known it? And yet the assurance was so sweet, so heavenly, so laden to her ears with divine music, that at this moment she would not even ask herself to disbelieve it. "If he does come to you, give him a chance again." Why;—yes! Though she never spoke a word of Miss Wanless without praise, though she had tutored herself to swear that Miss Wanless was the very wife for him, yet she knew herself too well not to know that she was better than Miss Wanless. For his sake, she could with a clear conscience—give him a chance again. The dear old parson! He had seen it all. He had known. He had appreciated. If it should ever come to pass that she was to be his daughter-in-law, he should have his reward. She would not tell herself that she expected him to come again; but, if he did come, she would give the parson his chance. Such was her idea at that moment. But she was forced to change it before long.

CHAPTER V.

THE INVITATION.

When Major Rossiter discussed his own conduct with himself as men are so often compelled to do by their own conscience, in opposition to their own wishes, he was not well pleased with himself. On his return home from India he had found himself possessed of a liberal income, and had begun to enjoy himself without thinking much about marrying. It is not often that a man looks for a wife because he has made up his mind that he wants the article. He roams about unshackled, till something, which at the time seems to be altogether desirable, presents itself to him ; and then he meditates marriage. So it had been with our Major. Alice had presented herself to him as something altogether desirable,—a something which, when it was touched and looked at, seemed to be so full of sweetnesses, that to him it was for the moment of all things the most charming. He was not a forward man,—one of those who can see a girl for the first time on a Monday, and propose to her on the Tuesday. When the idea first suggested itself to him of making Alice his wife he became reticent and undemonstrative. The kiss had in truth meant no more than Mrs. Tweed had said.

When he began to feel that he loved her, then he hardly dared to dream of kissing her.

But though he felt that he loved her,—liked perhaps it would be fairer to say in that early stage of his feelings,—better than any other woman, yet when he came to think of marriage, the importance of it all made him hesitate; and he was reminded, by little hints from others, and by words plain enough from one person, that Alice Dugdale was after all a common thing. There is a fitness in such matters,—so said Mrs. Rossiter,—and a propriety in like being married to like. Had it been his lot to be a village doctor, Alice would have suited him well. Destiny, however, had carried him,—the Major,—higher up, and would require him to live in London, among ornate people, with polished habits, and peculiar manners of their own. Would not Alice be out of her element in London? See the things among which she passed her life! Not a morsel of soap or a pound of sugar was used in the house, but what she gave it out. Her hours were passed in washing, teaching, and sewing for the children. In her very walks she was always pushing a perambulator. She was, no doubt, the doctor's daughter; but, in fact, she was the second Mrs. Dugdale's nursemaid. Nothing could be more praiseworthy. But there is a fitness in things; and he, the hero of Beetham, the Assistant Deputy Inspector-General of the British Cavalry, might surely do better than marry a praiseworthy nursery girl. It was thus that Mrs. Rossiter argued with her son, and her arguments were not without avail.

Then Georgiana Wanless had been, as it were, thrown at his head. When one is pelted with sugar-plums one can hardly resent the attack. He was clever enough to feel that he was pelted, but at first he liked the sweetmeats. A girl riding on horseback, with her back square to the horse's tail, with her reins well held, and a chimney-pot hat on her head, is an object, unfortunately, more attractive to the eyes of ordinary men, than a young woman pushing a perambulator with two babies. Unfortunately, I say, because in either case the young woman should be judged by her personal merits and not by externals. But the Major declared to himself that the personal merits would be affected by the externals. A girl who had pushed a perambulator for many years, would hardly have a soul above perambulators. There would be wanting the flavour of the aroma of romance, that something of poetic vagueness without which a girl can hardly be altogether charming to the senses of an appreciative lover. Then, a little later on, he asked himself whether Georgiana Wanless was romantic and poetic,—whether there was much of true aroma there.

But yet he thought that fate would require him to marry Georgiana Wanless, whom he certainly did not love, and to leave Alice to her perambulator,—Alice, whom he certainly did love. And as he thought of this, he was ill at ease with himself. It might be well that he should give up his Assistant Deputy Inspector-Generalship, go back to India, and so get rid of his two troubles together. Fate, as he personified fate to himself in this matter,—took the form of Lady Wanless. It made him sad to think that he was but a weak creature in the hands of an old woman, who wanted to use him for a certain purpose;—but he did not see his way of escaping. When he began to console himself by reflecting that he would have one of the handsomest women in London at his dinner-table he knew that he would be unable to escape.

About the middle of July he received the following letter from Lady Wanless:—

"DEAR MAJOR ROSSITER,—The girls have been at their father for the last ten days to have an archery meeting on the lawn, and have at last prevailed, though Sir Walter has all a father's abhorrence to have the lawn knocked about. Now it is settled. 'I'll see about it,' Sir Walter said at last, and when so much as that had been obtained, they all knew that the archery meeting was to be. Sir Walter likes his own way, and is not always to be persuaded. But when he has made the slightest show of concession, he never goes back from it. Then comes the question as to the day, which is now in course of discussion in full committee. In that matter Sir Walter is supposed to be excluded from any voice. 'It cannot matter to him what day of the week or what day of the month,' said Georgiana very irreverently. It will not, however, much matter to him so long as it is all over before St. Partridge comes round.

"The girls one and all declared that you must be here,—as one of the guests in the house. Our rooms will be mostly full of young ladies, but there will be one at any rate for you. Now, what day will suit you,—or rather what day will suit the Cavalry generally? Everything must of course depend on the Cavalry. The girls say that the Cavalry is sure to go out of town after the tenth of August. But they would put it off for a week longer rather than not have the Inspector-General. Would Wednesday 14th suit the Cavalry? They are all reading every word of my letter as it is written, and bid me say that if Thursday or Friday in that week, or Wednesday or Thursday in the next, will do better, the accommodation of the Cavalry shall be consulted. It cannot be on a Monday or Saturday because there would be some Sunday encroachment. On Tuesday we cannot get the band from Slowbridge.

"Now you know our great purpose and our little difficulties. One thing you cannot know,—how determined we are to accommodate ourselves to the Cavalry. *The meeting is not to take place without the Inspector-General.* So let us have an early answer from that august functionary. The girls think that the Inspector had better come down before the day, so as to make himself useful in preparing.

"Pray believe me, with Sir Walter's kind regards, yours most sincerely,

"MARGARET WANLESS."

The Major felt that the letter was very flattering, but that it was false and written for a certain purpose. He could read between the lines at every sentence of it. The festival was to be got up, not at the instance of the girls but of Lady Wanless herself, as a final trap for the catching of himself,—and perhaps for Mr. Burmeston. Those irreverent words had never come from Georgiana, who was too placid to have said them. He did not believe a word of the girls looking over the writing of the letter. In all such matters Lady Wanless had more life, more energy than her daughters. All that little fun about the Cavalry came from Lady Wanless herself. The girls were too like their father for such ebullitions. The little sparks of joke with which the names of the girls were connected,—with which in his hearing the name of Georgiana had been specially connected,—had, he was aware, their origin always with Lady Wanless. Georgiana had said this funny thing and that,—but Georgiana never spoke after that fashion in his hearing. The traps were plain to his eyes, and yet he knew that he would sooner or later be caught in the traps.

He took a day to think of it before he answered the letter, and meditated a military tour to Berlin just about the time. If so, he must be absent during the whole of August, so as to make his presence at the toxopholite meeting an impossibility. And yet at last he wrote and said that he would be there. There would be something mean in flight. After all, he need not ask the girl to be his wife unless he chose to do so.

He wrote a very pretty note to Lady Wanless saying that he would be at Brook Park on the 14th, as she had suggested.

Then he made a great resolution and swore an oath to himself,—that he would not be caught on that occasion, and that after this meeting he would go no more either to Brook Park or to Beetham for awhile. He would not marry the girl to whom he was quite indifferent, nor her who from her position was hardly qualified to be his wife. Then he went about his duties with a quieted conscience, and wedded himself for once and for always to the Cavalry.

Some tidings of the doings proposed by the Wanlesses had reached the parson's ears when he told Alice in the lane that his son was soon coming down to Beetham again, and that he was again going to Brook Park. Before July was over the tidings of the coming festivity had been spread over all that side of the county. Such a thing had not been done for many years,—not since Lady Wanless had been herself a young wife, with two sisters for whom husbands had to be,—and were provided. There were those who could still remember how well Lady Wanless had behaved on that occasion. Since those days hospitality on a large scale had not been rife at Brook Park—and the reason why it was so was well known. Sir Walter was determined not to embarrass himself further, and would do nothing that was expensive. It could not be but that there was great cause for such a deviation as this. Then the ladies of the neighbourhood put their heads together,—and some of the gentlemen,—and declared that a double stroke of business was to be done in regard to Major Rossiter and Mr. Burmeston. How great a relief that would be to the mother's anxiety if the three eldest girls could be married and got rid of all on the same day!

Beetham, which was ten miles from Brook Park, had a station of its own, whereas Slowbridge with its own station was only six miles from the house. The Major would fain have reached his destination by Slowbridge, so as to have avoided the chance of seeing Alice, were it not that his father and mother would have felt themselves aggrieved by such desertion. On this occasion his mother begged him to give them one night. She had much that she wished to say to him, and then of course he could have the parsonage horse and the parsonage phaeton to take him over to Brook Park free of expense. He did go down to Beetham, did spend an evening there, and did go on to the Park without having spoken to Alice Dugdale.

"Everybody says you are to marry Georgiana Wanless," said Mrs. Rossiter.

"If there were no other reason why I should not, the saying of everybody would be sufficient against it."

"That is unreasonable, John. The thing should be looked at itself, whether it is good or bad. It may be the case that Lady Wanless talks more than she ought to do. It may be the case that, as people say, she is looking out for husbands for her daughters. I don't know but that I should do the same if I had five of them on my hands and very little means for them. And if I did, how could I get a better husband for one of them than—such a one as Major John Rossiter?" Then she kissed his forehead.

"I hate the kind of thing altogether," said he. He pretended to be stern, but yet he showed that he was flattered by his mother's softness.

"It may well be, John, that such a match shall be desirable to them and to you too. If so, why should there not be a fair bargain between the two of you? You know that you admire the girl." He would not deny this, lest it should come to pass hereafter that she should become his wife. "And everybody knows that as far as birth goes there is not a family in the county stands higher. I am so proud of my boy that I wish to see him mated with the best."

He reached the parsonage that evening only just before dinner, and on the next morning he did not go out of the house till the phaeton came round to take him to Brook Park. "Are you not going up to see the old doctor?" said the parson after breakfast.

"No;—I think not. He is never at home, and the ladies are always surrounded by the children."

"She will take it amiss," said the father almost in a whisper.

"I will go as I come back," said he, blushing as he spoke at his own falsehood. For, if he held to his present purpose, he would return by Slowbridge. If Fate intended that there should be nothing further between him and Alice, it would certainly be much better that they should not be brought together any more. He knew too what his father meant, and was more unwilling to take counsel from his father even than his mother. Yet he blushed because he knew that he was false.

"Do not seem to slight her," said the old man. "She is too good for that."

Then he drove himself over to Brook Park, and, as he made his way by one of the innumerable turnings out of Beetham, he saw at one of the corners Alice, still with the children and still with the perambulator. He merely lifted his hat as he passed, but did not stop to speak to her.

CHAPTER VI.

THE ARCHERY MEETING.

THE Assistant Deputy Inspector-General, when he reached Brook Park, found that things were to be done on a great scale. The two drawing-rooms were filled with flowers, and the big dining-room was laid out for to-morrow's lunch, in preparation for those who would prefer the dining-room to the tent. Rossiter was first taken into the Baronet's own room, where Sir Walter kept his guns and administered justice. "This is a terrible bore, Rossiter," he said.

"It must disturb you a great deal, Sir Walter."

"Oh, dear—dreadfully! What would my old friend,

your father, think of having to do this kind of thing? Though, when I was at Christchurch and he at Wadham, we used to be gay enough. I'm not quite sure that I don't owe it to you."

"To me, Sir Walter!"

"I rather think you put the girls up to it." Then he laughed as though it were a very good joke and told the Major where he would find the ladies. He had been expressly desired by his wife to be genial to the Major, and had been as genial as he knew how.

Rossiter, as he went out on to the lawn, saw Mr. Burmeston, the brewer, walking with Edith, the third daughter. He could not but admire the strategy of Lady Wanless when he acknowledged to himself how well she managed all these things. The brewer would not have been allowed to walk with Gertrude, the fourth daughter, nor even with Maria, the naughty girl who liked the curate,—because it was Edith's turn. Edith was certainly the plainest of the family, and yet she had her turn. Lady Wanless was by far too good a mother to have favourites among her own children.

He then found the mother, the eldest daughter, and Gertrude overseeing the decoration of a tent, which had been put up as an addition to the dining-room. He expected to find Mr. Cobble, to whom he had taken a liking, a nice, pleasant, frank young country gentleman; but Mr. Cobble was not wanted for any express purpose, and might have been in the way. Mr. Cobble was landed and safe. Before long he found himself walking round the garden with Lady Wanless herself. The other girls, though they were to be his sisters, were never thrown into any special intimacy with him. "She will be down before long now that she knows you are here," said Lady Wanless. "She was fatigued a little, and I thought it better that she should lie down. She is so impressionable, you know." "She" was Georgiana. He knew that very well. But why should Georgiana be called "She" to him, by her mother? Had "She" been in truth engaged to him it would have been intelligible, enough. But there had been nothing of the kind. As "She" was thus dinned into his ears, he thought of the very small amount of conversation which had ever taken place between himself and the young lady.

Then there occurred to him an idea that he would tell Lady Wanless in so many words that there was a mistake. The doing so would require some courage, but he thought that he could summon up manliness for the purpose,—if only he could find the words and occasion. But though "She" were so frequently spoken of, still nothing was said which seemed to give him the opportunity required. It is hard for a man to have to reject a girl when she has been offered,—but harder to do so before the offer has in truth been made. "I am afraid there is a little mistake in your ideas as to me and your daughter." It was thus that he would have had to speak, and then to have endured the outpouring of her wrath, when she would have declared that the ideas were only in his own arrogant brain. He let it pass by and said nothing, and before long he was playing lawn-tennis with Georgiana, who did not seem to have been in the least fatigued.

"My dear, I will not have it," said Lady Wanless about an hour afterwards, coming up and disturbing the game. "Major Rossiter, you ought to know better." Whereupon she playfully took the racket out of the Major's hand. "Mamma is such an old bother," said Georgiana as she walked back to the house with her Major. The Major had on a previous occasion perceived that the second Miss Wanless rode very well, and now he saw that she was very stout at lawn-tennis; but he observed none of that peculiarity of mental or physical development which her mother had described as "impressionable." Nevertheless she was a handsome girl, and if to play at lawn-tennis would help to make a husband happy, so much at any rate she could do.

This took place on the day before the meeting,—before the great day. When the morning came the girls did not come down early to breakfast, and our hero found himself left alone with Mr. Burmeston. "You have known the family a long time," said the Major as they were sauntering about the gravel paths together, smoking their cigars.

"No, indeed," said Mr. Burmeston. "They only took me up about three months ago,—just before we went over to Owless. Very nice people;—don't you think so?"

"Very nice," said the Major.

"They stand so high in the county, and all that sort of thing. Birth does go a long way, you know."

"So it ought," said the Major.

"And though the Baronet does not do much in the world, he has been in the House, you know. All those things help." Then the Major understood that Mr. Burmeston had looked the thing in the face, and had determined that for certain considerations it was worth his while to lead one of the Miss Wanlesses to the hymeneal altar. In this Mr. Burmeston was behaving with more manliness than he,—who had almost made up his mind half-a-dozen times, and had never been satisfied with the way he had done it.

About twelve the visitors had begun to come, and Sophia with Mr. Cobble were very soon trying their arrows together. Sophia had not been allowed to have her lover on the previous day, but was now making up for it. That was all very well, but Lady Wanless was a little angry with her eldest daughter. Her success was insured for her. Her business was done. Seeing how many sacrifices had been made to her during the last twelvemonths, surely now she might have been active in aiding her sisters, instead of merely amusing herself.

The Major was not good at archery. He was no doubt an excellent Deputy Inspector-General of Cavalry; but if bows and arrows had still been the weapons used in any part of the British army, he would not, without further instruction, have been qualified to inspect that branch. Georgiana Wanless, on the other hand, was a proficient. Such shooting as she made was marvellous to look at. And she was a very image of Diana, as with her beautiful figure and regular features, dressed up to the work, she stood with her bow raised in her hand and let twang the arrows. The circle immediately outside the bull's-eye was the farthest from the mark she ever touched. But good as she was and bad as was the Major, nevertheless they were appointed always to shoot together. After a world of failures the Major would shoot no more,—but not the less did he go backwards and forwards with Georgiana when she changed from one end to the other, and found himself absolutely appointed to that task. It grew upon him during the whole day that this second Miss Wanless was supposed to be his own,—almost as much as was the elder the property of Mr. Cobble. Other young men would do no more than speak to her. And when once, after the great lunch in the tent, Lady Wanless came and put her hand affectionately upon his arm, and whispered some word into his ear in the presence of all the assembled guests, he knew that the entire county had recognised him as caught.

There was old Lady Deepbell there. How it was that towards the end of the day's delights Lady Deepbell got hold of him he never knew. Lady Deepbell had not been introduced to him, and yet she got hold of him. "Major Rossiter, you are the luckiest man of the day," she said to him.

"Pretty well," said he, affecting to laugh; "but why so?"

"She is the handsomest young woman out. There hasn't been one in London this season with such a figure."

"You are altogether wrong in your surmise, Lady Deepbell."

"No, no; I am right enough. I see it all. Of course the poor girl won't have any money; but then how nice it is when a gentleman like you is able to dispense with that. Perhaps they do take after their father a little, and he certainly is not bright; but upon my word, I think a girl is all the better for that. What's the good of having such a lot of talkee-talkee?"

"Lady Deepbell, you are alluding to a young lady without the slightest warrant," said the Major.

"Warrant enough;—warrant enough," said the old woman, toddling off.

Then young Cobble came to him, and talked to him as though he were a brother of the house. Young Cobble was an honest fellow, and quite in earnest in his matrimonial intentions. "We shall be delighted if you'll come to us on the first," said Cobble. The first of course meant the first of September. "We ain't so badly off just for a week's shooting. Sophia is to be there, and we'll get Georgiana too."

The Major was fond of shooting, and would have been glad to accept the offer; but it was out of the question that he should allow himself to be taken in at Cobble Hall under a false pretext. And was it not incumbent on him to make this young man understand that he had no pretensions whatever to the hand of the second Miss Wanless? "You are very good," said he.

"We should be delighted," said young Cobble.

"But I fear there is a mistake. I can't say anything more about it now because it doesn't do to name people;—but there is a mistake. Only for that I should have been delighted. Good-bye." Then he took his departure, leaving young Cobble in a state of mystified suspense.

The day lingered on to a great length. The archery and the lawn-tennis were continued till late after the so-called lunch, and towards the evening a few couples stood up to dance. It was evident to the Major that Burmeston and Edith were thoroughly comfortable together. Gertrude amused herself well, and even Maria was contented, though the curate as a matter of course was not there. Sophia with her legitimate lover was as happy as the day and evening were long. But there came a frown upon Georgiana's brow, and when at last the Major, as though forced by destiny, asked her to dance, she refused. It had seemed to her a matter of course that he should ask her, and at last he did;—but she refused. The evening with him was very long, and just as he thought that he would escape to bed, and was meditating how early he would be off on the morrow, Lady Wanless took possession of him and carried him off alone into one of the desolate chambers. "Is she very tired?" asked the anxious mother.

"Is who tired?" The Major at that moment would have given twenty guineas to have been in his lodgings near St. James's Street.

"My poor girl," said Lady Wanless, assuming a look of great solicitude.

It was vain for him to pretend not to know who was the "she" intended. "Oh, ah, yes; Miss Wanless."

"Georgiana."

"I think she is tired. She was shooting a great deal. Then there was a quadrille;—but she didn't dance. There has been a great deal to tire young ladies."

"You shouldn't have let her do so much."

How was he to get out of it? What was he to say? If a man is clearly asked his intentions he can say that he has not got any. That used to be the old fashion when a gentleman was supposed to be dilatory in declaring his purpose. But it gave the oscillating lover so easy an escape! It was like the sudden jerk of the hand of the unpractised fisherman: if the fish does not succumb at once it goes away down the stream and is no more heard of. But from this new process there is no mode of immediate escape. "I couldn't prevent her because she is nothing to me." That would have been the straightforward answer;—but one most difficult to make. "I hope she will be none the worse to-morrow morning," said the Major.

"I hope not, indeed. Oh, Major Rossiter!" The

mother's position was also difficult, as it is of no use to play with a fish too long without making an attempt to stick the hook into his gills.

"Lady Wanless!"

"What am I to say to you? I am sure you know my feelings. You know how sincere is Sir Walter's regard."

"I am very much flattered, Lady Wanless."

"That means nothing." This was true, but the Major did not mean to intend anything. "Of all my flock she is the fairest." That was true also. The Major would have been delighted to accede to the assertion of the young lady's beauty, if this might have been the end of it. "I had thought——"

"Had thought what, Lady Wanless?"

"If I am deceived in you, Major Rossiter, I never will believe in a man again. I have looked upon you as the very soul of honour."

"I trust that I have done nothing to lessen your good opinion."

"I do not know. I cannot say. Why do you answer me in this way about my child?" Then she held her hands together and looked up into his face imploringly. He owned to himself that she was a good actress. He was almost inclined to submit and to declare his passion for Georgiana. For the present that way out of the difficulty would have been so easy!

"You shall hear from me to-morrow morning," he said, almost solemnly.

"Shall I?" she asked, grasping his hand. "Oh,

my friend, let it be as I desire. My whole life shall be devoted to making you happy,—you and her." Then he was allowed to escape.

Lady Wanless, before she went to bed, was closeted for awhile with the eldest daughter. As Sophia was now almost as good as a married woman, she was received into closer counsel than the others. "Burmeston will do," she said; "but, as for that Cavalry man, he means it no more than the chair." The pity was that Burmeston might have been secured without the archery meeting, and that all the money, spent on behalf of the Major, should have been thrown away.

CHAPTER VII.

AFTER THE PARTY.

When the Major left Brook Park on the morning after the archery amusements he was quite sure of this,—that under no circumstances whatever would he be induced to ask Miss Georgiana Wanless to be his wife. He had promised to write a letter,—and he would write one instantly. He did not conceive it possible but that Lady Wanless should understand what would be the purport of that letter, although as she left him on the previous night she had pretended to hope otherwise. That her hopes had not been very high we know from the words which she spoke to Sophia in the privacy of her own room.

He had intended to return by Slowbridge, but when the morning came he changed his mind and went to Beetham. His reason for doing so was hardly plain, even to himself. He tried to make himself believe that the letter had better be written from Beetham,—hot, as it were, from the immediate neighbourhood,—than from London; but, as he thought of this, his mind was crowded with ideas of Alice Dugdale. He would not propose to Alice. At this moment, indeed, he was averse to matrimony, having been altogether disgusted with female society at Brook Park; but he had to acknowledge a sterling worth about Alice, and the existence of a genuine friendship between her and himself, which made it painful to him to leave the country without other recognition than that raising of his hat when he saw her at the corner of the lane. He had behaved badly in this Brook Park affair,—in having been tempted thither in opposition to those better instincts which had made Alice so pleasant a companion to him,—and was ashamed of himself. He did not think that he could go back to his former ideas. He was aware that Alice must think ill of him,—would not believe him to be now such as she had once thought him. England and London were distasteful to him. He would go abroad on that foreign service which he had proposed to himself. There was an opening for him to do so if he liked, and he could return to his present duties after a year or two. But he would see Alice again before he went. Thinking of all this, he drove himself back to Beetham.

On that morning tidings of the successful festivities at Brook Park reached the doctor's house. Tidings of the coming festivities, then of the preparations, and at last of the festal day itself, had reached Alice, so that it seemed to her that all Beetham talked of nothing else. Old Lady Deepbell had caught a cold, walking about on the lawn with hardly anything on her old shoulders,—stupid old woman,—and had sent for the doctor the first thing in the morning. "Positively settled," she had said to the doctor, "absolutely arranged, Dr. Dugdale. Lady Wanless told me so herself, and I congratulated the gentleman." She did not go on to say that the gentleman had denied the accusation,—but then she had not believed the denial. The doctor, coming home, had thought it his duty to tell Alice, and Alice had received the news with a smile. "I knew it would be so, father."

"And you?" This he said, holding her hand and looking tenderly into her eyes.

"Me! It will not hurt me. Not that I mean to tell a lie to you, father," she added after a moment. "A woman isn't hurt because she doesn't get a prize in the lottery. Had it ever come about, I dare say I should have liked him well enough."

"No more than that?"

"And why should it have come about?" she went on saying, avoiding her father's last question, determined not to lie if she could help it, but determined, also, to show no wound. "I think my position in life very happy, but it isn't one from which he would choose a wife."

"Why not, my dear?"

"A thousand reasons; I am always busy, and he would naturally like a young lady who had nothing to do." She understood the effect of the perambulator and the constant needle and thread. "Besides, though he might be all very well, he could never, I think, be as dear to me as the bairns. I should feel that I lost more than I got by going." This she knew to be a lie, but it was so important that her father should believe her to be contented with her home duties! And she was contented, though very unhappy. When her father kissed her, she smiled into his face,—oh, so sweetly, so pleasantly! And the old man thought that she could not have loved very deeply. Then she took herself to her own room, and sat awhile alone with a countenance much changed. The lines of sorrow about her brow were terrible. There was not a tear; but her mouth was close pressed, and her hand was working constantly by her side. She gazed at nothing, but sat with her eyes wide open, staring straight before her. Then she jumped up quickly, and striking her hand upon her heart, she spoke aloud to herself. "I will cure it," she said. "He is not worthy, and it should therefore be easier. Though he were worthy, I would cure it. Yes, Bobby, I am coming." Then she went about her work.

That might have been about noon. It was after their early dinner with the children that the Major came up to the doctor's house. He had reached the parsonage in time for a late breakfast, and had then written his letter. After that he had sat idling about on the lawn,—not on the best terms with his mother, to whom he had sworn that, under no circumstances, would he make Georgiana Wanless his wife. "I would sooner marry a girl from a troop of tight-rope dancers," he had said in his anger. Mrs. Rossiter knew that he intended to go up to the doctor's house, and therefore the immediate feeling between the mother and son was not pleasant. My readers, if they please, shall see the letter to Lady Wanless.

"My dear Lady Wanless,—It is a great grief to me to say that there has been, I fear, a misconception between you and me on a certain matter. This is the more a trouble to me because you and Sir Walter have been so very kind to me. From a word or two which fell from you last night I was led to fear that you suspected feelings on my part which I have never entertained, and aspirations to which I have never pretended. No man can be more alive than I am to the honour which has been suggested, but I feel bound to say that I am not in a condition to accept it.

"Pray believe me to be,
"Dear Lady Wanless,
"Yours always very faithfully,
"John Rossiter."

The letter, when it was written, was, to himself, very

unsatisfactory. It was full of ambiguous words and namby-pamby phraseology which disgusted him. But he did not know how to alter it for the better. It is hard to say an uncivil thing civilly without ambiguous namby-pamby language. He could not bring it out in straightforward stout English: "You want me to marry your daughter, but I won't do anything of the kind." So the letter was sent. The conduct of which he was really ashamed did not regard Miss Wanless, but Alice Dugdale.

At last, very slowly, he took himself up to the doctor's house. He hardly knew what it was that he meant to say when he found himself there, but he was sure that he did not mean to make an offer. Even had other things suited, there would have been something distasteful to him in doing this so quickly after the affair of Miss Wanless. He was in no frame now for making love; but yet it would be ungracious in him, he thought, to leave Beetham without seeing his old friend. He found the two ladies together, with the children still around them, sitting near a window which opened down to the ground. Mrs. Dugdale had a novel in hand, and, as usual, was leaning back in a rocking-chair. Alice had also a book open on the table before her, but she was bending over a sewing-machine. They had latterly divided the cares of the family between them. Mrs. Dugdale had brought the children into the world, and Alice had washed, clothed, and fed them when they were there. When the Major entered the room, Alice's mind was, of course, full of the tidings she had heard from her father,—which tidings, however, had not been communicated to Mrs. Dugdale.

Alice at first was very silent while Mrs. Dugdale asked as to the festivities. "It has been the grandest thing anywhere about here for a long time."

"And, like other grand things, a great bore," said the Major.

"I don't suppose you found it so, Major Rossiter," said the lady.

Then the conversation ran away into a description of what had been done during the day. He wished to make it understood that there was no permanent link binding him to Brook Park, but he hardly knew how to say it without going beyond the lines of ordinary conversation. At last there seemed to be an opening, —not exactly what he wished, but still an opening. "Brook Park is not exactly the place," said he, "at which I should ever feel myself quite at home." This was in answer to some chance word which had fallen from Mrs. Dugdale.

"I am sorry for that," said Alice. She would have given a guinea to bring the word back after it had been spoken. But spoken words cannot be brought back.

"Why sorry?" he asked, smiling.

"Because— Oh, because it is so likely that you may be there often."

"I don't know that at all."

"You have become so intimate with them!" said

Alice. "We are told in Beetham that the party was got up all for your honour."

So Sir Walter had told him, and so Maria, the naughty girl, had said also—"Only for your beaux yeux, Major Rossiter, we shouldn't have had any party at all." This had been said by Maria when she was laughing at him about her sister Georgiana. "I don't know how that may be," said the Major; "but all the same I shall never be at home at Brook Park."

"Don't you like the young ladies?" asked Mrs. Dugdale.

"Oh, yes; very much; and Lady Wanless; and Sir Walter. I like them all, in a way. But yet I shall never find myself at home at Brook Park."

Alice was very angry with him. He ought not to have gone there at all. He must have known that he could not be there without paining her. She thoroughly believed that he was engaged to marry the girl of whose family he spoke in this way. He had thought,—so it seemed to her,—that he might lessen the blow to her by making little of the great folk among whom his future lot was to be cast. But what could be more mean? He was not the John Rossiter to whom she had given her heart. There had been no such man. She had been mistaken. "I am afraid you are one of those," she said, "who, wherever they find themselves, at once begin to wish for something better."

"That is meant to be severe."

"My severity won't go for much."

"I am sure you have deserved it," said Mrs. Dugdale, most indiscreetly.

"Is this intended for an attack?" he asked, looking from one to the other.

"Not at all," said Alice, affecting to laugh. "I should have said nothing if I thought mamma would take it up so seriously. I was only sorry to hear you speak of your new friends so slightingly."

After that the conversation between them was very difficult, and he soon got up to go away. As he did so, he asked Alice to say a word to him out in the garden, having already explained to them both that it might be some time before he would be again down at Beetham. Alice rose slowly from her sewing-machine, and, putting on her hat, led the way with a composed and almost dignified step out through the window. Her heart was beating within her, but she looked as though she were mistress of every pulse. "Why did you say that to me?" he asked.

"Say what?"

"That I always wished for better things and better people than I found."

"Because I think you ambitious,—and discontented. There is nothing disgraceful in that, though it is not the character which I myself like the best."

"You meant to allude specially to the Wanlesses?"

"Because you have just come from there, and were speaking of them."

"And to one of that family specially?"

"No, Major Rossiter. There you are wrong. I

alluded to no one in particular. They are nothing to me. I do not know them; but I hear that they are kind and friendly people, with good manners and very handsome. Of course I know, as we all know everything of each other in this little place, that you have of late become very intimate with them. Then when I hear you aver that you are already discontented with them, I cannot help thinking that you are hard to please. I am sorry that mamma spoke of deserving. I did not intend to say anything so seriously."

"Alice!"

"Well, Major Rossiter."

"I wish I could make you understand me."

"I do not know that that would do any good. We have been old friends, and of course I hope that you may be happy. I must say good-bye now. I cannot go beyond the gate, because I am wanted to take the children out."

"Good-bye then. I hope you will not think ill of me."

"Why should I think ill of you? I think very well,—only that you are ambitious." As she said this, she laughed again, and then she left him.

He had been most anxious to tell her that he was not going to marry that girl, but he had not known how to do it. He could not bring himself to declare that he would not marry a girl when by such declaration he would have been forced to assume that he might marry her if he pleased. So he left Alice at the gate, and she went back to the house still convinced that he was betrothed to Georgiana Wanless.

CHAPTER VIII.

SIR WALTER UP IN LONDON.

THE Major, when he left the doctor's house, was more thoroughly in love with Alice than ever. There had been something in her gait as she led the way out through the window, and again, as with determined purpose she bade him speedily farewell at the gate, which forced him to acknowledge that the dragging of perambulators and the making of petticoats had not detracted from her feminine charm or from her feminine dignity. She had been dressed in her ordinary morning frock,—the very frock on which he had more than once seen the marks of Bobby's dirty heels; but she had pleased his eye better than Georgiana, clad in all the glory of her toxopholite array. The toxopholite feather had been very knowing, the tight leathern belt round her waist had been bright in colour and pretty in design. The looped-up dress, fit for the work in hand, had been gratifying. But with it all there had been the show of a thing got up for ornament and not for use. She was like a box of painted sugar-plums, very pretty to the eye, but of which no one wants to extract any for the purpose of eating them. Alice was like a housewife's store, kept beautifully in order, but intended chiefly for comfortable use. As he went up to London he began to doubt whether he would go abroad. Were he to let a few months pass by would not Alice be still there, and willing perhaps to receive him with more kindness when she should have heard that his follies at Brook Park were at an end?

Three days after his return, when he was sitting in his offices thinking perhaps more of Alice Dugdale than of the whole British Cavalry, a soldier who was in waiting brought a card to him. Sir Walter Wanless had come to call upon him. If he were disengaged Sir Walter would be glad to see him. He was not at all anxious to see Sir Walter; but there was no alternative, and Sir Walter was shown into the room.

In explaining the purport of Sir Walter's visit we must go back for a few minutes to Brook Park. When Sir Walter came down to breakfast on the morning after the festivities he was surprised to hear that Major Rossiter had taken his departure. There sat young Burmeston. He at any rate was safe. And there sat young Cobble, who by Sophia's aid had managed to get himself accommodated for the night, and all the other young people, including the five Wanless girls. The father, though not observant, could see that Georgiana was very glum. Lady Wanless herself affected a good-humour which hardly deceived him, and certainly did not deceive anyone else. "He was obliged to be off this morning, because of his duties," said Lady Wanless. "He told me that it was to be so, but I did not like to say anything about it yesterday." Georgiana turned up her nose, as much as to say that the going and coming of Major Rossiter was not a matter of much importance to any one there, and, least of all, to her. Except the father, there was not a person in the room who was not aware that Lady Wanless had missed her fish.

But she herself was not quite sure even yet that she had failed altogether. She was a woman who hated failure, and who seldom failed. She was brave of heart too, and able to fight a losing battle to the last. She was very angry with the Major, who she well knew was endeavouring to escape from her toils. But he would not on that account be the less useful as a son-in-law;—nor on that account was she the more willing to allow him to escape. With five daughters without fortunes it behoved her as a mother to be persistent. She would not give it up, but must turn the matter well in her mind before she took further steps. She feared that a simple invitation could hardly bring the Major back to Brook Park. Then there came the letter from the Major which did not make the matter easier.

"My dear," she said to her husband, sitting down opposite to him in his room, "that Major Rossiter isn't behaving quite as he ought to do."

"I'm not a bit surprised," said the Baronet angrily. "I never knew anybody from Wadham behave well."

"He's quite a gentleman, if you mean that," said

Lady Wanless; "and he's sure to do very well in the world; and poor Georgiana is really fond of him,—which doesn't surprise me in the least."

"Has he said anything to make her fond of him? I suppose she has gone and made a fool of herself,—like Maria."

"Not at all. He has said a great deal to her;—much more than he ought to have done, if he meant nothing. But the truth is, young men nowadays never know their own minds unless there is somebody to keep them up to the mark. You must go and see him."

"I!" said the afflicted father.

"Of course, my dear. A few judicious words in such a case may do so much. I would not ask Walter to go,"—Walter was the eldest son, who was with his regiment,—"because it might lead to quarrelling. I would not have anything of that kind, if only for the dear girl's sake. But what you would say would be known to nobody; and it might have the desired effect. Of course you will be very quiet,—and very serious also. Nobody could do it better than you will. There can be no doubt that he has trifled with the dear girl's affections. Why else has he been with her whenever he has been here? It was so visible on Wednesday that everybody was congratulating me. Old Lady Deepbell asked whether the day was fixed. I treated him quite as though it were settled. Young men do so often get these sudden starts of doubt. Then, sometimes, just a word afterwards will put it all right." In this way the Baronet was made to understand that he must go and see the Major.

He postponed the unwelcome task till his wife at last drove him out of the house. "My dear," she said, "will you let your child die broken-hearted for want of a word?" When it was put to him in that way he found himself obliged to go, though, to tell the truth, he could not find any sign of heart-breaking sorrow about his child. He was not allowed to speak to Georgiana herself, his wife telling him that the poor child would be unable to bear it.

Sir Walter, when he was shown into the Major's room, felt himself to be very ill able to conduct the business in hand, and to the Major himself the moment was one of considerable trouble. He had thought it possible that he might receive an answer to his letter, a reply that might be indignant, or piteous, admonitory, or simply abusive, as the case might be,—one which might too probably require a further correspondence; but it had never occurred to him that Sir Walter would come in person. But here he was,—in the room,—by no means with that pretended air of geniality with which he had last received the Major down at Brook Park. The greeting, however, between the gentlemen was courteous if not cordial, and then Sir Walter began his task. "We were quite surprised you should have left us so early that morning."

"I had told Lady Wanless."

"Yes; I know. Nevertheless we were surprised. Now, Major Rossiter, what do you mean to do about,—

about,—about this young lady?" The Major sat silent. He could not pretend to be ignorant what young lady was intended after the letter which he had himself written to Lady Wanless. "This, you know, is a very painful kind of thing, Major Rossiter."

"Very painful indeed, Sir Walter."

"When I remembered that I had been at Christchurch and your excellent father at Wadham both at the same time, I thought that I might trust you in my house without the slightest fear."

"I make bold to say, Sir Walter, that you were quite justified in that expectation, whether it was founded on your having been at Christchurch or on my position and character in the world." He knew that the scene would be easier to him if he could work himself up to a little indignation on his own part.

"And yet I am told,—I am told——"

"What are you told, Sir Walter?"

"There can, I think, be no doubt that you have—in point of fact, paid attention to my daughter." Sir Walter was a gentleman, and felt that the task imposed upon him grated against his better feelings.

"If you mean that I have taken steps to win her affections, you have been wrongly informed."

"That's what I do mean. Were you not received just now at Brook Park as,—as paying attention to her?"

"I hope not."

"You hope not, Major Rossiter?"

"I hope no such mistake was made. It certainly was not made by me. I felt myself much flattered by being received at your house. I wrote the other day a line or two to Lady Wanless and thought I had explained all this."

Sir Walter opened his eyes when he heard, for the first time, of the letter, but was sharp enough not to exhibit his ignorance at the moment. "I don't know about explaining," he said. "There are some things which can't be so very well explained. My wife assures me that that poor girl has been deceived,—cruelly deceived. Now I put it to you, Major Rossiter, what ought you as a gentleman to do?"

"Really, Sir Walter, you are not entitled to ask me any such question."

"Not on behalf of my own child?"

"I cannot go into the matter from that view of the case. I can only declare that I have said nothing and done nothing for which I can blame myself. I cannot understand how there should have been such a mistake; but it did not, at any rate, arise with me."

Then the Baronet sat dumb. He had been specially instructed not to give up the interview till he had obtained some sign of weakness from the enemy. If he could only induce the enemy to promise another visit to Brook Park that would be much. If he could obtain some expression of liking or admiration for the young lady that would be something. If he could induce the Major to allude to delay as being necessary, farther operations would be founded on that base. But nothing had been obtained. "It's the most,—the most,—the most astonishing thing I ever heard," he said at last.

"I do not know that I can say anything further."

"I'll tell you what," said the Baronet. "Come down and see Lady Wanless. The women understand these things much better than we do. Come down and talk it over with Lady Wanless. She won't propose anything that isn't proper." In answer to this the Major shook his head. "You won't?"

"It would do no good, Sir Walter. It would be painful to me, and must, I should say, be distressing to the young lady."

"Then you won't do anything!"

"There is nothing to be done."

"Upon my word, I never heard such a thing in all my life, Major Rossiter. You come down to my house; and then,—then,—then you won't,—you won't come again! To be sure he was at Wadham; but I did think your father's son would have behaved better." Then he picked up his hat from the floor and shuffled out of the room without another word.

Tidings that Sir Walter had been up to London and had called upon Major Rossiter made their way into Beetham and reached the ears of the Dugdales,—but not correct tidings as to the nature of the conversation. "I wonder when it will be," said Mrs. Dugdale to Alice. "As he has been up to town I suppose it'll be settled soon."

"The sooner the better for all parties," said Alice cheerily. "When a man and a woman have agreed together, I can't see why they shouldn't at once walk off to the church arm in arm."

"The lawyers have so much to do."

"Bother the lawyers! The parson ought to do all that is necessary, and the sooner the better. Then there would not be such paraphernalia of presents and gowns and eatings and drinkings, all of which is got up for the good of the tradesmen. If I were to be married, I should like to slip out round the corner, just as though I were going to get an extra loaf of bread from Mrs. Bakewell."

"That wouldn't do for my lady at Brook Park."

"I suppose not."

"Nor yet for the Major."

Then Alice shook her head and sighed, and took herself out to walk alone for a few minutes among the lanes. How could it be that he should be so different from that which she had taken him to be! It was now September, and she could remember an early evening in May, when the leaves were beginning to be full, and they were walking together with the spring air fresh around them, just where she was now creeping alone with the more perfect and less fresh beauty of the autumn around her. How different a person he seemed to her to be now from that which he had seemed to be then;—not different because he did not love her, but different because he was not fit to be loved! "Alice," he had then said, "you and I are alike in this, that simple, serviceable things are dear to both of us." The words had meant so much to her that she had never forgotten them. Was she simple and serviceable, so that she might be dear to him? She had been sure then that he was simple, and that he was serviceable, so that she could love him. It was thus that she had spoken of him to herself, thinking herself to be sure of his character. And now, before the summer was over, he was engaged to marry such a one as Georgiana Wanless and to become the hero of a fashionable wedding!

But she took pride to herself as she walked alone that she had already overcome the bitterness of the malady which, for a day or two, had been so heavy that she had feared for herself that it would oppress her. For a day or two after that farewell at the gate she had with a rigid purpose tied herself to every duty,—even to the duty of looking pleasant in her father's eyes, of joining in the children's games, of sharing the gossip of her stepmother. But this she had done with an agony that nearly crushed her. Now she had won her way through it, and could see her path before her. She had not cured altogether that wound in her heart; but she had assured herself that she could live on without further interference from the wound.

CHAPTER IX.

LADY DEEPBELL.

Then by degrees it began to be rumoured about the country, and at last through the lanes of Beetham itself, that the alliance between Major Rossiter and

Miss Georgiana Wanless was not quite a settled thing. Mr. Burmeston had whispered in Slowbridge that there was a screw loose, perhaps thinking that if another could escape, why not he also? Cobble, who had no idea of escaping, declared his conviction that Major Rossiter ought to be horsewhipped; but Lady Deepbell was the real town-crier who carried the news far and wide. But all of them heard it before Alice, and when others believed it Alice did not believe it,—or, indeed, care to believe or not to believe.

Lady Deepbell filled a middle situation, half way between the established superiority of Brook Park and the recognised humility of Beetham. Her title went for something; but her husband had been only a Civil Service Knight, who had deserved well of his country by a meritorious longevity. She lived in a pretty little cottage half way between Brook Park and Beetham, which was just large enough to enable her to talk of her grounds. She loved Brook Park dearly, and all the county people; but in her love for social intercourse generally she was unable to eschew the more frequent gatherings of the village. She was intimate not only with Mrs. Rossiter, but with the Tweeds and Dugdales and Simkinses, and, while she could enjoy greatly the grandeur of the Wanless aristocracy, so could she accommodate herself comfortably to the cosy gossip of the Beethamites. It was she who first spread the report in Beetham that Major Rossiter was,—as she called it,—"off."

She first mentioned the matter to Mrs. Rossiter

herself; but this she did in a manner more subdued than usual. The "alliance" had been high, and she was inclined to think that Mrs. Rossiter would be disappointed. "We did think, Mrs. Rossiter, that these young people at Brook Park had meant something the other day."

Mrs. Rossiter did not stand in awe of Lady Deepbell, and was not pleased at the allusion. "It would be much better if young people could be allowed to arrange their own affairs without so much tattling about it," she said angrily.

"That's all very well, but tongues will talk, you know, Mrs. Rossiter. I am sorry for both their sakes, because I thought that it would do very well."

"Very well indeed, if the young people, as you call them, liked each other."

"But I suppose it's over now, Mrs. Rossiter?"

"I really know nothing about it, Lady Deepbell." Then the old woman, quite satisfied after this that the "alliance" had fallen to the ground, went on to the Tweeds.

"I never thought it would come to much," said Mrs. Tweed.

"I don't see why it shouldn't," said Matilda Tweed. "Georgiana Wanless is good-looking in a certain way; but they none of them have a penny, and Major Rossiter is quite a fashionable man." The Tweeds were quite outside the Wanless pale; and it was the feeling of this that made Matilda love to talk about the second Miss Wanless by her Christian name.

"I suppose he will go back to Alice now," said Clara, the younger Tweed girl.

"I don't see that at all," said Mrs. Tweed.

"I never believed much in that story," said Lady Deepbell.

"Nor I either," said Matida. "He used to walk about with her, but what does that come to? The children were always with them. I never would believe that he was going to make so little of himself."

"But is it quite sure that all the affair at Brook Park will come to nothing, after the party and everything?" asked Mrs. Tweed.

"Quite positive," said Lady Deepbell authoritatively. "I am able to say certainly that that is all over." Then she toddled off and went to the Simkinses.

The rumour did not reach the doctor's house on that day. The conviction that Major Rossiter had behaved badly to Alice,—that Alice had been utterly thrown over by the Wanless "alliance," had been so strong, that even Lady Deepbell had not dared to go and probe wilfully that wound. The feeling in this respect had been so general that no one in Beetham had been hard-hearted enough to speak to Alice either of the triumph of Miss Wanless, or of the misconduct of the Major; and now Lady Deepbell was afraid to carry her story thither.

It was the doctor himself who first brought the tidings to the house, and did not do this till some days after Lady Deepbell had been in the village. "You had better not say anything to Alice about it." Such at first had been the doctor's injunction to his wife. "One way or the other, it will only be a trouble to her." Mrs. Dugdale, full of her secret, anxious to be obedient, thinking that the gentleman relieved from his second love, would be ready at once to be on again with his first, was so fluttered and fussy that Alice knew that there was something to be told. "You have got some great secret, mamma," she said.

"What secret, Alice?"

"I know you have. Don't wait for me to ask you to tell it. If it is to come, let it come."

"I'm not going to say anything."

"Very well, mamma. Then nothing shall be said."

"Alice, you are the most provoking young woman I ever had to deal with in my life. If I had twenty secrets I would not tell you one of them."

On the next morning Alice heard it all from her father. "I knew there was something by mamma's manner," she said.

"I told her not to say anything."

"So I suppose. But what does it matter to me, papa, whether Major Rossiter does or does not marry Miss Wanless? If he has given her his word, I am sure I hope that he will keep it."

"I don't suppose he ever did."

"Even then it doesn't matter. Papa, do not trouble yourself about him."

"But you?"

"I have gone through the fire, and have come out without being much scorched. Dear papa, I do so wish that you should understand it all. It is so nice to have some one to whom everything can be told. I did like him."

"And he?"

"I have nothing to say about that;—not a word. Girls, I suppose, are often foolish, and take things for more than they are intended to mean. I have no accusation to make against him. But I did,—I did allow myself to be weak. Then came this about Miss Wanless, and I was unhappy. I woke from a dream, and the waking was painful. But I have got over it. I do not think that you will ever know from your girl's manner that anything has been the matter with her."

"My brave girl!"

"But don't let mamma talk to me as though he could come back because the other girl has not suited him. He is welcome to the other girl,—welcome to do without her,—welcome to do with himself as it may best please him; but he shall not trouble me again." There was a stern strength in her voice as she said this, which forced her father to look at her almost with amazement. "Do not think that I am fierce, papa."

"Fierce, my darling!"

"But that I am in earnest. Of course, if he comes to Beetham we shall see him. But let him be like anybody else. Don't let it be supposed that because he flitted here once, and was made welcome, like a bird that comes in at the window, and then flitted away again, that he can be received in at the window just as before, should he fly this way any more. That's all, papa." Then, as before, she went off by herself,

—to give herself renewed strength by her solitary thinkings. She had so healed the flesh round that wound that there was no longer danger of mortification. She must now take care that there should be no further wound. The people around her would be sure to tell her of this breach between her late lover and the Wanless young lady. The Tweeds and the Simkinses, and old Lady Deepbell would be full of it. She must take care so to answer them at the first word that they should not dare to talk to her of Major Rossiter. She had cured herself so that she no longer staggered under the effects of the blow. Having done that, she would not allow herself to be subject to the little stings of the little creatures around her. She had had enough of love,—of a man's love, and would make herself happy now with Bobby and the other bairns.

"He'll be sure to come back," said Mrs Dugdale to her husband.

"We shall do no good by talking about it," said the doctor. "If you will take my advice, you will not mention his name to her. I fear that he is worthless and unworthy of mention." That might be very well, thought Mrs. Dugdale; but no one in the village doubted that he had at the very least £1,500 a year, and that he was a handsome man, and such a one as is not to be picked up under every hedge. The very men who go about the world most like butterflies before marriage "steady down the best" afterwards. These were her words as she discussed the matter with Mrs.

Tweed, and they both agreed that if the hero showed himself again at the doctor's house "bygones ought to be bygones."

Lady Wanless, even after her husband's return from London, declared to herself that even yet the game had not been altogether played out. Sir Walter, who had been her only possible direct messenger to the man himself, had been, she was aware, as bad a messenger as could have been selected. He could be neither authoritative nor persuasive. Therefore when he told her, on coming home, that it was easy to perceive that Major Rossiter's father could not have been educated at Christchurch, she did not feel very much disappointed. As her next step she determined to call on Mrs. Rossiter. If that should fail she must beard the lion in his den, and go herself to Major Rossiter at the Horse Guards. She did not doubt but that she would at least be able to say more than Sir Walter. Mrs. Rossiter, she was aware, was herself favourable to the match.

"My dear Mrs. Rossiter," she said in her most confidential manner, "there is a little something wrong among these young people, which I think you and I can put right if we put our heads together."

"If I know one of the young people," said Mrs. Rossiter, "it will be very hard to make him change his mind."

"He has been very attentive to the young lady."

"Of course I know nothing about it, Lady Wanless. I never saw them together."

"Dear Georgiana is so very quiet that she said nothing even to me, but I really thought that he had proposed to her. She won't say a word against him, but I believe he did. Now, Mrs. Rossiter, what has been the meaning of it?"

"How is a mother to answer for her son, Lady Wanless?"

"No;—of course not. I know that. Girls, of course, are different. But I thought that perhaps you might know something about it, for I did imagine you would like the connection."

"So I should. Why not? Nobody thinks more of birth than I do, and nothing in my opinion could have been nicer for John. But he does not see with my eyes. If I were to talk to him for a week it would have no effect."

"Is it that girl of the doctor's, Mrs. Rossiter?"

"I think not. My idea is that when he has turned it all over in his mind he has come to the conclusion that he will be better without a wife than with one."

"We might cure him of that, Mrs. Rossiter. If I could only have him down there at Brook Park for another week, I am sure he would come to." Mrs. Rossiter, however, could not say that she thought it probable that her son would be induced soon to pay another visit to Brook Park.

A week after this Lady Wanless absolutely did find her way into the Major's presence at the Horse Guards, —but without much success. The last words at that interview only shall be given to the reader,—the last words as they were spoken both by the lady and by the gentleman. "Then I am to see my girl die of a broken heart?" said Lady Wanless, with her handkerchief up to her eyes.

"I hope not, Lady Wanless; but in whatever way she might die, the fault would not be mine." There was a frown on the gentleman's brow as he said this which cowed even the lady.

As she went back to Slowbridge that afternoon, and then home to Brook Park, she determined at last that the game must be looked upon as played out. There was no longer any ground on which to stand and fight. Before she went to bed that night she sent for Georgiana. "My darling child," she said, "that man is unworthy of you."

"I always thought he was," said Georgiana. And so there was an end to that little episode in the family of the Wanlesses.

CHAPTER X.

THE BIRD THAT PECKED AT THE WINDOW.

The bird that had flown in at the window and had been made welcome, had flown away ungratefully. Let him come again pecking as he might at the window, no more crumbs of love should be thrown to him. Alice, with a steady purpose, had resolved on that. With all her humble ways, her continual darning of stockings, her cutting of bread and butter for the children, her pushing of the perambulator in the lanes, there was a pride about her, a knowledge of her own dignity as a woman, which could have been stronger in the bosom of no woman of title, of wealth, or of fashion. She claimed nothing. She had expected no admiration. She had been contented to take the world as it came to her, without thinking much of love or romance. When John Rossiter had first shown himself at Beetham, after his return from India, and when he had welcomed her so warmly, —too warmly,—as his old playfellow, no idea had occurred to her that he would ever be more to her than her old playfellow. Her own heart was too precious to herself to be given away idly to the first comer. Then the bird had flown in at the window, and it had been that the coming of the stranger had been very sweet to her. But, even for the stranger, she would not change her ways,—unless, perchance, some day she might appertain to the stranger. Then it would be her duty to fit herself entirely to him. In the meantime, when he gave her little hints that something of her domestic slavery might be discontinued, she would not abate a jot from her duties. If he liked to come with her when she pushed the children, let him come. If he cared to see her when she was darning a stocking or cutting bread and butter, let him pay his visits. If he thought those things derogatory, certainly let him stay away. So the thing had grown till she had found herself surprised, and taken, as it were, into a net,—caught in a pitfall of love. But she held her peace, stuck manfully to the perambulator, and was a little colder in her demeanour than heretofore. Whereupon Major Rossiter, as the reader is aware, made two visits to Brook Park. The bird might peck at the window, but he should never again be taken into the room.

But the bird, from the moment in which he had packed up his portmanteau at Brook Park, had determined that he would be taken in at the window again,—that he would at any rate return to the window, and peck at the glass with constancy, soliciting that it might be opened. As he now thought of the two girls, the womanliness of the one, as compared with the worldliness of the other, conquered him completely. There had never been a moment in which his heart had in truth inclined itself towards the young athlete of Brook Park,—never a moment, hardly a moment, in which his heart had been untrue to Alice. But glitter had for awhile prevailed with him, and he had, just for a moment, allowed himself to be discontented with the homely colour of unalloyed gold. He was thoroughly ashamed of himself, knowing well that he had given pain. He had learned, clearly enough, from what her father, mother, and others had said to him, that there were those who expected him to marry Alice Dugdale, and others who hoped that he would marry Georgiana Wanless. Now, at last, he could declare that no other love than that which was warm within his heart at present could ever have been possible to him. But he was aware that he had much to do to recover his footing.

Alice's face and her manner as she bade him good-bye at the gate were very clear before his eyes.

Two months passed by before he was again seen at Beetham. It had happened that he was, in truth, required elsewhere, on duty, during the period, and he took care to let it be known at Beetham that such was the case. Information to this effect was in some shape sent to Alice. Openly, she took no notice of it; but, inwardly, she said to herself that they who troubled themselves by sending her such tidings, troubled themselves in vain. "Men may come and men may go," she sang to herself, in a low voice. How little they knew her, to come to her with news as to Major Rossiter's coming and going!

Then one day he came. One morning early in December the absolute fact was told at the dinner table. "The Major is at the parsonage," said the maid-servant. Mrs. Dugdale looked at Alice, who continued, however, to distribute hashed mutton with an equanimity which betrayed no flaw.

After that not a word was said about him. The doctor had warned his wife to be silent; and though she would fain have spoken, she restrained herself. After dinner the usual work went on, and then the usual playing in the garden. The weather was dry and mild for the time of year, so that Alice was swinging two of the children when Major Rossiter came up through the gate. Minnie, who had been a favourite, ran to him, and he came slowly across the lawn to the tree on which the swing was hung. For a moment

Alice stopped her work that she might shake hands with him, and then at once went back to her place. "If I were to stop a moment before Bobby has had his turn," she said, "he would feel the injustice."

"No, I isn't," said Bobby. "Oo may go 'is time."

"But I don't want to go, Bobby, and Major Rossiter will find mamma in the drawing-room;" and Alice for a moment thought of getting her hat and going off from the place. Then she reflected that to run away would be cowardly. She did not mean to run away always because the man came. Had she not settled it with herself that the man should be nothing to her? Then she went on swinging the children,—very deliberately, in order that she might be sure of herself, that the man's coming had not even flurried her.

In ten minutes the Major was there again. It had been natural to suppose that he should not be detained long in conversation by Mrs. Dugdale. "May I swing one of them for a time?" he asked.

"Well, no; I think not. It is my allotted exercise, and I never give it up." But Minnie, who knew what a strong arm could do, was imperious, and the Major got possession of the swing.

Then of a sudden he stopped. "Alice," he said, "I want you to take a turn with me up the road."

"I am not going out at all to-day," she said. Her voice was steady and well preserved; but there was a slight rising of colour on her cheeks.

"But I wish it expressly. You must come to-day."

She could consider only for a moment,—but for a

moment she did think the matter over. If the man chose to speak to her seriously, she must listen to him, —once, and once only. So much he had a right to demand. When a bird of that kind pecks in that manner some attention must be paid to him. So she got her hat, and leading the way down the road, opened the gate and turned up the lane away from the street of the village. For some yards he did not speak. She, indeed, was the first to do so. "I cannot stay out very long, Major Rossiter; so, if there is anything——?

"There is a something, Alice." Of course she knew, but she was quite resolved. Resolved! Had not every moment of her life since last she had parted with him been given up to the strengthening of this resolution? Not a stitch had gone through the calico which had not been pulled the tighter by the tightening of her purpose! And now he was there. Oh, how more than earthly sweet it had been to have him there, when her resolutions had been of another kind! But she had been punished for that, and was strong against such future ills. "Alice, it had better come out simply. I love you, and have ever loved you with all my heart." Then there was a frown and a little trampling of the ground beneath her feet, but she said not a word. Oh, if it only could have come sooner,—a few weeks sooner! "I know what you would say to me, but I would have you listen to me, if possible, before you say it. I have given you cause to be angry with me."

"Oh no!" she cried, interrupting him.

"But I have never been untrue to you for a moment. You seemed to slight me."

"And if I did?"

"That may pass. If you should slight me now, I must bear it. Even though you should deliberately tell me that you cannot love me, I must bear that. But with such a load of love as I have at my heart, it must be told to you. Day and night it covers me from head to foot. I can think of nothing else. I dream that I have your hand in mine, but when I wake I think it can never be so."

There was an instinct with her at the moment to let her fingers glide into his; but it was shown only by the gathering together of her two hands, so that no rebellious fingers straying from her in that direction might betray her. "If you have never loved me, never can love me, say so, and I will go away." She should have spoken now, upon the instant; but she simply moved her foot upon the gravel and was silent. "That I should be punished might be right. If it could be possible that the punishment should extend to two, that could not be right."

She did not want to punish him,—only to be brave herself. If to be obdurate would in truth make him unhappy, then would it be right that she should still be firm? It would be bad enough, after so many self-assurances, to succumb at the first word; but for his sake,—for his sake,—would it not be possible to bear even that? "If you never have loved me, and never can love me, say so, and I will go." Even to herself, she had not pledged herself to lie. If he asked her to be his wife in the plain way, she could say that she would not. Then the way would be plain before her. But what reply was she to make in answer to such a question as this? Could she say that she had not loved him,—or did not love him? "Alice," he said, putting his hand up to her arm.

"No!"

"Alice, can you not forgive me?"

"I have forgiven."

"And will you not love me?"

She turned her face upon him with a purpose to frown, but the fulness of his eyes upon her was too much, and the frown gave way, and a tear came into her eye, and her lips trembled; and then she acknowledged to herself that her resolution had not been worth a straw to her.

It should be added that considerably before Alice's wedding, both Sophia and Georgiana Wanless were married,—Sophia, in due order, as of course, to young Cobble, and Georgiana to Mr. Burmeston, the brewer. This, as the reader will remember, was altogether unexpected; but it was a great and guiding principle with Lady Wanless that the girls should not be taken out of their turns.

THE END.

READ MORE IN PENGUIN

In every corner of the world, on every subject under the sun, Penguin represents quality and variety – the very best in publishing today.

For complete information about books available from Penguin – including Puffins, Penguin Classics and Arkana – and how to order them, write to us at the appropriate address below. Please note that for copyright reasons the selection of books varies from country to country.

In the United Kingdom: Please write to *Dept. JC, Penguin Books Ltd, FREEPOST, West Drayton, Middlesex UB7 OBR*

If you have any difficulty in obtaining a title, please send your order with the correct money, plus ten per cent for postage and packaging, to *PO Box No. 11, West Drayton, Middlesex UB7 OBR*

In the United States: Please write to *Penguin USA Inc., 375 Hudson Street, New York, NY 10014*

In Canada: Please write to *Penguin Books Canada Ltd, 10 Alcorn Avenue, Suite 300, Toronto, Ontario M4V 3B2*

In Australia: Please write to *Penguin Books Australia Ltd, 487 Maroondah Highway, Ringwood, Victoria 3134*

In New Zealand: Please write to *Penguin Books (NZ) Ltd,182–190 Wairau Road, Private Bag, Takapuna, Auckland 9*

In India: Please write to *Penguin Books India Pvt Ltd, 706 Eros Apartments, 56 Nehru Place, New Delhi 110 019*

In the Netherlands: Please write to *Penguin Books Netherlands B.V., Keizersgracht 231 NL–1016 DV Amsterdam*

In Germany: Please write to *Penguin Books Deutschland GmbH, Friedrichstrasse 10–12, W–6000 Frankfurt/Main 1*

In Spain: Please write to *Penguin Books S. A., C. San Bernardo 117–6° E–28015 Madrid*

In Italy: Please write to *Penguin Italia s.r.l., Via Felice Casati 20, I–20124 Milano*

In France: Please write to *Penguin France S. A., 17 rue Lejeune, F–31000 Toulouse*

In Japan: Please write to *Penguin Books Japan, Ishikiribashi Building, 2–5–4, Suido, Tokyo 112*

In Greece: Please write to *Penguin Hellas Ltd, Dimocritou 3, GR–106 71 Athens*

In South Africa: Please write to *Longman Penguin Southern Africa (Pty) Ltd, Private Bag X08, Bertsham 2013*

READ MORE IN PENGUIN

ELIZABETH GASKELL – A SELECTION

North and South
Edited by Dorothy Collin with an Introduction by Martin Dodsworth

Through the medium of its central characters, John Thornton and Margaret Hale, *North and South* becomes a profound comment on the need for reconciliation among the English classes, on the importance of suffering, and above all on the value of placing the dictates of personal conscience above social respectability.

Cranford/Cousin Phillis
Edited by Peter Keating

Its analysis of an early Victorian country town, captured at the crucial moment of transition in English society, besieged by forces it is incapable of understanding or, ultimately, withstanding, is sharply observed and acutely penetrating. Like *Cranford*, the nouvelle *Cousin Phillis* is concerned with 'phases of society' – the old values as against the new.

Wives and Daughters
Edited by Frank Glover Smith with an Introduction by Laurence Lerner

The story of Mr Gibson's new marriage and its influence on the lives of those closest to him is a work of rare charm, combining pathos with wit, intelligence, and a perceptiveness about people and their relationships equalled only by Jane Austen and George Eliot.

Mary Barton
Edited by Stephen Gill

Mary Barton depicts Manchester in the 'hungry forties' with appalling precision. Illustrated here is Elizabeth Gaskell's genius for making her characters so individually human in their responses to poverty and injustice that we are touched by an appeal that goes beyond government statistics and beyond time.

READ MORE IN PENGUIN

JANE AUSTEN – A SELECTION

Emma
Edited with an Introduction by Ronald Blythe

Dominating the novel as she dominates the small provincial world of Highbury, Emma's forays into the matchmaking arena bring her up sharply against the follies of her egotism and selfishness. The consequent crisis, her bitter regrets and the happy resolution are plotted with Jane Austen's incomparable art in this sharp and gloriously sparkling comedy of self-deceit and self-discovery.

Northanger Abbey
Edited by Anne Ehrenpreis

At Northanger Abbey Jane Austen's charmingly imperfect heroine, Catherine Morland, meets all the trappings of Gothic horror and imagines the worst. Fortunately she has at hand her own fundamental good sense and the irresistible but unsentimental hero, Henry Tilney.

Mansfield Park
Edited with an Introduction by Tony Tanner

In *Mansfield Park* Jane Austen draws on her cool irony and comic genius to full effect. Against her chosen backdrops, the story of the Crawfords, the Bertrams and Fanny Price, her quiet, suffering heroine, and their interlocking destinies, is played out with superb control, wit and profound psychological insight.

THE PENGUIN TROLLOPE

1. The Macdermots of Ballycloran (1847)
2. The Kellys and the O'Kellys: Or Landlords and Tenants (1848)
3. La Vendée: An Historical Romance (1850)
4. The Warden (1855)
5. Barchester Towers (1857)
6. The Three Clerks (1858)
7. Doctor Thorne (1858)
8. The Bertrams (1859)
9. Castle Richmond (1860)
10. Framley Parsonage (1861)
11. Tale of All Countries: First Series (1861)
12. Orley Farm (1862)
13. The Struggles of Brown, Jones and Robinson: By One of the Firm (1862)
14. Tales of All Countries: Second Series (1863)
15. Rachel Ray (1863)
16. The Small House at Allington (1864)
17. Can You Forgive Her? (1865)
18. Miss Mackenzie (1865)
19. The Belton Estate (1866)
20. Nina Balatka (1867)
21. The Last Chronicle of Barset (1867)
22. The Claverings (1867)
23. Lotta Schmidt and Other Stories (1867)
24. Linda Tressel (1868)
25. Phineas Finn: The Irish Member (1869)
26. He Knew He Was Right (1869)

THE PENGUIN TROLLOPE

27. The Vicar of Bullhampton (1870)
28. An Editor's Tales (1870)
29. Sir Harry Hotspur of Humblethwaite (1871)
30. Ralph the Heir (1871)
31. The Golden Lion of Granpère (1872)
32. The Eustace Diamonds (1873)
33. Phineas Redux (1874)
34. Lady Anna (1874)
35. Harry Heathcote of Gangoil: A Tale of Australian
    Bush Life (1874)
36. The Way We Live Now (1875)
37. The Prime Minister (1876)
38. The American Senator (1877)
39. Is He Popenjoy? (1878)
40. An Eye for an Eye (1879)
41. John Caldigate (1879)
42. Cousin Henry (1879)
43. The Duke's Children (1880)
44. Dr Wortle's School (1881)
45. Ayala's Angel (1881)
46. Why Frau Frohmann Raised Her Prices and Other Stories (1882)
47. Kept in the Dark (1882)
48. Marion Fay (1882)
49. The Fixed Period (1882)
50. Mr Scarborough's Family (1883)
51. The Landleaguers (1883)
52. An Old Man's Love (1884)
53. An Autobiography (1883)